THE Last Messenger OF Zitól

THE Last Messenger OF Zitól

CHELSEA DYRENG

SWEETWATER
BOOKS

An Imprint of Cedar Fort, Inc.
Springville, Utah

ISBN 13: 978-1-4621-1896-0

Published by Sweetwater Books, an imprint of Cedar Fort, Inc., 2373 W. 700 S., Springville, UT 84663
Distributed by Cedar Fort, Inc. www.cedarfort.com

LIBRARY OF CONGRESS CATALOGING-IN-PUBLICATION DATA ON FILE

Cover design by Michelle May Ledezma
Cover design © 2016 by Cedar Fort, Inc.
Edited and typeset by Justin Greer and Jessica Romrell

Printed in the United States of America

10 9 8 7 6 5 4 3 ₊2 1

Printed on acid-free paper

For my daughters

Introduction

Before we begin, I want you to understand that I am not a good person.

I keep a mirror on a chain around my neck so that I can admire my nose, my black hair, my bronze muscles, and my straight teeth. I like to eat imported foods that most of the population can't afford. When I taste something I do not like, I spit it into the open hand of the nearest servant, and he wraps it in a cloth to burn later in a sacred ceremony. I bathe twice a day in tiled pools, receive massages in steamed rooms, and on hot afternoons I am fanned by six slaves. I very seldom wear the same clothes twice, as my skin is accustomed only to fabrics that are fresh off the loom. Most of my thoughts are consumed with how I can amuse myself, and the rest are spent thinking about how others can amuse me.

I never think twice about lying to save my skin. I have little respect or patience for people who are poor, dirty, malnourished, old, lame, or female, and see them as obstacles to my happiness. I am not a good listener, and I am skeptical of anything that cannot be seen or proven before my own eyes. There was even a time when taking a life was as easy for me as pinching out the flame on a candle.

Cities have been named after me, statues have been carved of me, temples have been built for me, but always out of fear or coercion. To be plain, I am arrogant and cynical, and I have never done anything noble, kind, or unselfish.

That is why writing this book may be the only good thing I have ever done.

The book you are about to read is about a girl named Rishi and how she became the Messenger of my city. She was everything I am not: pure, honest, and above all, filled with virtue.

Which is exactly why she had to die.

CHAPTER 1

The Island

If it isn't night when you read this, close the book. Wait for the sun to melt into the horizon and for the first stars to prick through the purple sky. Light your fire and sit as close as you can to its warmth. Then you can begin reading again. For nighttime is the best time for story-telling. Rishi told me so.

In her village, when the sun was just a burning ember at the end of the ocean, the people gathered to listen. Some of the stories were true, some were not, and the best stories were an exquisite blend of both. Of course, no one could tell a story like Rishi's grandfather.

Yelgab was different from all the other grandfathers on the island. Not only was his name unusual, but long ago his ears had been pierced with plugs so that now they hung low and drooped almost past his chin. His lobes were so stretched he could fit an egg though them, which he did every so often, just to horrify his young listeners. His skin was darker and his nose slightly larger than the other islanders, traits he passed down to Rishi and her brothers. He was also the only person on the island with a foreign accent. When Rishi pestered him about why he talked in such a peculiar way he reminded her that he had been educated in the prestigious schools of Zitól. Of course, once the word *Zitól* left his lips Rishi and the others would beg for a story, and he was only too happy to oblige. He would then plunge into a tale of the dazzling, holy city, far away in the jungles of the mysterious mainland. He spoke of limestone temples, enormous pyramids, and kings who drank from golden cups. Rishi savored each detail as if it were a ripe berry. She thought his stories of Zitól were so magnificent that they made her island seem as stale as an old fish.

Every day Rishi found excuses to get her grandfather to tell his stories. If a bird landed in the village to steal a scrap of food, she would say, "Grandfather, tell me about the birds in Zitól." And he would describe great aviaries that housed birds of every kind—eagles, toucans, egrets, quetzals, swallows, and even tiny birds the size of bumblebees. ". . . And if you were a Zitóli child and you needed a beautiful feather to decorate your hair or tunic, all you would have to do was enter the aviary and clap your hands. Then the birds would fly down and land on your shoulder or at your feet. If you were gentle they would let you pull a feather or two before flying off again."

"Didn't that hurt the birds?" Rishi asked.

"Oh, no," her grandfather would say. "They just flew back up to their resting places to grow new ones. The high priests use these precious feathers in their ceremonial robes and the warriors use them in their headdresses. I once even saw a warrior captain wearing a cape made entirely with the feathers of hummingbirds."

"What do the women wear? Do they wear bead belts and cotton dresses like we do?"

"They wear their bead belts, of course, very much like your mother's. But their fabrics are much different than ours. They weave fabrics so fine that if I held it up to your face I would still be able to see your pretty smile. Even the breast of a bird isn't as soft as these cloths, and they dye them any color you can imagine. Then designs of jaguars, toucans, and butterflies are embroidered around the hems of the fabric with golden threads. They pin these fabrics around their waists, drape scarves around their shoulders, and hang glittering necklaces of topaz, ruby, and opal about their necks. But it is the children that look the most splendid, Rishi. The Zitóli people love their children more than any people that ever walked the earth, and they cover them in crimson, jade, and purple garments, pierce their ears with golden rings, and adorn their little feet with slippers lined with ocelot fur."

Rishi had no idea what ocelot fur was, but it sounded so much more wonderful than the crudely crafted sandals of palm leaves that she wore on her feet.

Yelgab continued, "They have special fruits that are cool and shiny to the touch, but when you eat them they make your mouth burn like fire."

Often Rishi thought Zitól was just *too* fantastic, and that her grandfather must be making it all up. But she didn't care. To her, all that really mattered was listening to the magic of his voice. And sometimes, if Rishi stared hard enough into the fire, she could smell the spicy air of the city, taste the heat of exotic peppers on her tongue, and see the fluid forms of the Zitóli people, dancing in full regalia, alive, vibrant, and *real*.

One night Yelgab wasn't at his usual spot at the fireside. When Rishi and some of the other children questioned her mother, the reply was, "He's not feeling well. I'm afraid there will be no stories tonight." There was a collective moan and some of the children meandered off to other campfires to seek a substitute.

Rishi's older brother Quash, who was sitting by the fire sharpening a stick, lifted his head and smiled. "I'll tell them a story, Mama."

Now, Rishi had three older brothers: Quash, Eno and Cotyl, and they were all quite horrible, but Quash was the most terrifying of all. He was monstrously huge and his hair hung over his shoulders like black snakes. For amusement he liked to lift Rishi up by her ears. So when an offer of a story came from *his* lips Rishi had to look at him twice, for she could hardly believe anything benevolent could originate from his mouth. Her mother, however, was delighted. "That is so kind of you, Quash," she gushed, for any time her sons showed a glimmer of humanity toward Rishi she couldn't help but be swept with emotion.

"It is my pleasure," he said. "I'd love to entertain my sister and her little friends."

With a contented sigh and a gentle pat on Quash's cheek, Rishi's mother disappeared into the hut to rest, leaving Rishi standing stiffly in the doorway, eyeing Quash in the same way a mouse watches a circling hawk.

"Come have a seat, Rish, and all you other little people," Quash said chummily, as he cut the shavings into the fire with his knife.

Rishi slowly moved to sit on a log close to the fire next to her friends Sepya and Venay, but still a safe distance away from her brother's flying shavings and flashing blade. Lantana, who had been lame since birth, limped after Rishi and nestled in next to her, and finally Isra, who had been beautiful since birth, sat apart from the others, arms folded and legs crossed. All of them watched Quash closely, ready to disperse like rabbits if he did anything unexpected.

"Have I ever told you about the lost girls from the island of Conicha?" Quash said, looking at Rishi and raising one eyebrow.

"You've never told me *any* story before, Quash," Rishi said.

"Hmm . . . that is a pity. It is probably because my stories are too scary for you."

Rishi folded her arms and lifted her chin. "You can't scare me."

"Well, would you like to hear it? You won't get bad dreams tonight, will you? I will try not to make it *too* frightening."

"Make it as frightening as you want," Rishi challenged. Bad dreams weren't a problem for her.

"Well, don't say I didn't warn you." He paused and put the end of his stick in the fire. "You know why you aren't supposed to wander out of the village after dark, don't you?"

"So that we don't get lost."

"Perhaps. But think about it. We live on a tiny island. How could you get lost? It is easy to find your way back to the village at night, especially with the fires burning." He pulled his stick out of the fire. It was now lit at the end and Rishi watched it as Quash hypnotically waved it in lazy circles over the flames. "No, there is another reason you are not supposed to wander off at night. The grown-ups haven't told you because they know you are young and they don't want to excite your sensitive imaginations." He pulled the stick toward his mouth and blew out the small flame. Smoke slithered around his shadowy face. "That means they don't want to *scare* you," he said, making his big black eyes bulge at Lantana who instantly quivered. "Consequently, as Rishi's older brother, that duty falls to me."

Everyone watched, mesmerized, as the smoke continued to flutter up from the tip of Quash's stick. Rishi waited impatiently for Quash to begin the story, but Quash stalled, staring open-mouthed at the smoke with feigned fascination.

Annoyed, Rishi asked, "So what is the *real* reason we aren't supposed leave the village after dark?"

"Because . . . of the *Snatchers*."

"Snatchers?"

"There is a rumor I heard on one of the other islands . . ." Quash was just old enough to visit neighboring islands with the men to trade pearls, a fact he liked to often repeat, even though the number of islands he'd visited so far totaled one. ". . . that one night, last summer, on a nearby island, a group of girls decided to leave the village and have some fun. They wanted to do some girly thing like dance under the moon. They waited until the grown-ups were all asleep. Then they tiptoed out to the beach. Unfortunately, they found that the moon was covered by clouds and the night was as black as the back of your eyelids. So they decided to start a fire, which was the *worst* thing they could have done."

"Why?"

"Because the Snatchers are drawn to light."

The girls shifted uneasily as they watched the glowing fire, which up until that moment had seemed so comforting.

Quash continued, "They sat around it, talking about all those silly things girls like to talk about when they think they are by themselves, not realizing that they were actually *luring* the Snatchers to them. Soon, dark shapes emerged out of the waves and crept onto the beach."

A chill ran up Rishi's spine and she put her arm around Lantana protectively. Sepya put her hands over her face. Venay turned, darting her moon-shaped eyes into the darkness behind them, just to be sure nothing was there.

Even the perpetually poised Isra secretly inserted the end of her braid into her mouth and started nervously chewing.

"Once they were on the beach the creatures waited, their hairy bodies crouching in the darkness while they watched the girls hungrily. Every time the girls laughed the creatures' smoldering eyes glowed red-hot, for that is why they came—to seize and silence the laughter of innocent, young girls.

"The girls told stories and jokes late into the night. They felt safe because the fire lit their faces and warmed their hands, but really the glow of the fire weakened their night eyes, obscuring everything beyond the circle of light. Meanwhile, the creatures silently crept toward the girls like giant tarantulas. When the Snatchers had them surrounded on every side, they started to make a low clicking noise, like this—" Quash rapidly clicked his teeth together— "That became louder and louder. There was a terrifying *hiiisssss!* And the creatures leaped out of the darkness and grabbed each girl by the throat, stopping their breath before they could scream. They dragged them down across the beach into the waves, never to be seen again. The next morning when the villagers woke, there was nothing left on the beach but smoking coals and the jagged trails of fingernail marks in the sand."

The fire cracked and snapped as Rishi's friends digested this imagery in horrified silence.

Quash smiled. "There was one girl, however, that escaped. The villagers found her hiding behind a rock, trembling. She wouldn't speak for weeks after that, and she never laughed again. When asked to describe what happened that night she would only say one word."

"And that was . . . ?" said Rishi.

"*Teeth.*"

"Teeth," the children repeated in whispers.

Rishi was silent for a moment. Quash blew lightly on the black end of his smoking stick and the coals flashed like a ruby.

"So what *really* happened to the girls?" Rishi asked.

"I told you. They were *snatched*."

"But why?" Rishi asked, thinking practically.

"Like I said, to steal their laughter."

"You can't steal someone's laughter," Rishi said. "You made that part up."

"Well then maybe they wanted to eat the flesh off their bones. Or to suck on their eyeballs. Or to use their skins to make canoes. I don't know why the girls disappeared. If I knew, I would be a Snatcher, wouldn't I?"

Lantana whimpered and buried her face in Rishi's shoulder.

Quash smiled to himself, clearly enjoying the atmosphere of terror he spawned. He picked up his knife and shaved the charred coals off the end of his burned stick. There was a long silence while the girls pictured Quash dragging them into the ocean with his teeth.

Finally Rishi stood up. "That is the dumbest story I've ever heard."

Quash shrugged. "All I'm saying is that you better not go out after dark or the Snatchers will get you. But, then—" he smiled, "with *your* weird eyes, Rishi, you'll probably be spared. They say the Snatchers only take the pretty girls."

The next night Quash retold the story to a larger group, adding some gory embellishments. His fame spread quickly and soon every evening the teenagers and children swarmed around the fire where Quash sat, spinning his tales of terror. Since he was keen on retaining his audience, each night the Snatchers acquired descriptive new features: sizzling eyes that could burn through skin, poisonous saliva that dripped from forked tongues, tusks the size of a man's arm and stained with clotted blood . . . Quash had never enjoyed the storytelling hour before, but now he had become the island celebrity. As he told Eno and Cotyl, he had discovered his *gift*.

The Snatcher stories also supplied Rishi's brothers a whole new medium in which to torment her and her friends. For weeks they would "play" Snatchers, flipping their eyelids inside out and stalking after the girls, moaning incoherently. Other times they'd hide behind rocks or trees and suddenly jump out in front of a group of girls, making them scream or wet themselves. They knew no mercy, harassing sensitive Sepya to tears, telling Venay she'd taste extra delicious because she was so plump, and even teasing Lantana that she would be the first to be snatched because of her lame foot. It was not uncommon for parents to hear cries in the night from frightened young girls whose imaginations had been commandeered by Quash's dark tales.

Rishi had to admit the stories did make her uneasy, and it didn't help to have her brothers terrorizing her friends. But at least Rishi didn't have to worry about the nightmares. Rishi never had nightmares. Rishi didn't even know what having a dream was like. She had never had one.

CHAPTER 2

Zitól

"Let me tell you something about public speaking," said Speaker Gula to me as we walked briskly along the corridor. We had to hurry; everyone was waiting for us.

Gula was wearing an emerald green cape over his white tunic that bulged out to make room for his belly. His hair was oiled and a golden band circled his head, perfectly matching the bands about his wrists. His ears were pierced in the traditional Zitóli fashion for a priest, with a large gaping hole in the lobe, so large I could have stuck my finger through it. Shiny nose rings dangled from one nostril, clinking together each time he took a step. To me, a boy of twelve years, he was everything I wanted to be.

I held my mask by the straps and it bounced against my leg as we walked. Gula hadn't noticed I wasn't wearing it yet and I wasn't going to put it on until I absolutely had to. For the moment, Gula had other things on his mind.

"The most important part of public speaking is the opening line. If you don't seize your audience's attention from the very beginning, you'll lose them. You might as well start singing lullabies."

"So what is a good way to begin?" I asked, elated that Speaker Gula was even conversing with me at all. He always became uncharacteristically giddy and talkative before he was to give a speech, and I wanted to take full advantage of this opportunity to learn from a master.

Gula took the mirror that hung on a chain around his double chin and gazed at himself. "There are several different ways I like to begin." He smoothed his hair and moistened his raging eyebrows that grew into triangles when he became angry.

"One way is with a captivating story. Another way is to ask your audience a perplexing question or to tease them with a tantalizing half-truth that you promise to resolve later. Sometimes, depending on the event, it is good to start out with something light, a joke for instance, to get the listeners to relate to you. Then, once you have them hooked, you use other devices. Voice inflections, rhetorical questions, drama . . . and one must never overlook the power of the *pause*. When you pause it makes the audience uncomfortable and creates suspense. *What will he say next?* they wonder. And then you dazzle them with your next breath of brilliance." He chuckled to himself. "Of course you must never overdo it. You must speak simply and plainly so that even the very stupidest person in the audience can understand your message. Above all, always make your audience believe they are the finest and most superb generation there ever was or ever will be. Your goal as a Speaker is to influence people. People will resist your influence if you are critical of them."

I nodded, committing what he said to memory. He went on.

"People want to be validated. They want to feel important. Once they feel like they are something special or, even better, something *superior*, then you can slowly guide them in the direction you want them to go. That is what I enjoy most about my duty as a Speaker, and as your regent: the molding of minds . . . the swaying of souls."

I nodded again.

"Just watch me, and you will see. A truly talented Speaker, one with years of experience like myself, can take *any* idea and convince an audience that it is truth. Above all, word choice is everything. Even *one* carefully placed word can be the catalyst that changes the opinions of thousands. Through words I can inspire people do anything I want them to do, or make them believe anything I want them to believe."

"Isn't that lying?" I asked.

"It is not lying," he said as he tucked away his mirror. "It is leadership."

We left the palace and entered the ball court through the private corridor that is only used by the Speakers and priests and their servants. I could hear the restless crowd, already gathered in the stands, and my stomach twisted in anticipation. Even though I truly was honored that Speaker Gula was teaching me about speaking, and I was ever so grateful for his tutelage, what I really wanted to see was the match.

By the time we arrived, the seats were packed with people. I followed Speaker Gula up the stone stairs to the Speakers' Box, a spacious stone balcony, where we would view the match from the choicest seats. Speaker Riplakish was already there. Gula still hadn't noticed that my mask wasn't on yet, and with the excitement of the game, I forgot all about it as well.

As I climbed the last step to the Speakers' Box, I heard a screech. It was Speaker Riplakish, with one slender hand poised over his mouth in alarm. "Put on your mask, boy, before someone sees you!" he gasped. In his astonishment at seeing me maskless, the Speaker must have smeared his lipstick, which turned his horrified expression into something quite funny. I laughed.

"This is nothing to joke about, young man," he said with a pout. "Now cover your face."

I sighed and reluctantly fit the carved mask over my face and breathed in the woody smell. "Will I *ever* be able to watch a game without this thing on my face?" said my muffled voice.

"In time, my son. But for now your power lies in your anonymity."

Today I had chosen the mask of the skunk. It was my least favorite, but it had the biggest eye holes and I planned on watching the game as clearly as possible. I wished I could watch without a disguise, like everyone else.

I slumped in my chair, for the moment sullen. "I wish the games were played more often," I mumbled.

"My dear boy," Riplakish said as he elegantly crossed his legs. "If we had the games more often we wouldn't have any team captains left in the city."

I sighed. It was always tragic if the team I was rooting for lost, for the captain especially. But then, it was for this reason that the game had so much intensity. It is not every day you are playing for your life.

The hot wind tossed the giant flags that bordered the Speakers' Box. A long, rectangular court spread out before us, lined on each side with a stone wall that was as high as two men standing on top of each other. The teams stood at attention on the grass court, the rubber ball resting between them, and the spectators looked down on them from the stands.

While I gazed at the scene I had an unsettling feeling that Speaker Riplakish was leaning closer to me than usual. I turned, and when I did his lips spread apart in a wide smile, showing his teeth, newly studded with glimmering jade. I blinked in surprise.

"Do you like them? I thought I would wait until you noticed, but I just got them today and I am too excited to keep it all to myself. What do you think?"

I nodded the mask and said the only thing that came to my mind, "Is it permanent?"

"That was the intention," he said, running his tongue slowly over them and smiling again for me. "I have something else to show you too." He put his hand into a large basket beside his chair and pulled out a jet-black object covered with fur. The fur mewed.

"What is it? A rat?"

"No. A cub. A jaguar cub."

My eyes widened. "Where did you get it?"

"It was brought to me as a gift. From one of my many admirers."

"You are going to keep it?" I asked.

"Of course. I think it could be useful in the future." Puckering up his thin, lipstick-smeared lips, Riplakish kissed the animal on the head. The animal shuddered. He placed the unfortunate thing in his lap and dug his long fingernails into its fur. It mewed in pain, but Riplakish did not seem to notice or care.

"I believe it is time to begin," said Speaker Gula, rising from his seat and clearing his mighty throat. He strode to the balcony. Seeing their cue, the heralds lifted and blew the conch horns and the chattering crowd silenced and turned their heads toward the Speakers' Box. With his hands raised out to the spectators, Speaker Gula began.

"Greetings, People of Zitól."

He let the words ring out, ricocheting off the walls of the ball court. The spectators were dressed in their finest clothing and jewels; each side trying to outdo the other's flamboyance. The players stood in two neat rows, hands behind their backs, wearing heavy leather pads and grim expressions. They all listened, their faces sober, their eyes transfixed to Gula's hands, which were outstretched, palms up, like he was waiting to catch something that was about to fall from the sky. Rain would have been nice. It was cloudless and hot and I hoped Speaker Gula, as magnificent a speaker as he was, wouldn't speak for too long.

"Look at the faces of these athletes," Gula began. "They are the faces of courage. They are the faces of strength. They are the faces of Zitól."

Pause.

"You, great people of Zitól, are a choice people. You are the greatest generation that has ever lived in this city. You, like these warriors, have great destinies that await you. You must find your destiny and seize it. Your destiny might be to work the fields for the sustenance of our city. Your destiny might be to provide textiles and metal works so that we may live richly and dress to the standard of our greatness. Each man and woman, fulfilling his or her destiny, brings honor to our city. Of course, we know the *greatest* destiny that any of us can contribute; it is a destiny that calls to us all. A destiny that beckons each of us to fulfill our duty to the gods. You know what it is, my good people."

Pause.

"It is that of tribute. It is that of *sacrifice*. Sacrifice is what keeps our crops lush and green. It is what brings us the cotton to make our fine clothes. It is what makes the golden corn grow tall. But without sacrifice the gods see us as mere cockroaches to crush. Without sacrifice the gods would lay waste to our city like hungry dragons. Without sacrifice the gods would tear us apart with their fingernails!" His voice grew shrill. "Without sacrifice, the sun would drop from the sky, the world would be rocked off balance!"

I leaned back in my chair. It looked like this would be a long one. After a while I began to yawn. "How long do you think Gula is going to speak?" I asked.

"*Speaker* Gula, Anointed One."

"How long do you think *Speaker* Gula is going to speak?" I repeated dutifully.

"He's wrapping up now, I think." Speaker Riplakish smiled. "They are getting restless, and a good Speaker can read an audience with his eyes."

". . . May you remember my words, for they will secure our way of life. The law of sacrifice brings forth great blessings. May the gods bless our lives, our temples, our city. Now . . . let the game begin!" The crowds on both sides of the court erupted in wild screaming. Hands stretched forth out of the audience. Scarves and banners appeared from nowhere and the teams marched into position.

I leaned forward in my seat.

CHAPTER 3
The Legend of the First Man

"Am I ugly?" Rishi asked her grandfather one afternoon while they ate. Quash, Eno, and Cotyl were gone oystering and had refused to take her along. Again.

"Does this have anything to do with your brothers?"

Rishi stirred her food around the bowl, trying to hold back tears. "Cotyl said I was as ugly as the underside of his tongue."

"Were they teasing you about your eye again?"

She nodded. This was a tender topic. Rishi knew she looked odd, for even though she belonged to a tribe of dark-skinned, dark-eyed people, the gods had played a mean trick on her: she was born with a blue eye. Or, as her brothers called it, a ghost eye.

Her grandfather sighed and shook his head. "Rishi, I'm going to tell you two things and I want you always to remember them. Always. Will you?"

"Yes," she said.

"Rishi, first of all, you are the *epitome* of beauty."

"I am?" said Rishi anxiously, hoping that "epitome" didn't mean "opposite."

"What that means is that you don't just look beautiful. You *are* beauty."

Rishi looked at him blankly.

"When a person is kind and virtuous and displays honor and tolerance—such as you do—'beauty' ceases to become a label that can come and go with your appearance. 'Beauty' is who you are. No matter what you look like, whether you are old or young, wide or thin, tall or short, blue eyed, brown eyed, or have one of each, that has no bearing on defining beauty. Even if you have a scar across your face, if your teeth fall out or if you lose your hair . . . your virtue makes you beautiful in a way that eclipses any physical trait. True beauty isn't a way to describe a person, it *is* a person."

Rishi gazed at him thoughtfully, searching his old, wrinkled face.

"What is the second thing I need to remember?"

"That you came from a long line of extremely handsome and beautiful people," he said, smiling and showing his last remaining teeth.

At storytelling hour when the youth gathered in unprecedented numbers to hear Quash's growing volumes about the Snatchers, Rishi loyally stayed near the fire outside her family's hut with the younger children and listened to the stories Yelgab told of Zitól.

"Tell my favorite Zitóli story, Grandfather," she asked, trying to ignore the exclamations of awe and fear that erupted every now and then from the older youth around Quash's campfire. "Tell us the one about the First Man and how Zitól was created."

"It wasn't how Zitól was created, Rishi," her grandfather said. "It is how the *world* was created." The old man cast his gaze up at the dark sky. "It happened a very long time ago, back when there were only a few intelligences in the heavens." No one needed to ask what "intelligences" were, for another one of Yelgab's peculiarities was that he liked to use old Zitóli words for things. All the children knew that when Yelgab said "intelligences," what he meant were the stars.

"Once," he began dramatically, "there was a man . . ."

He paused and surveyed the group. His gaze fell upon the face of the youngest child and he whispered loudly, ". . . and he was all alone."

"He ate alone. He walked alone. He worked alone. He thought alone. But he did not laugh, because it is hard to laugh alone, and he did not talk because it is hard to talk alone. But he did cry sometimes, for when you are alone crying comes easily.

"He told the gods, 'I need a companion. I need someone to work with and talk with and laugh with.'

"But the gods were doubtful. 'If we give you a companion, what will you do for us? Prove to us that you are worthy of a companion,' they told him.

"So the man made an altar out of limestone and marble and polished the top until it was so smooth it reflected the clouds in the sky.

"He said, 'Here, I have made this beautiful altar where I can worship you.'

"The gods said, 'This is not enough.'

"So the man built a village with many thatched huts and he dug a well and planted rows of corn. 'Here,' he said, 'I have made a village with water and food where there is a place for many people to live and a community can be built to worship you.'

"'That is not enough,' replied the gods.

"Then the man built stone buildings and roads. He built majestic temples and four-sided pyramids that rose high into the sky and were capped in gold.

"'Here are shining temples built to honor you and sanctify your holiness. Surely this is what you want.'

"But still, the gods said, 'That is not enough.'

"The man fell on his knees and groaned saying, 'What more can I do? I have done everything I can. I don't know what else I can give! What am I lacking? How can I prove I can be trusted?'

"He wept for many days. Then, with a heavy heart, he painted himself blue, the same blue as the sky. He climbed to the top of the highest temple. He stood with his arms raised above his head and called to the gods in anguish, 'Dear gods, I have one more thing I can give you. It is all that I have left, but I give it freely. I give you my broken heart.'"

Yelgab's face was upturned toward the stars and his arms were outstretched. He slowly lowered his hands and peered at the small glowing faces watching his every movement. "Now, why did he paint himself blue, my children?"

"Because it is the color of sacrifice," they murmured.

"And what happened after he offered his broken heart?"

"She came," whispered Rishi, smiling.

"That is right. The gods gave the man a woman. She had kind, soft eyes, strong hands, and warm arms. Now he had someone to work with, to walk with, to laugh with, and to love. The man was no longer alone, and the gods knew he would be happy because of the promise he made to them."

"And that is how Zitól was created!" said one of the children.

"Yes. The man and the woman had many children. As many children as there are intelligences in the sky. And they all lived in that beautiful city that the man built in his loneliness. They grew to become a great civilization. They called themselves the people of Zitól."

"These people were beautiful and virtuous and honest. They worked hard and were generous with everything they had. And this was because they were good, and so the gods blessed them. So if you want the gods to bless you, you be good too. You will do that, won't you?" Every head nodded earnestly. "Now, children, please recite to me the Seven Songs."

Grandfather often ended his stories that way. And whenever he came to the last part, his gentle brown eyes gazed so imploringly at each child that they felt as if they would never make a wrong choice for as long as they lived.

No one felt this more than Rishi.

For the rest of the evening Rishi sat hunched over, chin in hand, absorbed in deep, private contemplation. Other stories were requested and told, but the tales sailed over Rishi's head as unperceived as owls in the night sky. She was glad when the other children began to yawn, nod, and to be spirited away into the darkness by their parents. When finally she was left alone with her grandfather she straightened up and spoke.

"If Zitól is such a wonderful place, why did you leave?"

To indicate she expected an answer in detail she added another log to the dying fire.

Yelgab sighed and watched the flames lick the new log. His neck shrunk down into his shoulders and his breathing became heavy. For a moment he seemed kingdoms away.

"Grandfather?" she prompted.

"Things . . . changed," he said simply, his voice soaked with weariness.

They sat in silence for a few moments. Rishi, unsatisfied with the answer to her question, was about to stand and say good night when Yelgab spoke again.

"Don't you think this is a nice place to live, Rishi? We are on a beautiful island, surrounded by a ribbon of white sand and a blue sea filled with life and wealth that meets our every need. The ocean yields up its bounty to us and we are blessed with fat fish and white pearls, and we don't have to depend on the rain for our crops like the people in Zitól. *This* is paradise. Everyone we love is here. Why would we want to be any place else?"

"But you make Zitól sound so wonderful. Your stories make me shiver with happiness. It makes me wish I had been born in Zitól, instead of this boring old island."

He sighed. "Every place has its good and bad. But I'd say this island has a lot more good than most. There is nothing to fear here, nothing to worry about."

"What about . . ." Rishi paused. ". . . the Snatchers?"

"Ah . . . the Snatchers," said Grandfather, nodding his head slowly. He readjusted his position as if he were sitting on something uncomfortable.

"You know about the Snatchers?" she whispered.

"I am aware of their existence," he said gravely.

Rishi shivered. "See? That's another reason I wish we lived in Zitól."

"Do not base decisions on your fears, my love."

Rishi sighed, blowing air across her lips, making them flutter noisily.

"Perhaps your brothers will take you to Zitól someday. When you are older."

Rishi puckered her lips and raised one eyebrow.

"What is this expression you are giving me? Are you telling me that you wouldn't want to go with your brothers to Zitól?"

"They wouldn't want to go. *They* don't think it exists."

"Hm," her grandfather replied, rubbing his chin. "Is that so?"

"Couldn't *you* take me there?" Rishi pleaded. "So I could see it with my own eyes? Then we would come back . . ." and she would not only prove her brothers wrong, but she could dazzle everyone with her *own* stories and show off her *own* pair of ocelot slippers.

Yelgab smiled weakly, his expression filled with both warmth and deep shadow. "Rishi, I will never visit Zitól again. If you want to know the truth, I am not allowed in that city."

"Not *allowed?*" Rishi said. "What did you do?"

Yelgab gazed out toward the black ocean, toward the rising crescent moon. "I think it is what I *didn't* do, Rishi. But I don't regret it. Not at all." He smiled as he observed her puzzled expression. "If you do ever get the chance to go to Zitól, you will see what I mean. But for now you have a beautiful, rich life here on the island. Nothing in Zitól can compare with the peace and happiness I have found here."

Rishi frowned. The flames from the new log had died down, and her eyes reflected the smoldering coals.

"And don't let those brothers get to you. They are still boys. They think that in order to be strong they need to ignore their hearts. Someday they will understand that following the feelings that come into their hearts will give them their greatest power. Be patient with them, Rishi, for learning that can be awkward and painful. But when they do, they will no longer be boys; they will be men. And they will be your greatest allies."

Rishi thought that out of all the amazing tales Yelgab told, *that* was definitely the hardest to believe.

CHAPTER 4

Customs of Talom

Learning the Seven Songs was the sacred duty of each child on the island of Talom. Without the songs, the people of Talom would forget who they were and why they were born. Worst of all, they would forget where they were going. Rishi explained to me that the Songs were the thread that stitched friends to friends, children to their parents, and parents to each other. She couldn't remember a time when she didn't know the Seven Songs, as they were sung to her even as a suckling baby.

By the time the children were ten years old, they were expected to be able to recite the Songs word for word. This event was celebrated with a week of dancing, eating, and storytelling. On the last day of the celebrations, each child was to recite the Seven Songs in front of the councilmen and the entire village. If the child were male he received a spear. If the child were female she received her own bead belt. She would wear this around her waist for the rest of her life.

All the island women had bead belts. They were made from leather and decorated with small beads or shells. The belt was a symbol of honor and virtue, and a token of her womanhood. It was also a code, and a polite way to answer the delicate questions men were not permitted to ask a girl, but questions that were essential to know.

Hanging down from the side of the belt was a braided cord that swung at Rishi's hip. Rishi's mother gave her a beautiful bead the size of a man's thumb, made from polished whalebone and fixed it to the end of this rope. The bead was white, symbolizing purity. She would wear this until she married. Then she would give her white bead to her husband, for him to wear around his neck, symbolizing his pledge to protect and honor her virtue. In exchange, he would give her a bead of pure turquoise for her belt, signaling to other young men that she was now a married woman.

The first few days of the Recitation Celebration were a happy blur. Rishi loved the dancing, the music, and the attention all the villagers lavished on her. She was praised, complimented, and showered with little trinkets and gifts. And for the most part, her brothers were too wrapped up in their own lives to care much about the festivities, so they left Rishi alone—at least at first.

Finally the day that Rishi would receive her bead belt arrived. The entire village gathered at the place of assembly. Rishi sat on the platform next to her mother and the four members of the village council. Her hair was braided around her head, decorated with ribbons and tiny shells that stood out like stars against her black hair. She wore a new dress of creamy cotton that was too long and baggy for her slight body, something her new beit, now draped across her mother's lap, would improve.

Yelgab hobbled up to the platform, hushed everyone, and beckoned Rishi to come to the center. In his hand was a little bowl filled with yellow ochre. Dipping one finger into the bowl he marked a horizontal line over Rishi's nose and across her cheeks. "Now you look just like the beautiful young women of Zitól," he whispered in her ear.

Rishi grinned. Her heart felt huge, like it was filling her entire chest.

"Are you ready?" he asked.

Rishi nodded, her eyes bright. Her grandfather squeezed her shoulder and presented her to the audience. Then he left her to stand alone, facing the villagers.

Their expressions were encouraging, kind, beaming. To her delight, Eno, Cotyl, and Quash sat cross-legged at the foot of the platform, with what seemed to Rishi to be genuine smiles. The great swelling feeling of her heart spread through Rishi's body, filling her with happiness. She took a deep breath and began.

The words flowed easily, and she was only a phrase or two into the first song when suddenly she stopped. Something very small struck her shoulder. She glanced around her, but no one else seemed to notice. She continued.

She finished the first song and was well into the second when it happened again. Only this time, something hit her face and it stung so much that she had to lift her hand to her cheek. The villagers watched her, giving her encouraging smiles and some even mouthing the next word, as if she had forgotten.

But she hadn't forgotten. She knew the Songs better than any of her friends, and better than some adults, and she wanted to prove it. Cautiously, knowing that if something happened twice it was sure to happen a third time, she continued. She had hardly said five words when she was attacked again simultaneously in the neck and the forehead.

This time she heard the almost imperceptible *tap* of something tiny falling on the platform. She looked down. Resting near her feet was a black sunflower seed. She raised her head and cast a fatal stare at her brothers, whose faces were splitting with wide, unrepentant grins. Cotyl took something out of a bag at his side and slid it into his mouth.

Some girls, upon the discovery that their three older brothers were spitting sunflower seeds at them at the most important moment of their life, would have begun to cry. But not Rishi, and not today. This was *her* day. She knew the Seven Songs. She wasn't going to let her brothers ruin it with their stupid pranks.

She finished the second song and two more seeds flipped by her. By the fourth song the seeds were coming regularly and Rishi closed her eyes to focus on the words. Then during the fifth song the seeds stopped flying and Rishi took a glance at her brothers, only to find out they had been waiting for her to notice and all three unleashed seeds from their silent lips at once.

From that point to the end she was constantly being bombarded with the little stinging specks. It wasn't until she was halfway through the seventh song and the seeds littered the ground at her feet that her mother realized what was going on. But by then Rishi was on the last phrase, and, slowly and deliberately, she finished, flashing a look of triumph at her would-be assassins.

The villagers applauded her performance, and even her brothers smiled and flapped their hands together. Everyone became still when her mother wrapped the beautiful belt around her waist, tying it firmly on the side so that all could see the precious white bead. Then her mother took her by the shoulders and looked into her eyes.

"Rishi," she said in a low voice, "now *you* are a guardian of virtue. By wearing this bead you show the gods you can be trusted with the power of life. Remember this. For this is how we keep the balance of the world." She kissed Rishi's forehead.

As you can see, the significance of upholding chastity and virtue was reinforced, celebrated, and cemented into the mind of Rishi by her elders, and it was this indoctrination that caused so much trouble for me later.

CHAPTER 5
Customs of Zitól

S*it in your seat, Anointed One!"*

"But they almost scored!" I wailed.

I was on my knees, with my elbows on the limestone balcony, my fingers intertwined in my hair, ready to rip it all out if it would help my team score. The other team had just pitched the ball toward the stone ring fixed to the wall, but it bounced off the side of the ring, preventing them from making the one and only point of the game. That was too close. Another close call like that and my heart might stop beating. All the players moved off the field to rest and drink, and I crept back to my seat and sat on its edge and cracked my knuckles, too restless to lounge like the Speakers.

I readjusted my mask, which had turned sideways at the recent close call. The mask was getting hot and stuffy, and sweat seeped from my forehead and dripped off my chin, making the mask almost unbearable.

The game was beginning its third hour, and the sun was high in the sky, baking the brown shoulders and arms of everyone in the stands. People vigorously fanned their faces with large leaves as the sweat trickled down their cheeks, but no one considered leaving. We would all stay to the end, which would indeed be bitter for someone.

In the Speakers' Box we were shaded by a large fabric canopy and refreshed by a constant breeze provided by two servants with great feathered fans. A woman appeared at the stairs, carrying a tray of cut fruits and goblets filled with foaming chocolate.

Riplakish took a goblet from the tray and sipped. "Nadal, if you could just sit in your seat for the rest of the match, it would be appreciated. Standing, screaming, and pulling out your hair isn't going to help your team to win. Besides, I am rooting for the other side and you're making it profoundly difficult for me to enjoy the game."

"I know, Speaker, I just get so nervous. The stakes are so high."

The woman offered me something from the tray, but I declined. This was not a time to be distracted.

"You are cheering for my team, aren't you, Speaker Gula?"

Gula smiled. "Of course, my boy. You know I always side with you. But Speaker Riplakish is right that it is important for you to calm yourself. You must act more godlike, if possible."

I groaned and slouched back into my chair. "No one is watching me. Everyone is watching the game," I mumbled.

"People are *always* watching the Speakers and you must remember that you are anointed to one day become King: the holiest of us all."

The players finished their break and jogged back onto the field. I wiped my sweating palms on my tunic and moved back to the edge of my seat. The ball was launched into the sky. One of my players hit it with his head and it went spinning through the air. It hit the chest of a man on the other team, and he deflected it to his teammate. Since it was against the rules to hit the ball with your hands or feet, he skillfully "caught" it using his shoulder and the side of his head. He thrust it to another teammate and it was tossed from player to player until finally a strong man butted it up against the wall where it ricocheted off and sailed through the stone ring. A tremendous roar erupted on one side of the court as the winning side threw their arms toward the sky.

"Noooo!" came my muffled wail.

I covered the mask's eye holes with my hands. Speaker Gula patted me consolingly. "Better luck next time," he sighed. In my grief I could hear Riplakish's rapid clapping.

When I lifted my head my team was on their knees in the grass, some beating the ground, some with tears running down their stained faces. Only the team captain was still standing and staring at the stone ring, still as a statue. Meanwhile, the other team strutted around the field, shaking their tongues, slapping their chests, and making fierce battle faces to the spectators. The losing team captain finally pulled his eyes away from the stone ring, swallowed hard, and walked to the center of the field to stand alone.

"Splendid game!" Speaker Riplakish said cheerfully, still clapping his hands. "Wasn't that exciting? I suppose it is my turn today, is it not?" He looked at Speaker Gula expectantly.

"Go ahead. I'm afraid I'm not in the mood. I would hurry if I were you, Speaker. You know the people can only restrain themselves for so long," said Gula.

Riplakish took one last drink from his goblet, dabbed away the chocolate from the corner of his mouth, and stood. "How do I look?" he asked, smoothing his robes.

Gula nodded approvingly. I noticed he did not tell Riplakish about the smeared lipstick. Under normal circumstances I would have been amused, but at this moment I couldn't care less what Riplakish looked like.

"Anointed One, take care of my kitten while I'm gone," he said, handing me the ball of fur.

I couldn't do anything but stare at him blankly, his words not making sense in the mush of disappointment that used to be my brain. I nodded the mask up and down and cradled the trembling animal.

"I'll be back in a mooo-ment," Riplakish sang, waving his fingers.

He left and I slumped back in my chair, feeling as limp as a fallen flag. The game wasn't over yet. The most anticipated events were yet to come.

No one had left the stands, and the noise in the court gradually died down into an anxious silence. We were waiting. Riplakish soon appeared on the field, and everyone's eyes followed him as he glided out into the center of the green, his feet whispering across the grass, his white robes billowing behind him like clouds. In his slender hand flashed a machete.

On the side of the victorious team, people were leaning forward, some of them silently getting out of their seats to come down to the railing, the only thing that kept them from falling off the stone wall and onto the field. The losing side became increasingly tense, clutching the jewels that hung from their necks and the bracelets on their arms. I saw one woman pull her rings off and place them in her mouth. They were bracing themselves.

The losing captain knelt on his knees as Riplakish approached. No words were said. Riplakish simply removed the man's headdress and put his hand on the top of the man's head, clutching a handful of hair. Then he raised the machete and with one quick movement sliced through the captain's neck.

Riplakish held up the head high in the air as the body flopped over to the side. This was their cue. With a loud roar, the winning fans moved like a great wave over the railing. People were leaping and falling off the wall, swarming over the court and climbing up the opposite wall like hundreds of cockroaches.

The losing fans tried desperately to exit the stands as members of the advancing mob were hoisted up over the barrier. Finally, in a great surge, the winners billowed up over the wall in a wave of black heads. They spread through the stands, overtaking the losers.

In no time, the winning fans had stripped the opposing side of all their jewelry, all their precious feathers, and most of their fine clothing. In this game the losers lose everything.

This was the custom in Zitól.

CHAPTER 6

The Screen-Fold Book

Rishi entered her grandfather's hut, bringing some fried fish and potatoes for his dinner. She found him sitting with a large wooden box on his lap. She put the plate of food down and sat next to him, leaning over his shoulder. The box was made of dark, polished wood. Inside was a beautiful knife with a mother-of-pearl handle, sheathed in an eelskin scabbard. She had seen the knife before, for it was one of the only things he had brought with him from Zitól. Yelgab pulled it out of its sheath, admiring the blade of razor-sharp obsidian. He never used it for fishing or for work, though he kept it constantly sharpened. It was very special to him, for, he told Rishi many times, it had once saved his life. But Rishi was more interested in the other item in the box.

"What is that?" she asked, pointing to the other object. Her grandfather put down the knife and carefully lifted out the painted papers.

Rishi had never seen anything like them. The pages were as long as her forearm and each page was decorated with vibrant illustrations and figures. When folded up it could fit neatly in the box. But when it was unfolded, it opened like a screen and became very long. The smooth, white surface was pliable, but stiff enough to not wrinkle like fabric.

"This is a book. I brought it with me from Zitól. It is made from a buckskin hide that has been bleached and pounded very thin. It has the Zitóli calendar and many of the characters. It also has the Seven Songs."

"The Zitóli people know the Seven Songs too? Can you read it? What does it say?" Rishi asked.

Her grandfather chuckled. "One question at a time. Here, look at this. Do you see this character?"

Rishi knelt and saw the head of a serpent with fierce eyes and a gaping mouth. The whole image was shaped in a cube, as were the other pictures on the page.

"This is a hieroglyph. It is a picture that represents something. In this case, this image means *clever*. But if the serpent had a tongue extending from its mouth it would mean *cunning*." He turned the page. "Here is another one that people often mistranslate." He pointed to a hieroglyph of a heart over a background of a swirling pattern of wave-like designs. "This means *heart* or *soul*. And here . . ." His finger slid over to a similar picture next to it. It was also a picture of a heart, but it was resting in the palm of a hand. ". . . this picture means a literal heart. As in, 'I skinned a rabbit and ate its heart.'" Rishi nodded her head. She knew about rabbit hearts. They were delicious.

"Do all the people in Zitóli know how to read this kind of writing?"

"Yes—the children were taught from a very young age to read."

"Why don't you teach us to read, Grandfather?"

"Because we do not have a way to make buckskin paper here on our island, and the stone here is not good for chiseling. That is why I have all the children memorize the Seven Songs, so that it is right up here." He tapped on his temple. "That way you will never lose it, and it will stay with you your whole life. When you have children you can help them learn the songs. But . . . if you really want," he paused tentatively, "I could teach you how to read these characters. I could teach you to read this whole book."

"You could?" Rishi was delighted.

So it was agreed. Every afternoon when Rishi brought her grandfather his lunch, they would eat together and browse through his amazing book. Rishi was fascinated. Her grandfather was careful to only teach her a little at a time, fearing that too much would make her bored and lose interest. He had tried to teach her older brothers to read the characters, but they were never patient or curious enough. He hadn't thought of teaching Rishi at all, thinking that she too would be uninterested. But his efforts to limit her only made her more inquisitive, and she studied his book with passionate diligence.

She loved reading the picture-words. It thrilled her to decipher meaning out of the simple lines and pictures. As she became more and more literate, she treasured this secret language she shared with her grandfather that she knew her brothers envied. Now there was at least one thing in which she had the advantage, though how that would help her against their constant tormenting, she did not know.

CHAPTER 7
My Great Opportunity

We think it is a bad idea," they were saying. "He is still too young." We were in the throne room, and I sat, dangling my legs on the oversized throne. I was maskless, for here in the palace was I permitted to be myself. It was only in front of the people that I was to be anonymous.

On my left was Speaker Riplakish, on my right was Speaker Gula, both sitting on their thrones. Facing us in the rostrum that curved around the perimeter of the chamber sat a dozen priests.

Their bickering was nothing new. The priests and the Speakers generally liked to argue with each other on policies and treaties and laws. I didn't care much for their meetings, since my thoughts at that time centered on the next ball game or a pretty face I'd seen in the city. But this time they had my full attention. After all, they were arguing about my competence.

"We can't have a fourteen-year-old speaking to the people. He has not yet gained the wisdom of the world. He is not prepared. The people would tear him to pieces."

"When will it be time, then?" said another priest. "The people are restless and desire a king. We've been without a king for too long."

Another spoke. "Yes—even a young king is better than no king."

Speaker Gula nodded as he listened to the opinions of the priests. Finally he lifted his hands and the voices abated. Sometimes I wondered if the clouds would part when Gula raised his massive arms to the sky.

He cleared his throat, making his great double chin quake. "Squabbling like this makes us weak. We all know he will one day be the king. I believe there is no need to rush into something as important as this. The boy is not yet ready. He has much to learn. His time will come, and until then Speaker Riplakish and I will continue to manage the affairs of the kingdom."

"But will he be ready when he is of age?" the priests insisted. "He should be doing something to prepare."

I thought it strange how they were speaking of me as if I were not right there, sitting in front of them. Why could they not ask me? I knew the answer to my own question, though. The Speakers didn't just speak for the people. They spoke for me too. And speaking for me meant they spoke for the gods.

"But he needs to be preparing now. He needs to be educated. He should at least be practicing his speaking," said Tungan, one of the youngest and most vocal priests.

"And to whom should he speak?" said Speaker Riplakish.

"To us!" answered some of the priests.

"Yes," said Tungan. "Give him one month. Have him prepare a lecture and give it to us, the priests. Then we will know whether he is ready or not."

I gulped.

I glanced sideways at Gula and then at Riplakish. I thought at first they were both looking at me, but then I realized they were really looking at each other.

Speaker Gula licked his lips and leaned back into his cushioned seat. "Very well then. Did you hear that, Anointed One? One month from now, on the fourth day of the month of the Crocodile, you will give your first speech."

Later that afternoon I sat cross-legged on my bed, thinking. What would I talk about, especially in front of the priests and Speakers? They knew far more than I did about every subject imaginable. If I performed well, would they really turn the kingdom into my hands? A thrill ran through my body as I thought about being king. I imagined being the one who spoke at all the gatherings. The one the people looked to for guidance and direction. I nodded to myself . . . I could do this.

But what to speak about? The Speakers usually talked about the same subjects: the gods, what the gods wanted from us, how angered the gods can get, how disobedience to the gods brings eternal torture and pain in the underworld. Sometimes they would talk about the Great Coward or the need for more sacrifices. None of these topics appealed to me. Besides, I had heard them all before. If I was to truly prove to them that I was ready, I had to find a topic that was new, stimulating, perhaps even . . . revolutionary.

The Speakers gave me one month. During that time I tried to approach Speaker Gula and Speaker Riplakish to ask for their advice. But whenever I asked them, they seemed preoccupied and dismissed me with irritated waves, as if I were some buzzing insect. Since the "Anointed One" wasn't really allowed to talk to anyone besides them, I was on my own.

I decided to go out. I changed out of my white clothes and into the dull brown tunic and cape I kept hidden in my closet. Tonight I would go down to the city. Perhaps there I would find the inspiration I needed for my speech.

CHAPTER 8

Strange Visitors

Rishi's eyes opened to blackness. Her heart was beating like the wings of a frightened bird and her entire body trembled. She sat up, hugged her knees and looked around, her eyes wide with fear. Slowly things began to look familiar. She was in her hut; her mother and her brothers were all around, sleeping. She was safe. The beach, the terror, and the wolves were all gone. Just vapors of memory. Slowly, as the reality of her surroundings became more believable, she understood.

So this is what it was like to dream.

She lay back down, and then sat right back up. She didn't want to relive the dream, for it still lurked in her mind like a stingray in the sand. She slowly got to her feet and tiptoed around her snoring brothers' bodies and out into the night air.

Then she crept out under the starry night sky, took four quick leaps, and ducked into Yelgab's hut.

"Grandfather," she whispered, *"Grandfather."* But his sleep was peaceful and deep, and he was impossible to wake. She curled up next to his warm body, her back against his, keeping her eyes open for as long as she could until finally the feeling of her dream faded and her mind slipped back into an uneasy sleep.

When Rishi awoke, her grandfather was gone and his mat was cold. She rubbed her eyes. The imprint of the dream was still in her mind. She needed to tell someone. But who? She couldn't tell her mother—she'd worry. She couldn't tell her brothers either. That was obvious.

"Where's Grandfather?" Rishi asked her mother, who was starting a fire.

"He's been called to council."

"So early?"

"Canoes arrived before dawn with strangers who wished to speak with the village leaders. They are only here for a short time. It seemed urgent."

Rishi ran down the trail to the council lodge and saw a half dozen unfamiliar men coming out. Their meeting must have just ended. The visitors had darker skin than the people on her island, and as they filed out of the lodge their faces were very solemn and grave, as if they were leaving a funeral. They were followed by the councilmen, who wore equally grim countenances. Finally, Rishi recognized Yelgab's bent figure in the doorway.

"Grandfather!" She ran up to him through the crowd of men and tugged at his tunic.

"Not now, Rishi. Hush."

At the rebuke, Rishi drew back behind Yelgab, but he opened his hand for her to hold as he addressed the strangers.

"We will do all we can to help you. You are welcome to go from hut to hut, if you wish," he added. "We have nothing to hide."

The other councilmen nodded in agreement.

"It is not necessary," said one of the strangers. "We know they are not here." There was an awkward silence. Timidly, Rishi observed the hopeless faces of the men around her. They looked like the saddest men in the world. Finally the leader murmured to his companions, "We must be going."

Grandfather then said, "You must be hungry. Let us fill your bellies."

"Thank you, Yelgab. You have all been kind to us, but we must go."

"Then let us fill your canoes with food for your journey," said another councilmen.

"That would be most appreciated, since we have other islands to visit."

The men trudged across the sand to where the strangers' canoes were beached. Rishi followed at a respectful distance, walking among their long shadows that slanted across the beach in the crisp morning light. After filling their boats with fruits and salted fish, the men bid farewell to the councilmen. "Thank you again," said the leader. "Please remember what we said. And . . ." He glanced at Rishi. ". . . protect what you have."

The councilmen watched in silence as the men climbed into the canoes and paddled away toward the bright rising sun. Finally, the councilmen turned to walk up the beach, shaking their heads and talking softly to each other, all except her grandfather, who sighed deeply and turned to Rishi.

"Now what was it that you wanted to tell me?"

"You'll never believe it, Grandfather. You know how I never, ever have dreams? Well, last night I had a dream! But it was a terrible dream.

It all started when I saw this strange cloud in the sky. It had a funny shape . . ." Rishi prattled on, even though she could feel by the way he kept looking out at the ocean that her grandfather was not listening. ". . . and then I woke up and I was so scared and that is why I came to sleep in your hut. Grandfather?"

He was staring at the sea, and he did not answer her.

"Grandfather?"

"Hmm?" he said.

"What did you think about my dream?" she said in exasperation.

"I'm glad you had a dream," he murmured as he watched the departing canoes. It was then that Rishi noticed, in the light of the golden sun, that his eyes were glittering with tears.

"Grandfather?" she asked, following his gaze.

"Yes, Rishi."

"What were those men looking for?"

"They are looking for their daughters."

CHAPTER 9

The Dream Child

We should not overreact," a councilman told the villagers later that day.

They had called an assembly. It was only that morning that the strangers had come and gone, and the councilmen felt their village needed to prepare. And in order to prepare, the people needed to know the truth.

Rishi was sitting in the group, crammed between Quash and a large woman who was nursing a baby. Every now and then Quash would wet his finger in his mouth, put his arm around Rishi, and stick it in her ear.

Calmly, Rishi's grandfather and the other three men had explained that the early morning visitors were from a distant island, and came bearing a strange tale.

One night, a group of warriors with blackened faces attacked their island. The village was ransacked; their huts were pillaged and burned. Anything valuable was taken or destroyed. Finally, the marauders left, taking with them every girl they could carry.

"So the rumors are true, then."

"The Snatchers really exist."

Quash jabbed Rishi in the shoulder. "See?" he hissed in her ear. "I told you."

The councilman continued, "It is true that these bandits—the, ah, *Snatchers* as some of you call them—are real. But there are many islands in the sea. It is unlikely that they would ever come to ours."

"But what if they do?"

"Then we must be prepared," reassured the councilman. "We have a plan."

He explained: the northern shore of the island was studded with high black cliffs and below the cliffs was a series of caverns that the villagers used for shelter from hurricanes. It was decided that young men would be placed at lookout points around the island, taking turns to serve as sentinels to watch the sea. If they saw anything unusual on the

33

water, they were to sound a conch horn and all villagers were to head for the caves, in case of an attack.

The plan was implemented that very day, with Rishi's brothers serving as sentinels for three of the posts. In the days afterward, the drill was practiced several times, and this finally put the villagers' minds at ease.

Even so, for weeks Rishi's mother would not let her daughter go anywhere alone, and made her brothers be her escorts when they weren't serving as sentinel or doing their other duties. Rishi didn't know which was more dangerous: being kidnapped by Snatchers or being left alone with her brothers. Luckily, her mother also considered Yelgab a competent protector (even though to Rishi he seemed as old as the sun and as fragile as a footprint) and so she spent most of her time by his side, listening to his stories and learning Zitóli characters.

Her dream repeated itself two more times in the coming weeks, wedging itself in her mind all day like a stubborn splinter. She yearned to tell it to her grandfather again, knowing he had not truly heard her the first time.

"Grandfather," she said one day when they were alone. "I've been dreaming."

"I remember you said that, the day the men came looking for their daughters. That is a good thing. It is very healthy to dream. It means the gods have blessed you with a vigorous imagination."

"But Grandfather, it is always the *same* dream. And it always wakes me up. It terrifies me, Grandfather."

"Let's hear it again, then. Dreams are always less scary once they are spoken out loud."

Rishi took a deep breath. "It always begins with me, sitting on the beach, alone. The sand is white and warm. The sky is blue and perfect with only an odd-looking cloud, shaped like a pink seahorse, floating in the distance. When I look down again, I see that I am holding handfuls of colored stones. I lay them each on the sand, in a row. Among these colored stones I find white stones that look like my white bead."

She looked to see if Grandfather was paying attention. His brown eyes were fixed on her face, and this time she could tell he was listening.

"These white stones seem special, like little moons, so I group them together and put them on my right. I put the colored stones on my left. But then, Grandfather, I have a bad feeling, like something is going to happen. Above me, in the sky, the seahorse cloud is still there. I look up and down the beach, wondering what it is that makes me feel uneasy, but everything is the same as before. Then I look out into the ocean. The waves are breaking along the sand as usual, but something is different. When I look closer I start to see shapes in the white water. With each new wave the shapes become clearer until finally I realize that the waves are not waves at all."

"What are they?"

"They are wolves, Grandfather. Their jaws are opened and frothing, and each new wave brings the wolves farther and farther up the beach until they break out of the water and start running at me in a great foaming pack. Their bodies are white and liquid and their jaws hang open and I can see their tongues and white teeth." Rishi stopped to catch her breath. By now her voice was trembling and her eyes were wide.

"Remember it is only a dream, Rishi," her grandfather reassured her, a look of captivation on his face. "But you must finish. Please go on."

Rishi swallowed and closed her eyes. "I want to run, but my body is stuck right were I am. They are coming nearer, galloping up the beach, sometimes stopping to sniff the ground like they are looking for something." Rishi swallowed. "I can feel they are looking for me and they are going to eat me alive. Then they see me and start sprinting toward me. I close my eyes and I hear them snapping their teeth. I can feel water on my face. And then . . . everything is quiet." Rishi had been twisting her tunic in her hands. "When I open my eyes everything is always still and beautiful again, just like it had been before the wolves came, except one thing: the colored stones are still on the sand, but all of the white stones are gone."

When she finished, she knew her grandfather had understood her, for the look on his face frightened her.

"Rishi, is it true that you have never dreamed a dream at all until this one?"

"Never. This is the only dream I've ever had."

"Then it is true," he said in a quiet voice.

"What is true?"

"You are a dream child."

"A dream child?" Rishi felt her body shiver as she said the words. "What is that? It is it bad?"

"No, not at all. A dream child is what the Zitóli people call children like you who are born with a blue eye . . . and who can dream the future. It is a gift."

"There are other children who look like me?"

"I've heard of several. But I've only known of one other."

"And could the child you knew see into the future?"

"Yes," said Yelgab, looking at the ground. "She could."

"But if my dream is telling me the future, what does it mean? Will I see stones on the beach? Will wolves come out of the water?"

"I don't know, my child. Only the dream child can learn to interpret their own dreams," said Yelgab seriously. "But I do think it means that you must never go to the beach alone."

CHAPTER 10

Dangerous Ideas

I walked through the torch-lit streets of Zitól maskless, knowing no one would recognize me. The Speakers always did an excellent job of making sure I was thoroughly disguised at all public events. It was for my protection, they said, because the Anointed One is too holy to be seen by common people. When I wore the mask, I was taking on the image of the gods, the Speakers explained to me. I always thought that was strange, since I seldom felt holy, and *never* godlike. What I really wanted was to just be myself.

The city was an excellent place to escape the profound pressure of pretending to be a god. There the laughter and the women and the fermented drinks were abundant. Dark corners hid dark deeds and everyone seemed to have an interesting secret of some kind. Because no one knew my face, I was never more hidden than when I was without my mask. I could walk the dark streets freely, mingling with the people without any fear of being discovered. The only concern I had, lingering in the back of my mind, was that I needed to arrive back in my tower before anyone discovered I was gone.

But tonight was not as carefree as it was in the past, for tonight a thought pressed on my mind. What would be the topic of my first great speech? What could I say to impress the Speakers and priests? I knew that I did not have the commanding presence of Speaker Gula or the eloquence of Speaker Riplakish. But what if I presented an idea that had never been considered? What if my idea could make up for my inexperience?

I ran my palm along the side of a stone building, letting my fingers fall into the hieroglyphs written there. In the city, writing was everywhere: carved on the walls, chiseled over the doorways, engraved on the temples. It was all ancient, and no one now could understand it except for the Speakers. The writing looked like pictures, but that did not make them any easier to interpret. The Speakers taught me that the gods wrote it when the city was first built. Some of my earliest memories were of the Speakers telling me terrifying stories about the gods and what they did to people who were disobedient. As I grew, I often found it easier to pretend the gods didn't exist. On this particular evening I found myself wondering, as usual, what the writing said and if it were important. If Speaker Riplakish were here, he could tell me.

Then the idea came to me.

I turned back to the palace and started to run, hoping that Riplakish would be up late in the library.

It was always a little disconcerting going down to the library, down the narrow stairwell that opens up to a series of shadowy dark corridors, down past the skittering cockroaches that were the size of small mice and the spiders that took pleasure in weaving cobwebs right at face level. The aversion I had to books in my younger years had a good deal to do with my association of books with black creeping things.

Sometimes Riplakish would come here to study from the ancient texts. I always knew he was here if the stairwell was lit with torches. Sure enough, he was sitting at the thick table, stacked with scrolls and folios and plates made from pounded ore. Sitting beside him was the priest Tungan. Before entering, I cleared my throat and clapped my hands to request entry.

The two men looked up. "Who's there?" the Speaker said, narrowing his eyes into the darkness. I could immediately see that I had caught Riplakish at a bad moment—he was without his makeup, and his face looked ghastly, like a pineapple past its prime.

I stepped down the last step and entered the room. "Only me," I said.

"Hello, my boy," he said, not cheerfully. "You are up late tonight. How is your speech coming along?"

"That is why I came to see you. Do you . . . do you have time?"

He looked at Tungan, who shrugged and leaned back in his chair.

Tungan was the newest of the priests, though he was still ten years older than me. He was an imposing, striking man who wore a gold ring through his nose and shaved the sides of his head. He had charisma and a natural confidence that set him apart from the other priests. Gula and Riplakish noticed right away that he had great potential. I knew they were grooming him to become one of my Speakers. He had already given several public speeches and was being taught to read the ancient texts. In time he would be anointed and I would have three advisors instead of two. Lucky me.

"We were just finishing, weren't we, Tungan?" Riplakish said. "It is late, though, and I am tired, but if you *absolutely* need my opinion, and if you can keep it brief, I will listen." Riplakish always made it sound like it was terribly inconvenient to even spend two minutes looking at me, but he was the only one I could ask at this late hour.

I plunged in. "What do all the writings say?" I asked.

"Ah . . . could you be more specific? What writings?"

"*All* the writings. The writings on the walls in the city, the writing on the temple, these," I gestured to the paper and books and scrolls that filled the room.

"Why, they say a multitude of things. You've probably heard a significant amount of it from Speaker Gula and me. We are constantly quoting from them in our speeches. The rest would take me hours to read and explain to you, and I really don't have the time. It is hard enough trying to explain it to the people in a way they can understand."

"Then why not teach the people to read? Then you wouldn't have to always be trying to explain things to them."

Riplakish gave an exasperated sigh. He closed his eyes and rubbed his face, as if my words had just given him the worst headache he'd ever had. "And what does this have to do with your speech?" he asked with closed eyes, his thumb and middle finger pinching the bridge of his nose.

"I think we should teach the *people* to read. *That* is the topic I have chosen."

Riplakish let his hands fall down onto the desk with a thump. His face had a peculiar expression, as if I had just asked if I could set fire to his hair. I wondered if I had made a mistake.

His jaw tightened. He inhaled slowly—and loudly—through his nose, staring at me. I took a step back. Tungan, sensing the prelude to an explosion, interjected.

"You know, holy one," he said, leaning toward Riplakish's ear. "You could have him *try*, just to see what would happen."

Riplakish blinked, and when he did I could tell something flashed across his mind, and instead of letting out all of his air in the usual long lecture, he exhaled through his mouth and a strange smile curved his lips. His eyebrows relaxed, and his entire expression softened into something that could almost be called fatherly. Almost.

"I think . . . you've chosen an *excellent* topic," he said.

Tungan smiled.

"Are you sure?" I asked, doubting his sincerity. After all, a moment ago he looked as if he was going to choke me.

"Definitely. I think the priests and Speaker Gula will be enthralled. It is a stirring idea, and priests may be talking about it for a long time."

"You think so?" I asked.

"I *know* so." He smiled, the jade studs glistening. "Now, go off to your chamber and start practicing. You know what I always say, content is important, but it is the *delivery* that really matters."

"Yes, you are right, Speaker Riplakish. Thank you for your help."

"I am always at your service, my future king," he said, bowing his head slightly.

I left the library, elated.

I spent many days and nights preparing my speech. I practiced in my tower, trying out different phrases on my tongue and trying to memorize the ones that sounded the best. I spoke to the drapes, to my bed, to the birds that landed on the balcony, as if they were priests of the court. I polished my performance, perfecting it until I could utter it in my sleep.

The fourth day in the month of the Crocodile finally arrived. As I entered the throne room, dressed in my royal robes, the priests and Speakers stood. Immediately I noticed—with great displeasure—that Raven was in attendance. I had not expected this. I glanced at Riplakish for an explanation, and he answered with his jade-encrusted smile. I felt Raven's golden eyes follow me as I walked across the room and up the steps of the rostrum to my gilded throne. I turned to face the court and she was still staring. When I sat she licked her lips.

Any handsomeness Riplakish's jaguar may have inherited from her species disappeared as she grew, or rather languished, under Riplakish's care, for the Speaker took pride in starving his pet. He often told me he did not want her to become "a great, fat nuisance." It was good, he said, to feed her sparingly, for it kept the *fire* in her eyes. It only took one glance at her to know for a surety that the "fire" was there, hot and seething.

In the years since he had acquired her, Raven had become Riplakish's secret weapon, his favorite instrument of torment. To make up for her bony and sickly appearance, he had her fit with a golden collar, inlaid with opal and turquoise. During meetings and hearings, she paced the steps of the rostrum incessantly, covering as much ground as her short, heavy chain would allow. She hissed at prisoners pleading for mercy and snarled at peasants who couldn't pay tribute. The more disruptive she was, the more delighted Riplakish became. Of course, she sometimes distressed even the priests, so Gula would not allow her presence at *every* meeting. She was only used on occasions when Riplakish needed to intimidate, confuse, and terrorize.

I realized, as I sat in my throne, that this was one of those moments.

Speaker Gula began the meeting. After some brief announcements, introductions, and formal explanations of what was about to take place, I was directed to stand in the middle of the circular room, the same place where I had seen prisoners and thieves stand to plead their innocence. Leaving the safety of my throne, I slowly made my way down the steps, taking care to carve a path out of Raven's swiping range. Once I reached the mosaic of the sun that spread across the floor, I turned to face my audience.

"Very well, Anointed One," Gula said. "You may begin when you are ready."

The priests stared. Raven snarled. I took a deep breath.

They were intimidating, these well-educated men, all dressed in white with feathers in their hair and rings dangling from their noses and ear lobes. No one smiled or gave any indication that they wished for my success. I looked at Speaker Riplakish for a shot of encouragement, and indeed he had a small smile on his face, but his eyes seemed rounder and more penetrating than usual. Too penetrating.

"I—I have come to talk—I mean, to *speak* to you all today," I said, stumbling over my well-rehearsed opening sentence. All saliva evaporated from my mouth and my tongue felt as agile as a baked brick. "I am going to speak to you about the importance of—the importance of —" Out of the corner of my eye I saw Speaker Gula open his jowls in an exaggerated yawn. Some priests leaned back in their seats, and one rolled his eyes to the ceiling. I shook my head and cleared my throat. I would start again.

"I have come to speak to you about a proposal." I lifted my chin and straightened my shoulders. I tried to look confident, authoritative. "My proposal would help everyone in the city become more obedient and more . . . more . . ." What was the right word here? ". . . *compliant* with our cultural ideals. In addition, the people will all come to a knowledge for themselves that what we teach them is the truth, and I believe their lives will be better and more productive with this confidence."

At least they were all paying attention now. Even Raven sat still and erect, eyeing me shrewdly while flicking her ears and batting her tail hard against the stone floor. I continued. "I have always been taught that the gods have written upon the walls of our ancient city the laws we are to perform. The gods expect us to obey these laws with exactness, that our city might be preserved from their anger." Several of the priests nodded.

"My proposal is simple, though it may take months or even a year to be carried out. After that, it will take ongoing care to ensure everyone has mastered the skill." I looked at the Speakers, and their eyes made me nervous, so I looked at the priests instead. "I think that everyone would benefit, and our city would become stronger, if *everyone* were taught—" I inserted a pause here for drama, hoping to please Speaker Gula. "—if everyone were taught to read the ancient writings. And I *also* propose," I added quickly before anyone could protest, "that we have schools where children can learn, too, so that they will grow to become knowledgeable adults. Then not only would we be able to have the spoken word go out to the people, but we would have a written word too." I started to get excited with my own idea. "We could have people who would write down what the Speakers say and then other people that could be couriers to bring the words to those who are too far away to hear, or even to neighboring villages and kingdoms. With written communication, we could strengthen alliances with other tribes and make the kingdom of Zitól even grander than it is now." I was done but I had forgotten how to finish. "That is what I think," I said lamely. "That is all. I'm finished. Amen."

I surveyed my audience. They couldn't have looked more surprised if I had taken off my sandals and started eating them. Clearly, I had made an impression.

"Are you finished?" came Speaker Gula's low, gravely voice.

"Yes, holy Speaker," I said.

"Good." He leaned forward. "Then let me tell you why that idea is ridiculous."

This last word sent a cold chill vibrating through my core. With a foreboding sense of doom, I turned my face toward Gula, giving one long, painful blink. I knew, from watching his performances in the past, that this was just his opening statement. His eyebrows started to rise into their triangular shape and all I could do was stand and steady myself against the hurricane.

First he talked about how I was young and inexperienced and how I did not have the wisdom to even *imagine* the consequences of ideas like this. That the words written in stone were words from the *gods* and that only those who speak for the gods, the Speakers, were worthy enough to interpret them. That having everyone read would bring grave doctrinal misunderstandings, for there would be too many interpretations on how to perform the rituals. Confusion would abound. Rebellion would ensue. He went on and on until his words became a faraway sound to me and all I could concentrate on was the peculiar way his fish-like eyes bulged from his ever-reddening face. When I glanced to Riplakish for some sort of rescue, he began to file his fingernails.

Finally, when Gula became so infuriated he couldn't speak and I was certain his fish eyes would pop out of his head and hit me in the face, he opened the floor to the others. For over an hour they took turns criticizing me on everything from my diction to my posture. I was obviously not ready for the throne, they said. Nor did I exhibit sufficient leadership even on the most basic level. What kind of ruler would entertain such dangerous ideas? Raven added to the insults by laying her ears back and hissing disapprovingly.

By the time they were finished, my confidence had turned to slime. Ultimately the Speakers dismissed the meeting as a completely failed experiment. The topic of my future as a leader would not be brought up again for years.

They couldn't have done more to silence me than if they had cut out my tongue. I slunk back to my tower like a salted slug, shamed and spiteful. I told myself that I didn't need to speak, and that my very presence still commanded respect. But I knew my presence would only go so far if I couldn't open my mouth.

After that I was as influential as a statue. Meals were still served me, clothes were still brought to me, but from that time forth I became the Great Anonymous. I kept to my tower, as shamed as a plucked turkey. When I did venture down to the palace, I passed through like a phantom, aloof and irrelevant, speaking to no one. Increasingly it became clear to all what my purpose was. Someday I would become the king, everyone knew that, and to the beautiful nation of the Zitóli people I would one day become the "head" of the kingdom. But the Speakers and priests would always remain my neck, turning my head to see only what they wanted me to see. My purpose was purely ornamental. I was simply a symbol. A figurehead. A mascot.

The next few years were dark years, and I never attended another meeting again.

And, for a time, this is where my part of the story ends.

CHAPTER 11

Rishi Becomes a True Brother

Over the next few years, Rishi's brothers' gangly frames filled out. Their arms and legs became thick and muscular, their chests wide and strong, and their brown skin as smooth and tight as the skin of a tomato. Most of their energy was spent finding ways to avoid work in all its forms, but they still took their turns standing sentinel, just as all the boys did on the island. They also still teased Rishi, but she couldn't help notice that the words had lost their bite. Perhaps they had become nicer. Or perhaps she had become stronger.

At sixteen, she now was taller than her mother and wore her hair in one braid instead of two. Her breasts and hips filled out the baggy parts of her dress and she tied a blue band across her forehead, to match her eye, for now that she was older, she was proud of what made her unique.

By now the Snatchers were old news. Rumors of recent kidnappings from other islands were nonexistent, and the gossip that was still passed among the traders was the same old gossip heard before. Even Quash eventually ran out of gory details for his stories and his audience disbanded to other firesides. Only the duty of the sentinels still survived, and that was only because the villagers needed something to keep the boys out of trouble. The Snatchers ended up being a myth after all. And of course, if that were truly the case, our story would end here.

"I'm coming with you today," stated Rishi as she trotted after her brothers, carrying an oyster basket.

"Fine. Come," Eno said without enthusiasm.

Rishi ran ahead of them to the shore. Eager to be useful, she tugged at the canoe to move it toward the water. It hardly budged.

The boys stood and watched, letting her try until it became too painful for them. Finally Quash said, "Get in, weakling." Then he picked up the end of the canoe with one arm and dragged it, with Rishi inside, to the water.

They pushed off and Rishi glanced up at the sky—as always—looking for any peculiar clouds. Her dream still haunted her and she was always wary of what she might see on the horizon. Many dreamless months would pass, and just when Rishi thought she had outgrown the dream, it would appear again and she would relive everything. The cloud. The stones. The wolves. She'd wake, shivering with fear, knowing that even though her eyes were open, the dark spirit of the dream would continue to follow her throughout the day like a hungry dog. Once, in a moment of weakness, she told her brothers about the dream, adding that Grandfather had called her a dream child. They listened intently until she was finished and then rolled around on the ground laughing and snorting. She just shook her head and wondered if they would ever grow up.

But there were no clouds today, so Rishi breathed a sigh of relief. All was well. She closed her eyes and enjoyed the breeze in her face and the spray of the plunging paddles as they skimmed along the surface to the cove.

The cove was perfectly calm. They anchored and let their paddles clatter into the canoe. Then all four of them took their baskets and splashed overboard. Rishi, thanks to Eno's patient teaching, could now hold her breath long enough to gather almost as many oysters as her brothers. She could never beat Eno, however. He was king.

"How can you stay under for so long? You must have bigger lungs," Rishi said when Eno surfaced. She had been treading the water for a full thirty seconds before he appeared.

Eno spat water out of his mouth. "Maybe, but I doubt it. Quash has bigger lungs than me and I can always beat him," he said, emptying two handfuls of oysters into his basket.

"So what is your trick? How do you do it?"

"Practice," Eno said as he climbed into the canoe. He towed in his basket, almost sinking with oysters. His expression became thoughtful. "Although there is something else that helps, I think."

Eno held the boat steady while Rishi flung one leg over the side and pulled herself in. "What is it?" She asked, expecting another joke.

"The Seven Songs."

Rishi was confused. "What?" she said. She leaned over the side to squeeze the water out of her braid.

Eno glanced over his shoulder at the spot where Cotyl and Quash were still diving. He lowered his voice.

"When I first started diving I tried to see how many of the Seven Songs I could recite. I first dove until I could go through one in my head. Then two . . . now I can say all seven."

Rishi's eyebrows raised in surprise. "*You* recite the Seven Songs to yourself?" Eno? Her brother? The one who used to light her braids on fire and fling her dolls out into the ocean?

"What is wrong with that?"

"I don't know. It just seems odd that someone like *you* would . . ." Rishi didn't know how to end her sentence in a complimentary way.

Eno grinned. "I will tell you a secret, Rishi."

"What?"

"I believe the songs have power."

Well, of course, thought Rishi. Everyone knew that.

"What I mean is, I think that when you sing the songs the gods *really* listen. I think that when I sing the songs as I am diving the gods give me more strength than I have."

Rishi felt a rush spread through her body. It was kind of like water, kind of like wind. She knew that what Eno said was true. And from the look in Eno's eyes, he had felt it too.

The feeling lasted only a moment. Just then Cotyl and Quash surfaced and clamored into the boat. Rishi began towing in her basket. Eno reached for a paddle.

"You two look like you were having a deep conversation," said Quash eagerly. "Might I join you?"

Eno smiled. "Rishi here was doubting that we know all the Seven Songs."

Quash put his hand to his heart in astonishment. "I'm hurt, Rishi."

"I didn't really say that exactly," said Rishi.

"You think we are not good people," Cotyl said, frowning.

"Well, I—"

"She was telling me that she thinks we are heartless brothers, with souls of stone," Eno explained.

"That's not what I—"

"Rishi, what must we do to prove we are gentle and kind siblings?" said Quash.

"And that we love you from the heart of our bottoms?" added Cotyl slyly.

"I know!" Quash's face brightened. "Let's take her to the cliff!"

Rishi's eyes widened at the word "cliff" and she looked at Eno in alarm. He gave her a wink. "Yes," he said. "I think it is time. Her initiation is long overdue."

"I think I've been initiated enough times, thank you very much," Rishi replied, trying to lift her heavy basket into the canoe. Cotyl reached over and gripped the handle.

"Here, let me help you with that, scream child," he said. With one arm he pulled the dripping basket out of the water and let it land in the canoe with a clatter.

"This is a different kind of initiation. This is what you have to do to become a true brother," Eno said. "We all had to do it."

Rishi paused. A true brother?

"I think she'll be too scared," Quash muttered.

"Will not," Rishi stated. "I can do whatever you can do." She would do anything if it made her a true brother. Anything.

They paddled the canoe over to the cliffs and wedged the rope between some rocks. Then they climbed out of the canoe and up the black wall.

"Where are you going?" Rishi called after them.

"Don't ask, just follow," was the reply.

She tentatively stepped out of the canoe and gingerly lifted one leg onto a ledge. The black rock looked jagged and slippery, but years of waves on the cliff had softened the ledges and her feet easily found places to lift her body up the rock face.

When they reached the top, Rishi saw that the cliff was a long, narrow precipice that jutted out into the lagoon. The water seemed as far below as the sky seemed as far above. Rishi felt dizzy as the wind tossed her hair, and she stood a safe distance away from the boys, just in case one of them thought it would be fun to see how far she could fly.

"What are you doing way over there?" Cotyl asked her. "We aren't going to throw you off."

"Not yet, anyway," Quash added.

"Come over here and look," said Eno.

Rishi shuffled closer to her brothers as Eno pointed his finger out to the huge rock formations.

"Do you see the arch that the cliff makes?" Rishi could see a nearby cliff that jutted out from the land, forming an arch over the water. The width of the space in the arch was about the size of a long canoe.

"I see it."

"Now look at the water. Do you see the way it swirls and eddies here below us?"

"Yes."

"That is a current. It comes from underground. It is cool and swift, and if you dive right there, it will push you forward under the arch. It is like swimming in an underwater river."

Rishi smiled dubiously up at Eno, Cotyl, and Quash, nervous about what they were suggesting. "You first," she said.

"If you insist." Eno stepped to the edge of the precipice and stood, holding his arms perpendicular to his body. Rishi watched his torso expand as he took a deep breath in through his nose and exhaled through his mouth. Then he breathed in sharply, bent his knees, and sprang off the cliff. With his back arched, his arms spread out, and his legs straight, he seemed to fall for hours. At the last moment he placed his hands together and pierced the surface of the water like an arrow. The three observers watched his shadow speed under the arch until he surfaced, on the other side. After catching his breath, he whipped the water from his hair, cupped one hand to his mouth and called, "Who's next?"

Cotyl stepped to the edge next, facing Rishi, with his back to the ocean. Giving Rishi a wink, he squatted and leaped backward, spinning and twisting in the air before dropping soundlessly into the crystal waters below, hardly leaving a ripple out of place.

Now it was just Quash and Rishi left. Quash backed up as far as he could on the cliff top and started running. When he reached the edge he thrust his body out into space and made one slow rotation before plunging into the water with a mighty splash.

Rishi watched them, wanting to throw up.

"Are you coming?" Eno called out to her.

"Or are you too scared?" said Cotyl.

She looked down. It was a long way. Rishi had never jumped from so high before.

"Don't be such a girl!" Quash cried out.

She put her feet side by side on the edge of the cliff and tried to steady her nerves. Her body was shaking, but she told herself it wasn't from fear, but from the brisk wind on her wet skin.

"I guess she'll never be one of us after all," Eno said loudly to the other two, and they all hooted.

Rishi held out her arms the way Eno had done. Then she put her arms down and backed away to take a running start like Quash had done. When she got to the edge she skidded to a halt. She was not even going to *consider* attempting Cotyl's back flip. Finally she sighed and put her hands on her hips. She was going to have to do this her way or no way at all. Closing her eyes, she took a deep breath and leaped.

She fell—legs kicking, arms flailing, and throat shrieking. She felt as if her stomach had climbed into her ears. She hit the water with a *slap* and an intense pain flashed through her body. The current swirled around her like a living thing and pushed her forward through the water. Tumbling and rolling, not knowing which way was up or down, she floundered until strong arms finally caught her and pulled her to the air.

Coughing and choking, she wiped the water from her eyes, opening them to see her brothers treading the water around her, grinning.

"I don't think anyone has made a jump quite like that before," Eno said.

"I liked the shrieking bit," added Cotyl.

"Great feeling, isn't it?" Quash asked. "It is like . . . being skinned alive."

"Yeah. Great feeling." Rishi nodded, thinking she never wanted to do anything like that again in her entire life.

"I'm impressed, Rishi," said Eno. "We never brought you here because we always thought you'd be too scared. After all, it took Quash half a day up on that cliff before he would jump off," Eno said.

"Did not," replied Quash.

"Well, it helped to watch you all jump first," Rishi admitted.

"Your form could use some work," said Cotyl.

"But it was a good first attempt," said Eno.

"For a girl," said Quash.

And so goes the complexities of sibling love: intense, devoted, and life-threatening.

CHAPTER 12

Yelgab's Secret

It was night. The light from the oil lamp in Rishi's mother's hand lit the inside of the hut with stark shadows, and Rishi leaned against her mother for comfort as she watched her grandfather's chest slowly rise and fall.

Yelgab's weak, withered body was propped up by blankets and mats. Next to him, Eno, Cotyl and Quash sat shoulder to shoulder, their long legs pulled up against their big frames to make room for each other in the cramped space. Their heads hung between their arms or rested on their knees, and in the gloom of the hut their uncharacteristically sober expressions made them look much older.

Yelgab took a sharp breath and opened his eyes. He gazed in wonder at the solemn faces surrounding him. "Something important must be happening," he said, blinking and looking around in anxiety. Then his face relaxed, and his wrinkles fell back into line. "Ah. I see. I am about to die. And you've all come to watch me step from this life into the realm of the gods. Very well, very well." He smacked his lips together a few times against his gums and settled into the blankets.

"Listen to my voice one last time, then. I have taught you the Seven Songs. These will protect you your entire life if you live by them and study out what they mean. There are some who will say that they are silly proverbs—" Everyone waited while Yelgab wheezed. "But they are not proverbs, they are truths."

Rishi's mother offered him a cup of water but he refused.

"Boys," he said, waving a trembling finger at Rishi's brothers. "You are strong and you have good hearts, but you are lazy. You have ancestors who depend on you. Do not be less than you are. Remember, someday you will each have a wife to honor and protect. Until then, protect the virtue of your little sister. She is in your charge now. Honor her, and you will bring honor to yourselves."

He wheezed again, wincing in pain. His sunken eyes were draped with dark shadows, his skin hung loose on his skeletal bones. Tears formed in Rishi's eyes. This is not how she wanted to remember her grandfather.

"I have one final wish," he said, looking towards the roof.

Rishi could sense her brothers holding their breath.

"I want you to take apart this hut."

Eno leaned forward. "What was that, Grandfather?"

"I want you to take it all apart . . . the walls, the roof, everything. I no longer have need of it. I don't want to see it anymore. I don't want it to be in my way."

"Very well," said Eno. "We shall do that first thing in the morning."

"No," said Yelgab. "Now."

The brothers hesitated, looking first at each other and then at their mother, wondering if they should really start taking apart the only protection their dying grandfather had from the elements.

She nodded. "Do what he says, my sons."

The boys gathered themselves and walked outside into the dark. Rishi could hear them drag the skins off the roof and start lifting away the sticks. As they worked bits of bark fell on Yelgab's face and Rishi and her mother quickly found a blanket to hold over him to protect him from falling debris. Stick by stick the hut was dismantled, and when the last pole had been removed Rishi and her mother moved away the blanket. Starlight fell across Yelgab's face as he looked up at the sky, ablaze with stars, and his mouth opened in rapturous awe. "There they are. Look at them! Look at them! Tell me, what do you see?"

"Intelligences," whispered Rishi.

"Yes," said Yelgab. "Every intelligence you see in the sky is a person who died and has reached their divine potential. They look down on us, watching us, hoping we will one day join them. That is how we know they love us, my children. The gods are not a group of lofty, unknowable beings; they are our ancestors. The ones who love us most."

A warm sea breeze blew against their skin and ruffled their hair as the family gazed in silence at the sky, each lost in the beauty of the night.

"Everything is best understood when put in context of the stars. I have tried to live my life so that one day I can be worthy enough to join them, and if the gods let me add my light to the dark sky, I will be watching you, waiting for when you can join me."

Rishi took her grandfather's hand and smiled through her tears. This was how she wanted to remember her grandfather.

Yelgab relaxed his head and his eyes became glossy. "Oh, my children," he said, closing his eyes and pressing out silver tears. "You are my necklace of precious stones. I could fill the sky with my love for you."

Rishi felt his chest rise and fall in a satisfied sigh, and then it rose no more.

The next morning Rishi helped her mother dress her grandfather in his burial shroud. It seemed strange to think that this still form so recently held the spirit of her grandfather. Without his breath it was as if it were just a shell, and that her real grandfather was on the beach or eating by the fire or telling a story. Wherever her grandfather was, Rishi thought, he was not here.

Rishi's mother had a bowl of clean water and fragrant herbs. She dipped a sponge into the bowl and slowly wrung out the water. Gently taking Yelgab's hand, she tenderly washed down his arms and hands and every finger. Rishi sat still and quiet, holding her dry sponge in her lap, watching every movement her mother made.

Her mother smoothed the sponge over his forehead. She let the sponge glide over the closed eyelids, one at a time, and then over his cheeks and down his neck. Then she paused, glanced at her daughter and said, "Rishi, I'm going to show you something." She put the sponge down and with a piece of obsidian carefully cut through Yelgab's tunic and opened the flaps of fabric, revealing his chest. When she did, Rishi put her hand to her mouth and gasped.

Down the side of her grandfather's chest was a jagged scar as long as her forearm. It looked as if someone had taken a knife and tried to slash open his chest, or a shark had tried to bite him in half. Rishi's mother touched the ugly scar with her fingertips, glancing up at Rishi's bewildered face.

"What happened?" Rishi whispered.

Her mother slowly shook her head. "I don't know, Rishi," she said. "I only know it happened when he was a young man in Zitól. He never spoke to me about it. I only know because I once saw him undress for a swim. I think he wanted to take this secret with him to the grave, but for some reason I feel that you need to know." Rishi tried to not look at the scar etched like a vulgar scream on her grandfather's gentle body, but her eyes kept flitting back to it.

After she finished washing the body, her mother took out the clean white burial shroud. As gently as if he were still alive, Rishi's mother worked the shroud under his frail body and pulled it out around him. Then, starting at his feet she sewed it together with a small bone needle. Before she sewed up the chest, she placed small bundles of food inside the shroud; food for his journey to the heavens. She opened Yelgab's wooden box containing his special treasures. Taking out the knife, she gently placed it on his chest, with his hand wrapped around the mother-of-pearl handle. She also took the screen-fold book, but just before she tucked it in the folds of the shroud Rishi asked, "Mama, can I keep that?"

She nodded, and placed the book in Rishi's hands. Then, as was the custom, she took a piece of polished jade, opened Yelgab's mouth and placed the jade inside. After closing his mouth she finished sewing the shroud until she completely encased him in a white cocoon.

That evening the body was burned.

CHAPTER 13

The Final Prank

Rishi woke with a strange feeling. She dressed and tied her bead belt around her waist, and stepped out. The morning felt fresh and clean compared to the warm stuffiness of the hut. Out of habit, she glanced over at the place where her grandfather's dwelling had been. It had been several weeks since his death, and the poles and skins had been repurposed for other structures. Now, blades of grass were starting to grow over the bare circle on the ground. She sighed and looked at the sky. The last of the night's stars were almost dissolved into the approaching blue-white dawn, preparing for the sun's grand appearance. The smells of hot food brought Rishi to the fire and she stood next to her mother, warming her hands.

Her mother ladled beans into a bowl for Rishi and steam curled up into the air.

What is it about this morning? she wondered as the warm food filled her belly. Was something supposed to happen today? Was there something she had forgotten? She couldn't shake the anxious feelings that seemed to flutter inside her like moths.

"Where are the boys?" Rishi asked.

"Cotyl took the night watch as sentinel. I think the other two woke up early to join him."

Rishi finished her breakfast and her mother handed her a bowl filled to the rim with beans, with two empty bowls nested beneath it. "Rishi, take this to your brothers. They are at the east watch."

Dutifully, Rishi held the warm bowls to her chest and began hiking the trail through the dunes to the eastern shore. As she walked, she wondered if the boys had seen anything on the horizon. It had been years since the traders came with their news about the Snatchers and the village implemented their evacuation plan. It was almost as if the Snatchers had disappeared . . . or never existed in the first place. A smile parted Rishi's lips when she remembered how Quash's Snatcher stories used to scare her when she was young.

Once she reached the beach, she stepped gingerly along the sand, avoiding the dark piles of glossy kelp that had washed up in the night and breathing in the fresh sea breezes as they tossed her hair. Finally she found them arranged just as she suspected they would be: sleeping around the conch horn with their heads resting on their hands like large, hairy babies. With a sigh Rishi sat down and ladled the steaming beans into the three bowls, making sure one had a little more than the others. This was her secret way of rewarding the last brother who was nice to her. Yesterday Cotyl had complimented her on the basket she was making, so today was his day to receive a little extra. She sat and held her knees, waiting for the sun come up over the ocean and still wondering what it was about this day that made her feel so uneasy.

As the sun blinked its way over the horizon, the warm rays spread out over the sleeping brothers and with a great display of loud yawning and stretching, they gradually woke. They rubbed their eyes, and upon seeing Rishi sitting with three warm bowls of beans, Eno murmured cheerfully, "Brothers, look. Here is a beautiful maiden offering me food on the beach. Is this heaven?"

"Very funny," said Rishi, handing out the bowls. "You are all supposed to be vigilant."

"We just took a little break. You have no idea how exhausting it is to watch the ocean," said Cotyl, stretching and yawning.

"I'm sure it is," said Rishi.

Cotyl took his bowl of beans. "You're lucky," he said. "You are a girl and you don't have to be a sentinel."

"Yeah," said Quash. "Girls get all the easy jobs . . . cooking, cleaning, playing games with little kids . . ."

". . . bearing children . . . ," added Rishi.

"Well," said Quash, "If *I* were a woman, I'd make my husband have the babies."

"You'd be one ugly woman," said Cotyl.

"I think boys get to do all of the interesting things," said Rishi. "You get to sail to faraway islands and fish in deep waters. You are stronger than us girls and get to defend the island while we hide in caves. Just like right now—as sentinels you are the *guardians* of our people. It is up to *you* to protect us. Our lives are in *your* hands. Doesn't that make you feel important?"

"It makes me feel tired," said Quash.

"Rishi, guarding the island is boring," yawned Cotyl. "Nothing ever happens. It's a waste of valuable resources, if you ask me." He raised his arm, flexing one of his resources.

"Well, one of these days you'll grow up and do something important," Rishi sighed. "You can't stay lazy forever."

"I actually think I *could* be lazy forever," said Quash with grave sincerity, packing a large spoonful of beans into his mouth and looking out at the ocean. He swung his head back toward Rishi and said, "Especially if I had you to take care of me."

"You have some beans on your cheek," said Rishi.

Instead of wiping the beans off, Quash took another spoonful and smeared it on his nose. "Is that better?"

"Are you saying that we lack ambition, little sister?" asked Eno.

"I just think you are capable of more, that's all."

"Shows what you know," answered Eno, running his fingers through his stiff hair so it pointed straight up at the sky. He looked out at the ocean wistfully. "Someday, I am going to be a great warrior."

"You realize that you have to *do* something great in order to become a great warrior, don't you?" said Rishi. "Something unselfish, brave . . . magnanimous."

"Magnanimous," repeated Quash. "That is a great word, Rishi. Did you make that one up?"

Eno swallowed a spoonful of beans and said thoughtfully, "I wouldn't mind if something exciting happened on my watch. I'd love to catch a glimpse of the Snatchers and finally be the one to blow the conch and warn everyone."

"Maybe something *did* happen during your watch, only you were asleep and you missed it," said Rishi.

"You got to blow the conch for the drill last week, Eno," said Cotyl, who had already finished his beans and was lazily digging a hole in the sand with his empty bowl.

"That isn't the same," Eno said.

"Oh. So you are serious about this warrior talk. You actually want to be a hero," said Cotyl.

"Yeah. I guess." Eno shrugged.

"It wouldn't be so bad to save hundreds of people's lives," agreed Quash.

"Yes," said Rishi with a smile, "and imagine what all the girls in the village would think."

"That does it," exclaimed Eno with resolution. "I will never sleep through my watch again."

"So Eno wants to be a warrior someday. What do you want to be, Quash?" Rishi asked, trying to fan the motivational fire while it was beginning to glow.

"I don't know . . . I guess it might be interesting to explore and discover new islands," Quash said, and then he turned to Cotyl. "You've been pretty quiet over there, brother. How about you? What do you want to be?"

Cotyl was now digging with more purpose, using his empty bowl as a scoop, and now both forearms disappeared completely into the hole. Without stopping he grinned and said, "I want to be a Snatcher."

Rishi rolled her eyes.

"Hey Rishi," said Eno, his tone suddenly serious. "Do the girls ever talk about us? You know, does . . . Isra . . . ever . . . ," he raised his eyebrows up and down, "mention me?"

"Maybe," Rishi said, disgusted. She would never admit it to them, but her friends *did* talk about her brothers. All the time. "Isra is very beautiful, but she isn't very nice."

"Bah—that isn't important. I don't care what my future wife acts like, as long as she's good-looking."

Rishi glared at him.

"Besides, my motives are completely unselfish. Everyone knows you owe it to your children to marry a beautiful wife."

"You will change your mind after she complains all day and never does any work and just wants to comb her hair."

"Yes . . . her silky, soft hair . . . ," Eno cooed.

"Yes, and she still *chews* on it when she thinks no one is looking."

At this, Eno frowned. "She does?"

Rishi stood up and brushed the sand off the back of her dress. "Well, while you watch for Snatchers and dream about girls who would make your future miserable, I'm going back to the village to help Mama . . . unless you want to switch and let me watch for a while. I'm sure Mother would love to have *you* fetch water and wash out the bowls."

Cotyl pulled his head out of his hole. "Stay for a while more, little Rishi," he said, winking at Quash.

Quash smiled slightly and added, "Yeah, Rishi-Wishi. Keep us company."

"Well . . . all right." She sat back down on the sand. They were silent and thoughtful as they all watched Cotyl deepen his hole.

"You know, Rishi, you're not as annoying as you used to be," said Eno after a while.

"Um . . . thanks, Eno."

"Or as whiny," added Cotyl from inside his hole.

"I appreciate that."

"You're not as ugly, either," said Quash.

"You are all so *very* kind," replied Rishi, with her sweetest voice.

"Actually," said Eno seriously, "we *are* kind. When was the last time we tried to drown you?"

"Or tie you up?" Quash added.

"You have to admit, Rishi, we have improved as brothers."

"I suppose," said Rishi, trying to sound noncommittal, but agreeing whole-heartedly. They were kinder.

Cotyl had disappeared entirely inside his hole, but sand was still flying out.

"Say, Cotyl, what are you making there?" Eno said, peering down into the pit.

"I just thought I'd catch myself a little fishy."

"What kind of fishy?"

Cotyl's head appeared, grinning. "A Rishi-fishy."

Rishi gulped and was on her feet in a second, sprinting across the beach, with all three boys in pursuit. Within moments they caught her and dragged her back to Cotyl's pit, her arms flailing and legs kicking.

"Don't—you—dare!" she yelled, half shouting, half laughing.

"But you sound like you're having so much fun, Rish," Cotyl said as he tried to pull her legs together so she'd stop kicking him in the face.

"There is no way the three of you can get me into that hole!"

"You're right, Rishi, it would only take *one* of us to get you in the hole."

With this, Rishi extracted one leg and kicked Cotyl's hands so that Cotyl lost his grip and she wriggled free, crawling along the sand. But as soon as she got her feet under her again, one of them grabbed her ankle and brought her down with a thud. Eno clamped her legs together like a vice and Quash pinned her arms to her torso until finally all she could do was shriek. Cotyl was at the hole, and for all their roughness, they set her in the hole as if she were as delicate as a shell. Then Cotyl started pushing sand into the hole and packing it around her feet, knees, and waist.

"Keep her arms down and we'll pack it around her sides."

"Stop it! I'll tell Mama!" Rishi yelled.

"I don't think Mama can hear you from here, Rish," Quash said.

"Grandfather told you to be *nice* to me!"

They all stopped for a moment, panting for breath, and still holding Rishi in place.

"Did he?" asked Eno seriously to the other two.

They pondered this. Suddenly Quash perked up. "No . . . ," he said. "I distinctly remember Grandfather telling us to protect her *virtue*, which is not the same thing as being nice. Tell you what, Rishi. We'll stop if you can tell us the password."

Rishi groaned. She hated this game.

"Come on, just guess."

"How about 'I smell like a whale carcass'?" That was a password they had made her use in the past.

"Nice try, but wrong. One more chance."

"Ummm . . . 'Quash is the strongest man alive.'" Another old password.

"Sorry," said Quash. "The answer was '*magnanimous*.'"

The other two boys groaned and hit him with clods of sand. Then they resumed packing sand around Rishi's body. Rishi was now screaming and laughing so hard she didn't have any energy to struggle. She wasn't nervous or terrified like she had been when she was a child. Now she enjoyed the attention, and played her part with gusto.

Finally her brothers pushed the sand around her shoulders and her neck until it reached her chin.

Rishi was still shouting threats as Eno stepped back and said thoughtfully, "Should we stop there or cover up her head too?"

"I say we stuff her mouth with sand," said Quash. "It will stop her awful screeching."

Rishi instantly shut her mouth and glared at them.

"Good girl," Eno said.

Under the sand, Rishi's body was in a kneeling position, her arms down at her sides, with the sand packed so tight around her body that she couldn't even wiggle her hand.

Her brothers smoothed the sand around her. Cotyl brushed the sand off his hands and gently pulled Rishi's hair away from her face and set it in a dark mass behind her.

"Hmm . . . it needs something else," said Eno, walking around Rishi. Then he took a stick and drew large petals around Rishi's head.

"A pretty girl inside a pretty flower," said Quash, admiring Eno's work.

"Okay, boys, it's been fun. Now you can dig me out." Rishi said, spitting a few grains of sand out of her mouth.

Eno ignored her. "How long should we leave her here?" he asked.

"Well, she *did* want to watch for Snatchers, and your watch is next, right, Eno?" Cotyl said slyly.

"And after that it is my watch. She could take mine too," chimed Quash.

"Excellent," said Eno, clapping his hands together. "Here is your horn, Rishi." He set the conch next to her on the sand.

"Have a nice watch!" said Cotyl.

"Let us know if you see any Snatchers!"

The boys disappeared behind her, snickering.

"Come back, Eno!" Rishi shouted. It was hard to take a deep breath with the sand packed around her like this. "Cotyl, dig me out right now! Don't leave me! Quash, come back!" She listened as their voices got farther and farther away and it wasn't long before all she could hear were the undulating waves of the ocean.

The hilarity of the moment wore off soon and Rishi laughed uneasily at her predicament. A seagull flew down from the sky and landed next to her, cocking his head, this way and that.

"Go away," said Rishi.

But the gull did not. It cawed loudly, padded up to Rishi and started to peck at her forehead. Rishi screamed and the bird flapped its great wings in her face before flying away.

This is ridiculous, she thought. She could just imagine how she appeared, this severed head sitting out on the beach watching the sunrise. It was kind of funny, she thought. Kind of. It would be much more funny if she were still laughing.

Rishi strained her ears, trying to hear above the sound of the waves for voices. They were probably going to let her think they'd gone, only to sneak up behind her and scare her. She couldn't believe they'd do this—when they were all older now and getting to be such good friends. They *were* good friends, though. That is why she knew that at any moment they would be back to finish their joke and help her out. They'd tease her and laugh and tell her what a good sport she was. She'd laugh too—though not as comfortably—and she'd forgive them, of course, and then they would resume their watch and Rishi could go back to the village and help her mother. Yes. That is what would happen. She just needed to be patient.

The sun was getting higher and finally it was high enough that it was not shining directly into Rishi's eyes. It really was a perfectly clear day, with a cool sea breeze, and if there was any day to be buried in the sand up to your neck, this was as good a day as any, Rishi decided. The breeze was warm and fresh, the sea stretched out before her in a fluid blanket of turquoise. Rishi tried to smile. All was well. One day this would be a hilarious memory they could all laugh about. *Remember when you all buried me in the sand? Ha, ha, that was so funny. I thought you were never coming back for me . . .*

It wasn't until then that Rishi noticed a strange little cloud in the sky, shaped like a seahorse.

CHAPTER 14

Alone

At that instant, all feelings of kindness, reconciliation, and forgiveness that Rishi was trying to muster up for her brothers vanished like a drop of water on a hot coal. Panic flooded her paralyzed body and she began shouting their names, over and over. Where were they? Why wouldn't they come back?

She couldn't move at all. Cotyl had dug the hole in damp sand and it fixed her in place like cement. Rishi could twist her head from side to side, but that was all she could do. After a while, she stopped shouting and tried to calm herself. Panic only increased the absurdity of the situation. After all, the only thing more ridiculous than a head on a beach was a head on the beach that was screaming. She tried to take a deep breath, even though her lungs were packed tight in the sand. If they weren't going to come back, then she would have to just free herself. She could move one of her fingers back and forth. If she just kept moving that finger, perhaps she could start moving her hand. If she could move her hand, then she could move her arm, and if she could move her arm— even one—she would be free, and then she would never speak to those three idiots again.

The seahorse cloud floated just above the horizon. It glowed golden-pink, looking innocent and benign. Rishi's finger was moving, but it was just creating a cavern for itself in the sand. The rest of her hand still refused to budge. *Calm yourself*, Rishi thought. *You are worrying over nothing.* She avoided looking at the rolling surf, afraid of what she might see. Perhaps if she didn't look at the waves, nothing would happen. Besides, Rishi reasoned, there were no stones around. In her dream there were stones lined out on the sand, but there were only bits and pieces of shells and kelp scattered about her, as far as she could see. There was nothing to fear. That was just a dream, like anyone else's dream, weird and bizarre.

Would her mother notice she was gone? Probably not until later. Perhaps someone would come to the beach? But she was on the eastern shore. All the fishing and oystering was done on the other shores, closer to the village. In fact, villagers hardly ever came to this shore unless they were serving as sentinels. And the next two sentinels were her darling brothers. Her heart raced. She could be here all day.

Against her will, tears began to spill out of her eyes. This only frustrated her more, as she had no way to wipe her face and they dripped onto her lips and down her chin and neck. She forced herself to control her emotions. The last thing she wanted was her brothers to return to her when she was crying like a baby.

But she could not stop the tears anymore, and they gushed out of her eyes, accompanied by loud choking sobs. She cried until her head ached. And for all that crying, it hadn't improved her situation at all. She was still stuck. She closed her eyes tightly, trying to squeeze out the last of the tears, and let out an exasperated shudder. Then, in between two large, noisy sniffs, she heard something. Composing herself as much as she could, she held her breath and listened.

It was a high wail, far away and faint.

Could it be? If it was, then she would surely hear it again.

She listened intently, to be sure. She barely breathed. Sure enough, there it was again, far away, but clear and piercing. It was a conch horn.

CHAPTER 15

The Snatchers

Her brothers left a conch on the beach that was too far away from her to even think of blowing. Her eyes were drawn to it, though, and she watched it as she listened to its sister wailing somewhere across the island. Her mind raced to decipher the implications.

Rishi knew there were only two reasons the horn could be blowing. One, they were having a drill. But they had just had a drill last week. Usually there was only a drill every few months. The second reason was that someone saw something approaching the beach. It could be a friendly vessel, of course. Traders, friendly canoes from other islands . . . those were possibilities.

And then, there was the other possibility, but she dared not think of that.

Eventually the conch stopped sounding. Everything seemed peaceful again except for the feeling of dread that sat like rotten fruit in the pit of Rishi's stomach.

An hour went by.

And another.

Before long, the sun was above her in the sky, baking the skin on her scalp where had parted her hair. The day was half over. Why had no one come for her? Did anyone even realize she was missing?

The light breeze had shifted and was blowing from behind her, bringing with it a dark haze. Rishi breathed in a faint woody, peppery smell and wispy grey things started falling from the sky. All around her the things floated down until Rishi realized the smell was smoke and the grey specks floating around her were ash.

Then it happened. She could feel them coming before she heard them. The ground trembled and vibrated with the energy of their steps. She turned her head around as much as she could and out of the corner of her eye she saw three familiar figures racing down the ridge and across the sand. Relief flooded her body. Her brothers had come back for her!

But there were no smiles on their faces now. As soon as they reached Rishi, they shoved their hands into the sand and started digging frantically.

"What's going on?" Rishi asked, bewildered.

"Hurry—hurry," Cotyl panted. "Got—to get—her out."

They were out of breath; their bodies dripped with sweat and ash littered their black hair. Cotyl dug his hands into the sand so hard he scratched Rishi's back, and Quash pulled sand away from her shoulders and chest, finally freeing her arms.

"Pull your arms out," Eno ordered.

Her shoulders were completely uncovered but her arms would not work. All feeling in her arms was gone, and even though nothing prevented them from coming out, they were lifeless.

"I can't move them," Rishi said.

Fear flashed across Eno's face and he glanced back toward the village.

"We have to get you out. You really can't move your arms?"

Rishi had been buried in the sand for over three hours. Her body was almost completely without sensation.

"Just pull her out," Quash growled. He and Eno pulled on her arms while Cotyl worked around her hips and legs. Quash bent down and put his great, warm arms under her shoulders, pulling her free of the hole. As she leaned over his shoulder Rishi noticed bright red blood ooze out a small hole in Quash's back.

"Hurry!" Cotyl said, looking behind him at the empty ridge.

Quash pulled Rishi to her feet and the three boys started running across the beach, away from the village trail. But Rishi couldn't run; she couldn't even stand. Her legs were just starting to come back to life and they felt electrified and stinging.

"Run, Rishi!" they called back to her.

"I can't!" she wailed. Her legs gave way under her and she stumbled into the sand. Her brothers stopped and looked over their shoulders, their eyes wide with fear. Smoke was now billowing from beyond the ridge, from the village.

Quash ran back to Rishi and heaved her onto his shoulder. They took off again, sprinting as fast as they could across the wet sand. Rishi jostled up and down on Quash's back, feeling like all her teeth were coming loose. Bracing herself, and lifting her head, she searched the bouncing landscape behind them. Way back on the ridge, silhouetted against the sky was a cluster of dark forms. All of the sudden Rishi heard a *whiz* through the air and something lodged itself in Quash's back. Rishi screamed, horrified, and immediately pulled it out of his skin. It was a dart. A second later Cotyl cried out, gripping his arm. Another dart.

Darts began flying through the air like tiny spears. Rishi looked back to the ridge where the forms started running toward them, holding long sticks. Every now and then one of them stopped and raised the stick to his mouth. A second later Rishi would hear that whizzing sound and a dart found its target in her brothers' flesh.

The brothers ran. Instead of traveling up through the dry sand to get further inland where they might have been safe, they sprinted down the wet, packed beach like wild rabbits, without a plan or destination. Rishi could tell Quash was getting tired, as his pace was unsteady. Another dart stuck into his lower back and Rishi again pulled it out and flung it away. Blood drizzled down, staining his loincloth. Then she noticed three darts in his buttocks and two more sticking from the back of his thigh. His breathing became loud and forced and Rishi could feel him start to limp. Finally his legs buckled underneath him and he fell, smashing Rishi's body into the hard sand.

Rishi crawled out from under Quash and leaned over him, pulling out all the darts she could find. Blood oozed from the punctures, dripping down his brown skin in bright scarlet streaks. He looked up at Rishi with a face so filled with terror that she hardly recognized him. "*Run,*" he said.

Just then Eno's arms grabbed her around the waist and pulled her to her feet.

"Get out of here, Rishi! They don't want us, they want *you!*" He pulled her arm. Rishi looked at him in horror. He had darts sticking out of his chest, his neck, his torso like a cactus. His eyes were wild with desperation. Cotyl was there too, his body also stippled with the poisonous darts.

Their pursuers were close now, so close that Rishi could hear their voices and the slap of their feet on the wet sand.

Cotyl grabbed Rishi's other arm and the two brothers dragged her forward until her feet found their balance and she ran along with them. Then three more darts hit Cotyl in the neck and he crumbled to the ground. Eno continued to pull Rishi away, tears streaming down his face, but by then the poison overwhelmed his body and finally he, too, collapsed with a moan into the sand. Once Eno fell, Rishi's will to escape disappeared and she could do nothing but stand and stare at the trail of her brothers' bodies.

CHAPTER 16
The White Stones Are Stolen

Trembling, Rishi sank to her knees. She did not care what happened to her. She leaned over Eno's quivering body and frantically pulled the darts out of his skin. Just before she reached the last dart, she was yanked away and pulled roughly to her feet. Her arms were twisted behind her back and someone began lashing her wrists together. Rishi hung her head and closed her eyes, not knowing what else to do. She felt a tug on her waist. Rishi's bead still dangled from her belt and she opened her eyes to see a dark, dirty hand rolling the bead around in its stubby fingers. The fingers brushed off the sand, revealing its brilliant whiteness. A voice called out something and the hand held the bead so the others could see. There was a loud cheer. It was then that Rishi lifted her eyes to look at her captors.

They were hideous. Wild, thick hair sprang from their ugly heads in matted locks, festooned with bits of shell, mud, and colored beads, looking like a mass of debris that had washed up on the beach. Ragged, stained loincloths were wrapped carelessly about their waists. Their dark-skinned bodies were painted to look like skeletons, and their faces were smeared with pitch. One was missing a chunk of his ear; another was missing a hand.

They were stocky but not tall—most were only a little taller than Rishi. Her brothers would have towered over them, if their magnificent bodies were not lying lifeless on the sand. A rotting smell of carrion emitted from these strange men that was so intense that it burned Rishi's nostrils with its rancid acidity, and their eyes had a dull, glazed look to them, as if the human part of the soul was missing.

But as Rishi continued to analyze the group something strange started to happen. Their fierceness dissolved into astonishment. Some even took a step backward. They began to talk to each other, their voices low and guarded, and they took the amulets that hung from their necks and pressed them to their lips. One pointed at her face.

The man who was tying Rishi's hands noticed their apprehension. He placed his hands on her shoulders and forced her around. As soon as they stood eye to eye he quickly yanked away his hands and stumbled backward into his companions. His face was that of one who had just seen a ghost.

The men gathered together, talking in an unfamiliar language and casting leery glances at Rishi. Rishi wondered who their leader was, as none of them seemed to be in charge.

After much grunting and nodding the men finished their discussion. One came up behind her and skittishly poked her in the back with his blow gun, forcing her forward. The others walked along beside him, but a safe distance from Rishi, as if she had a disease.

In this manner Rishi was prodded across the beach, passing the fleeing footsteps of her brothers and the remnants of the hole in which she had spent the morning. *My legs work fine now*, she thought bitterly, *now that there is no reason to run.* They walked up over the ridge. Rishi tried to look back at her brothers before they left the beach, but she was shoved forward.

Once over the ridge, the village came into view, or, at least, what was left of it. Black smoke billowed from the charred huts, and Rishi could feel the heat from the fires as she was driven past the broken pottery, destroyed looms, burned clothing, smashed melons, and other debris scattered along the ground. She tried to slow her pace—to peer through the smoke and flames for a glimpse of her people—but she couldn't see anyone and the stick constantly jabbed at her to move on. The village seemed deserted. In her heart Rishi prayed that her people were in the caves, safe.

The men pushed Rishi past the smoking village and down to the bay where she saw a gathering of people. As she got closer, she saw it was more strangers.

Their canoes—almost a dozen—were beached on the shore.

Another sharp pain in Rishi's back pushed her forward, toward the cluster of men. At the center was a tall figure, wearing a tattered headpiece of dingy turkey feathers. Like the others, this man's face was painted completely black, and a bone was threaded through the septum of his squashed nose. Around his neck hung a necklace of rodent skulls. Rishi knew by the way the other men cowered around him that he was the leader. He stood with his fists on his hips, rolling something around in his mouth, and watched as Rishi was placed before him.

The man's eyes coursed up her body and for the first time in her life Rishi felt shamed. He grunted, as if finding her acceptable. Casually, he motioned to the other men to put her in a canoe, and turned to walk toward the canoes himself.

Rishi then noticed that in several of the canoes there were girls—her friends from the village. The other canoes were filled with spears, boxes, pelts, and gourds . . . contraband taken from her village. Rishi even saw her precious screen-fold book, sitting precariously at the top of one pile, its pages ruffling in the breeze.

The leader was almost to the canoes when he realized no one was following him. He turned to see his men, still gathered around Rishi, immovable and wary. He shouted at them impatiently, holding up his hands, his fingers splayed in exasperation. The men fidgeted, but still did not move, eyeing Rishi as if she were poisonous. The leader screamed at them again. One of them mumbled something and pointed to Rishi's face.

The leader narrowed his eyes suspiciously and walked back up to Rishi, unsheathing his knife. Rishi stiffened as she saw the weapon coming toward her. He put the tip of the knife under her chin, forcing her to look into his dark face. He was so close she could see the sweat coming out of the large pores on his upper lip and breathe the noxious air coming from his flared nostrils. She closed her eyes tightly. She wished she could part her lips to breathe and avoid the rotten, rat-like odor coming from his body, but the tip of the knife had already pricked her skin and she dared not move, not even to swallow. His hand roughly palmed her forehead. With his thumb he forced open her brown eye. Then he lifted the lid to the right eye, and Rishi's blue iris stared up at him. Uttering an exclamation of surprise, he released her. He took a step back and gazed at her in astonishment, as if she had two heads sprouting from her neck.

He stared at her for a long time, his eyes narrowed and his mouth twisted in apprehension, and he, too, fingered the smooth amulet that hung on his chest. The other men were silent, awaiting a decision. Rishi wondered if he was frightened of her, like the others were. If he was, then perhaps they would leave her here. Once they were gone she could go find her mother in the caves and tell her about how her brothers . . . her mean, obnoxious, annoying and wonderful, amazing brothers gave their lives for her . . .

Thinking of her brothers brought tears to Rishi's eyes, and before she could control them, they overflowed and spilled down her cheeks. Her tears had an instant effect on the man with the black face. He lowered his knife and his face relaxed. One corner of his mouth lifted in amusement and then he slowly opened his mouth, revealing the most hideous smile Rishi had ever seen. His mouth was filled with jagged white teeth, each sharpened to a point so that his mouth looked like that of a shark. She felt weak and her knees almost gave out on her. He spoke to the others, sneering at them. Even without understanding their language Rishi could tell what he was doing. He was mocking them, shaming them for being afraid of a crying girl.

After barking out some orders, his men finally piled into the canoes. The man with the shark mouth grabbed Rishi by the arm so hard she cried out in pain as he pulled her into his canoe.

As the canoes were pushed off the shore and started through the water, Rishi tried to catch the attention of the other girls. She could see Lantana and Isra but they only looked down, their usual cheerful laughing faces somber and tear-stained. It was then that she remembered her dream. She remembered that all the white stones disappeared from the beach. Rishi understood now. She and her friends were the white stones. And now the white stones were about to disappear.

The canoe loaded with the villagers' possessions passed by Rishi, and she saw her grandfather's book teeter back and forth on top of the pile until it toppled off and splashed into the water.

CHAPTER 17

The Song of Grief

Shark Mouth made Rishi sit in the bow of the boat and seated himself right behind her. Two other men sat in the back of the canoe, content to be far away from Rishi and her strange eyes.

The canoes traveled swiftly over the water. Every now and then Shark Mouth suspended his dripping paddle over Rishi's head, soaking her head and dress with seawater. The first time he did this it startled Rishi so much that Shark Mouth laughed. After that Rishi held her peace when he dripped water over her, unflinching, until he finally lost interest and spent his time using his paddle for what it was made for.

All day they paddled, following the sun until it turned blood red and dripped through the slits in the clouds and into the ocean. Then heaven pulled its black cape over the sky, covering the earth in a vast, starlit dome. The night air was warm and the paddles moved the boats over the waves like strange fish. Smooth, glossy dolphins followed the canoes, their backs awash in moonlight.

Rishi turned her eyes upward, to the sky, something she would often do in the desperate days to follow. Up there nothing had changed: all was still and silent and serene. The stars were brilliant tonight, just as they had been on the evenings she had sat on the beach with her grandfather. If all the things he told her were true, then his star was up there, somewhere. Was he watching her? Despair filled her heart as she realized that her brothers' stars would be among them as well.

Ahead of the canoes, far off and low on the horizon, there was a star that was different. Its golden light faded and flickered. The light grew into several lights as they came nearer and, before long, Rishi saw fires glowing on a black shoreline. She heard a drumbeat coming from one of the canoes and the paddlers all started to row in time to the drum, letting out a loud groan each time they pulled the canoes forward. The eerie cadence gave Rishi a feeling of ominous foreboding. Rishi's hair swept back from her face as the canoes picked up speed. They paddled through the breaking waves, and once the canoes touched ground, the men leaped out and dragged their boats up onto the sand.

Rishi was pulled from the boat and herded together with the other girls from her village. No one spoke, but their eyes all expressed the same message: *I'm glad I am not alone.*

A figure holding a torch walked toward them. The night wind was strong and it whipped Rishi's hair around her face, so she pulled it back with her hand to see. The person was large and well-bosomed. The wind made the woman's dress stick to the front of her large body and flap wildly in the back. She greeted Shark Mouth, and after speaking together they walked over to the captive girls. The guards stepped back and the woman held the torch high, examining each girl. When the torch passed before Rishi, Shark Mouth muttered something to the woman in his strange whiny language. The torch came closer to Rishi's face and she felt its heat so intensely that it stung her eyes. The woman cupped her hand under Rishi's chin. In a voice that was used to being obeyed she said, "Look up."

Rishi lifted her eyes.

The woman's face was close and the light from the torch cast shadows all about her features, making her look like a monster. Rishi could see her large, squashed nose, full lips, and painted eyelids. Her eyes were like wells—black and deep with tiny fires dancing at the bottom. She peered into Rishi's face with an intensity that made Rishi's knees weak.

Finally the woman had seen enough. "Remarkable," she whispered. Then, after a pause she asked, "Are you blind?"

"No," Rishi answered.

"Your eyes have always been this way?" asked the woman.

"Yes," said Rishi.

"Simply fantastic," the woman murmured. Then she uttered a low chuckle. "The people are going to *love* this."

She turned to Shark Mouth and said something to him. He and the other men drove the girls up the beach, past a large bonfire, and came to where the sand mixed with the soil of the earth and became hard. Here there was a large animal pen. It had bars all around it, and more bars crisscrossed over the top. Into this pen the girls were pushed. The men left them and walked down the beach to stand around the large fire not far from the enclosure. The fire made their shadows long and eerie, like the rays of a black sun. They began to talk and laugh, and the smells of cooking meat rose up from the fire. Every now and then, one of the men would turn back and look at the pen. Oddly, they had left the gate open.

"Where are we?" whispered Lantana.

"I don't know," answered Venay.

"What will they do with us?" said Sepya, a tremor running through her voice.

"We will be all right," Rishi said, trying to calm the girls. "We still have each other. Perhaps we can find a way to escape and go back to our families. I'm sure there is a way. Surely the gods will help us."

Every head turned to look at Rishi. They were silent, but by the light of the full moon she could see their faces, and their expressions told Rishi she had just said something wrong.

"What *families*?" said Isra, staring at her with fierce, black eyes.

"Back at the caves—" Rishi explained, perplexed at Isra's tone. "I heard the conch shell sound, and I knew everyone had gone to the caves."

"We *were* safe in the caves," Isra said, her voice rising. "But thanks to your brothers, now our families are all *dead*."

"I—I don't understand," Rishi said. Not her mother too. Oh gods above, please not her mother.

Venay spoke. Her voice was softer, but Rishi could tell she was doing everything she could to control her feelings. "The conch shell *did* sound, Rishi. And we all did exactly what we were supposed to do. Everyone was in the caves, even your brothers. But then—"

"Your brothers said they needed to leave," added Sepya. Rishi felt as if a rock was in her stomach, and each time the girls spoke, the rock became larger and heavier.

"They said that you were still out there, on the east beach," continued Venay. "But it was too late by then. We knew the Snatchers had landed their canoes and the councilmen wouldn't let anyone out of the cave. But your brothers were . . . were—" she tried to find the right word.

"—*lunatics*," Isra spat out. "They wouldn't listen. They started yelling and no one could get them to shut up. They said they were going to go find you, that they knew right where you were—"

Rishi wanted to plug her ears.

"Our fathers tried to hold them in the cave but they were too stubborn and they ran out like complete idiots."

"It wasn't long before the Snatchers saw them and discovered our hiding place," added Venay, her round face grave. "They entered the caves with their long knives . . ." Rishi felt her insides collapsing. "They pinned everyone up against the cave walls, and no one could escape." All the girls in the pen were sniffing and crying now.

"We were the *only ones* they did not kill, Rishi," said Lantana softly.

Isra spoke again, her voice so furious Rishi hardly recognized it. "There is no one left on our island, Rishi, *no one*. And it is all your fault! I hate you, Rishi! I hate you!" She lunged at Rishi but the other girls pulled her away until she collapsed and curled up in a ball, sobbing.

Rishi was silent, replaying the events of the horrible day before in her mind. She had thought that her brothers were honorable for coming to her rescue, giving their lives to try to save hers. But if what her friends said was true, then they had really disgraced her. Shame filled her body like polluted water. It would have been better if they had left her in the sand to be discovered by the Snatchers. Then at least everyone else would have been safe. Because of her and her brothers the entire village was slain. It was unforgivable. She backed into a corner of the pen and sat, hugging her knees, wanting to die. At least her brothers could hide their humiliation in death. She would have to live with it.

After that, no one spoke for a long time. Some lay down, trying to find a comfortable way to spend the night on the hard, sandy ground. Others leaned up against the cage. After a while someone started to sing.

> *My wings are broken;*
> *I dissolve into myself.*
> *My heart beats, slow and painful.*
> *I am lost.*
> *My future is a black mist.*
> *I give my will to the gods*
> *And show them my bleeding heart.*
> *Only they can make it whole again.*

It was Lantana, and she sang one of the Seven Songs, the Song of Grief. Rishi had sung this song dozens of times for rituals and funerals and was often quizzed on it by her grandfather. But she never understood the depth of its meaning, until now.

Lantana's soft, despondent voice echoed the feelings of despair in the hearts of the girls. They grouped together in the cage, comforting each other, but leaving Rishi alone in her corner. Rishi listened to the sweet voice and the bitter words. As she listened, she clenched her fists and made a promise that somehow, some way she would make it up to her people. Somehow she would pay for what had happened. And somehow she had to show the gods that her brothers had not meant any harm, that her brothers were only trying to save her. She closed her eyes, letting the music wash over her, breaking her already broken heart. She felt as if she could fill a canoe with her tears.

CHAPTER 18

Three Survivors

Quash tried to open his eyes, but it was too bright, so he closed them again.

Something was nudging him in the ribs. It was very annoying. He decided to grab it, but when he tried to move his arm, it felt floppy and weak. "This must be what it feels like to be a girl," he murmured.

"Get up," said a voice. Quash sat up and blinked his eyes. He could see some familiar feet standing before him. Eno's feet.

"Eno. Tell me something. Why do I feel so lousy?"

"Because the poison from the darts hasn't worn off yet, and you are covered with blistering scabs."

"No. There is something else. I feel lousy inside, not outside," he said to the feet.

There was a pause. Then Eno said, "Because they took Rishi."

Quash looked at the ground and nodded. "Ah . . . yes. That is it."

Quash slowly worked his way up to a standing position, his big body swaying a little at first. He grimaced as he raised his arm to shield his eyes from the sun and look around. Cotyl was a little ways away, lying on the beach like a huge dead starfish.

"He's alive," murmured Eno, "in case you were wondering."

"That is good," said Quash. They both tottered over to Cotyl. They lifted up his arms and started dragging him across the beach until he woke up, cursing them.

They hobbled slowly and painfully up the beach, like three ancient men. The ocean's waves had now filled up the hole that Cotyl had dug for Rishi, and except for a small, unremarkable dent in the beach, it was almost imperceptible. They passed the spot, each observing it and saying nothing.

They walked up the path over the ridge and stopped for a moment to view the huts, black and burned. They walked through the village and up to the caves. When they surveyed the interior, Cotyl braced himself against the wall. Quash covered his face. Eno fell to his knees and pounded the sand with his fists. Their cries echoed in the cave for hours.

Each young man left the cave on his own and wandered in aimless trails around the destroyed village, until he eventually reunited with the other two at the place of assembly. They sat with their backs to each other, their heads in their hands. The only sound was the squawking of the gulls that swarmed the village to pick at rotting food.

Finally Cotyl wiped his face and stood up. He marched over to one of the remaining huts and cracked its frame. Then he dismantled the wooden poles and palm thatching. Making a crude sledge, he layered the palms and wood and dragged it toward the cave. Eno and Quash observed him in silence but then reluctantly stood and did the same.

The three brothers painstakingly organized the bodies so they lay side by side, each individual in his or her family group.

"Four are missing." Eno observed after looking over the families carefully. "Isra, Lantana, Sepya, and Venay."

"And Rishi," said Quash. "Five."

They continued to work silently, covering all the bodies with wood. By the time they finished the funeral pyre, it was dark. They kissed their mother's face, and they lit the fire.

"*My wings are broken, I dissolve into myself . . .*" Eno started to sing in a broken tone.

The other two joined in as the flames filled the cave, engulfing the dried palms, the wood, and the people they loved.

They staggered back to the place of assembly, their muscles aching, their eyes red from the fire and swollen from the tears. They collapsed on the platform, looking up at the sky, the smell of the fire still riding the air. That night the stars seemed especially numerous. It hurt to look at them.

Suddenly Eno stood up and started walking away.

"Hey," said Cotyl. "Where are you going?"

"Where do you think I'm going?" he said as he picked up a spear. "I'm going to find our sister."

CHAPTER 19

Mama Xoca

Lantana had only been singing for a few moments when one of the men turned and broke away from the fire. He cupped his hand around his mouth and yelled at the girls, and then shook his fist. Lantana's song came to an abrupt end and the other men around the fire snickered.

Rishi laid her head on the sand and closed her eyes. The desire to sleep was overwhelming, but her mind would not rest. It wasn't until the sky started to lighten that Rishi finally drifted off.

When she opened her eyes, the sun had already made its way past the horizon and was well into the blue sky.

The cage was situated on the edge of a thick forest, so that one side of the pen looked into the darkness between the trunks of palm trees and green ferns. The beach spread out on the other side, and beyond the sand they could see the turquoise water sparkling in the morning light. Between them and the sea was the black circle of the fire that had burned the night before. Several of the men were awake; others were still sleeping in the sand. The door to the pen was still wide open.

Around noon Shark Mouth approached the opening of the pen, motioning for the girls to come out. Escorted by Shark Mouth and two other men, they were led into the shady forest. A winding trail took them through a grove of guava trees, overgrown with vines and underbrush, and brought them to the entrance of a dilapidated lodge. It was larger than any of the structures on Rishi's island, and looked as though it hadn't been lived in for years. The sun-bleached wooden planks that made up the walls leaned precariously. Saplings grew out of the roof, part of which was caved in, squishing the entrance into half the size it had once been. The entire building was beaten and weatherworn, a dilapidated survivor of many years of storms and hurricanes.

Rishi thought they would pass the structure and head deeper into the woods, but they were led right into it, the men making the girls duck through the slanted doorway and into the dark.

After entering, the room opened up into a large cavity, cave-like and claustrophobic, smelling of sweet smoke and rotting leaves. Hazy sunbeams fell through the holes in the patchy, palm-covered roof, dappling the dirt floor with bits of light. While their eyes adjusted to the darkness, a thick, sultry voice called to them from the end of the chamber.

"My daughters. Come forward. Do not be afraid," the heavily accented voice beckoned. Rishi knew that accent. It was the same as her grandfather's, only thicker, huskier, and female.

The girls inched forward, in and out of the smoky sunbeams, toward the source of the greeting.

Slowly, through the haze, a wicker chair appeared. On the chair, surrounded by faded, threadbare pillows, was the woman they'd seen from the night before. A dark purple dress wrapped across her great bosoms and under her arms, leaving her fleshy shoulders bare. Her wiry black and grey hair was pulled back from her face in a bun and a wilted crocus blossom sagged over one ear like a dead butterfly. Around her neck was a leather strap from which hung an amber amulet, similar to the ones their captors wore, only larger. Her wide face was pockmarked and waxy and she sat holding a long pipe, emitting wisps of blue smoke that floated up around her face. To Rishi, she looked and smelled like a large rotting flower.

"Welcome," she said, her face blossoming into an overdone smile. "Welcome to Mama Xoca's summer home. Before we become acquainted, Mama Xoca must apologize for the coarse manner in which she knows you've been treated. It was necessary, you see, to get you here, but you will be handled with more gentleness in the future, if you are obedient."

Who is Mama Xoca? Rishi wondered.

The woman went on, "Mama Xoca's dog men can be rather . . ." She paused to breathe in her pipe, ". . . rough." As she said the word, smoke came tumbling out of her nose and mouth like a grey waterfall. "They are like animals . . . completely at the mercy of their urges. Incapable of self-control. Vacant minds mastered by virile bodies."

"Because of this, they will do anything for a reward, especially if it will give their bodies pleasure. And this is how Mama Xoca controls them—by giving them a 'bone.' As long as Mama Xoca throws them this bone, they will do anything she asks of them. It is important, you see, to guide their carnal natures in a productive direction . . . otherwise they can become rather . . . destructive."

Finally Rishi realized that every time the woman said "Mama Xoca" she was referring to herself.

"And when that doesn't work . . ." The great woman stood. With one hand she grasped the amulet hanging from her neck. With the other she pointed a fat finger at one of the dog men. Nonsense words came gurgling up out of her throat, and Rishi felt chills crawl up her back and shoulders. The strong man immediately cowered and receded into the dark corner, whimpering like a puppy. She slowly lowered her arm and let go of the amulet. She then turned to the girls. ". . . superstition will."

While the dog man cowered in the corner, Mama Xoca circled the girls, looking at their faces, touching their hair, scanning their bodies. Shark Mouth watched with increasing anticipation: it was almost time for him to receive his reward.

"Let us see what potential we have before us. Here we have the Pretty One," she stroked Isra's luscious hair. "And," she mused, strolling past Venay, "you must be the Fat One." Venay's countenance fell. Moving on to Sepya, the woman smeared away a tear that was rolling down the girl's cheek. "I see that you are the Sad One," she said with a pout. She made a circle around Rishi and crossed her eyes "You are the Odd One. And you . . ." She stopped before Lantana.

"Come here, child," Mama Xoca purred. Shark Mouth made a strange noise that sounded almost like a muffled laugh as he wiped saliva from his mouth. Lantana looked back at her friends and then at Mama Xoca. Timidly she took three steps toward the woman, dragging her misshapen foot.

"Ahhh . . . just as Mama suspected . . . an imperfection," she lamented with a frown. "Mama Xoca is sorry, little potato skin." She heaved a grand sigh. "But today *you* will have to be the bone." She pushed Lantana toward Shark Mouth whose arms slithered around her like two snakes.

"Save me!" Lantana screamed. The other girls stood petrified with fear, not knowing what to do, while Lantana sank to the ground, reaching out to them. Shark Mouth hoisted her back up and lifted her over his shoulder. He walked to the entrance of the lodge and disappeared through the bright doorway. The other dog man followed, and finally the third man, who was still in the corner, skittered out of the lodge like a frightened monkey. The girls listened helplessly as Lantana's terrified screams faded away into the jungle.

Several of the girls began to cry softly. Mama Xoca sat back in her chair, watching the girls' reactions without remorse. With a cloth, she dabbed the sweat from her forehead and clicked her tongue. "What is this? Tears? But there is no need for *you* to fear now . . . now that those nasty men are gone and it is just us girls. Don't worry, she'll return to you later today. They won't *kill* her, of course," she said, smiling sweetly. "We shall become good friends in the days ahead. You shall be cared for, fed, and Mama Xoca will look after you as she would her own daughters. She also will protect you from those brutes, as long as you remember one simple rule: *do as Mama says.* Believe me . . . you don't want to become *the bone.*" She paused, her smile was gone and without it her made-up face looked mask-like and hideous. "For you shall never be quite the same afterward. But let's not talk about that . . . Mama Xoca doesn't want to depress you, after all you've been through already. Let's put the past behind us. As they say in the city, 'The past is for pessimists, the future is for fools, but we are people of the present!'" Putting her pipe to her lips, she inhaled deeply and then exhaled. "Are you curious about what Mama Xoca has planned for you? In two days, my little goldfish, we will begin our journey to a place that surpasses anything your primitive island brains could conjure up. A place where dreams come true. Perhaps even on your insignificant island you might have heard of the great city of Zitól?"

Rishi breathed in sharply.

The woman leaned forward, "*Well, have you?*" she growled. Several of the girls nodded, for they all knew Yelgab's stories.

"Mama Xoca should hope so. Mama is relieved to know that even island people aren't completely ignorant of the real world." She blew out a long stream of smoke, and Rishi couldn't help inhaling the sickly sweet vapors. "You may leave now. Go back to your chambers, and Mama Xoca will have someone bring you something to eat. And when you are tempted to try to escape, just think about your little friend who is at this moment losing something very precious to her. Leave me now, my seashells."

The girls turned, anxious to get away.

"Wait!" cried the woman. She pointed her pipe at Rishi. "You with the blue eye. Stay here."

Rishi felt as if cold water had just been poured down her back, and her heart started to beat hard in her chest. Perhaps Mama Xoca would find her to be "imperfect" as well and call back the dog men.

"Come closer, strange one, and look into Mama Xoca's eyes." Rishi stepped closer to the chair. Mama Xoca leaned forward and peered at Rishi like a mole looking at sunlight for the first time.

Rishi watched as the woman's eyes flitted back and forth. Her mouth was hanging open and Rishi could smell her yellow teeth. The smoke swirled around, caressing Rishi's face. She felt as at if any moment she would vomit. She stepped away.

"I've been thinking about you," Mama Xoca said, cocking her head to the side and narrowing her eyes. "You know you frighten them, don't you?"

"Who?" said Rishi.

"My dog men," she smiled. "They think you are *magical*." She flared her hands when she said the word "magical," and then she giggled, making her large body bounce. She stepped back and slumped into her seat like a great, smirking manatee. "Mama Xoca has heard of people like you—people with a mystic eye. 'Dream children' they call you. They say you can see things that others can't, that you can tell the future and communicate with the sky. Can you tell the future, child? Are you a dream child? Tell Mama Xoca's future." She leaned forward and smiled, showing her pink gums. "How much money will Mama make on you in the big city?" She waited for an answer but Rishi kept her lips pinned together.

Finally the woman slumped back down. "No . . . ," she said, disappointed. "You can't tell the future; you seem much too fearful. After all, if you *really* knew what awaits you in Zitól you would not be afraid," she said pleasantly. "Relax, Crazy Eyes. Your future is as bright as a flashing mirror. Mama Xoca has taken you out of obscurity. Soon you will be set on a pedestal in the world's most magnificent city. You will be beautiful and famous. Mama Xoca is famous in Zitól, you know. At Mama's side you shall be a glittering prize. That is something every woman desires, is it not? To be sought after? Men all over the city will do anything just to look at your radiant face, your wholesome body . . ." Then she laughed and inhaled her pipe, exhaling the smoke into Rishi's face. "See? Mama's telling *your* future. It looks as though Mama Xoca is the dream child, now, does it not?"

"You are going to sell us as slaves?" Rishi asked.

"Slaves!" The woman gasped in mock horror. Then her voice lowered, "*Hush*, child! How could you *say* that word? How would your little friends feel if they were to hear you say such an awful thing? No, no . . . Mama Xoca never deals with *slaves*. Slaves are worthless . . . What would a slave sell for? No, little mushroom, Mama lives by a much higher standard. A slave would sell for a bag of pumpkin seeds. You and your pristine friends, you will sell for *rubies*."

"No decent person would buy and sell people. Especially someone from Zitól," said Rishi firmly.

The woman's head rolled back and she howled with laughter. "Decent?" she said, wiping the tears out of her eyes. "No one in Zitól has said the word 'decent' in forty years. Believe Mama when she says she will have no difficulty finding a buyer. You island girls are always the same, at first. You cling to your religious traditions and your stupid beads . . . but life will wear you down. Make no mistake, you will be sold, one way or another. And the whiter the bead, the higher the price."

Rishi felt a fire burn inside her. "Virtue cannot be bought and sold."

"That is what you think. Just you wait, Crazy Eyes, you will see. Zitól is a magnificent place. Either it will change you, or it will break you."

CHAPTER 20

Stolen Laughter

By the time Rishi came back to the pen—what Mama Xoca called their "chambers"—everyone had eaten. Lantana had not yet returned. The girls treated Rishi with stone-faced courtesy, and although they saved her some food, they did not speak to her.

Rishi felt miserable and alone. She tried to tell them about her conversation with the strange woman, but they continued to shun her.

The morning dragged on as the sun climbed tediously into the sky. There was still no sign of Lantana.

It was afternoon when they heard a rustling in the forest and Shark Mouth appeared, pulling Lantana by the arm. He shoved her into the pen where she crumpled to the ground like a used garment. All the girls gathered around her, blocking Rishi from helping.

"Oh, Lantana, what happened to you?" Venay asked in a soft voice. Lantana curled up and lay with her head in Venay's lap and let Venay stroke her hair. She smelled terrible. She smelled like the dog men.

Even from Rishi's vantage, she could see the scratches up and down Lantana's legs and arms. Her eye was swollen, and a smear of dried blood came out from beneath her shoulder sleeve. Her dirty cheeks were streaked with the signs of crying, but there were no tears now, and no words came from her mouth. Rishi remembered the words from Quash's old Snatcher stories: *They come to seize and silence the laughter of innocent, young girls.*

Rishi's chest burned with anger. Something needed to be done. They couldn't just let bad things keep happening to them; they had to act. And perhaps if Rishi could get them out of this mess, she could redeem herself. There was only one thing to do.

"We need to escape," Rishi said.

All four faces turned toward hers, but only Isra spoke.

"Are you crazy?" she said. "Do you see what they did to Lantana? Do you *see* this?" She pulled up Lantana's sleeve, revealing a curved row of teeth marks.

Lantana, who was staring straight ahead, brushed Isra's hand away.

Isra continued, "First of all, Rishi, *how* would we escape?"

Rishi pointed to the open gate.

"Don't you think there is a *reason* they leave it open?" Isra said. "They *want* us to try to escape so that they can catch us again and that crazy woman will give them another one of us as their 'bone.' And even if we did escape, where would we go? Thanks to you we have no family, no home, no village."

"Those men are like animals, Rishi," Venay added. "They will hunt us down. They could probably sniff out our trail."

"Perhaps one of us could escape and go and bring back help," Rishi said. "But we have to do something. She plans on selling us! The woman told me 'the whiter the bead, the higher the price.'"

"I know how to solve that," Isra said. She snapped the cord off her bead belt and flung the bead out into the sand.

All the girls gasped. Lantana had seen what had happened too, and she sat herself up, looking after the discarded bead in horror. "Isra, Isra, what have you done?" she whispered, her first words since she returned.

"It is just a stupid bead," Isra mumbled.

It was at this moment that everyone finally noticed Lantana's bead. Perhaps they hadn't noticed it before because it was obscured in the folds of her dress or because they were looking at her bruised body, but now they all saw it. The white bead made from polished bone was gone. In its place, tied with a messy knot, was a brown, wooden bead.

Lantana saw them gaping. She fingered the drab bead self-consciously and tucked it back in the folds of her dress.

"Where did you get that?" Rishi asked quietly.

"Mama Xoca. She tied it on my belt after . . . after that man—the one with the sharp teeth—" she shuddered, "took away my white one."

No one knew what to say.

Venay put her arms around Lantana's shoulders and rocked her. She looked at Rishi. "Do what you want, Rishi. We won't be coming with you. But we won't stop you, either."

In the evening Mama Xoca came, with Shark Mouth at her heels. The girls' stomachs burned with hunger when they saw the large bowl Mama Xoca held against her hip.

"I've come to wish all my little white blossoms a pleasant night," she said cheerily. "Please feel free to move anywhere in your chambers you'd like." She cackled at her joke. Shark Mouth stood behind her, arms folded, expressionless.

"Oh, I almost forgot, here is your dinner." Reaching into the bowl, she pulled out handfuls of corn kernels and threw them through the bars of the pen, as if she were feeding birds. After releasing a few handfuls she turned the bowl upside down over the top of the pen and scraped the last of the corn so that it rained down on the girls' heads.

Mama Xoca watched the girls pick the corn out of the sand. She sighed, "Aren't they adorable? They look just like little sparrows pecking for bugs." She turned to Shark Mouth. "Keep the gate open," she said loud enough for the girls to hear. "Let's see what they do. Mama Xoca wants to see if their parents taught them obedience." Mama Xoca turned her back and sauntered back into the forest, swinging her bowl and her hips. Shark Mouth joined the other dog men who were starting to light the fire.

The girls combed through the sand, picking out the corn as carefully as if they were picking lice out of a friend's hair. At first they brushed the sand off each kernel, but they were so ravenously hungry that they eventually were content to just eat the corn along with the gritty sand.

Meanwhile, Rishi stared at the open gate. It tortured her. All she had to do was walk through that opening and she'd be free.

"Don't do it," Venay whispered, watching her.

"But we could leave," Rishi said. "Right now. Tonight." She could barely contain herself; she felt her spirit darting around inside her body, trying to fly like a bird that knows it is about to be released.

"You are forgetting the dog men, Rishi, with their knives and their blow guns and their machetes."

"But haven't you noticed? They have no weapons. Ever since we came here they have not had so much as a knife. I think Mama Xoca keeps their weapons so they can't attack her."

Venay's eyes glanced down the beach at the growing group of dog men that were gathering around the fire to eat. "Rishi, think about what they could do to you even *without* weapons. And remember what the woman told us? They *want* us to escape. It is a trap."

"But they are all busy right now," said Rishi. "See? No one is even paying attention to us."

"I bet she's put men in the bushes to watch us," Sepya said. A breeze ruffled the girls' hair and even though it was a warm night some of them shivered.

"So you are all just going to sit here in an unlocked cage and not try to escape?" Rishi asked.

The girls nodded, all except Isra, who sat leaning her head against the bars, scowling and chewing the end of her braid.

Rishi crept closer to the opening.

"Stop, Rishi," Lantana said, her voice soft but urgent. She was the only one at this point who Rishi would listen to. "At least wait a little longer, to be sure."

Rishi looked at her and, with a reluctant sigh, pulled her hands away from the gate and wrapped them around her knees.

All evening the dog men gathered firewood. Even after they had what would be sufficient for a good fire, they continued adding more until the mass of dead logs and branches was taller than some of the men. The girls watched the growing pile with the realization that it was going to be a long, sleepless night.

At sunset the fire was kindled. At first it was just large enough for the men to cook their dinner. But after they had eaten, they piled more and more wood, turning their cooking fire into a roaring blaze and blacking out the stars. Even from their cage, the girls could feel the fire's heat.

The men gathered around this fire, some sitting, some standing, and their long shadows stretched into monstrous shapes. A gourd filled with some liquid was passed around, and the more they drank, the louder and wilder they became. They howled and cursed and laughed in their strange language. Sometimes they turned to the girls and shouted indecipherable words, their voices slurred and threatening.

Then two of the men left the fire and staggered up to the cage. They peered in at the girls like smiling goblins. Then, to the girls' horror, the two men crawled inside the pen.

On their hands and knees the men growled at the girls, uttering slimy words. They puckered up their lips at Isra and made kissing sounds. The girls backed into the corner, terrified. One man lunged at them, making them scream and scuttle around the pen in fear while the other one blocked the open door. Suddenly the men stopped. They were listening to something.

A rustling sound came from the trees. The two men looked at each other, and one of them muttered the word "Xoca." Again the trees rustled, sending them scrambling out of the pen as fast as they could. They plodded through the deep sand down to the fire, looking over their shoulders before joining the others.

Just then, a shadow darted out of the bushes. At first Rishi thought it might be Mama Xoca, but it was taller and moved much too fast, and it started rushing toward the cage. This was too much for Rishi and she hid her face in her hands. She could hear heavy breathing while the cage rattled.

After a few moments there was silence. Rishi lifted her head and looked around, half expecting to see the shadow inside the pen, but there was no one except the other girls who, except Isra, still had their faces covered. Isra was staring at the doorway of the pen. "Look," she said.

Rishi followed her gaze. She blinked her eyes several times and squinted, trying to make sure she was seeing things correctly in the darkness. But her eyes told the truth: no longer was the cage door open. It was shut. *Lashed* shut. Rishi and Isra looked at each other.

Slowly Rishi crawled over to the gate. Sure enough, a rope was tied tightly around the gate door, securing it.

Something else was holding the gate closed, but it was tied loosely and it came apart in Rishi's hand when she tugged on it. It was a braided leather rope with something hard and smooth hanging at the end.

"What is that?" Isra whispered behind her. By now the other girls were watching too. Rishi turned around and placed it in Isra's hand. "It is yours," Rishi said.

Isra took the leather rope and held it in her hands, turning her white bead over and over.

"My bead?" she said in disbelief. "How . . . ?"

"It either belongs to you or one of the dog men. My bet would be that it is yours."

"But who tied that?" asked Lantana, pointing to the closed gate.

No one had time to answer because the two dog men that had tormented them before were once again striding up to the cage. There were some astonished grunts when they found they could not enter the pen, and they rattled the gate in protest. One of them tried to undo the knot but in the darkness it was impossible, and neither had a knife. Ironically, now that the gate was shut, the girls were finally safe.

Grumbling, the two decided it was not worth the effort and walked back down to the others. The fire was lower now, and the dog men had started a game of who could jump over the fire without getting burned, which completely captivated everyone's attention, even the girls in the pen. But every now and then Rishi's eyes glanced at the knot in the gate, and a tiny, hopeful question took seed in her heart.

What if . . . ?

CHAPTER 21

Escape

It was late in the morning when one of the men finally brought water and food. Breakfast was stale corn cakes and cold, charred fish so covered with ash that it looked as if it had been dropped into the fire the night before.

When the dog man saw the knot, he left and brought Shark Mouth, who sat next to the gate and ripped the knot apart with his teeth. He opened the gate wide and snarled at the girls. Then they left without shutting the gate. And, for the first time since they had arrived in this strange place, not a single dog man was on the beach.

"Let's go," said Rishi.

"You are joking, right?" said Venay.

"No, I'm serious. Let's go right now. No one is here. We will run as fast as we can down the beach and hide in the jungle."

"Don't do it," said Sepya, starting to tear up.

Lantana said nothing but looked at Rishi, her face pale and tormented.

"What about you, Isra?" Rishi said. "Will you come with me? I *know* I can get help," Rishi said, thinking of last night's mysterious knot-tier.

"I think you are crazy, Rishi," said Isra.

"Listen," said Rishi. "We may not have another chance. If we are going escape, we need to do it now. Maybe they are all at a meeting or something. Maybe they went to gather food."

Isra's eyebrow rose. "Maybe they are all in that bush over there, listening to every stupid word that is coming out of your mouth."

"Just think about it," Rishi pleaded.

Isra pursed her lips. She turned and gazed around at the empty beach, into the forest and down by the surf. *At least she is considering it,* Rishi thought.

"Look—their canoes are just right there," said Isra, nodding toward the far end of the beach. "We could just push one into the water . . ."

"Yes!" said Rishi. Of course! Why hadn't she thought of that? "That is exactly what we should do."

"A lot better than your suicide mission of running down the beach and into a jungle we know nothing about. At least we *know* the sea."

"You are right. Your idea is a lot better." At this point Rishi would say anything to Isra if she could just get her and the rest of the girls to come with her.

Isra's shrewd gaze traveled back and forth between the canoes and Rishi. Everyone waited breathlessly for her decision.

Finally Isra nodded at Rishi. "I'll go."

Rishi smiled. The other girls looked at each other, stricken with the choice before them.

"Those canoes are too big for you two to paddle all by yourselves," said Venay slowly. "You will need help . . . I'll come too."

Now there were three going. Rishi looked at Lantana and Sepya. Lantana's face was white but she nodded her head. "I'll go."

Sepya folded her arms and scowled, but a smile played on her lips. "Well, I can't stay here all by myself, can I?"

Rishi felt a rush of happiness. "Let's do it, then. Together."

"You know, we don't have any food," panted Venay as they ran toward the ocean.

"Or water," added Lantana as she struggled to keep up.

"It doesn't matter," said Rishi recklessly. "We have a canoe."

They ran as fast as they could down the beach, keeping their eyes on the canoes. They surrounded one large canoe and carried it awkwardly to the water. Once it was in the water it glided effortlessly.

"There are only three paddles," said Isra.

Rishi cringed and glanced back at the other canoes. There wasn't time. Any moment the dog men might see they were missing. "We'll use what we've got. We can't go back now," she said. "Get in and I'll push you out further."

The girls piled into the canoe while Rishi walked it into the surf. The waves were small at first, breaking just at her knees. Rishi continued to guide the boat further out, and when the water was at her belt, she climbed into the boat.

The waves quickly increased in size and those with paddles dug them into the water with all their strength. Larger waves washed over them, drenching them and leaving water in the hull. Rishi's hair stuck to her face like the legs of an octopus.

"Here comes another wave," shouted Isra. "Paddle hard!"

The wave rolled toward them, swelling and picking up speed. Rishi prayed that it would peak after they passed it, but the wave sloped ominously. Having two paddlers on one side made things worse, for they couldn't keep the long canoe straight in the water. At the last moment it turned sideways, just as the huge wave started to crest.

The boat was sucked into the swelling wave, spilling out the girls and paddles, and then crushing them with a deafening roar. Rishi tumbled end over end through white bubbles, her head smashing against the sandy bottom and then smashing against the churning canoe. With her legs she searched for the ground as the wave continued to throw her toward the beach. She broke through the surface, gasping for air. Finally her toes brushed the sand and she staggered to her feet while rubbing her eyes and coughing seawater out of her lungs. Just when she was about to open her eyes, she felt the water pulling her backward and heard the unmistakable rumbling of another breaking wave. It slammed into her back and swallowed her, rolled her around again, and then finally let her go.

This time she crawled out of the ocean on her hands and knees, while salt water gushed from her nose and mouth and the vestiges of the wave lapped around her, languid and benign. Scattered about her were the remains of their miserable escape attempt. The canoe was overturned in the shallow water, the paddles were nowhere to be seen, and all of her friends were strewn about on the beach like palm fronds after a storm. Another wave came in, pushing one of the missing paddles until it floated right up to Rishi, nudging her knees, as if offering a pathetic apology. She heard laughter and when she looked up her heart dropped. At least a dozen dog men lounged on the dry sand, taking great pleasure in the pitiful scene.

Shark Mouth stood and sauntered toward Rishi, a delighted sneer on his face. Rishi rose to her feet, bringing the paddle with her. This wasn't over yet.

With both hands she lifted the paddle over her shoulder, turning the blade so that it faced her enemy. Shark Mouth didn't stop walking, and his grin became wider. Around his neck Rishi saw Lantana's white bead and anger rippled through her body. Tightening her grasp on the shaft of the paddle, she aimed for his chin, pulled back, and swung.

Shark Mouth easily caught the end of the paddle with one hand and laughed as if he were playing a game with a baby. He yanked it from Rishi's grip, jerking her forward, and she splashed into the shallow water. A loud crack sounded above her as Shark Mouth broke the paddle over his knee like a twig and flung the pieces into the ocean. Rishi stood and tried to run, but the folds of her wet dress clung together, ensnaring her legs, and she fell again into the water. Finally, Shark Mouth grabbed her by the scalp and pulled her across the sand by her hair.

When Rishi opened her eyes again, she was lying on the dry sand near the pen. Her head throbbed in pain and she had to feel her hair to make sure it was still attached.

Sepya and Lantana were beside her, Sepya groaning and Lantana looking around, dazed. Soon Venay was added to the group and finally Isra's body was dumped next to Rishi, pale and lifeless.

The dog men surrounded the five girls, covering them with their shadows. The thought of running away was unfathomable at this moment and Rishi lay there, just trying to concentrate on breathing without pain.

"Get out of Mama Xoca's way, dogs," came Mama Xoca's voice. "Show me the girls. You better not have injured any of them." The men shuffled out of the way as Mama Xoca pushed through.

She wore a yellow tunic and carried a red fan. A look of relief settled over her features after she counted the girls. "Well, at least you are all here."

Shark Mouth stood beside her, breathing heavily, his dark skin beaded with sweat. Rishi forced herself up into a kneeling position. The other girls were all sitting up by now too, except for Isra, who remained motionless on the sand. "What's wrong with her?" Mama Xoca pointed her fan at Isra. "She's still breathing, I hope."

"She's breathing," said Rishi. "Barely."

"I hope you all enjoyed your swim. Tell me, my little sea bubbles, was it refreshing?" She shook her head and clicked her tongue. "Well, it is time for someone else to have some fun now. Do you see this man, here?" She gestured to Shark Mouth, who was still panting. "Do you see him? This brave, strong, loyal servant of Mama Xoca? Look at him. Look at how eager he is to execute the consequences of your disobedience."

Rishi's eyes turned down to the sand and she prayed. She prayed like she had never prayed before. There must be a way out of this, if only she could think of something.

Mama Xoca was speaking with Shark Mouth in his own language. She asked him a question, and Rishi knew what it was. She was asking him whom of all the girls he wanted to take as his bone. His grotesque smile broadened and without hesitating he grunted and pointed to Isra.

With a gracious nod and gesture, Mama Xoca granted permission and he advanced toward the unconscious girl. Instantly Rishi scrambled across the sand, throwing herself between Shark Mouth and Isra.

"Stop!" she cried. She wasn't going to let anything else happen to her friends on account of her. She had already done enough damage.

Of course, Shark Mouth didn't stop. Instead, he palmed her head and shoved her, face first, into the sand.

Before Shark Mouth could gather up Isra's limp body, however, he was stopped by Mama Xoca's sharp voice calling to him. "Wait, my pet," she said, raising her hand. "Let's hear what the girl has to say." Shark Mouth growled, but stepped back.

"What is the matter, Crazy Eyes?" Mama Xoca said, directing her attention on Rishi. "Are you insulted that Mama Xoca's faithful servant didn't choose *you*?"

Rishi ignored the ridiculous question. "If you let him take her she will not have her bead any more and she will not sell for as much in Zitól. You will forfeit the money you would have received. Isra is the most beautiful of all of us and she will bring you a handsome price if you let her keep her bead."

Mama Xoca paused, and tapped her fan thoughtfully on her cheek. "There is truth to what you say . . . ," said the woman. "So maybe Mama Xoca should let him have *you*, Crazy Eyes. What would your answer be to that?"

Rishi swallowed. "I will also bring you more money if you let me keep my bead and my virtue, you said so yourself. *All* of us will be more valuable . . . if left unharmed." The girls cast worried glances from Rishi to Mama Xoca, their eyes wide and faces pale.

As Shark Mouth listened to Rishi and Mama Xoca his expression grew dark. Not because he understood what Rishi was saying, but because he could tell Mama Xoca was listening.

Mama Xoca shifted her weight and fanned herself. Shark Mouth frowned and cracked his knuckles. Rishi held her breath. It might be her fault that they were all here, but she wasn't going to let her friends down anymore. No matter what happened, she promised herself that from now on, she would protect them.

Mama Xoca's eyes narrowed. "That is a good argument, Crazy Eyes, but if Mama Xoca doesn't correct your bad behavior now, you will think you can get away with anything. *Someone* must pay for your disobedience . . . that is why I will let him have . . ." She bit her lower lip as she decided, ". . . that one. Again." And she pointed the fan at Lantana who immediately shrank, trembling. "She is worthless now anyway," Mama Xoca said.

No! Rishi groaned inside herself. This was not what she wanted! She didn't think that by deflecting attention from Isra that Lantana would again be punished. Why couldn't she get anything right? Rishi frantically tried to think of something else.

But she didn't have to. A strange rumbling sound made the hair on Rishi's arms stand on end. She thought at first the sound was coming from the sea or from the earth, but it was coming from Shark Mouth's throat.

His arms became rigid, his fists clenched. He thrust a pointed finger at Isra.

"No," said Mama Xoca coolly, not bothering to translate. "Mama Xoca is keeping her. *You* take *this* one." But Shark Mouth didn't need a translation. He growled and pointed again.

"*No!*" said Mama Xoca so sharply that some of the girls jumped.

Shark Mouth snarled, his black eyes flashing. The girls clung to the sand, petrified, as their eyes darted back and forth between Shark Mouth to Mama Xoca, not sure who was the most terrifying.

This time Mama Xoca spoke very slowly, enunciating each word with cold, crisp tones. "*No.* You-take-*that*-one," she nodded at Lantana, "*or none at all.*"

A thick vein appeared on Shark Mouth's forehead and began to pulse. His face tightened, reddened and steamed. His nostrils widened, his eyes burned hatred, and Rishi felt that at any moment he would leap on Mama Xoca and rip her apart.

But Mama Xoca did not waver, step back, or even blink. Instead she stared coolly at the animal man, while the other dog men watched, eyes frozen wide, muscles tense and ready to defend their leader, whomever it should be.

Shark Mouth opened his mouth and roared. Rishi could see deep into the black cavern of his throat. A flock of birds flew from their perches in the trees above. When he finished, he rushed at the girls, snarling and growling. He did not touch them, however. Instead he ran, seething, to the pen. Grasping the bars, he ripped the side of the cage out of the sand. With his hands he crushed the rods and flung the pieces into the forest. The other dog men watched, cowering back, just like the girls. When he finished, he looked at Rishi with eyes filled with wrath. He spat into the sand and then stormed into the forest.

Mama Xoca observed the scene unruffled, with a hint of amusement on her lips. When he was gone, she chuckled. "Good riddance," she said. She turned to what remained of the pen. Pointing to the damage, she said something to the dog men. A few of them left the group.

In a few moments they were back with new poles. They pounded these deep into the ground and fixed the damage to the top of the pen. The girls watched, miserably. When the dog men were finished, Mama Xoca said, "All right, everyone, your palace is repaired. Time to get back in. Don't forget to take your friend with you," she said as though she were pleasantly herding chickens. "I'm sure she'll wake up soon and when she does you can tell her about all the fun she missed. Get a good rest everyone, for tomorrow is a big day. We will be off on our way to Zitól!" The way she said it made it sound like they were all about to start a grand adventure together.

And so they were, for somewhere in the forest was an animal who had been denied his bone.

CHAPTER 22

A New Dream

The next day the group entered the steamy, dense forest and the jungle embraced the travelers like prey. It was a dark world, full of shadows. Trees blocked out the sky and suffocated the breeze. Every shape and size of tree trunk grew out of the black earth, covered with moss and dripping with loops of sprawling vines. Glossy leaves the size of small children sprang out on huge stems. Large, waxy flowers graced the shrubs, emitting odd, suffocating fragrances that made Rishi feel sick when she passed them. The ground was black and spongy; the air was so humid Rishi felt like she was constantly dripping.

The jungle was eerily alive with human sounds. Wild turkeys thumped out quick drumbeats. The black forms of monkeys darted about in the canopy above, shrieking like angry women. Unseen birds called out to each other, their shrieks like the screams of babies. Underneath the drumming, shrieking, and screaming was the constant drone of cicadas and the eternal dripping of water on leaves.

The girls followed their captors through this maze of darkness with their hands bound, burdens across their backs, and Mama Xoca walking close behind. She was the only one who did not carry a bundle. Instead, she carried two things: a wooden case with a handle, and a long, black machete.

Every so often Rishi would hear something dash through the underbrush or angrily rattle the branches above her, but when she turned to look she saw nothing except leaves bouncing on their stems or a quivering branch. She shivered as she thought of the jaguars she'd heard about in her grandfather's stories, and she imagined them crouching, ready to spring out and sink their teeth into her neck.

But what worried Rishi the most was the light she sometimes saw, far back in the trees. Not small, like insect lights, but larger and orange, the kind of light that only comes from a fire. From time to time Rishi caught Mama Xoca and some of the dog men staring at this light, though they never seemed to discuss it.

At night the men tied Mama Xoca's hammock to two trees and she slept, one arm wrapped around the mysterious box she carried, the other around the machete. Everyone else found a place on the moist, crawling ground. The trees completely blocked out the light from the moon and stars, leaving them smothered in a sticky, wet darkness that seemed to cling like tar. It was also a deafening darkness; all night twigs snapped, wings beat, water dripped, insects chirped, turning the night into a black cacophony of unknown terrors.

In the midst of this, Rishi dreamed a new dream.

She was alone in the forest. She was looking for something. She looked all over the ground and it was not there. She parted bushes and looked behind trees. She couldn't find it anywhere. She didn't know what she was looking for, she just knew she desperately needed it, for if she didn't find it, something terrible would happen. Her heartbeat quickened with a sense of urgency. She started to run through the forest, looking all around, feeling that it was near and that she would soon find it if only she kept searching.

Then she saw a large, wide tree with gray bark and thick branches that grew out and then back to the ground, like a man who is too tired to hold up his arms. There was a hole in the trunk of this tree, and Rishi felt relief and excitement, for somehow she knew that the object of her desire was *in that hole*. She came closer to the tree and reached her hand into the dark cavity. But before she could pull out the object, the dream began to ripple and fade and disappear.

She found herself sitting on the ground, curled up around her knees, feeling a great loss that she could not obtain that object. Darkness surrounded her, so dark that she could not tell if her eyes were open or shut.

But she could hear. Something was near her, breathing, sniffing her neck. Then she felt small points of pressure tighten on her shoulder. It was bothering her; she wanted it to stop. It pressed down harder through her tunic and into her skin. It wasn't a hand . . . It was smaller and sharper, like . . . teeth.

Rishi's eyes flew open and she sat up, looking around her in panic. The pressure on her shoulder disappeared. Where was she? She spotted the glowing fire and the forms of her friends sleeping around her. Beyond them were the bodies of snoring dog men. Mama Xoca was in her hammock. It must have been a dream, she thought. But it seemed so real. She reached up to touch the spot on her tunic where she had felt the pressure. It was wet.

Over at the fire Rishi could see one of the dog men stirring the coals with a stick. He crouched on the other side of fire, staring at her. When their eyes met he continued to stare at her until finally she shuddered and looked away.

By the third day Rishi's feet were blistered and swollen. Sepya had a red rash on her legs, and Venay could barely walk. They were all covered with insect bites that itched so much it made them want to tear off their skin. "Stop scratching," Mama Xoca growled at them. "You will scar."

Each day it became more apparent that they were following a path. Before long it was wide enough that two people could walk side by side. The roots and dead trees that clogged the trail before were gone and the path was more or less level. Even the steep parts of the trail were fitted with stone steps. Before, Mama Xoca relied on the dog men to cut a path through the jungle with her precious machete, but now that the path was clear, the weapon seldom left the belt around her waist. When they stopped to drink or eat, Rishi and the other girls watched it as it hung about her hips, tantalizing them.

Rishi wondered what she would do if she was able to gain possession of that weapon. What would she do first? Stab Mama Xoca? Slit her throat? She played out the scenario in her mind and shivered. Rishi wouldn't do that. But if she ever gained possession of that weapon, she knew what she would do. She would give it to Isra. Isra would know what to do with it.

But even if they were able to take care of Mama Xoca, there were still the dog men.

"Why are men born stronger than women?" grumbled Isra one night after the dog men were asleep and Mama Xoca was snoring in her hammock. "They are taller than us, faster than us, meaner than us . . ."

"Smellier than us," Sepya said.

Rishi agreed. If there was anything she learned from her brothers, it was that when it came to physical strength, women were powerless.

"You would think there would be *something* we could do," mused Venay.

Rishi sighed, thinking of her brothers. If it was true that they may have survived, then why didn't they show themselves? Why didn't they help her? Ever since that night on the beach when the gate was mysteriously tied shut, Rishi had expected that at any moment her brothers would pop out of the bushes and save them all. But with each day that passed, she was beginning to wonder if the miraculous knot was just another dream. She knew she couldn't rely on the hope that her brothers would come to her rescue. If she and her friends were to protect themselves, they would have to take matters into their own hands.

CHAPTER 23

An Enemy Returns

Turquoise butterflies as big as Rishi's hand floated lazily alongside the girls as they walked, each girl flanked by two dog men. They passed snakes coiled on branches, clouds of biting flies, and small fuzzy animals nestled in the trees that stared at them with large, unblinking eyes. Flamboyant birds flew from branch to vine, vine to branch, their lavish tail feathers streaming behind them like hair ribbons. Every now and then the group would pass an open spot where sunlight spilled though the forest canopy in beams that looked so thick Rishi thought that if she could only grab one she could pull the sun down into this dark, wet place.

The girls were led through thick forests, across spongy swamps, and up mossy cliffs. The path wound through rock canyons where hundreds of tiny waterfalls veined their way down the lush green cliffs, dripping with the earth's pulse.

For food they ate fruit and nuts, and sometimes large worms, whose soft bodies gave an unsettling crunch when chewed. Other times one of the dog men would catch a turkey. They'd roast this over the fire, and when the juices from the turkey leaked out and sizzled in the coals and the delicious warm fragrance floated in the air, the dog men would take the turkey from the spit and cut the best parts out for Mama Xoca, who undaintily ate it in her lap. The men would eat the rest, smacking their lips together like animals and gnawing the bones clean until the meat and its wonderful smell were just a memory. The girls were tossed a few morsels of leftover fat and bones.

Every evening Mama Xoca would lay in her hammock and smoke her pipe, and if the mysterious fire appeared in the forest, she would arrange her great body so she could watch it until everyone else fell asleep.

One night there was no light to watch, so Mama Xoca retired earlier than usual, filling out her hammock like a massive caterpillar beginning its metamorphosis into a great, ugly moth.

It was a hot, steamy evening, and the dog men were skittish. They kept looking out into the forest, cracking their knuckles and whispering to each other. After Mama Xoca was asleep, one dog man stood next to her hammock for a long time.

"What is he doing?" whispered Sepya.

"I don't know. Maybe he's guarding her." Rishi shrugged.

"From who? Us?"

The girls continued their usual nightly forest routine of clearing a spot on the ground to sleep. Meanwhile, the dog men built up the fire until it was uncomfortably large, making the hot jungle air unbearable. Then, when the fire blazed so brightly that it illuminated everything from the crawling lines of ants to the leaves of the canopy above, the dog men stepped into the forest and disappeared.

"Ohhh . . . I hate it when they do this," Sepya whimpered.

Harboring a growing feeling of dread, but not knowing what else to do, the girls lay down. They expected the dog men to come back any moment but they didn't. Though the girls were exhausted, sleep did not come. The fire was big and blindingly bright. The forest was unusually silent tonight, as if everything was hiding. The only sound they could hear was the crackling of the fire's tall flames, flapping like flags.

A twig snapped in the darkness and Rishi sat up.

"What was that?" she whispered.

"Just your imagination," said Sepya. "I hope."

Lantana and Sepya gathered close to Rishi and the three of them listened while Isra and Venay still lay on the ground, their eyes wide open.

"I know it is kind of a strange thing to say," Sepya said slowly, "but I would feel safer if they all came back."

Rishi agreed. Although the fire made it easier to see each other, it made the jungle terrifyingly black. Shadows were everywhere, seeming to move and jump as the fire waved, playing tricks on Rishi's eyes. Even Mama Xoca's hammock, still as a stone, cast a monstrous silhouette.

"It is probably just a—" Rishi began, but she was interrupted by another snap, and a black form passed through the plants.

"Did you see that?" Lantana said in a strangled voice.

Now Venay and Isra sat up.

"Maybe we should wake Mama Xoca," Sepya said.

Isra scowled at her. "She's not on our side, remember?"

"But at least she seems interested in keeping us alive."

"It is probably just an animal," Rishi said.

"A big animal," Sepya whispered, as all of the girls moved closer together.

Slowly, Rishi picked up a heavy stick and stood. Narrowing her eyes, she peered into the direction she thought the animal had gone. She tried to listen, but all she could hear was the roaring fire and the pounding of her heart.

With the stick raised, she walked around the fire, listening, watching. There were no sounds, and all she could see were shadows. After a few moments she relaxed her grip on the stick and let her arm fall to her side. Whatever it was must have run away. It was just an animal. It was gone.

She walked over to the girls and was about to sit down when suddenly she stopped.

"What is it, Rishi?" Venay asked.

"I smell something," she said. It was thick, foul, and unmistakably familiar.

"Oh no," Lantana wailed, catching the scent.

All at once footsteps sounded all around them, crashing through the underbrush. The girls would have run, but the footsteps seemed to be coming from everywhere. The sounds came closer and faster until a dark shape leaped like an animal out of the shadows. It sailed through the air, landing on Isra and knocking her to the ground.

Isra screamed as the shadow pinned her down with his hands and bent down to bite her neck. Shark Mouth had returned to claim his prize.

CHAPTER 24

The Longest Night

Screams filled the air. Rishi lost all mobility as she watched Shark Mouth overtake Isra. Then she remembered she still carried a stick. She ran up to him and cracked the stick across his back as hard as she could. He didn't even look at her.

More shadows leaped out of the forest, and the other dog men appeared, their faces and chests painted like skeletons, just like the day they burned the village. One grabbed Rishi's stick from her and shoved her against a tree so hard she cried out in pain. Somehow, Isra had wriggled free from Shark Mouth's grasp and was crawling away, trying to stand, but Shark Mouth grabbed her ankle and raked her over the root-covered ground back to him.

This time Rishi jumped on his back and reached around his neck, pulling tight against his throat. Shark Mouth shook his shoulders furiously, trying to shake her off and grasp Isra at the same time, but Rishi was fixed to him like a clam and Isra pulled herself far enough away to get a leg loose and kick her attacker in the face. Snarling, Shark Mouth's hands covered his broken nose and Rishi tightened her grip around his throat.

The other girls around her were shouting and crying out, trying to fight their own battles. Rishi glanced desperately at Mama Xoca's hammock, serenely still.

With his free hands Shark Mouth peeled Rishi off his back, dumped her to the ground, and kicked her toward the fire. Rishi pulled a smoldering log out of the flames and staggered to her feet just as she heard Sepya shriek. A man was pushing her to the ground. Holding the log, Rishi charged at Sepya's perpetrator, laying the lit end on the man's naked back. He yelped and let Sepya go. Sepya made it several paces, only to be caught in the grip of another man. Rishi expected the man she had burned to turn and grab her, but he went after Lantana, who was crouched against a tree. He snatched her wrist and started to drag her off in the forest. Rishi caught hold of his arm, but he easily twisted free and then pushed her into the dirt.

"Run, Rishi!" Lantana yelled just before the dog man clinched his hands around her neck. Rishi scrambled to her feet and watched the hopeless scene of chaos all around her. She couldn't run and leave her friends here. But she couldn't fight all of these men by herself, either. And even though the girls continued to kick and fight and scream, Rishi knew their strength wouldn't last long.

Then a realization struck her. Why weren't they attacking *her*? They were pushing her away, but it was clear that it was the *other* girls they wanted. Were they still afraid of her? Rishi remembered how Mama Xoca had controlled the dog man with only her words and an amulet. Could she do the same thing? But what would she say?

Instantly, words flashed into her mind. They were the words of the Song of the Bead, the song always sung at bead ceremonies to the young girls. Rishi tried to think of something else, a different song, one that was stronger, more forceful, but at that moment, it was as if she had forgotten all of the other songs. The Song of the Bead was all she had.

Doubtful and nervous, but knowing this was her only option, she put herself in the middle of the fray, next to the fire and blurted out, "*My daughters!*"

No one paid attention.

She held up her hands. "*My daughters!*" she shouted again. Some of the men turned their heads toward her.

Rishi stood as straight and tall as she could. She knew the words meant nothing to the dog men. But that didn't mean that the words weren't powerful. Hadn't she been taught that her whole life? Did not Eno himself tell her that he felt the power of the songs as he dove for oysters? If the gods blessed him in his pursuit for pearls, surely they could help rescue her friends' lives. Rishi opened her mouth and continued the song and the words she knew by heart:

> *Though you are a young girl,*
> *Your strength is as strong as the sea.*
> *In your eyes lies the light of the future.*
> *And what you are to be.*
> *You are as white as a blossom*
> *Your face is a golden sun*
> *Your smile is that of the sparkling waves.*
> *In your voice hope is won.*

All of the men were watching her now, puzzled. The girls were listening, too, and had stopped screaming.

Once she saw that she had everyone's attention, she tempered her voice. From experience, she knew that men never take shrieking women seriously. If you really want a man to listen to you, her mother told her once, *whisper.*

Rishi repeated the song again, whispering this time, and began to walk, chanting the words like a spell and forcing eye contact with each dog man she passed. It didn't matter that the cheery, sunny words did not fit the chaotic setting; her enemies did not know the meaning of the words. All that mattered was that her friends knew what she was saying.

Just as Mama Xoca would grasp the amulet that hung around her neck, Rishi grasped her white bead with one hand. The dog men watched her, transfixed, but still clutching her friends. For a moment Rishi wondered what she would do next, if this didn't work. But her worries were swept away when she heard Lantana's voice.

"*Be strong, my daughter,*" she sang out.

The corner of Rishi's mouth lifted in a half smile. She locked eyes with Lantana and together they chanted the next lines.

May your life be full, faithful, and long.

Encouraged, Venay joined in. Then Sepya and Isra.

Find your voice, my daughter
Though you are small, your voice is strong.

The combination of their voices together rang through the darkness, and it was as if the whole forest listened to their words.

The girls started the verse over again and as they did, Rishi cut out and spoke between lines. "Look them in the eyes, my island sisters," she said, her heart pounding, "Tell them *who we are.*"

The girls turned as one and stared into the faces of their attackers. With narrowed eyes they repeated the words, keeping their voices low and steady.

I am as white as a blossom!
My face is a golden sun!

Rishi continued, "Don't let your eyes waver from theirs. Let the fear leave your body and enter *theirs.*"

My smile is that of the sparkling waves!
In my voice hope is won!

With growing anxiety, men loosened their hold on the girls and instead fingered the amulets that hung around their necks. With eyes wide and fearful, they watched Rishi, some visibly trembling as they backed away from the girls who now seemed possessed. The chanting continued.

Rishi felt filled with power.

Only Isra was still being held now, by Shark Mouth. He did not seem as overwhelmed by Rishi's voice as the others.

All of the sudden one of the men turned and tore off into the forest. Then another ran away, crashing into a tree as he tried to make his escape. Shark Mouth shouted at them, but his words had no effect, for the other two fled like their feet had been set on fire.

Rishi turned to Shark Mouth, pulling together all of her courage. "Don't stop, my sisters! We must make our voices one!"

Now all the girls faced Shark Mouth who was still holding Isra, his hands on her shoulders and one knee on her chest. Rishi walked toward him. The other girls walked toward him. Rishi pointed at him. The other girls pointed at him. They came closer and closer, surrounding him and filling the night with the power of their words. Finally Shark Mouth took his hands off Isra, and backed up into a squat. Slowly he stood and stepped away as Isra lifted herself to her feet, turned, and joined her sisters.

My face is a golden sun!
Though I am small, my voice is strong!

Shark Mouth slowly backed up against a large tree. But something was wrong. Rishi could tell he was not afraid like the other men had been. With an unreadable expression, he scanned the girls' faces until he came to Rishi. He stared hard at her, narrowing his eyes. *He knows,* she thought. *He knows I don't really have power over him.* Without meaning to, she faltered the words of the song, weakening the rhythm of the chant. Shark Mouth's eyes glittered, and Rishi knew the spell she had worked so hard to cast was broken.

He lunged at Rishi, catching her by the throat. Then he spun her around, slamming her back into the tree. The girls scattered like fish, and instantly the magic vanished.

Once again, fear ruled the night.

Shark Mouth caught Isra by the shoulders and again forced her to the ground, determined to finish what he set out to do.

Rishi sat up, dazed, and saw Shark Mouth leaning over Isra, pressing his mouth against her closed lips. Rishi knew she had to do something, but she was exhausted and out of ideas. The situation was beyond what she and her friends could handle now, and she needed help from another place. There was only one thing left to try.

She closed her eyes and tried to imagine the sky on a clear night, with the stars scattered like sand on an ebony shore. In her mind she called out to this sky, the sky she could not see but knew was there. *Please, help us,* she called out to the unseen stars. *Don't leave us alone.*

And then, when she opened her eyes, she saw it. It had been here the entire time. Why hadn't she seen it before?

Rising just beyond Shark Mouth and Isra, there was a large grey tree, with thick branches that grew out from the trunk and then bent down to rest on the ground, like a man too tired to lift his arms . . . and there in the center of the trunk was a *hole.*

Just like her dream.

Rishi was so awestruck by this miracle that she couldn't even move until she heard Isra start screaming. Suddenly remembering the urgency of the situation, Rishi picked herself up and dashed to the tree. She didn't know what it was, but she knew *it* was there, and *it* would save them. She thrust her hand into the hole and immediately she clutched something long and hard. She pulled it out. It was a knife.

Rishi grasped the familiar mother-of-pearl handle and drew it out of its eel skin sheath. Her grandfather's blade glimmered in the night: long, polished, and willing. The other girls gaped in astonishment.

"Rishi, you just pulled a *knife* out of a *tree!*" exclaimed Sepya, her eyes big as pumpkins.

Isra was still screaming.

Rishi couldn't stop staring at the blade.

"Hurry, Rishi!" Sepya shouted. "Use it!"

Rishi looked at Shark Mouth, still struggling to keep the squirming Isra in one place. His back was there, smooth and wide, an easy kill. All she had to do was take three steps forward and thrust it through his skin. It would be as simple as pushing a stick into the sand. That was all she had to do. Push the stick into the sand.

Isra was screaming.

"*Use it!*" cried Venay.

Rishi closed her eyes . . . *a stick into the sand.*
"NOW, RISHI!" Sepya wailed.
Isra was screaming, screaming, screaming . . .

Before we continue, it is important for you to understand that Rishi could never kill anything. She would fight to save her friends; she would scratch and bite and kick to save herself . . . but to actually *kill* someone? It was not in her nature or power. I would have been able to use the knife without a second thought. You probably would have too. Rishi, however, could not.

But the gods are wise, and they knew this. The knife was for Rishi *to find*, not for Rishi *to use.* As you will see, the gods are efficient, and excel at granting several prayers at once.

Back to where we were—Isra was screaming.

To the horror of her companions, Rishi's hands trembled and she dropped the weapon. It fell between her feet, piercing the black earth.

In the time it took for Rishi to blink, the knife was swept away by another hand. A voice rang out into the night, "*Though I am small, my voice is strong!*" And gentle, clubfooted Lantana plunged the knife into Shark Mouth's back.

His body went limp and he collapsed against Isra, crushing her. In an instant, everything became quiet.

"Help!" Isra gasped.

The girls rolled Shark Mouth off her and she scooted away. They sat in silence for a moment, listening only to the throb of their hearts in their necks while regarding the body of the dead man with guarded horror, half expecting him to suddenly leap up once more and gnash his pointed teeth.

A muffled sound came from Mama Xoca's hammock, which was now wriggling like a netted whale. Rishi stood, still trembling, and approached the hammock. The opening had been sewn shut with layers of crudely sewn stitches. Now Rishi understood: the dog man hadn't been guarding the woman at all; he had been ensnaring her.

Something prodded at the seam from the inside of the hammock until suddenly the stitches were ripped apart. Mama Xoca appeared, waving her machete, her face dripping with sweat, her eyes ablaze.

"What is going on? Who trapped Mama Xoca?"

Once Mama Xoca fully untangled herself from the hammock and had two feet on the ground, she marched toward the girls, waving her weapon above her head. She froze when she saw Shark Mouth's body, with his expressionless face staring blankly up at the forest canopy. Her arm lowered and the machete dropped to the ground. Insects hummed in the jungle while the girls waited, breathless and terrified for her reaction. Then Mama Xoca turned to the girls. She viewed their grimy clothes, their ravaged hair, their smudged faces, and the blood across their cheeks and arms. Their appearance told the story.

She put one hand on her hip. "Who killed him?" she asked.

No one dared look at Lantana.

Mama Xoca stooped to pick up her machete. She strode up to the body and pushed it over with her foot. She saw the bloody wound on his back, but the knife had vanished. She narrowed her eyes. "From the looks of the way this turned out, Mama Xoca guesses that you are still virgins?"

The girls slowly nodded their heads.

"Well, *that* is a relief. And what did you do with the rest of the men? More invisible weapons?"

No one said anything.

Suddenly Mama Xoca spit on Shark Mouth's body. "Good riddance," she said. She turned to the girls. "I suppose in some ways you have done Mama Xoca a favor. We will talk about this in the morning."

She staggered back to her hammock, leaving the girls alone with the dead man.

For a long time, the girls lay with their eyes wide open. After a while, Rishi reached for Lantana's hand and squeezed it. "Thank you, Lantana," she whispered.

Lantana said nothing. But she squeezed back.

Rishi watched the insects float above her, lit by the dying fire. She shifted her focus beyond them to a tiny crack in the canopy of trees where she thought she could see a star glittering in the midnight blue sky. "Thank you, Grandfather," Rishi whispered as her eyes grew heavy and finally closed.

The strong smell of medicinal herbs hung in the air when the girls opened their bleary eyes. Sunlight was trickling through the layers of leafy ceiling, and ants and roaches were already exploring Shark Mouth's body.

Sitting by the fire on an alarmingly fragile-looking stool, Mama Xoca stirred a small pot filled with boiling water. Every so often she added leaves and powders to the pot.

The mysterious wooden case she had been carrying since they left the beach was opened at her feet. Next to this was a mat on which sat dozens of small gourd bottles with cork stoppers. Using a forked stick, Mama Xoca pulled the boiling brew off the fire and set it to the side.

"You." She pointed to a yawning Isra. "Come here."

Isra hesitated, but then made her way to Mama Xoca, flinching in pain with every movement.

Mama Xoca leaned over, picked up one of the bottles, removed the stopper, and tapped a thick paste onto her fingers. Rubbing the paste together, she inspected Isra's body. Isra had two black eyes, abrasions up and down her arms, insect bites on her legs, and teeth marks on her neck. Mama Xoca rubbed the paste on each wound and cut, working it into Isra's skin. She took the shriveled leaves from the pot of hot water and told Isra to hold them against her bruised eyes.

"You realize now that you have a choice," Mama Xoca said as she worked. "Mama has no way to force you to stay with her now. You can run. You can hide yourself in the jungle and take your chances against the fire ants, the jaguars, and the poisonwood trees. You can try to survive by eating the forest fruits, half of which are poisonous and will kill you only after three days of intense vomiting. You can flee to a neighboring village where they will rob you of your virginity before they ask you your name. Or . . . you can stay with me."

Finished with Isra, she pointed to Lantana, making them switch places. Putting more paste on her hands and inspecting a deep gash on Lantana's shoulder, she continued. "I will keep you safe. I will feed you. I will heal every scratch and bruise on your body." She paused and looked up at them. "And I will make you an oath that by the time we get to the city, your skin will be as flawless as it was the day you were born."

Rishi realized this was the first time Mama Xoca had used the word "I."

Mama Xoca did not say anything after that, but silently tended to each girl, as gently and thoroughly as any mother.

CHAPTER 25

Golden Temples

Kingdom of Zitól, 10.

Those were the words Rishi read on the stone marker they came to the next day. Mama Xoca walked past it with not so much as a glance, but Rishi felt a wave of hope. Everything inside her told her that in Zitól she would find refuge; in Zitól she would be safe. Mama Xoca *had* to be wrong about this city.

After the first marker, the landscape began to change. The forest thinned. The dirt path became a limestone road. The canopy of trees overhead gradually thinned and Rishi could see the sky again. By the next stone marker, *Kingdom of Zitól, 5*, the road had become a causeway. It was raised up from the forest floor, built upon a wall of stones, and was perfectly level. When the road spanned depressions in the land, its sides were as tall as eight men. Rishi could see the tops of the trees as they walked and she watched the monkeys swinging on the draping vines. Then, when there was a hill, the highway was even with the ground. In this way, although the land was shaped in gentle contours, they never had to walk uphill or down.

From time to time they saw other people on the road, carrying burdens on their backs, with the strap around their foreheads. Sometimes they would issue a greeting to Mama Xoca. Always their eyes lingered on the beads swinging at the girls' hips.

As they traveled, more and more people entered the highway. When the highway was level with the ground, travelers came in from trails emerging from trees or cornfields. When the land lay below the walls of the highway, the people entered from stone stairways that were built adjacent to the outside walls. All were going in the same direction, and everyone carried something on their back. Some carried bushels of sticks or tapestries rolled up in piles. Others had fruits or vegetables. Many had loads of corn and potatoes and huge bundles of white cotton. One man had a cage on his back filled with wild turkeys. Everyone was coming to sell, trade, or pay tribute in Zitól.

There were also beggars that sat along the highway, as well as clusters of young warriors with fierce expressions and painted faces and chests. Once, when Mama Xoca stopped to make corn cakes (for people created cooking fires right there on the highway), a group of slaves passed by, their hands all lashed to one long rope. Rishi watched them pass, wondering where they came from and if any were from the islands. They all wore belts with beads swinging back and forth. None of them were white.

They passed another marker: *Kingdom of Zitól, 3.*

Rishi watched the sun set over the distant road in front of her. The sky was awash with colors of orchids and plumerias. The sun rested for a few moments on the zenith of the road, winking at her through the bundles carried on people's backs. She had no doubt that tomorrow they would enter the city. There were too many travelers for it not to be so.

On this night Mama Xoca didn't stop once it was dark. She pulled the five girls along under the indigo sky until only the moon illuminated the stone highway.

Up ahead Rishi could see a large pavilion with square columns and a thatched roof.

Mama Xoca led them into the crowded structure and found a place for them to spread out. People were warming themselves by small fires, finishing their evening meals, and curling up next to their bundles, trying to find enough room to get comfortable on the stone floor but still protect their valuables. Some watched the girls as they found a place to rest. Rishi could hear people whispering Xoca's name.

Mama Xoca settled the girls near the back of the pavilion and the girls gratefully loosened their loads. The night was cooler than usual and Rishi shivered and hugged her knees close to her body. There was a group next to them, a group of women with loads of dried corncobs. They had a bright fire and they laughed and joked with one another. One of them took out a bundle of sharp sticks and handed them out to her companions. They each fit a corncob on a stick and held it in the fire. Before long there was a loud pop. Then another. Rishi and the other girls peered through the shoulders of the boisterous women. The popping was coming from the roasting corn. Puffs of white flew out of their fire, and the woman scooped them up with their hands and tossed them into their mouths, laughing as they crunched the white puffs.

A few stray pieces of the popcorn popped out of the women's circle and landed before Rishi. She handed them out to the other girls, and they put the puffs into their mouth and slowly tried the new flavor, savoring the soft, squeaky crunch.

Deep into the night people talked and chatted. One by one Mama Xoca and the other girls fell asleep. But Rishi could not. Lantana shifted next to her restlessly. Finally she turned toward Rishi.

"Rishi, are you awake?"

"Yes."

"Are you afraid of what will happen when we get to the city?"

"No."

Lantana propped herself up on her elbow. "You aren't?"

"No. My grandfather always told me that Zitól is a place of beauty and goodness. We will be safe there."

Lantana didn't say anything. Then Rishi remembered.

"I have something for you," Rishi said and sat up. She reached into the folds of her tunic.

"What is it?" asked Lantana, sitting up.

"Hold out your hand."

Rishi put the object into Lantana's hand. Lantana gasped.

"It is my white bead! How did you—?"

"I took it from his neck the morning after he attacked us. I think you earned it back. Let me tie it on your belt."

Lantana put the bead back in Rishi's hand.

"I can't," she said.

"Why not?"

"I am not worthy of it."

"Lantana, you are still virtuous."

Lantana shook her head.

"No, Rishi, I'm not. I was defiled."

"But it wasn't your choice. It was against your will. It doesn't count."

"It may not count to you, but I can still feel it in here." She tapped her chest. "He took something from me, Rishi, and I will never be the same."

Lantana lay back down and rolled over, leaving Rishi alone, still holding the bead.

When she awoke, Rishi's clothes were damp with dew. All around her there were bodies stirring. Mist engulfed the pavilion and Rishi huddled closer to the other girls for warmth until Mama Xoca got up and shook them all awake.

Rishi stood, rubbing her hands up and down her freezing arms. All around the pavilion people were rising, yawning, and loading up their valuable cargos with purposeful, quiet eagerness. Even with the chill, no one bothered to resurrect the coals in the fires.

Mama Xoca handed each girl a corn cake, made the night before, gritty and tasteless. "Eat it while we walk," she said.

People were leaving the pavilion rapidly, disappearing into the mist. Mama Xoca secured the girls together, ensuring that her "goods" didn't become separated from her in the migration of strangers.

They came out onto the highway and became part of the flow of figures appearing and disappearing in the white morning mist. It seemed they traversed this way for hours, the bundles on their backs bobbing along the misty river of travelers.

Gradually the mist lifted, settling only in the wrinkles and creases of a gigantic plain. Rishi focused her eyes on the retreating fog in the distance. She knew the city was there before her, hidden in those clouds. When she finally saw the glimmer of something jutting up into the pewter sky, her heart skipped a beat.

She fixed her eyes on the object until she saw another one, a little ways away from the first, and then another. She could count four now, aloft like great stone heads facing each other over a veil of cool mist. The morning sun was rising behind her, spreading warmth along her back and highlighting the massive heads, and when the sun finally broke over the crest of land, the objects suddenly reflected the sun's golden light in a brilliant, blinding flash. Rishi knew what they were now. They were the gilded tops of the pyramids of Zitól, exactly as her grandfather described.

The sun's light stripped the mantle of mist away from the pyramids, unveiling their huge sloping shoulders. Smaller pyramids and temples appeared, clustering around the four towering structures like children surrounding their parents.

As the sun rose behind them, the girls followed their long, stretched shadows that pointed the way to the city. Rishi swallowed hard, and she couldn't help the hot feeling in her chest and the rush of tears that came to her eyes. She couldn't believe she was really here, looking at the pyramids of Zitól. It was more magnificent than she imagined. This scene had been described to her over and over, but she never truly believed she would be a part of it. It was the place she had yearned for, obsessed over as a child, and hoped to see with her own eyes. And now that she was actually gazing at the majestic city it seemed as familiar to her as her grandfather's face. This was the ancient city of her ancestors. Was it all as her grandfather said it was, with benevolent people who were as generous as they were wealthy? *Surely it must have changed a little since he had been here,* she thought. As Rishi drank in the dazzling view, she couldn't help but feel that this was surely a place of happiness and enchantment. It was as if she were headed to paradise, and her heart was on the verge of bursting.

The throng pushed forward, energized by the sight of the city. All aching muscles and blistered feet were forgotten at the sight of the shining pyramids.

By the time they reached the outside wall, the sun had erased away any memory of the morning's chill. Sweat gathered around the strap on Rishi's forehead, forcing her to continually adjust her load.

It is required of all who wish to enter the city of Zitól to state their name and intentions for their visit, and sometimes, especially at times of festivals, this could take an entire day. For most of the morning they waited in line, and Rishi spent the time staring up at the walls and imagining what amazing things she would see on the other side.

Finally they came to the gate, as tall as three men and made of thick wood. Over the gate were carvings and symbols. Rishi's eyes eagerly swept over the carvings and she smiled as she recognized characters from her grandfather's book. Any city that bears the images of the gods over their gates must be a place of safety, she determined. Now the only thing keeping Rishi from her city of dreams was a table, flanked by two ominous-looking guards holding pointed spears. Seated at the table was a man in a white robe with tattoos swirling up his arms. Before him lay many pieces of parchment. Rishi hoped that perhaps when Mama Xoca stated her business the man might realize that Rishi and the other girls were being held against their will. Perhaps somehow Rishi could give the man some signal that they were in trouble.

"State your name and business," said the man without looking up. He was still marking the papers for the last travelers.

Mama Xoca cleared her throat. The man made a final mark and then raised his head. "Why, Madame Xoca!" he exclaimed in surprise. "We were wondering when you were going to arrive. These are the maidens, I presume? You don't have as many as usual." He counted them and then wrote something on his paper.

Mama Xoca smiled and winked. "A lean year."

The man took a moment to gaze at the girls, his eyes pausing on Isra a moment longer than the rest. "Exquisite as pearls," he commented. He leaned toward Mama Xoca and whispered behind his hand, "You know, I've always wondered how you can be sure that they are virgins."

Mama Xoca smiled. "There are ways," she said mysteriously.

"Yes, yes, I'm sure there are," he mused. "Well, go on through the gates. We all know *your* business. I will send a runner to tell everyone you've arrived. I assume one of these young women will become the next Messenger?" His eyebrows raised.

Mama Xoca nodded serenely.

"Delightful. Pass through the gate. I know you have much to do to get them prepared."

Mama Xoca led the girls toward the gate. Rishi tried to give the man an expression of alarm, even mouthing the word, "Help!" but he just smiled and waved her through toward the great wooden door that was opening for them.

CHAPTER 26

The City of Zitól

After passing through the gate, they entered a large plaza shaped like a half moon. In the center was a fountain and as they passed Rishi could see red and orange goldfish as long as her arm swimming around like bits of trapped sunlight. Mama Xoca led them up one of the streets that branched off from the plaza. As they entered the narrow corridor, stone structures rose all about them, sheltering the girls in their cool shadows. Colorful designs zigzagged across the walls. On some buildings there were great murals of birds, turtles, and jaguars, painted in dark, deep red, cobalt, and vermilion.

Rishi gazed at the woven tapestries that covered every doorway, and the stonework and the carved hieroglyphs that adorned the face of every building and were written on every corner. Some of the buildings rose two or three stories high and Rishi had to crane back her neck to see them as she passed. They wound along the streets until they stopped at a large building. Over the doorway there was a stone that read, "Bathing Pools." Wisps of steam seeped out of the cracks of the tapestry that covered the doorway. A woman parted the tapestry, greeted Mama Xoca by name, and let them into the building.

Inside, they stepped into a tiled courtyard surrounding a large, square pool of water. The pool was as smooth as oil and hot steam lazily curled up from its surface toward the blue sky.

Out of the mist came five exotic-looking women. Their hair was tied up on their heads, glistening with droplets of water. They, too, had belts around their waists, but instead of white beads, deep purple beads hung at their sides. The beads were so large and luscious they seemed edible.

One of the women approached Rishi and took her hand. "Come with me," she whispered in a voice as gentle as a cloud, "and I will make you beautiful."

Their old clothing was removed and smooth hands guided them to the pool. Mama Xoca's medicine had truly healed their wounds, for there were no scars on their bodies.

Rishi placed one foot into the hot pool, then the other. The heat stung at first, but the pain melted away quickly and Rishi stepped down again so the water was at her knees. One more step and Rishi was waist-deep in the pool. She sat down, leaned against the wall, and closed her eyes.

Had she just entered heaven? Hot water enveloped her body and tiny bubbles fizzed around her skin. A delicate perfume filled Rishi's nostrils and she opened her eyes to see the women setting giant lily blossoms on the water. Mama Xoca was nowhere to be seen. The girls glanced at each other with enchanted expressions and cautious smiles. "I wasn't expecting *this*," whispered Sepya.

I was, Rishi thought. She lowered herself further into the water, letting it caress her shoulders. Then she closed her eyes and slid under the surface, feeling as if she could melt into the pool and become water herself. Being here in this beautiful place made the terror of the dog men and the sorrow of her lost village seem far away and dreamlike, almost as if it had never happened.

When the women came back, they each had a basket and beckoned the girls to sit on the edge of the pool.

The air felt cool on her skin as Rishi sat on the towel the woman set down for her. "Hold out your hand," Rishi's bather directed. Her palm was filled with cream that smelled of blossoms and vanilla bean. "Smooth this over your skin." Rishi spread the cream over her arms and legs, making her skin feel softer than it had felt when she was a young child, and then dipped her leg back into the water, washing the cream off. Meanwhile, the bather took out a sponge and gently scrubbed Rishi's neck, shoulders, and back. Then she reached in her basket and pulled out an avocado. Breaking it open, she scooped out the green flesh and rubbed it in her hands, mixing it with oils until it was a supple cream. She slowly massaged it into Rishi's hair, spreading it all the way to the ends. With her fingers, she gradually worked out all the snarls until she could pull her fingers through without a catch. She poured water over Rishi's head, rinsing it thoroughly and leaving it smooth and fragrant. Then she deftly wrapped a cloth around Rishi's hair and piled it on top of her head.

Taking Rishi's hand, she helped her stand and held out another large, white cloth to wrap around Rishi's dripping body as she stepped out of the pool. Rishi dried her feet, legs, arms, and face. While Rishi tried to keep the cloth wrapped around her essential parts, the woman rubbed her legs, arms, and body with more sweet-smelling oils. She untied the wrap around Rishi's hair and let the towel hang on her shoulders. Using a comb and sharp razor, she carefully trimmed off the broken ends. Every now and then Rishi looked over her shoulder to see her friends being combed and polished and cleaned as well. The woman worked a white cream into Rishi's hair that smelled like the ocean and coconuts and mist.

They were led out of the steam and into another room where the woman helped Rishi step into a cool, light green tunic that was so soft and supple that Rishi hardly felt she was wearing anything at all. The tunic was laced up the front. Garlands of marigolds were placed on each girl's head, and gold ribbons were plaited through their hair. Bowls of yellow ochre were brought out and a horizontal line was painted across each girl's nose and cheeks, the same way Rishi's grandfather had done so long ago. Thick, polished gold bracelets were fastened on their wrists and when Rishi looked into them and saw her own reflection, a shiver ran down her spine. *I am now a woman of Zitól*, she thought.

Then everything seemed to be finished and the girls beheld each other as if they were new people. But something was missing. Rishi felt around her waist. Her belt! But just as she started to worry, a woman walked in, carrying the belts. They had been cleaned and the beads had been polished. Rishi gratefully took her belt and tied it around her waist. Now she was complete.

Mama Xoca appeared, looking fresh and greatly improved as well. Her hair was coiled on top of her head like vines, and she wore earrings that were so long and heavy they stretched her earlobes and brushed against her shoulders. Her dress was a flaming red tunic with a yellow sash that crisscrossed between her bosoms and around her waist.

"This is more like it." She nodded, pleased. "*Now* you look more like Mama Xoca's girls. Word has spread, my hummingbirds, and soon you will make your grand appearance. The whole city knows you are here and they are waiting for you."

The girls looked at each other, completely mystified . . . and flattered.

"Come on now, stand up straight. Hold your heads high. And whenever you start to feel sorry for yourselves, just remember that today you are the most beautiful and sought-after women in the world. You want to make Mama Xoca proud, don't you?"

The girls didn't know how to respond to this question, but some of them nodded obediently. The bath had done wonders for their perception of their predicament and they were starting to believe that there might actually be a positive outcome to all their sufferings. So far their Zitóli experience had been exquisite. They felt blissfully confused.

"Where are we going?" Isra asked.

"To the amphitheater. Don't look so worried, my dear. You won't have to do anything but walk, stand, smile, and show off your pretty white beads. Mama Xoca will do *all* the talking. When the time comes—and you'll know when that is—you must stand as still as you possibly can. Very, *very* still, do you understand?"

The girls did not understand and looked at her blankly, but she did not elaborate.

Instead, she led them to the tapestry door. "You must follow Mama Xoca closely," she warned, looking them each in the eyes. "There is no telling what might happen to you if you are found in the city without protection."

Mama Xoca led the five women out into the hot afternoon sun. They walked in a line, one after the other, their beads swinging at their hips. Through the streets of the city, through plazas and past windows they walked, and everywhere they went people stopped to watch them. Some even began to follow. Everywhere Rishi could hear them whispering, "The Messenger . . ."

With each step Rishi felt more confident that everything was going to be all right. She gazed at the inquisitive faces around her, faces that—except for the color of her eye—reflected the same features of her and her mother and her grandfather. These people were *her* people, and this city was *her* city. This was the place where she had always belonged.

The people of Zitól look forward all year long to the arrival of Mama Xoca's bright-eyed maidens, and the farther the girls traveled into the city, the more people began to trail them. By the time Mama Xoca led them into the enormous amphitheater, people were already swarming into the stands, jostling each other for the best seats.

But even with all their urgency and excitement, the spectators took great care to avoid the special section in the middle of the audience, set apart by a low railing, which held ornately decorated seats. These special seats remained untouched.

Clattering rattles and drums burst into a vigorous tempo, and out of nowhere a troupe of dancers and musicians tumbled out onto the flat, hard-packed stage and began a circular dance. They wore colors of the sunset, and their jeweled wrists and necks glittered as they swayed to the rhythm. Fiery torches appeared and the dancers tossed them back and forth to each other to the delight of the spectators. The girls were so mesmerized by the scene, that they kept bumping into each other as they tried to walk and look at the same time.

Rishi felt like if she opened her eyes any wider they'd pop out of her head. None of them had seen so many people at once, nor had they seen anyone who danced with fire. The atmosphere was becoming more electric by the moment. The five mystified island girls knew that for better or for worse, something significant was about to happen to them.

Mama Xoca led the young women to a long bench near the stage where they continued to watch the performers dance. Everything was so festive that they couldn't help but smile, and Venay and Sepya even clapped their hands to the beat of the drum. Rishi swept her eyes over the vast audience. The people were finely dressed. The men had clean tunics, gold bracelets, and earrings. Some had nosepieces and head-bands. The women were dressed in blouses and skirts so colorful they seemed as if they were wearing rainbows. Their hair was braided and piled on their heads in the same style as Mama Xoca's and the gold on their necks glittered in the afternoon sun.

Mama Xoca squatted in front of the girls so they could hear her voice over the music, which was gradually getting louder and more raucous.

"When Mama Xoca calls out your name you will come to the center of the stage and stand in a row. Be good girls and be sure to give the audience your best smiles." She demonstrated by giving them a wide, exaggerated grin. The girls had no idea she even knew their names. "Whatever you do, keep your head high, your tummy tucked in, and your shoulders back. Remember, this is the most important moment of your life. You want to look as good as you can so they will pick you as the Messenger."

"The what?" Rishi shouted back.

"The Messenger!" said Mama Xoca. "This is a—" but the music swelled and they couldn't hear the last word. The girls looked at each other for clarification, but no one understood.

"What?" yelled Isra, cupping her hands around her mouth. "What did you say?"

"This is a CONTEST!" shouted Mama Xoca. "And only one of you will win!"

CHAPTER 27

Mama Xoca's Exotic Maidens of Paradise

A burly, bald, bare-chested man wearing a long white skirt and a jade necklace approached Mama Xoca. His smile revealed a row of gold teeth.

The man leaned over, saying something in her ear. She nodded. They spoke this way for several moments, sometimes gesturing toward the girls on the bench. All at once there was a loud droning sound that vibrated the ground and rattled Rishi's ribs. The dancers spun to the ground and vacated the stage. Mama Xoca returned to the bench and sat, and the bare-chested man strode to the center of the stage. The loud drone ceased and the audience was hushed and alert.

The man cleared his throat and bellowed, "The Holy Speakers!"

All heads turned back toward the top of the amphitheater. There at the top of the stairs were three men, dressed in tunics of pristine white. The first was tall and slender, the next was enormously wide, and the third was a mix between the two. All three had crowns of emerald-colored quetzal feathers, red and orange capes, and layers of gold strewn about their necks and dripping down their chests. Behind them were young men carrying enormous plumed fans. This regal procession marched down the stairs while the audience observed in silent deference. They settled in the specially reserved seats. The men with the fans stood back and began waving their mighty plumes gracefully up and down and the audience exhaled at once as if they had all been holding their breath.

The crowd's attention eagerly turned back to the stage, where the bare-chested man was raising his arms.

"Welcome, citizens of Zitól!" he bellowed. "The month of the Jaguar has finally arrived, and the time has come to select the new Messenger. Mama Xoca has once again brought to us her exotic maidens from the distant isles. In a moment they will be on this stage, and you shall be witnesses to not only their enchanting beauty, but also their unwavering courage!" The crowd roared in approval.

Rishi leaned closer to Mama Xoca. "What does the Messenger do?" she whispered. The others girls leaned in to hear.

"Shh!" was the answer.

The man continued, "We will introduce them to you now . . . Madame Xoca." The man gestured to the bench. Like a very fat bird, Mama Xoca stood and slowly swayed to the stage. Rishi felt as if her stomach was filled with jellyfish.

"Good afternoon, oh noble Zitól!" she gushed, raising her thick, flapping arms to the crowd. "Did you miss Mama Xoca?"

They cheered.

"Mama can't hear you," she teased.

They shouted and stomped their feet. Some stood. The noise was so loud that the bench Rishi sat on trembled. The two older Speakers nodded to each other, eyebrows raised, as if amused by Mama Xoca's eccentric gusto.

"Mama Xoca hopes you've all been good and minding your manners."

The audience snickered. Someone shouted out something obscene.

Mama Xoca raised her hands, her palms facing the audience, "Now, now. Let's not be nasty." Then she held one hand to her mouth like she was telling a secret. "We mustn't upset the *virgins*." Everyone laughed.

"Who would like to meet Mama Xoca's girls? Mama Xoca's daughters of paradise?"

The people thundered back their enthusiastic answer in another wave of deafening sound. The girls all looked at each other, embarrassed by the attention, not sure whether they should smile or sob.

"Good," said Mama Xoca. "We shall begin." Opening her arms wide, as if to embrace the entire audience, she announced in a voice so loud it seemed to shake the walls, "Noble Speakers! Good citizens of Zitól! May I present to you Venay, Keeper of Pearls!"

Venay's eyes popped open at the sound of her name and the new title Mama Xoca had conjured up for her. She stared desperately at her friends who stared back at her, everyone equally alarmed. "What do I do?" she asked as her cheeks flushed bright red.

The impatient crowd began to chant, "Ven-ay, Ven-ay, Ven-ay!"

Venay's hands came to her face and she looked out at her friends from between her fingers. "What do I do? What do I do?" she squealed.

Mama Xoca took her by the hand and pulled her to the stage and the audience laughed and cheered. Mama Xoca led her to the far end of the stage where Venay stood awkwardly, looking like she wished the ground would swallow her.

Mama Xoca called out the next name, "Isra, Vision of the Waves!"

Without any hesitation, Isra stood, and with her chin up, she slowly and majestically walked to Mama Xoca as if she were a balancing a jar of water on her head. Rishi didn't know what qualities were supposed to make up a Messenger from Zitól, but from watching the captivated expressions the people gave Isra as she crossed the stage, Rishi knew that from the crown of her silken hair to the swing of her hips, Isra had it. Mama Xoca smiled broadly as Isra came nearer to her and she guided her to a spot a few paces from Venay.

"Sepya, Treasure of the Sea!" Mama Xoca announced. Taking a hint from Isra's lead, Sepya, too, raised her head and marched out on the stage bravely, although not with Isra's grace, and did not receive Isra's awed reception. Now it was only Rishi and Lantana left.

"Lantana, Singer of the Islands." Lantana stood, her neck blotchy from her nerves. With a nervous, fragile smile at Rishi, she started her journey across the stage, dragging her club foot, the brown wooden bead jumping up and down like a pet frog.

The crowd's reaction was immediate. Zitóli crowds are not the type to applaud for the sake of courtesy, and if anything, their blisteringly stark honesty is their only virtue. Hisses and boos echoed throughout the amphitheater and Rishi could see Lantana's shoulders slump.

Rishi had no time to react before she was summoned.

"And finally, Rishi—" Mama Xoca paused until the audience was completely still, ". . . Child of Dreams." There was no cheering this time, only whispers, as Rishi stood and crossed the stage, feeling embarrassed and self-conscious. Remembering the way Isra had floated across the stage, she managed to carry herself reasonably well, and finally she reached her spot and faced the audience. The people in the first few rows stared at Rishi with fascination, while the others that sat farther back strained their necks and squinted their eyes to see. It had been a long time since they had seen a dream child.

Once all the girls were standing in a line across the stage, Mama Xoca announced, "People of Zitól, your candidates for Messenger!" and the audience cheered.

The noise quickly dissipated as one of the Speakers rose from his seat. All eyes watched the slender figure as he elegantly lowered himself down the steps with the methodical poise of a long-legged crane. As he came closer, Rishi could see that his eyes were outlined in black, and his lips, which seemed to be suppressing a smile, were painted crimson. He lighted onto the stage, swept his eyes across the girls, and turned to face the audience, gazing at the people in silence for what seemed to Rishi a very long time. Then, slowly he raised his manicured hands and spoke.

"Thank you. Thank you, beloved people of Zitól for uniting together at this special place to witness the first phase of the Messenger's journey to her destiny."

He did not boom and bellow his words like Mama Xoca; he did not have to. The amphitheater, like all of the courtyards, temples, and plazas in Zitól was designed to amplify every nuance of a Speaker's voice. This gave the Speakers the luxury of creating the perfect tone for their speeches, and on this occasion, Speaker Riplakish's voice was smooth as oil, his carefully crafted words dripped like honey, and he spoke patiently, pausing in between each sentence to allow his message to marinate.

"The royal Messenger is not any ordinary woman. First of all, she must be a pure and untarnished virgin. As you all know, in our city this type of woman is as precious and rare as a fleeting white blossom." He said this with an apologetic smile, as if it was some private joke between him and the people, and Rishi wondered what that meant.

"*Most* of the women standing here before you on this stage possess this distinction." Out of the corner of her eye Rishi saw Lantana shift uneasily. "But there is more that a Messenger of Zitól must exhibit than just virtue. She must be fearless. She must put the needs of her people over her own sense of self-preservation. But most of all, she must have the discipline to remain still and composed while looking down into the gaping mouth of death."

The girls glanced at each other in apprehension. What was he talking about?

"Keep smiling!" Mama Xoca mimed from the bench. The Speaker continued.

"The Messenger must be willing to submit to the will of the gods, even if it means leaving behind everything she knows and loves, cleaving to nothing except her integrity. Only a woman with these rare, singular characteristics will be chosen. The time has come to test these women, to discover which of them, if any, is worthy to be called the Messenger." He clapped his hands together. "Bring out the meat!"

The bewildered girls watched as a man with a basket entered the stage. Walking up to Sepya, he reached into the basket, pulled out a slab of fresh meat, and handed it to her. Sepya was so surprised she immediately dropped it, much to the consternation of the audience. It only took a few hecklers to get Sepya to quickly pick the meat up off the ground and hold it warily out in front of her with both hands while the blood seeped around her wrists and dripped to the ground. Meat was handed out to each of the girls and they grasped the gruesome gifts in their hands, looking pale.

The audience was leaning forward, eager, and Rishi could feel thousands of eyes watching her as she held the moist meat. She remembered Mama Xoca's words to stay very still, so she did, even though her heart was pounding. But now what? She turned to the Speaker for some clue. As if reading her mind, he raised his arms up in the air and with a loud voice shouted, "Release the jaguar!"

CHAPTER 28

The Sacred Duty of the Messenger

The girls heard a rattling sound behind them and a cage was brought onto the stage, carried on poles by several men. The men set the cage down and left the stage, so that only the girls and the Speaker remained. Mama Xoca had already retreated. Riplakish always tried to add extra drama whenever he could, and he walked over to the cage and proclaimed with a dramatic flourish, "Behold! The cat!"

As if they had rehearsed it beforehand, Riplakish's jaguar answered him with a searing scream. All the girls jumped. Jiggling the cage door skyward, he opened it little by little until the eager animal slinked out of its pen, like black dye spilling out onto the ground.

The cat was wiry and lean with grossly prominent ribs. Her coat, lacking the luster it would have had with a proper diet, had been purposely oiled so that in the sun it shone like polished obsidian. The jaguar let out another scream and opened her nostrils to the air. As she took in the smell of fresh meat, her tail swished and her eyes widened in ravenous anticipation.

This, of course is Raven, whom I told you about before.

Lowering his voice for only the girls' ears, the Speaker said, "I should warn you that she as not been fed for two days. Hold the meat out for her. Anyone who drops the meat from this point on is disqualified."

Immediately Lantana dropped the meat and stepped away. She knew she had already lost, and didn't care. The cat whirled around at the sound of the meat hitting the dirt. It took her only two leaps to cross the stage and pounce on her prize. Everyone watched as she clutched it between her paws, ripped it, and swallowed it down. Rishi closed her eyes and cringed, and the meat she was holding almost slipped from her trembling hands. She stole a glance at Isra whose lovely brow was beaded with sweat. The girl's queenly demeanor was replaced with a look of tempered panic. When she noticed Rishi watching her, her chin lifted in determination.

The crowd did not like that Lantana had given in so easily. They heckled and booed her as Speaker Riplakish led her off the stage.

After licking her paws, the jaguar sauntered around the remaining four girls, her bony hips jutting out with each step. When she passed Sepya she slid her tail around the girl's legs and Sepya let out a whimper that quaked her entire body. Her cries grew more anxious as the cat sniffed at the meat, and just as Raven opened her mouth to snatch the morsel, Sepya shrieked and threw her hands up, flinging the meat in the air. The jaguar leaped and caught it before it touched the ground. Sepya's bloody hands came to her face and she continued screaming hysterically over and over as Raven ripped apart the offering. She was taken off the stage, still screaming.

Just then Venay flung her meat across the stage and the jaguar chased after it, this time gulping the slab in one bite. Venay, too, was escorted away.

Now it was only Rishi and Isra. Flies buzzed around the meat that was getting heavier and heavier in Rishi's hands. The cat swayed toward Isra, her yellow eyes never leaving the girl's face. Isra trembled but held the meat flat on the palms of her hands. Raven sniffed at it, and then with flared nostrils sniffed up Isra's arm. The animal's ear flicked and then it daintily pulled the meat from her hands and devoured it at Isra's feet.

Isra exhaled and slowly lowered her trembling arms as the audience erupted with cheers. When Raven was finished, she looked up at Isra, licking her lips and twitching her long, white whiskers as if asking for more. Isra did nothing but look straight ahead, so Raven turned her attention to the last girl on stage.

Rishi reminded herself that at least now the jaguar wasn't as hungry. She took a deep breath and tried to calm her sprinting heartbeat. The cat's cold nose brushed against her ankles and then up to her arms. With her bristled tongue Raven licked off the blood that oozed around Rishi's wrists. It felt like a thousand little razors scraping off her skin. Rishi bit her lip to keep from crying out in pain.

After cleaning Rishi's arms, the cat sunk its jaws into the meat and pulled it from Rishi's hands. Raven lay down with the meat caught between her front paws and ate in contentment. Finally full (for the first time in weeks), she rolled on her side and closed her eyes.

"It appears we have two winners!" the Speaker declared, and the audience roared.

Rishi glanced at Isra, giving her a hopeful smile, but Isra ignored her and smiled instead at the audience. Again, a deep droning sound from the trumpets filled the air. Speaker Riplakish walked up the stairs of the amphitheater, and Rishi and Isra followed at his heels, escorted by Mama Xoca, whose large hands grasped both girls' arms. Halfway up the stairs the other Speakers met them and they all continued to the top as a caravan.

"I thought only *one* of us could win," Isra mumbled to Mama Xoca.

"Only one of you shall. You both made it through the initial selection. Tomorrow, after the ceremony, you will be interviewed by the Speakers."

"What about the others?" Rishi asked. "What will happen to them?"

"Oh, don't worry about them," panted Mama Xoca as they climbed. "I will make sure they all find excellent homes." But something in the way Mama Xoca said this made Rishi feel uneasy.

Together they climbed the steps of the amphitheater, as the curious Zitólis watched them as if they were celebrities, and Rishi could not help staring back. They had rings and jewels all over their faces—in their ears, their nostrils, and their eyebrows. Their faces were tattooed with designs and feathers decorated their hair. Up close the people were both beautiful and terrifying.

When they reached the top of the amphitheater, Rishi saw three huge chairs affixed to horizontal poles. Burly men in loincloths stood, arms folded, around the chairs. The Speakers each climbed into one of these seats, which were then hoisted onto the shoulders of the men. Still feeling the pressure on her arm from Mama Xoca, Rishi followed the litters through the city.

They meandered up the streets, and Rishi watched the sweat run down the tight, brown muscles of the men carrying the litter in front of her. Between buildings, she caught glimpses of the pyramids. Each time the litter approached a man or woman on the street they stopped, bowed their heads, and with their fingers pointing up waved their right hand in quick circles in the air until the Speakers' litters passed.

They turned a corner and Rishi could see they were walking in the shadow of one of the four pyramids. She gazed in awe at the ascending platforms that rose right up to the clouds. Then they walked straight into the heart of the temple plaza, the sight of which took her breath away.

It was unlike anything she had ever seen before. The four temples stood facing each other, surrounding a spacious, flat mall paved with great stones. In the center of the mall was a large, circular platform raised up above the ground with stairs that partially wound around it like a snail.

The stone paving was brilliant white, and there was not a weed nor blade of grass that poked between the perfectly fit seams. Lifting her eyes, she gazed at the surrounding temples that towered around her, pointing up to the sky. They were identical, with four sides, tiered platforms, and a steep stone staircase that led to the top. The exception was the east pyramid, which was much taller and grander than the rest. Up the center of the staircases were platforms that held charred wood and ashes. Men in white tunics were busy sweeping the black debris off the temple steps, replacing the ashes with large pots of exotic flowers. At the pinnacle of each pyramid, flanked by colorful flapping flags, was a stone shelter with a large opening into a dark, obscure chamber.

As they passed the largest temple, Rishi noticed that there were words carved into the steps, words she instantly recognized. She wanted to linger in the plaza, to climb the temple staircases, and explore the tops of the temples, but the procession did not stop. They continued across the plaza diagonally and soon Rishi was back in the shadows of the city.

The way became steeper, and soon they were traveling up a wide ramp that snaked up a hill overflowing with hanging gardens. Lush ferns, palm trees, and aromatic flowers draped sumptuously around the edges of the path, their sweet fragrance coaxing Rishi and Isra farther up.

When they reached the top of the hill, Rishi found herself on a broad terrace of an ornate palace bathed in the crimson light of the setting sun. Now that they were above the trees and buildings, Rishi could see the huge expanse of the sky arching from horizon to horizon, something she hadn't seen since she'd left the ocean. Looking down, they could see some of the tallest city buildings and pyramids poking their heads through the canopy of trees.

The litter was lowered and the Speakers stepped off and addressed Mama Xoca, who was still catching her breath from the climb. "The sun is getting low, and we have much to do before tomorrow," Riplakish said. "Leave the young women with Leema. They can stay in the Messenger's tower tonight, and we will choose between them tomorrow, after the ceremony."

He turned to leave.

"And when will Mama Xoca receive payment?" Mama Xoca said, louder than necessary.

The Speaker stopped and rotated. Meeting Mama Xoca's eyes, he gave a slow nod. "Tomorrow, Madame. We will pay you tomorrow."

A servant appeared on the terrace. She was short and old, with a complexion like the bark of a tree, and Mama Xoca greeted the woman the way one might acknowledge a termite. Rishi could see the contempt was mutual. "Hello, Leema," Mama Xoca said coolly. "Do not forget that until Mama Xoca is paid, they still belong to Mama Xoca."

Unimpressed by the larger woman's threat, the servant eyed Mama Xoca with disdain and waved Rishi and Isra to follow her, leaving Mama Xoca standing outside the palace, alone and fuming.

The girls were led around the terrace to a great doorway. Guards unlatched the heavy wooden doors and they opened into a grand, rectangular courtyard rimmed with apartments. On either side of the courtyard were two high, square-sided towers, covered in thick vines. One was slightly higher than the other.

Rishi and Isra followed Leema across the courtyard to the shorter of the two towers, at the base of which was the entrance, concealed by an intricately woven tapestry. Leema pulled back the tapestry and the girls walked into a dark, damp chamber. It was small, with only enough room to fit a bed, a stool, some baskets, and a small loom. The place had a putrid smell, like a wet rag that had been left in a corner for too long. As Rishi's eyes adjusted to the light, she saw that adjacent to the wall there was a stairway of stone that wound up the tower in a spiral.

"This is where I sleep," the woman said, gesturing around her. "You will stay upstairs."

She led them up the stone staircase. The walls were smooth and cool. Light spilled from an opening above them. When they reached the top, they climbed out into a huge chamber. "This is the Tower of the Messenger," said Leema as they stepped up into the room.

The two girls caught their breath. It was large and open, with no walls, only pillars that rimmed the perimeter, connected together by a stone railing. White, semi-transparent curtains draped artfully from pillar to pillar, imparting a feeling of privacy, but still letting in rose-colored light from all sides. Through the curtains they could see the hazy shape of the setting sun in the west. All about the room were mirrors and tasseled cushions. Soft rugs and tapestries softened and warmed the stone floor. In the center of the room was a circular pool of water, with lily pads and pink lotus flowers floating on the surface. Rishi looked up and saw that the ceiling was a huge dome, shimmering with tiny blue and green tiles. She had never seen any place so glorious and heavenly, and she was afraid to touch anything, so she just stood drinking it all in, breathless.

"Whichever of you is chosen as the Messenger, this will be your home for the next year." Rishi heard Isra inhale sharply.

Rishi then noticed that part of the room was divided by a sheer curtain. Beyond this curtain Rishi could see the figure of a woman lounging on cushions with her face looking down toward the city. "Who is she?" Rishi asked Leema in a whisper.

"That is the current Messenger. But this is her last night here. Do not approach her or speak to her. She is preparing herself, and she must concentrate." The figure on the other side of the veil turned her head toward them for a moment and then continued to gaze out at the city.

"What is she preparing herself for?" asked Rishi.

"Silly girl, don't you know? She is preparing herself for the ceremony, the whole *reason* why she is here. Tomorrow she will take a message to the gods." Then she added, "I'm sure you are both hungry. I will return shortly with something for you to eat."

Rishi and Isra were both drawn to the railing and gazed rapturously at the beauty of the city below.

Leema returned carrying a tray filled with diced fruits, avocados, tomatoes, salted meat, and corn tortillas. The girls were ravenous and began eating at once. Later, Leema came up again, holding mugs filled with cool watermelon juice.

Food had never appeared so glorious nor tasted so wonderful to Rishi. The fruits had already been peeled and each segment had a different succulent taste. She filled the tortillas with the meat and avocado, and with each bite she could feel her body regaining its strength. The two goblets filled with sweet, cold juice were rimmed with sapphires. She could tell the food was having the same effect on Isra, and for the first time since the jaguar contest she seemed to relax.

When Rishi couldn't eat another bite she sighed with contentment. She thought of the other girl through the curtain.

She cleared her throat. "Would you like something to eat?" Rishi asked loudly.

The girl turned her head and Rishi and Isra could hear the tinkling sound of tiny bells. She gave a deep sigh as if Rishi had just asked her a question that had no answer. Then she laid her head on her arms.

"We aren't supposed to talk to her, remember?" whispered Isra.

Rishi looked at the tray, still layered with food. She took one of the plates and filled it with fruits and meat. Standing, she took the plate to the curtain and bent down. She touched the fabric of the curtain. It was so thin and transparent, it was as if it had been woven from the silken strands of spiderwebs. She lifted it just enough to push the tray of food underneath to the Messenger's side of the room.

"Just in case you feel hungry later," she said softly.

That night Rishi and Isra slept on pillows as soft as a songbird's breast. When Rishi opened her eyes and found herself looking up at the tiled dome that glittered like the sunlit ocean, she knew, for the first time since she'd been taken from the island, that she was safe.

The morning sky was cloudless and the rising sun gilded the curtains in golden light. Rishi stretched. Through the curtain she could see that the Messenger was already awake and sitting on a chair before a mirror, slowly brushing her hair. The plate filled with fruit was still sitting inside the curtain. Except for some flies buzzing around it, the food was untouched.

Steps sounded in the stairwell and soon Leema's head surfaced. She walked into the room, passing Rishi and Isra, who watched her through sleepy, half-open eyes. She found the opening in the curtain and slipped through to the other side.

"It is time," she murmured to the girl. The girl stood. Leema parted the curtain and the girl walked through.

Rishi knew it was rude to stare, but she could not pull her eyes away from the girl. She was perhaps the most beautiful person she'd ever seen. Her elegantly shaped face was graced with large, brown eyes and full lashes and when she looked down her eyelids glittered with turquoise dust. Her black hair was pulled back and covered with a delicate, beaded hairnet, and strands of pearls dangled down her forehead. Her dress was as pale blue as an afternoon moon and it whispered when she walked. She wore a sash around her waist beaded with tiny pearls. Hanging from the sash on a length of blue ribbon was a pure white bead.

Rishi had the strongest desire to speak to her, to become her friend, but the girl's eyes stayed on the ground as she followed Leema down into the stairwell.

"I wonder where she is going," Rishi thought out loud.

"Wherever it is, she doesn't look very excited," Isra said, rubbing her eyes and yawning. "She is probably annoyed that we moved into her room."

Rishi and Isra spent the morning gazing out the great windows of the tower to the world below. The view was incredible. Never before had Rishi looked *down* on birds as they flew. The temples were bathed in amber light and a warm breeze rustled the tall palms. From all around, Rishi could smell the early morning smells of dew and perfumed flowers. Looking on the temple tops of Zitól made Rishi feel almost happy. If only she hadn't been forced to make such a great sacrifice to get here.

"What do you think that is?" said Isra. She was on the opposite side of the room, looking out to the west. Rishi walked across the room and stood beside her. This side of the tower overlooked miles of forest and jungle with mountains far in the distance.

"What?" Rishi asked.

"That big round hole, filled with water."

Rishi gazed out over the landscape and saw it. It was large hole in the earth. It was almost perfectly round, and had very steep sides that dropped down into a pool of blue-green water that reflected the clouds in the sky. A wide road led to its rim. A growing number of people were walking on the road, all headed toward this large hole.

"I wonder where they are all going," Isra said.

"Perhaps they are going swimming," murmured Rishi. Of course, she did not know that no one in Zitól knows how to swim.

Breakfast was served with even more delicious food. Every now and then they gazed through the curtain to the Messenger's side of the tower, but dared not lift the curtain. Somehow they felt that side of the room was forbidden.

"So which one of us do you think is going to be the Messenger?" Isra asked abruptly as she poured golden honey over her corn cake. Rishi looked up, surprised at Isra's bluntness. She was grateful her own mouth was full, giving her time to think about her answer. She chewed and then took a long drink from her cup.

"Perhaps they will choose both of us," Rishi said, giving a slight shrug. "It might get lonely up here after a while. I would rather stay together. Wouldn't you?"

"You heard Mama Xoca, though," Isra said between bites. "She said that only one would win. I wonder what they will have us do *this* time to decide who is more worthy."

It made Rishi's chest tighten to talk about this, about one of them winning and the other losing. She gazed at the beautiful room and thought how wonderful it would be to live here, to be fed like royalty every day. Whatever it was that the Messenger did to deserve these beautiful surroundings was obviously important. Rishi had to admit that she wanted to have that privilege, but she didn't want to have to fight her friend over it.

"It doesn't matter to me," Rishi said, trying to sound as if it really didn't matter. "I just want all the girls from our island to be in a place where they are safe and happy."

Isra took a drink. "Well, I'm glad you don't care, because *I* want to be the Messenger."

After breakfast they heard Leema's footsteps climbing the tower for the third time that morning. This time when she entered the chamber she appeared weary and exhausted. She had blue paint smudged on her hands and clothes.

"We must get you two ready as well, for you will be part of the procession to the cenote."

"What is the cenote?" asked Rishi. The woman strode to the west side of the tower and pulled the curtains. She pointed down to the pool of water that Rishi and Isra had noticed earlier. "*That* is the cenote," she said.

Then she leaned over and pulled a tasseled rope that hung from the top of the curtain dividing the room. The curtain parted and Rishi and Isra watched as the Messenger's half of the room was revealed. Leema briskly walked over and rummaged through the Messenger's baskets, pulling out the girl's tunics, jewelry, and hairbrushes. The side of the room that Rishi and Isra had respectfully avoided was now thrown open as if the girl was never going to come back for her things. Once Leema had found everything she was looking for, she put them beside the large mirror and turned to Isra. "Well, come here. You need to be dressed if you are going to be in the Messenger's procession."

Leema briskly combed through their hair and gave them blue tunics from the Messenger's baskets to wear. Additional bracelets snapped around Rishi's wrists and ankles, and jeweled neckbands were clasped around their throats. After they fastened their bead belts, the woman wrapped headbands around each girl's forehead with bright blue macaw feathers springing from the back.

"There," said the woman wearily. "You are finished, and just in time. I think the procession is almost ready. Follow me, please." Rishi followed Leema to the dim stairwell. Isra lingered at the mirror for a moment longer before joining them.

The palace courtyard that had been empty the day before was now filled with busy servants and white-robed priests. Like ants around a berry, the people of the courtyard busied themselves around a large chair in the center of the courtyard. Rishi recognized it as the golden litter that one of the Speakers had used the day before.

Rishi stood on her tiptoes, trying to see better. Finally there was an opening in the crowd and Rishi had a perfect view of the Messenger, sitting in the chair.

The girl was transformed. Her dress was strewn with pearls and her bead belt was prominently displayed on her lap. On her head was an enormous headpiece blossoming with blue and green feathers that fanned out in a colossal crest. Each time she turned her head the iridescent feathers glistened in the sunlight. Long hoop earrings dangled from her ears and her eyes were outlined in black, making them appear large and deer-like. Her eyelids were painted the iridescent color of morpho wings and beneath her eyes on both sides were rows of diamonds speckling her cheekbones like stars. But most astonishing was her skin. Her face, her neck, her hands, and every part of her body that Rishi could see was painted blue.

Blue.

Not a light blue or a dark blue, but a vibrant, dazzling blue like the color of a cloudless sky. A memory flashed through Rishi's mind. There was something significant about that color, if Rishi could only remember . . .

Blasting conch horns extinguished Rishi's thoughts and the three Speakers stepped out into the courtyard. They too were crowned with large headpieces and lavish regalia. Their white robes seemed almost blinding in the bright sun. They were princely, regal, and splendid. All those in the courtyard bowed their heads and circled their right hands in the air like the people had done in the street.

A procession was formed. A man with a large drum tied to his waist stood at the front. The two Speakers were next, followed by the six men who carried the Messenger on their shoulders. Rishi and Isra were bustled forward to their place behind the Messenger's litter, and were directed to humbly bow their heads as they walked. Behind the girls were a dozen priests dressed with their white mantles and tunics.

At the signal of a second droning conch shell, the man with the drum steadily beat out a rhythm and the group started to walk. The procession headed down a stone ramp at the back of the palace, walking at a painfully slow pace. From time to time Rishi looked up and watched the Messenger's feathered headdress, bobbing as the litter worked its way down the hill.

Boom, boom, boom went the drum as Rishi's slippered feet stepped in time. People lined the ramp, quiet and solemn, and a grim feeling began to creep into Rishi's heart like mold onto bread. Something was not right, she thought. When they reached the bottom of the hill they started on the wide road to the cenote. Throngs of somber-faced people lined the road and some threw white petals and palms out onto the flat stones. When the procession passed they gathered behind, becoming part of the march.

They reached the cenote and slowly circled its rim. It was larger up close, for Rishi's entire village could have fit into its cavernous pit. The sides were steep walls of limestone rock, white as bone. Long, draping plants hung like the hair of a giantess into the deep hole. Below, the jade green water was still and clear, so clear she could see some of the rock cliffs extending down under the surface. Rishi felt light-headed.

Jutting out over the cenote like a great horn was a stone staircase that led up to a precarious platform. When the procession had finished its journey around the hole and reached these stairs, the drums finally ceased and the conch shells went silent. All around the cenote the people gathered, standing so close to the edge Rishi thought that someone would surely fall in. Rishi could see they were holding things—handfuls of gold jewelry and cups, and heavy bags.

The Speakers helped the Messenger out of the litter. They escorted her slowly up the twelve steps to the platform. As Rishi watched, the grim, moldy feeling in her heart became a ringing alarm. She and Isra locked eyes, and from the way the color drained from Isra's face, Rishi knew they both had the same terrifying realization.

Speaker Gula raised his fat arms high above his head. "Citizens of Zitól!" he said. The walls of the cenote cavern amplified his voice, giving his words a strange and other-worldly resonance.

"We gather here today to witness this singular sacrifice."

Sacrifice. Rishi remembered now. Blue was the color of sacrifice in her grandfather's story about the First Man. Rishi's eyes scanned the words and characters on the steps of the platform, quickly reading the inscriptions.

"Many centuries ago our ancient predecessors carved on this platform the rituals required to receive the gods' greatest blessings. For one year this perfect and chaste young maiden has lived in seclusion, fed with the finest foods, indulged with every luxury we have to offer. During this time she has prepared herself spiritually for this moment when she gives up the one thing that the gods most desire: her life.

"The sacrifice of this young woman's life will satisfy two purposes; First, with her body she will pay precious tribute to our gods, for they are hungry gods, and sacrifice is prerequisite to their generosity. Second, with her spirit she shall enter the doorway to the underworld, bearing a special message. This year we shall ask the Messenger to plead with the gods to protect us from our enemies and to continue to send the life-giving rain to water our fields. Oh people of Zitól, she is only moments away from speaking with the gods. May all of us be so worthy of such an honor!

"We are pleased that many of you brought your own precious sacrifices to help aid the Messenger in her petition. Every piece of gold, every gemstone, every pearl will help loosen the grasp the gods have on the skies, persuading them to let rain fall generously on the earth. Bless you. For you shall be rewarded for your sacrifices. And now—behold, the Messenger!"

He turned to face the young woman.

"Messenger of Zitól," he said in a booming voice, even though the girl was standing right in front of him. "Ask the gods to grant us another year of rain and sun for our crops. Beg them to protect our great city. Thank the gods for their preservation of our traditions and culture!" The Messenger's face was composed, but Rishi could see the violent trembling of her hands. Then drums began again, quiet and slow.

Carefully, the Speaker lifted the feathered headdress off the Messenger's head, making her suddenly appear tiny and fragile. The tempo of the drums increased and Rishi felt her body go numb as she realized that the Speaker was tying the girl's hands behind her back. When he finished, he guided the Messenger to the edge of the platform. Rishi wanted to close her eyes but they were paralyzed open. Then, as the drums reached a deafening roar, shaking the very pebbles at Rishi's feet, the Speaker laid his hands on the Messenger's slender shoulders. Abruptly the drums ceased and the world was silent.

Centuries passed. No one moved. No one spoke. No one breathed.

Thousands of eyes fixated on the fat hands that held the girl's shoulders. Rishi's mouth was completely dry; her body had turned to stone.

Then, with the gentlest push, a push that took minimal effort, a push that in a different setting might displace the girl's balance only a step, the Speaker sent the Messenger's body off into nothingness.

For a moment she seemed to miraculously hover in the air over the cenote. Then she descended downward like a dying star, her dress whipping around her feet. Rishi felt her own stomach drop, as if she were falling too. She closed her eyes and heard the splash. When she opened them again, she only saw the undulating circles that spread outward from the point where the girl's body disappeared into the water. Rishi's hands came to her face. She felt as if she could hardly breathe.

The drums started up again in a flurry of beats and the people began throwing objects into the well—gold cups and necklaces, jewels, breastplates, spears, ears of corn, and heavy bags—until the surface of the cenote frothed. Then it was all over.

The multitude broke up in smaller groups as people turned to walk back to the city. Before taking her eyes from the gaping hole Isra elbowed Rishi and whispered, "*You* can be the Messenger."

CHAPTER 29

Bags of Rubies

The procession regrouped; the drummers, the Speakers, and everyone else found their places again. The drummers' mallets pounded
the pace that would take them back to the palace, but Rishi could not
make her wobbling legs match the cadence. She dragged her feet along
the road, her heart beating wildly, her head spinning. In her mind she
searched through the memories of her childhood to find any story, any
sentence, any clue from her grandfather's wondrous tales that hinted at
a Messenger for the people of Zitól. It was obviously significant. How
had he failed to mention it? She shook her head. It didn't make sense.

It was noon by the time the procession returned to the palace,
and clouds had begun to gather. Rishi and Isra were not taken to the
Messenger's tower. Instead Leema led them right through the courtyard, stopping only to take a burning stick from the coals in the large
fire pit. In the center of one row of apartments stood two large wooden
doors, carved with hieroglyphs of the gods. These were the only true
doors in the palace; all of the other openings to rooms were covered
with hanging tapestries. Two servants opened the large, creaking doors,
revealing stairs wide enough that the three of them could ascend side by
side. At the top of the stairs was a red curtain.

"This is the throne room," Leema said. She pulled the curtain back
and waved the girls in with the glowing stick. It was completely black
behind the tapestry and the girls hesitated.

"Go on in. I will come in after you and light the room."

Rishi felt Isra push her forward into the darkness, and Leema followed behind them. Once in the room, Leema dropped the curtain.
They watched Leema's glowing stick travel around in the darkness like
a floating red eye. Suddenly the red flickered and sputtered and orange
flames unraveled themselves onto a torch fastened to the wall, sending
light and shadows across the chamber. Leema walked to another torch
and more light illuminated the room. Gradually as each of the seven
torches were lit, the room revealed itself.

They were in a round chamber, made up of two levels. Rishi and Isra stood on the lower level, which was a circular space with no furniture and no ornamentation except for a mosaic on the ground. Opposite them were three steps leading up to the second level; a rostrum that held four large thrones. One was much larger than the others and substantially more grand, and looked as if it were made of solid gold.

On either side of these thrones, also elevated, were what Rishi had first thought were crouching animals. But as the light increased she realized they were only reclining chairs, draped with animal furs. There were six on either side of the thrones. The curving walls behind these seats were covered with heavy curtains, and in front of the seats was a stone lattice railing, separating them from the circular area in which Rishi and Isra stood. Surrounded by these empty seats that would soon be filled with her interrogators, Rishi felt a feeling of doom. If only she had known how many hours the two of us would spend together in this place, perhaps she would have felt differently.

The girls looked back at Leema for some sort of direction. "Patience," she said. "They will be coming." With nothing to do but wait, Rishi cast her gaze down to her feet. There was a round mosaic of the sun that spread out upon the floor of the chamber, surrounded by hundreds of white tile stars.

It was only a few moments before they heard footsteps and the red curtain was pushed aside. Men came striding into the room, filing up the steps into the rostrum and settling into the plush seats. Rishi recognized the man that had been at the front gate and greeted Mama Xoca, as well as the bald, bare-chested man (although now his chest was covered by his white tunic) who officiated at the amphitheater. Other faces she recognized from the procession. The men continued to stream in until all the reclining seats were filled. Then came the three Speakers, still dressed in their ceremonial clothing except for their headdresses that had been removed, leaving red indentations on their foreheads. As they passed Rishi, the air swirled around her, thick with perfume. They went up the steps and sat on the thrones, leaving the large golden throne empty. Who would sit in the golden throne? Rishi looked back to the curtain expectantly.

But she was disappointed. The last person to come through the tapestry door was Mama Xoca, in a long, emerald green sarong. There were no seats left for her (besides the throne, which clearly belonged to someone more significant) and she stood in the back against the curtain, next to Leema.

Finally, a servant walked in, leading the black jaguar on a thick chain. He fastened the chain to a metal ring protruding from the steps. The feline sat and scrutinized the visitors while the end of her tail beat against the floor disapprovingly.

"Welcome, maidens," said the large Speaker. "I am Speaker Gula. This is Speaker Riplakish," he said, gesturing across the empty throne to the other older Speaker with the lipstick and eye paint. Then he motioned to his left at the Speaker with the shaved hair and gold nose ring. "And this is Speaker Tungan. We are the representatives for our gracious and holy ruler," he said, motioning to the empty seat, "who is half-god and is therefore too holy to be seen in public."

This ironic, oft-repeated introduction never failed to amuse me.

"Surrounding the room on either side are the priests of Zitól." Gula continued. Apparently he thought Mama Xoca and Leema needed no introduction. "We are pleased that two of you were able to pass the Test of the Jaguar, as this is only the second year we have tried that method and I think it once again proved to be quite exciting." The priests nodded approvingly. "How very impressed we are that both of you had enough tenacity to stand your ground before Speaker Riplakish's pet. I'm sure you'll find the next part of the selection process much less perilous. It is only a short, simple interview." Rishi could feel all the priests lean forward in their chairs, like vultures hovering over a sick animal.

"The Sacrifice of the Messenger is the most sacred of all our rituals. She must be spotless and pure. Once she is chosen, she is separated from society for one year, during which time she is prepared to meet the gods. She is given the finest of foods, the grandest accommodations, and the strictest seclusion so that she may meditate on the noble task placed before her. We will need to ask you some questions to verify your worthiness for this great and sacred privilege. When we are finished, one of you will become the Messenger. The other . . . will become a concubine."

His last word stung and Rishi felt her knees buckle.

"Are you ready?"

No, thought Rishi.

"We will begin with you." Speaker Gula pointed a plumed scepter at Isra. "What is your name?"

"Isra," she said, her voice quivering ever so slightly.

"Where did you come from, Maiden Isra?"

Isra cleared her throat. "An island. The island of Talom."

"And what did you learn on this island?"

Isra didn't understand the question. "What all of the other girls learned, I suppose . . . shelling oysters, gathering food, learning to weave like our mothers."

"Why then do you wear a white bead?"

"This?" Isra said, lifting her bead with trembling fingers. "It is just . . . a decoration. It is just something girls like to wear on our island."

Gula cleared his throat and looked sternly at Isra. "We understand that primitive tribal cultures often wear outward symbols of their inner purity. I hope you will excuse the formality, but I must ask you. Are you a virgin?"

Isra did not answer.

"Your bead seems to indicate that you are, but we desire to hear it from your lips. Are you a virgin, Maiden Isra?"

Isra paused a moment longer, and then said, "No."

The room filled with whispers. From behind them came a grunt of displeasure from Mama Xoca. Rishi turned to Isra in surprise, but Isra stared straight ahead.

"Silence," Speaker Gula said. He narrowed his eyes at Isra, "Are you certain of this?"

Isra fumbled. "Yes . . . yes, I am certain; one doesn't forget something . . . like *that*."

More whispers and mutterings echoed through the room and Rishi looked at the ground. She knew Isra was lying. They had known each other since they were born. Rishi had been her companion and friend her whole life. The only person Isra had ever liked was her brother Eno, and she knew they could barely say two sentences to each other without blushing. She and the other girls fought to defend Isra in the jungle. Rishi knew Isra was every bit as pure as she was.

"Well then," said Speaker Gula, frowning deeply at Isra. "That terminates the questioning for you. We will now direct our questions to your friend."

Rishi felt her knees go weak.

"What is your name?"

"Rishi."

"Where do you come from?"

"From the island of Talom."

"And what did you learn on your island?"

Rishi paused. Then said, "I learned the Seven Songs."

A murmur spread among the priests and they leaned forward.

"Do you know of them?" Rishi asked.

"Indeed," said Gula with reverence, his eyes gleaming in the torch-light. "They are very ancient and holy. Tell me, dear maiden, is this why you wear a white bead? Because of these Seven Songs?"

"Yes. It is part of the traditions of my people. It is how we keep the balance of the—"

"Look up at me when you speak," Gula interrupted her. Rishi raised her eyes to meet his. "Open your eyes *wider*, maiden." After examining her face for a long time, he leaned back and drummed his fingers on his armrest. Finally he turned to his companions. "Riplakish, Tungan, tell me. Would you say she is beautiful? Do you think she is attractive enough to be the Messenger?"

Rishi's lips parted in consternation. She could feel sweat gather under her headband.

Riplakish stroked his chin with his carefully manicured fingers. "I am not so sure. From far away she is quite striking, but up close I would have to admit her features are extremely abnormal."

"Perhaps the gods will reject her as an offering," Tungan added. "Her imperfection could bring calamity on us all."

"You are all *imbeciles*," boomed a familiar voice. "It is not an imper-fection. It is a gift!" Everyone turned as Mama Xoca stepped into the center of the room. With a rag she mopped sweat from her forehead and then waved it at Rishi. "She is a *dream child*. Do you know what a dream child is? Do you not know your own legends? She is *the most* qualified to do the task, and you know it." With each word Mama Xoca's face increased in redness.

Taken aback, Gula, Riplakish, and Tungan leaned together for a few moments, murmuring low. The heat in the room was becoming unbear-able. Rishi shifted her feet. Finally Gula relaxed and nodded to Mama Xoca. "Thank you, Madame. Of course, you are correct. We indeed find the girl acceptable, and with her great and unique gift the gods will surely bless us for her sacrifice . . . that is, if she can answer the final question." He turned to Rishi. "And now, sweet maiden, I must ask you: are you, or are you not a virgin?"

In the moment before she spoke, many things flashed through Rishi's mind. She remembered the bead ceremony when her mother had tied the white bead around her waist. She remembered how her dying grandfather asked her brothers to promise to protect her virtue. She remembered the crumpled feeling she felt after Lantana had been given to the dog men and then the later feeling of triumph she had when her determination repelled Shark Mouth and his men. Above all, through her mind flowed the songs she had been taught as a child: that virtue was power, and virtue was strength. If there was any time she needed power and strength, it was now, in this city of unfulfilled expectations. She could not abandon virtue now.

She held her head up and matched Speaker Gula's steady gaze. "Yes. I am a virgin."

There was a communal exhale in the room.

"What a relief!" exclaimed Speaker Riplakish to no one in particular as he leaned back and began fanning himself. "This entire Messenger process is such an ordeal and I don't think I could stand to do it more than once a year. *Bless you, child!* I can't wait to get into the steam room."

Ignoring him, Speaker Gula stood and in loud voice said, "Priests of Zitól, we have found our new Messenger! Have her taken back to the tower so she can be made comfortable," he said. "The other one we will give to the captain of the guard. He's been asking me for a woman."

The priests, smiling like coyotes, turned to congratulate each other. Speaker Gula adjourned the meeting and the men rose from their seats to leave.

Rishi felt Isra take her hand. "I'm truly sorry you have to do this, Rishi," Isra said as tears filled her eyes.

Rishi pulled Isra tightly into her arms. "No, Isra," she said, whispering in her ear. "I'm sorry you have to."

Suddenly Mama Xoca's voice rang out once again from the back of the room, halting the exodus of priests.

"Excuuuse me," she sang. "Excuuuse me. Mama Xoca thinks you have forgotten something."

The room became quiet. The Speakers, who were standing, smiled courteously and sat down again.

"Of *course*, Madame. How could we be so thoughtless? Here—" Gula pulled out two pouches from his robes. "Two bags of rubies—your payment. Although it really only should be one, since only *one* is a maiden."

"Two bags—you cheat me!" Mama Xoca glared at Gula. "That girl is worth far more so than any other maiden that Mama Xoca has ever brought to you. You should be paying Mama *three bags*—just for her!" But she snatched the two bags anyway and hustled out unceremoniously, without a word or glance at Rishi or Isra.

CHAPTER 30
Rishi Throws Her Slippers

After Leema led Rishi back to the Messenger's tower—her tower, now—and left her alone, the first thing Rishi did was open the sheer curtain that divided the room in half. She walked over to the other side. There was a small table with a padded chair. There were baskets of beautiful linens and more jewelry than Rishi knew existed in the world. She walked to the railing and looked out. From this side of the tower she could see down into the courtyard, and down onto the roofs of the Speakers' apartments. The only thing she could not look down on was the tower opposite hers, which stood slightly taller.

She had always been taught that staying virtuous would be a protection to her. She'd done all she could to remain pure. She sang the songs of virtue and stayed true to their guidance. She had seen their power in the forest. When she sang the songs, she was comforted and felt an overwhelming sense of peace and reassurance. And now, because she had kept herself pure, she was destined to die?

Rishi would do anything the gods asked of her. She would even sacrifice her life, if that was what they required. But the more she learned about this strange city, the more she was filled with confusion. The personalities of these gods were very different from the ones she had known. Her gods were gods of protection and love. They gave guidance and reassurance, and Rishi saw herself as their child. The gods of this city were fierce and demanding, and the words she'd read on the walls around the city and the inscriptions she saw on the temple steps just made her more perplexed.

The Speakers had mentioned their ruler was half-god. What did that mean? She leaned on the balcony and studied the other tower, wondering if it was the residence of the elusive half-god that never sat on his throne. She sighed. Nothing made sense.

Rishi rearranged some of the furniture; she slept; she ate. There were three goldfish in the pond and she named them after her brothers, and when she really felt lonely she talked to them. She wondered if the other Messenger had named them and talked to them too.

But mostly Rishi piled the cushions next to the balcony and watched people. The courtyard below was always busy and she could see everything that went on. Sometimes she gazed up at the other tower, but the curtains were always drawn. When she looked to the east she saw the heads of the four pyramids, pristine and glorious. She avoided looking out the west side of the tower, toward the jungle and the cenote. The cenote was something she dared not think about for a while.

Leema brought her food three times a day. Every day it was different, but it was always mouthwatering and fresh and sprinkled with spices. Sometimes Leema brought other items, like jewelry, beaded tunics, or shawls made of the softest fabric Rishi had ever felt.

Once Leema brought her a wooden box that was exquisitely carved with images of suns and moons and smelled of cedar. Inside were two beautifully embroidered satin slippers. They were bright crimson and lined with white fur, and they cradled her feet in luxurious warmth. Rishi was grateful to have something to protect her feet from the chill of the stone floor in the early morning, and she was honored to be the recipient of something so lovely.

When she wasn't watching people, she sat and watched the goldfish. One of them seemed extra smart and would come to the surface every time Rishi approached. This is the one Rishi named Eno. Cotyl was quicker and more nervous than the other two, and the largest fish was, of course, Quash. She always shared her food with the fish.

On one particular afternoon, after she had fed the fish, she heard footsteps coming up the tower. It was an odd time for Leema to come by, but Rishi craved some change in her routine and looked forward to any visit, even if it was from her grouchy chaperone.

But when she lifted her head she was startled to see that it wasn't Leema at all. It was a man. One of the Speakers. Rishi sat up straight, putting her hands in her lap.

"Greetings, Messenger," said the Speaker.

Rishi nodded primly.

"My name is Speaker Tungan. I have come to see how you've been faring up here, in your solitude." He walked to the side of the tower, pulled back the curtains, and gazed out at the city. "Magnificent view of a magnificent city," he murmured. His hands were behind him, and Rishi noticed that in addition to the gold ring through his nose, he also had gold rings on almost every one of his fingers. "Well, Messenger, are you happy up here in your nest?" he asked her, without turning around. Rishi didn't answer. She had an uneasy feeling that the reason the man had come to see her was not to make sure she was happy.

The man pivoted slowly and watched her for a moment. He was not bad-looking, Rishi decided. The lines around his eyes and mouth suggested he was still ten years older than she was, but still much younger than the other two Speakers. He had a handsome profile, a fine nose, and broad shoulders. He looked as if he could have been an athlete at one time, but the gentle padding around his waist hinted that the days of strenuous activity were behind him.

Rishi waited for him to say something, but he kept staring at her with one corner of his mouth lifted in a strange smile. Rishi did not like that smile. Her cheeks burned and she looked down. She suddenly felt embarrassed even though she didn't know why. As she ran her hand along the top of the water, a fish came to the surface, brushing her fingers.

"I see you're enjoying my gift." At the sound of his voice the fish disappeared into the lilies. Rishi was confused at first. What gift? Then she saw the Speaker looking at the red slippers on her feet.

"Do they fit?" he asked, walking closer. He stooped down and traced the satin with his finger. Then his finger moved up to stroke Rishi's ankle.

Now, I have so far given you an account of how Rishi had been mistreated, wrestled, and pounded on by her brothers. I have described how she was dragged across the sand and tossed to the ground by Shark Mouth. But never, never did she feel more violated than she did by Tungan's soft caress up her ankle. She recoiled and pulled her feet away, tucking them under the folds of her dress. Blood rushed to her cheeks, making them bloom red.

Tungan gave a quiet chuckle. He stood and began leisurely pacing around the room, looking at the drapes, fingering the tasseled pillows, contemplating the blue dome above them. The silence was thick. He helped himself to some fruit on the tray.

"Is the food to your liking?" he finally asked cheerily, mouth full.

Rishi said nothing.

"And the tower . . . is it comfortable?"

Rishi looked back into the water. Her heart was beating hard in her chest now. The fish were still hidden.

Tungan paced slowly around the chamber, his hands behind his back. He took some more food from the tray. "I understand that this new experience might be difficult for you, Messenger," he said. "What you need to remember is that this is an *honor*."

"Sacrifice only means something if it is voluntary," she said quietly.

"Ah! She speaks!" Tungan clapped his hands and praised the ceiling. "And as for sacrifice being worth something only if it is willing, well, that may or may not be true," he said. "But *I* wasn't talking about sacrifice."

He paused, waiting for Rishi to ask him what he was talking about, but Rishi was silent.

"I was talking about the honor of being in my presence."

Rishi narrowed her eyes. It sounded like something her brothers would say as a joke, but this man was completely serious.

He went on. "I am a holy Speaker. To even be in the same room with me is a sacred experience." He looked her straight in her eyes. "To do *anything* with me is a sacred experience. Now I understand that you are probably not ready yet, and I will not force you. Believe me when I tell you that in a few weeks you will be *begging* me to come to you. And you *will* want me, Messenger, you can be sure of that. I have powerful methods of persuasion."

Rishi felt her cheeks grow hotter, but still she said nothing.

"I know what you are thinking," he continued. "You are wondering why I would come and ask for your virtue when your virtue is why you are to be sacrificed in the first place. But don't worry, my child. You still would be virtuous. In fact, after being with someone as holy as me, you would be even *more* virtuous." Tungan smiled and put another chunk of fruit in his mouth. "I am a patient man, Messenger, and it doesn't matter if it takes some time for you to see things my way . . . Besides, I like women to be on the slender side."

He came close to Rishi, and she stiffened. He brushed back her hair from her face and let his fingertips slide down her cheek and down her neck. "I don't know how we could have ever doubted your loveliness. You truly are beautiful."

"I am more than beautiful," Rishi said. "I am *clean*."

Tungan let out a hearty laugh, puffing his fruity breath into her face. "And you are spirited," he said stepping back. "I like that. Think about my offer. I will return."

Rishi sat rigid on the edge of the pond and listened to his steps fade down the stairwell. She heard him say something to Leema, but she could not distinguish the words. When she felt sure the man was gone, Rishi took the slippers from off her feet and flung each one out of a different side of the tower.

CHAPTER 31

Are You Afraid of Blood?

After the Speaker's visit, Rishi's menu abruptly changed. The next morning there were no fresh-cut fruits or vegetables on the tray that Leema brought, neither was there meat, and every day since then food came only twice a day and usually consisted of corn tortillas and beans. The only variety was in the way it was arranged. *So this is Tungan's method of persuasion,* Rishi thought.

Two weeks later Tungan came back to Rishi's tower, asking her if she was ready. She refused. He left, still confident that eventually she would come to see things his way. Soon afterward the corn tortillas were also removed from the menu. After another week the only food that Leema brought up the stairs were trays of tasteless wafers and refried beans and sometimes an overripe fruit. Rishi's stomach constantly burned with emptiness.

Sometimes good smells of sizzling onions and meat came floating up from Leema's room at the bottom of the stairs, torturing Rishi. Once Rishi ventured down the stairs to beg for food, but the woman chased her back upstairs with her wooden spoon.

It was hard to think of anything else. It didn't help that she had no occupation but watching servants carrying baskets of bread and corn, and platters filled with food up into the apartments of the Speakers and the priests. Her only other form of amusement was watching the gold-fish swim in the pond or taking a brush to her hair. Both the fish and the brush were starting to look delicious.

At first Rishi would use sleep to help herself forget about her hunger. She went to bed early and slept as late as she could. She took a nap in the afternoon. Then she started dreaming of food too. And because we know that Rishi didn't have just ordinary dreams like you and me, there was always something else in her dreams too. Some clue as to what would soon come to pass. And this time it involved a strange, little old woman.

Sometimes the old woman in her dreams was swimming in a sea of berries, smiling. In other dreams, the old woman was picking steaming tamales from a tree.

In one particular dream, the old woman was standing outside, under a vast sky of gathering clouds. The rain started to drip out of the clouds, but instead of coming down as water droplets, it came down as honey cakes. The woman watched the honey cakes fall, uninterested, while Rishi salivated from behind a small rock. Then somewhere drums started to beat and the woman became alert and looked up at the sky. She bent her knees and held out her apron, as if she were expecting to catch a very large cake. But instead of a cake, out of the sky fell a baby.

The baby landed safely into the old woman's apron, and the drums stopped. She embraced it, briefly holding it close to her cheek, and then set the baby down at her feet. She looked up again. The drums sounded and again the woman held out her apron. Another baby fell from the sky. Rishi watched, mesmerized.

Babies continued to fall, one at a time. The woman had to maneuver herself around to be in the right spot to catch each baby safely. Sometimes she got to the baby in time, and sometimes she didn't and the baby hit the ground, shattered like a broken pot, and vanished. When this happened, Rishi felt a tremendous sadness coming from the woman. But then the drumming would resume and the woman knew there would be another baby falling and made herself ready.

The beat of the drums quickened and several babies started to fall at once. Rishi sat behind the rock, her body tense, hoping that the woman could get to each baby in time. But she had to let some babies fall in order to catch others. It didn't occur to Rishi to help until it was all over.

The drums stopped and so did the raining babies. The woman, calm but breathless, gathered up all the babies she had caught and held them in her arms like a huge bunch of flowers. She was about to walk away when she turned her head toward Rishi, who was still sitting on the ground, behind the rock that was too small to conceal her. Suddenly feeling ashamed for not coming to help, Rishi looked away. But just before she did, their eyes met and Rishi saw that the woman had one blue eye.

This startled Rishi so much that she woke. Groggy and disoriented, she sat up and rubbed her eyes while her mind tried to untangle her dream from reality. The tamale tree was a dream. The falling babies were a dream. The woman with the blue eye was a dream. But the drums . . . why could she still hear drums?

She looked around and saw that the pillars on the east side of the tower had a faint red blush on their sides, and an orange glow stained the dark sky.

She crawled over the pillows to the railing of the tower, pushed back the curtains, and looked out into the night.

The four temples were ablaze with torches, and large fires filed up the center of each staircase. Figures were climbing up and down the stone steps like spiders. There was a gigantic fire blazing in the center of the temple plaza and all around it were the red-hued silhouettes of people. Rishi knew she wasn't dreaming anymore. The deep sounds of the drums made her tower vibrate and she doubted if anyone in the city could sleep through the commotion.

She ducked back under the curtains. She had to get a closer look.

Silently, she disappeared into the stairwell, carefully feeling her way down the steps. When she reached the bottom she could hear Leema's soft snore. She tiptoed across the small room and felt for the opening and the tapestry. As she lifted the edge, there was a jangling sound and Rishi froze. Leema muttered something and turned over in her bed. Rishi felt down the tapestry to the bottom. There were bells sewn to the bottom of the tapestry, no doubt to alert Leema if Rishi tried to escape. Clutching the bells in her hand, Rishi carefully eased her way under the tapestry and stepped over the threshold. Still holding on to the bells at the bottom of the tapestry, she gently lowered them back to where they hung, inside Leema's doorway. But she released the bells too quickly and they hit the stone threshold with a loud clatter.

A gnarled hand shot out from behind the tapestry, catching Rishi by the wrist and yanking her back inside.

"Where are you going?" snapped Leema's voice in the dark.

"I—I—promise I'll come right back," said Rishi. "I woke to the sound of the drums, and I just wanted to see what is going on down there."

"You can't leave this tower," snarled Leema, dragging Rishi back toward the stairs.

"I promise you, I'll be back," said Rishi.

"Ha!" the woman cackled and pushed her to the steps. Rishi fell on her hands and knees. "You were trying to escape," she said. "Now get to your room."

Suddenly a tremendous BOOM BOOM BOOM sounded from the drums and the crowd roared again. Leema and Rishi froze as they listened to the commotion. When it was over Rishi began to rise and walk up the stairs.

"Wait," Leema said, tapping her chin with a gnarled finger. "*Where were you planning on going?*"

"To the temples, to see what is happening," said Rishi.

"You mean you do not *know*?" the old woman asked, peering at her through the semi-darkness.

Rishi shook her head, her eyes wide and honest.

With her buckteeth pressing against her lower lip, Leema scrutinized Rishi with narrow, rodent-like eyes. A debate was going on inside the woman's head. Rishi did not know if she should climb back up to her room or stay where she was. The silence was made more uncomfortable as Rishi noticed Leema's breathing became louder and faster through her nose. Then, leaning close to Rishi's face, she said in an eager whisper, her eyes glittering, "Are you afraid of blood?"

Rishi refused to let herself be shocked by such a question. "No," she said without hesitation. Rishi did not like to admit she was afraid of anything.

Leema threw back her head and her laughter rang up and down the stairwell.

"Come!" said the old woman, grabbing Rishi's hand and pulling her down the steps. "You want to see the temples? You shall see the temples. I will show you." She grabbed a cape off a hook and flung it around her shoulders.

Up until this point Rishi had only seen Leema as a hunched over, quite miserable-looking woman who only spoke in short, grumpy eruptions. But now she was a different creature. She jumped around the chamber, grinning and whooping. She took another cape from a dark corner, danced around with it and then gleefully pitched it at Rishi's face.

"Put that on!" she exclaimed.

The more she watched Leema's display of overwhelming delight, the less interested Rishi became about the drums and glowing lights below. Rishi's curiosity to see the temples was vanishing quickly, and she dropped the cape and retreated backward up the stairwell, eager to put space between her and this madwoman. But Leema caught her hand and shoved the cape back into Rishi's chest.

"Put it on! Do you want to be *ravaged*?"

"I changed my mind," Rishi stammered. "I don't want to go. I prefer to stay here."

Leema stopped her celebrations and grabbed Rishi's wrist, yanking her down to her level.

"Listen to me, girl. I have guarded the Messenger's tower for more years than you have been breathing. I have not seen the sacrifices in all those years because I have to be *here*, with *you* while everyone else leaves. You think you are a prisoner? That is a lie. *I* am the prisoner. Tonight I will indulge myself, but since I cannot leave you here, you must come with me. *Put the cape on.* If you are recognized, we will both be killed."

Not knowing what else to do Rishi reluctantly put the cape over her shoulders and pulled the hood over her head. Taking a strip of leather, Leema cinched it tight around Rishi's wrist and tied the other end around her own. Then, with a loud clatter of bells she pushed aside the curtain and they stepped out into the moonlight.

Like ghosts, they crossed through the courtyard. The night air was suffocatingly thick and humid. There were no lights; all the rooms in the palace were dark. Everyone, it seemed, was down below.

Leema pulled Rishi around the palace compound and through the palace gates.

Rishi could barely keep up with the swift feet of the woman, who now and then let out a gleeful giggle as she leaped down the road. More and more Rishi was regretting ever leaving her room.

When they reached the bottom of the hill, they ducked in and out of the dark, deserted streets. As they neared the temple plaza, the crowd's tumultuous murmur grew more distinct. Drums pounded out a cadence, and the crowd issued a loud roar. Rishi's spirit was on edge and every part of her screamed that she should not be here. Several times she stopped and tried to convince Leema to return to the palace, but Rishi, weak with hunger, was no match for the determined old woman who tugged her forward. "Walk, or I'll drag you," the woman said.

They were very near the plaza now, and Rishi could smell the smoke and hear the roar of the fire. It still took Leema several wrong turns to find the way to the plaza, for it had truly been a long time since she had been free to roam in the city. Everywhere they turned they could still see the glow of orange smoke billowing out from behind the silhouette of a building, blocking the way, and each dead end received Leema's furious cursings. Leema continued to cut through the alleys, sensing a path through the darkness like a mole.

Finally they came to a wide corridor that led to the temples. Up ahead there were hundreds of people gathered in the plaza, overflowing into the road. Over their heads flickered the bright orange flames of the biggest fire Rishi had ever seen.

The old woman yanked Rishi's arm, forcing her to bend low near Leema's mouth.

"You must listen to me," she hissed. "If you get lost you will be raped or trampled. Do not leave my side. I am your only protection. Remember this, and the evening will be pleasant and delightful for both of us."

Pleasant and delightful? Rishi couldn't believe this was happening. Even if she had been able to escape from her tower and get this far, she never would have pressed herself into the rioting crowd that massed before them. The images of dark silhouettes before her, highlighted in fiery orange and waving their arms in the air, were enough to satisfy her curiosity. Something dreadful was happening here. Deep in her bones she could feel evil in the night and she longed to escape. She felt she was being pulled into a den of demons.

Leema's grip on her wrist was like iron, and she dragged Rishi toward the fringe of the crowd and entered the wall of people. As Rishi rubbed up against the hot skin and the half-naked bodies of the people around her, she could hardly believe these were the same people she'd seen in the amphitheater. Gone were the fine, rainbow-colored linens and layers of sparking jewelry. Tonight they were practically clothes-less—even the women's clothing was disheveled and hung about their bodies like rags, exposing their shoulders, torsos, and legs. The men were wearing nothing but loincloths, and some had painted themselves with black, geometric designs.

The mingled smells of ashes, incense, and sweat were thick in the air, and through the gaps in the crowd Rishi caught glimpses of the top of the temple, lit up like a stage. Bare-chested men beat huge drums while beside them, the two Speakers stood next to a stone table. They wore their enormous headdresses of feathers—the same ones they'd worn to the sacrifice of the Messenger—but this time their pristine white robes were smeared in crimson.

"Let the next sacrifice approach!" shouted one of the Speakers. The entire crowd began a low chant and Rishi could sense a feeling of terrible foreboding. The chanting grew louder as Rishi was drawn through the revelers, following Leema's dark shape as quickly as she could and agonizing over the pain in her wrist. The crowd was so massive that it overflowed up the lower stairs of the other temples. Leema reached the western temple and climbed the steps, hauling Rishi after her. Finally she came to a place where they could see out over the heads. Rishi turned around to look out across the plaza. Leema had found the perfect view.

Over the vast sea of people, the towering orange temples looked nothing like the majestic buildings she had seen by day, and instead like massive, spined dragons. Across from her, climbing up the steps of the greatest pyramid, were two priests and a man covered with blue paint. As they ascended the pyramid, the chanting of the multitude grew louder and more aggressive.

Because his hands were tied behind his back, the blue man's balance was skewed and he stumbled several times. When he tripped, another man, following behind with a spear, jabbed him in the back. Each time this happened, the clamor of the voracious crowd boiled with exuberant cheers.

Rishi's heartbeat quickened. A potent feeling of evil hung over the plaza, as suffocating and real as the clouds that loomed above the pyramids. Rishi felt hot and sick, and perspiration beaded her face. But just as it had been at the cenote, the horror before her was so mesmerizing and so absolutely inconceivable that she could not take her eyes away from the scene.

By the time the blue man and the priests reached the top of the temple, the crowd's chanting blended into a din of hysteria. People were screaming and waving their arms. Some were stacked on each other's shoulders, their expressions wild and fierce, their mouths gaping open, wagging their pierced tongues. It didn't matter that the sound of the drums was swallowed up in the crowd's frenzy, for Rishi could still feel its commanding beat rattling in her chest.

At the top of the temple, the blue man's feet were bound and he was laid on a stone table. Even from where she stood, Rishi could see his chest heaving up and down.

The Speakers raised their arms in the sky. The crowd did likewise, raising their hands and hushing, until the only sounds in the plaza were the roar of the great bonfire and the sobbing of the blue man on the table.

"Great gods of the universe!" shouted one of the Speakers, his voice clear and crisp in the sudden silence. "We stand before you in humility and meekness with a willing sacrifice that we might demonstrate to you our faithfulness."

Somewhere in the distance, thunder boomed.

"In stone it is written that you require complete sacrifice and the surrender of a beating heart to prove our sincere devotion to you."

Rishi's eyes grew wide. Then the hair on her arms stood on end as the Speaker pulled a stained knife out of his belt and with both hands raised it in the air. The victim's body thrashed on the table, and the other priests held him down.

"And with this enduring and eternal sacrifice, oh magnificent gods, *send us rain!*"

His arms came down, plunging the blade into the blue man's chest. Rishi could feel herself cry out, but she heard nothing, for her scream was lost in the thousands of other screams that shattered the night. Rishi cupped her hand over her mouth to keep from screaming again as the Speaker held up a pulsating red mass in his hands and the people beat the air with a thousand fists. Crimson lines of blood oozed down his raised arm and into his sleeve.

The crowd was hysterical.

Next to her, Leema hoisted her arms—and Rishi's—in the air. "It is better than I remember!" she shrieked at the sky.

Rishi tucked her head down into her hood, put her hand on her chest and tried to breathe. "I can't believe what I just saw," she gasped.

"Come," Leema said. "We must get back before anyone else. At least I had a taste." She pulled Rishi back down the pyramid steps and they pushed through the dense crowd. Individuals who were not still shouting and screaming were staring hypnotically at the copious rush of blood dripping down the steps of the temple. They were not in the mood to be jostled, and an elbow struck Rishi in the eye. She staggered back, holding her face in pain, and followed Leema through the people until they left them behind and retraced their path up the dark streets.

Thunder boomed above them as she stumbled after Leema. By the time they entered the palace courtyard, Rishi's eye was swelling and her head throbbed.

It wasn't until they reached the tower that Leema finally let her go. Rishi collapsed against the stone wall, trying to catch her breath and massaging her wrist. Leema watched her and chuckled.

"Did you enjoy it? Was it not a grand sight? Were the Speakers not magnificent?"

"How often does that happen?" Rishi panted. "Do they do this every year, like the sacrifice of the Messenger?"

"No, this ritual is much more often. It is performed the first night of every month. Was it not pleasing to you?" Leema asked.

"It was disgusting to me," Rishi said. "Those men are not Speakers. They are butchers."

Leema let out a loud cackle. "Perhaps . . . but they say they are only doing the will of the gods."

Thunder boomed again and drops of rain began to fall on Rishi's arms and face. Leema looked up in the sky and smiled. "Here it comes," she said.

"What?"

"The rain. Is that not what the sacrifices are for?"

Rishi felt sick.

"You get back in the tower now," Leema said. "Perhaps you will think twice next time about satisfying your curiosity. But if you want," she said, smiling, "we will go again next month."

Rishi ignored her and crawled into the tower, knowing that she would never go again. In her mind the fresh images kept repeating themselves over and over. She saw the knife falling down into the man's chest, his back arching in agony. Tears streamed out of Rishi's eyes. She felt defiled, even though she had done nothing but watch.

She entered her room just as a massive clap of thunder cracked over the city, making the tower tremble. For a moment everything—the pyramids, the people, the streets, the palace—was as bright as day.

Her body was exhausted, but her head was too filled with darkness to relax. She avoided looking out at the east side of the tower: the drums were still sounding down at the temple plaza; the crowd was beginning another slow chant. Rishi knew that another blue figure was now being guided up the stairs to meet his doom.

Rishi quickly shut all the curtains in the tower, trying to block out as much sound and light as possible. Just before she closed the curtain on the side overlooking the courtyard, she stopped and caught her breath.

There was a light in the other tower.

Rishi's hands clutched the curtain, her eyes fixated to that light. So not *everyone* was at the temple plaza that night. A soft pattering sound began on the roof of the dome. Within a few minutes the rain came down in thick, thundering sheets.

Leaving the drape open a crack, she dragged some pillows and a blanket near the railing. Curling up against a pillar, she held the drape open just enough to see the solitary light glowing through the downpour.

The rain brought some measure of comfort. *The sacrifices will* have *to stop now*, she thought. They couldn't keep the fires lit in rain like this. Perhaps someone would be spared to live a little longer. But there was something about the rain that bothered her too. No . . . not bothered her . . . *disturbed* her, down into her very bones. It was that the people were giving up sacrifices to the gods so the gods would send rain.

And the rain came.

CHAPTER 32

The Golden Comb

The month of the Hummingbird, the month of Grass, and the month of the Crocodile came and went. Three temple sacrifices that Rishi tried to muffle with pillows pressed to her ears. Sometimes at night she would see the other tower, its solitary light gleaming, and she would watch it until her eyes were so heavy she could no longer hold them open.

One afternoon, a week before the month of the Flower, Rishi saw Leema coming across the courtyard, toward the Messenger's tower. Three musicians followed her: one carried a drum, the other some chimes, and the last had rattles that shook with each step. The small group entered the tower and soon Rishi heard their steps clamoring up the stairwell. She turned and faced the opening, expectant and curious. She prayed that whatever this change of routine was, somehow it would involve food.

The four entered the room.

"It is time to learn the dance for the Flower Festival," Leema announced.

Rishi said nothing in response, for Leema's tone made it clear that refusal was not an option.

Silently, Rishi watched as Leema busily arranged the musicians in the corner. When she was satisfied, she tossed some pillows and cushions aside to clear a space for her to stand. "Watch carefully," Leema said, straightening her posture and flaring her hands dramatically in front of her face.

The musicians began a slow, tremulous rhythm and Leema began to move. She started with her wide hips, swiveling to the beat; her hands came up into the air, swaying back and forth like waving palm trees. The music sped up and Leema contorted and gesticulated in strange movements, sometimes bending down so far Rishi could see into her jiggling bosoms and other times gyrating so ridiculously that Rishi couldn't help biting her lip to hide her smile. Finally the music stopped, and Leema struck a seductive pose, her chest heaving and her eyelashes aflutter.

Rishi was speechless.

Leema slowly lowered her raisiny arms, resuming her usual crustiness. "Now, your turn."

"My turn?" Rishi panicked. Rishi couldn't dance like *that*.

"You *must* learn this dance for the Flower Festival. It is the Dance of the Messenger, and every Messenger from the beginning has learned it. It represents the dance you will do for the gods when you enter the cenote." *A fitting description*, Rishi thought. The dance did resemble someone drowning.

"You will dance this before all of the people of Zitól, the Speakers, and the priests. Not only that," the woman lowered her voice, "but I have heard that the *Anointed One* will be there. He hardly ever goes to any festival, on account of his holiness. This is a very important occasion."

"The Anointed One?" Rishi asked. So she would finally see the man from the tower.

Leema nodded with a grin, showing her buckteeth. "Now, let's begin."

Every afternoon Leema came with the musicians and taught Rishi the steps to the dance. Rishi felt absurd, but she imitated the steps to the best of her ability, all the while thinking how her brothers would mock her if they could see her. Rishi's reluctance prevented her from achieving the skill level Leema was hoping for, and Leema did nothing to mask her displeasure, often slapping Rishi's hands in frustration. Rishi sometimes practiced after Leema left, swaying her hips and striking the poses in the mirror, but she always gave up and fell back into the cushions, feeling ridiculous.

The day before the festival, Leema came once more, this time to sit and watch Rishi perform.

The music began and Rishi swiveled her hips and wiggled her arms . . . she did everything Leema asked. But before the song came to an end Leema was pulling her hair out in frustration.

"You are a *disgrace*," she said.

Rishi nodded. Yes, as far as this dance was concerned, she was an absolute, unequivocal disgrace.

"You must *act* like you are in the underworld, speaking to the gods!" she said passionately. "The gods are busy people! You must do something to get their attention. The gods are men, are they not? There is only one way to get the attention of a man. You must be passionate, imploring, *seductive.* It is tradition!"

Rishi blinked, dumbfounded.

Leema threw her hands up in the air. "I'm finished with you. No wonder you remained a virgin. Your body is like a pile of sticks. You dance like a beetle. Why would anyone ever want to make love to you?"

She marched out of the room, and the musicians followed at her heels.

Rishi kicked at some cushions and sat down. Something wasn't right here. The dance of the Messenger was to convince the gods by seduction? If she had a chance to meet with the gods and plead with them on behalf of the people, that would not be the method she would choose.

She thought about that all through the evening. Tomorrow was the festival. Would she decide to try to be more seductive or would she remain beetle-like? The dance was impossible for her to do. Besides, it didn't make sense for a virgin to dance like a harlot. *So how* should *a virgin dance?* she thought. She and her friends had danced at many village festivals. Rishi knew she was not the best dancer, but she always enjoyed it. Perhaps she could change the dance into something that made her feel more . . . like herself. If she broke the tradition they might punish her. But was there anything worse than being locked up in a tower with no food and then tied up and thrown into a deep underground pool?

"Well then," she said out loud to the fish in the pool. "I suppose I have nothing to lose. I think it is time for the Messenger to have a new tradition."

Dawn arrived too soon. Rishi noticed that Leema decided to supplement her usual breakfast of wafers with a corn tortilla, dried meat, potato skins, and an ear of boiled corn, for which she was grateful. She chewed slowly, savoring each bite while she tried to come up with a plan. Although she had made her decision to change the dance, she still didn't exactly know how.

People all over the palace were preparing for the festival. The steam rooms and bathhouse were filled, so Leema took Rishi into a private room to bathe.

After Rishi washed, Leema dried her with a towel and rubbed sweet lotions into her skin. Then Leema brought out the dress.

"You shall wear this," Leema said, holding up the azure-colored fabric, trimmed with tassels and bells.

Rishi couldn't believe her eyes. "That? But—it is so . . . short." The dress had only enough fabric to cover a spider monkey.

"That is the point. You are to show off your body."

"I don't want to show off my body."

"But you have a perfectly fine body."

"That is exactly why I don't want to show it to everyone. My body is *sacred*."

"*My body is sacred*." The woman mimicked in a high, whiny voice. "Relax, you sweetsop. You are not showing *everything*. The best parts will still be covered up."

"But—"

"In you go," she said as she pulled it over Rishi's head. The dress was the size of a small towel. It crossed her chest, leaving one arm bare, and fit snugly around the waist. It barely covered her backside, ending high mid-thigh.

"I can't wear this," Rishi said. "I feel naked."

"Wear it. Or you *will* go naked. Believe me, they will like that even more."

Pressing her lips in a line and clenching her fists, Rishi fumed but said nothing. Meanwhile, Leema plaited her black hair, crowned her with a gold beaded headband, and fixed it in the back with a shiny golden comb. "Close your eyes," she commanded. With her thumb Leema smeared blue paint over Rishi's eyelid and down her cheek. Then she did the same to the to the other side. Finally she tied Rishi's bead belt around her waist. Rishi thought it bitterly ironic that her bead hung lower than her dress.

"Remember," said Leema as she pushed her out the door, "*passion*."

There would be a procession to the temples. This time five magnificent litters lined up in a row down the center of the courtyard. The first one was made of solid gold, and Rishi guessed this was for the mysterious Anointed One. The Messenger's litter was behind that, and then came the three Speakers. All the litters were covered in fresh flowers.

Feeling as exposed and vulnerable as a freshly peeled banana, Rishi stepped into the litter and seated herself on the embroidered cushion, making sure she kept her bare knees pressed together. She noticed a basket of pumpkin seeds at her feet. She set the basket on the bare part of her legs to substitute for her clothing.

Just as the servants added the last flowers and finished lighting the urns of incense that hung from the litters, the young man appeared in the doorway of his tower. And Rishi almost missed it.

Later she told me she had been expecting some sort of fanfare and announcement, trumpets blowing, when the Anointed One revealed himself. Instead, the only thing that clued her in on his arrival was the flock of women who quickly passed her litter. She watched them hurry by and leaned to the side just in time to see one of the women conceal the young man's face with the painted mask of a falcon. Two others set a magnificent plume of fiery red and orange feathers on his head. Oil was rubbed into his skin and then several women gathered around him with cups and straws. Placing the straws to their lips, they blew gold dust all over his oiled body until his arms, chest, and legs glittered. Wide necklaces of jade and turquoise were placed around his neck, hanging low on his gilded chest. He stepped into his litter, disappearing behind the great throne. Rishi could only see the top of his headdress that arched over the back of his chair like a blazing sun. She chided herself for not watching the opening of his tower close enough to get a good glimpse of his face. But then, other than the makeup women, no one in the courtyard seemed to give the man a second glance.

Marble-muscled men stepped beside the litters and slowly raised them up. Rishi gripped the sides of her seat as it rocked back and forth. Like a great lumbering caterpillar, the procession made its way out of the courtyard and down the hill. This march was different than the solemn procession to the cenote. This time the people that bordered the streets were loud and festive. They waved flowers in the air as the litters passed.

Rishi saw that the Anointed One was throwing something out into the crowd. The pumpkin seeds. Rishi took a handful and threw it out into the street. People cheered and clapped. She threw out more. People were craning to look at her and smiling, waving their hands, "Messenger, here! Here!" and she threw more pumpkin seeds out to the boisterous crowd. She smiled. It felt so good to smile.

When they arrived in the temple plaza they made a large circle around the center of the huge square. Rishi marveled at how different it seemed from the night of the temple sacrifices. Gone was the giant bonfire. Gone were the torches and blood and smothering feeling of evil. Now the sun blazed in the clear morning sky and only frivolity and celebration reverberated throughout the great plaza. The people, fully clothed and boisterous, were smiling and merry. Flowers and streamers hung from poles, and women danced in circles, tossing flower petals and glittering trinkets. Men held T-shaped poles that carried rainbow-hued birds of all sizes, squawking and flapping their colorful, clipped wings. Rishi thought how much children would enjoy this festival, but she didn't see one child anywhere in the plaza. Now that she thought of it, she hadn't seen a child in Zitól at all, even as she watched from her tower. Where *were* all the children?

The procession came to a halt in front of the circular platform in the center of the plaza, known as the Speakers' Circle. During temple sacrifices, the Speakers' Circle is where the great bonfire is placed. But on all other occasions this is the spot for the Speakers to address the people. On this day, tables were set on the Speakers' Circle, with plates, goblets and lilies, orchids, and marigolds. Overlooking everything was a very tall throne that had been placed behind the table, so tall that a ladder was required to reach the seat.

Rishi's litter was set on the ground and the Speakers helped her out and escorted her up stone steps to one of the seats at the table. Rishi was placed at the end of the table, and, to her disappointment, so was Speaker Tungan.

Last of all, the mysterious Anointed One rose from his litter, and as he did, the multitudes of people bent low to the ground, pressing their hands and faces against the plaza floor, and a great hush fell.

"Bow your head, Messenger," said Speaker Tungan.

Rishi lowered her head. The Anointed One strode onto the circle and walked behind the Speaker's table. His feathered cape brushed Rishi as he passed. He climbed the tall throne. It was so silent Rishi could hear the squeak of his hands as he grasped the rungs. When he finally sat and raised his plumed scepter, the trumpeters blew their horns and the people lifted their heads. The area before the Speakers' Circle cleared and the dances began.

Costumed dancers came tumbling out onto the cleared space. They leaped and juggled, and balanced on each other's shoulders. When they were finished, women with bells jingling at their ankles filed out and danced together, holding hands in circles. Later the stage was filled with strong, athletic men dressed as birds or jungle animals. They spun and leaped.

During these dances, food arrived on large platters and the Speakers were served steaming tamales, fried tortillas, and spicy salsas. Cut pineapple, papaya, guava, tomatoes, and passion fruit were arranged in rainbows on great plates. Next to them were placed leafy green salads, beets, pumpkin, and squash. A display of roasted turkey and baked iguana, brazed to perfection, created the steaming centerpiece. But most of all there was corn. Blue corn, white corn, and corn the color of gold, arranged in baskets and bowls and cooked in every manner imaginable: cobbed, fried, popped, and mashed. With each new platter of food Rishi's eyes grew larger. Overwhelmed with the abundance of smells, the array of colors, and the promise of a full stomach, she was so happy she almost started to cry.

"This should be a pleasant change for you, Messenger," Tungan murmured to Rishi under his breath.

A thick, dark brown liquid was poured into Rishi's cup. She smelled it.

"Chocolate," Tungan said. "It is a delicacy. Only served to the holy." Rishi held the cup to her lips and sipped a little. It was cold and tasted earthy and bitter. She forced herself to swallow and grimaced at the powerful aftertaste that made her shoulders quiver.

The Speaker smiled. "It is an acquired taste," he said.

Huge slabs of roasted meat were brought to the table and the Speakers selected the cuts they wanted. With large knives, the servants sheared off generous, juicy portions and carefully laid the meat on their plates. Other servants with elegant fans made of green, white, and scarlet feathers stood behind Rishi and the Speakers, fanning the flies away from the Speakers' oily, pungent hair. Rishi stole a glance up at the gilded falcon-man perched above them.

"Isn't *he* going to eat?" Rishi whispered to Tungan.

"Who?"

"*Him.*" She gestured up and behind them with her spoon.

He shook his head. "Oh, no, he will not eat. He is a *god*," he said this with a smirk, as if he were letting her in on a private joke.

She turned and looked up at the masked man. From her angle she could only see the bottom of his sandals and his legs from the knee down. The soles of his sandals looked like anyone else's soles. The gold dust blowers had missed a spot behind his left calf and she could see recently scratched mosquito bites on his ankles. The gods might not need food, but apparently they were still susceptible to insects.

Her stomach growled and Rishi turned back to the glorious food. Tungan was packing an overflowing tortilla into his mouth. When he finished chewing he wiped the sauce from his lips and said, "I hope you realize that you *could* have food like this every day."

Rishi didn't answer him, for she was sinking her teeth into a juicy slice of passion fruit. As she savored the sweetness Tungan said, "I'm looking forward to your dance."

Rishi swallowed and put the rest of the fruit back on her plate. Her appetite vanished. In all the excitement about the food and the golden falcon-man she'd forgotten all about the dance. She suddenly felt sick, knowing she still didn't know exactly what she would do. And she'd have to do it *in this dress!*

"What is the matter?" Tungan asked. "Aren't you hungry?" She didn't want to talk right now; she needed to concentrate. What dance could she do? She thought back to when she was a child, and the dances she'd learned in her village. But that reminded her of something else.

"Why are there no children here?" she asked abruptly.

The Speaker gazed at her without blinking. She could see his mind forming the perfect sentence before it was released from his mouth.

"They are . . . in a better place," he said. "A place where they feel more comfortable."

"Do they ever walk the streets or come to festivals?" Rishi asked.

The man sighed importantly. "Messenger, some of our festivals are too mature for the tender, young feelings of children."

"Your festivals are not mature. They are barbaric."

"Are you questioning our rituals, Messenger?"

"My life is at the mercy of your rituals, Speaker, so naturally I question them."

"Our ways are the ways of the gods. We perform the rites that are carved in stone."

"I would like to see these stone carvings," said Rishi.

"Why? It wouldn't make a difference."

"I would like to read them for myself."

The Speaker laughed. "Read them? Let me inform you about the ways of Zitól, Messenger. It is illegal to read."

"How can it be illegal to read? Once you can read, you can read. You can't stop someone from reading. It is like telling someone to stop breathing. It can't be unlearned."

"Let me rephrase myself, then. It is *prohibited* for anyone but the priests and Speakers to be educated to read or interpret the sacred stone writings."

"Oh," Rishi said, looking over the vast crowd before them. "So no one even knows *how* to read?"

"They know everything they need to know. The general public does not have the time nor the discipline to spend on such things."

"I would think wise rulers would want intelligent people."

"We find it easier to bear this burden of knowledge for them."

"I see," said Rishi.

Tungan took a sideways glance at Speaker Gula and Speaker Riplakish, who were deep in discussion, then he leaned toward Rishi and lowered his voice. "You look stunning in that dress, Messenger. Have you . . . have you reconsidered my offer?"

"No."

"Why not? Tell me why you refuse me."

"You want just one reason? Or should I give you fifty?"

"Let's start with one."

"You don't love me."

"Easily remedied." He dabbed his mouth with a napkin. "I promise to love you 'til the day you die," he said, smiling like he had said something incredibly clever. He had something green caught in his teeth.

Rishi didn't have a chance to answer, for the music and dancing stopped and Speaker Gula walked to the front of the platform and began addressing the crowd. Rishi gazed at the wonderful food being served all around her and lamented that she was too nervous to eat any of it.

Gula's speech went on and on. He talked of rain and crops and sacrifice . . . The sun was getting warmer now and Rishi felt the effects of her sleepless night making her eyelids heavy.

Suddenly her eyes popped open and she was wide awake.

Tungan's hand was on her bare knee.

She glared up at him and tried to push his hand away. He only looked amused and stared straight ahead, tightening his grip. No one could see what was happening because of the cloth over the table. Rishi couldn't move her seat; it was large and solid and too heavy for her to move without drawing attention to herself.

Her nostrils flared. "Stop it," she hissed.

He only smiled and continued trespassing on Rishi's leg. Her heart raced. She was trapped. Gula didn't seem to be approaching any closing remarks. Rishi couldn't stand up and leave in the middle of his speech. Besides, where would she go? She looked around the platform surrounded by guards.

Tungan's fingers moved around her knee, rubbing and stroking her skin. When she tried again to push his hand away he squeezed her leg so tightly it hurt. Rishi wanted to scream but what would happen if she did? Would anyone come to help her? Would anyone believe her when she told them what Tungan was trying to do? And—worst of all—would they even care?

Rishi's blood started coursing through her body as his hand moved up to her thigh. How could she let herself become cornered like this?

"Stop it," Rishi said as demandingly as a whisper would allow.

"Relax," he murmured with a smile.

She pushed his hand away again, but he was too strong. *Something has to be done,* Rishi thought, *now.* She needed something—anything—to make him stop. If only she had a knife, a blade . . . any object that would inflict pain. She could see knives on the table, but they were out of her reach.

Then she remembered the golden comb in her hair. Reaching up, she discreetly pulled it out. For a few moments she held it in her hand, finding the best grip. She took a very deep breath. It was now or never.

In one swift movement she lifted her arm and jammed the comb into Tungan's forearm. "I *said,*" she whispered, pushing the teeth deep into his skin, "*stop it.*"

Tungan gave a piercing shriek and stood, upsetting his chair. The echoes of his scream reverberated off the walls of the pyramids and every head in the plaza turned, and every pair of eyes shifted from Gula to Tungan.

Speaker Gula stopped speaking and turned around, his mouth still half open. Tungan covered his arm with his hand.

"Speaker Tungan?" asked Gula.

Tungan glared down at Rishi, his eyes blazing, while she shoved forkfuls of meat into her mouth and vigorously chewed, watching the standoff between Gula and Tungan like a curious, munching chipmunk.

"I was just . . . I am . . . fine. Forgive me, Speaker Gula. Please, continue."

Tungan composed himself and sat, surreptitiously wrapping a napkin around his arm.

Gula's speech resumed. Rishi continued eating, her appetite returning with a vengeance. No one seemed to notice the way her hands shook or the way her cheeks glowed like bright red cherries.

Except me.

CHAPTER 33

The Dance of the Messenger

Unfortunately the interruption didn't abridge Speaker Gula's discourse; he continued explaining the many ways the gods could dismember a man's body before devouring it with their hairy tongues. It was a speech he often repeated, and as he put it, was "one of his most motivational." And indeed, he held the rapt attention of the people, even though their expressions were of fear, horror, and disgust.

Rishi's hair had come loose and her comb was nowhere to be seen—Tungan had knocked it out of her hands and it clattered to the ground somewhere under the table. She discreetly combed her hair out with her fingers. At least she didn't have to worry about Tungan touching her. For now.

Later she told me that it was moments like this when she missed her family the most. She realized now what she had always taken for granted: her security. On her island there was order, and everyone knew how to respect and show love appropriately. Here it seemed that the ones who were respected the most were the least respectful. How long would she be able to last? How long could she protect herself? Would she be able to keep herself a virgin until she was sacrificed?

Rishi remembered one of the Seven Songs. The fourth one—the one about protection. Suddenly, Rishi knew what she needed to do for her dance.

Speaker Gula finally finished his speech. Relieved, everyone seemed to perk up a bit, anxious for the festivities to resume. Now they were announcing the Dance of the Messenger, and all eyes focused on Rishi.

Her body was still trembling from her recent escape from Tungan's roving hand. She tried to tug her dress a little lower over her exposed brown legs, ashamed that she had to stand before the multitude in such nothingness. A fly buzzed in her ear and the servant behind her gently fanned it away with the plumes. Rishi turned to him.

"May I borrow these?" she asked, taking the two great fans from the surprised man. She walked around the table, to the front of the circle.

There was no way she could cover herself with the fans the entire dance. Instead Rishi hoped that the fans could at least be a distraction from her bare skin. Hundreds of faces watched her, anticipating the desperate, sensual dance of the Messenger's plea before the gods. Rishi felt her throat tighten. Her knees became so weak it was as if they had disappeared altogether.

She felt like jumping off the platform and running for her life, and she might have, if the drummer hadn't already started beating out the slow, gentle rhythm that introduced her dance. Leema had told her to face the Speakers and the Anointed One when she did her dance. But that would mean having her backside face the hundreds of people in the audience. If she faced the audience, her backside would face the Speakers, and that was worse. If this was truly to be a dance for the gods, she thought, she would have to perform her dance for *them*. She looked up into the blue above her. Yes. She would perform her dance for the sky.

Rishi bowed her head and pulled the fans before her face. When the chimes began their strange, mystic melody Rishi slowly opened the fans to reveal her lowered head and closed eyes. Slowly she raised her head upward. *"Dear gods, this is my dance,"* she whispered. Tentatively she guided the fans through the air, stretching as far as she could, watching them sweep the sky. *"This is my prayer to you."* The familiar words fell from her lips as naturally as tears, and she savored the wave of serenity that rippled through her body as she began her song. Her arms moved up and down, making the fans shimmer and tremble to the beautiful music. *"I have no spear, no sword, no shield for protection."* Rishi stepped forward, holding the fans at her hips, and brushed the ground with her sparkling slippers. *"I only have truth and courage and virtue for my weapons."* The beat increased slightly and her fans followed suit, swaying and gliding through the air like the wings of an eagle. *"Shield me with the power of truth, oh gods."* She held the fans around her face and then circled them up into the air. The music became even faster and Rishi stretched her arms out and started to spin, flaring the tassels on her skirt. *"Make my courage incorruptible."* The drums became louder and more intense. *"Make my message unquestionable,"* she said, spinning and spinning as she came to the last lines. *"Help me remember that even if I lose my life . . ."* Stray feathers flew off, whirling, drifting around her like falling blossoms. She turned her face up to the sky, her eyes closed, but a wide smile spread on her face. She was just a blur of color now and the music surged to the roaring climax. *". . . I will never lose my soul."* Then all at once Rishi spun to the ground and the music ceased.

The silence that followed the last slap of the drum was profound.

No word was spoken; no one moved. All were like blocks of wood, watching the last of the floating feathers drift to the ground around the girl who had danced like an eagle and was now tucked beneath the fans like a swan.

In her small shelter, Rishi could hear nothing but her own heavy breathing. "Thank you," she panted, closing her eyes and resting her forehead on the ground. "Thank you for helping me."

As Rishi regained her breath she desired to see the faces of the audience, but she did not want to break the spell that her dance had cast on her own racing heart. Somehow she could *feel* that they had heard her. Somehow she knew the starlit gods beyond the blue veil of sky could hear her and were aware of her. They were not terrifying gods, as the Speakers said. She lifted her eyes to glance at the first row of people and scanned their faces. There were looks of interest and wonder. Then a face caught her by surprise. She blinked her eyes. *It couldn't be*, she thought.

A hood partially obscured the old woman's hair but Rishi could see into her face and her one blue eye. The old woman smiled and lifted one crooked finger to her lips, giving Rishi the sign not to tell. Rishi blinked and the woman was gone.

A hand grasped Rishi's arm. Looking up, she saw Speaker Tungan. "Shall we get you back to your seat, Messenger?" he asked.

Rishi didn't reply. She could only think of the old woman with the hood. The woman with an eye like hers. The old woman from her dream who caught babies that fell from the sky.

By the time the festival was over and the procession lumbered back to the palace, Rishi was completely exhausted. She collapsed on the pillows in her tower and watched the blue ceiling shimmer in the light of the sinking sun.

She couldn't tell what kind of effect her dance had on the people. There had been no cheer, no applause, and, thankfully, no laughter . . . There had been no reaction that she could use to measure her success or failure. Was it childish? Were the feathers too ostentatious? Did she end up looking like a beetle after all?

She didn't know how she appeared, and she didn't care, because she knew how she *felt*. She felt as if she had been lifted up on wings. She felt strength and power. And when she had looked into the faces of the people, she hadn't seen the glazed stare she witnessed while Speaker

Gula was giving his lecture. Their faces looked different . . . brighter, curious, and full of wonder. Yes, it was a good dance, Rishi decided. A very good dance. If in the end she must die, at least the gods had allowed her this one victory.

CHAPTER 34

Rishi Finds
Something to Eat

Rishi expected retaliation from Speaker Tungan, and it came. The next time Leema brought food, Rishi received four crackers, a goblet of water, and a sprig of mint.

Several days passed, and every morning and every evening Leema brought Rishi the same meal of crackers and water. At first Rishi ate the crackers slowly, to make them last as long as possible. But after four days, just looking at the crackers was nauseating and she crushed them over the fish pond.

The future seemed bleak for the Messenger, and Rishi was sure she would die much earlier than the people of Zitól expected, for she languished in her chamber, with hardly enough energy to raise her body from the pillows she slept on. She felt forgotten by everyone. Each day she slept longer and longer, rose from her pillows less and less, until there seemed to be no point in rising at all.

But she was correct when she assumed that the gods had seen her dance and were aware of her, for they were indeed mindful of her every breath, and on the next Night of Sacrifices they would set in motion a series of events that would forever change the lives of us both. This was accomplished in the most satisfying way: Leema became sick.

I don't remember her ever getting sick before, but that particular day she was sicker than a rat. Rishi listened to her coughing and hacking all through the afternoon, and in the evening, the woman failed to bring Rishi her nightly meal of crackers. Instead, coughs and moans echoed up the stairwell until finally, late in the evening, the moaning stopped.

The moment the sounds of misery ceased Rishi sat up. Some instinct inside of her told her that this was her chance. Tonight, no matter what happened, she would find food.

Wobbling to her feet, she put on some slippers and staggered down the stairs, leaning on the wall for support. The bottom of the tower was completely black except for the thin strip of blue light that outlined the hanging tapestry. Rishi peered into the shadows where Leema slept. Though she could see nothing in the dark corner, she could hear the suffering, congested breaths of a woman languishing from a nasal curse. Carefully, Rishi stepped across the room to the tapestry. Being extremely mindful of the bells this time, she lifted the cloth and squeezed through the opening. One of the bells gave a light *tink* against the threshold and Rishi froze, one foot in the tower, one foot out.

The old woman stirred and moaned. She rolled over. She rolled over again. She muttered. And then she was still.

Rishi exhaled and pulled the rest of her body out of the tower and into the open air.

As soon as she put two feet in the courtyard, Rishi could smell it. It was a faint, warm aroma of spices and something sweet. She first went to the door where she had most often seen the food going in and out. But when she got there, she lifted the tapestry only to find a locked gate. Her stomach growled in defeat.

Following the smell, she came to another door. She lifted the tapestry and walked in, but it was only a bathhouse. She wandered out to the courtyard again and decided to walk up the outside stairs that led to the second floor apartments. Though it was a short climb, it made her head spin, and she paused at the top of the stairs to grip the railing and steady herself.

She crept along the balcony, passing several tapestry doors. She let herself in under the flap of one and walked through what she knew must be the room of one of the Speakers. The chamber was huge and spacious with a great bed in the center, but the air in the room was stale and clothing was strewn about in heaps. On the bed was a jumbled knot of sheets, and an overturned goblet had spilled a dark stain of wine on the mattress. Dirty dishes lay in piles on the floor, which she would have gladly gleaned if they weren't currently being licked by several feral-looking cats that paused to eye her with annoyance before they resumed their meal. There was no food here. She went back.

She staggered down the stone steps to the courtyard, feeling weaker than ever, almost to the point of falling to her knees and crawling. She passed the great wooden doors of the throne room, where she and Isra had last parted. There was light spilling out from under the door and she caught a hint of the sweet, spicy scent she had been following. Grasping the handle, she pulled the door open, and when she did, her nose was rewarded with an increase of the wonderful smell she had been seeking.

She knew that no matter who or what was in the throne room, nothing would stop her from finding the source of that smell.

Meanwhile, I sat on my throne, cross-legged, never suspecting there was a shadowy figure lurking in the courtyard, hunting down my midnight snack. I stabbed another chunk of pineapple with my skewer. On the table next to me was a lamp, and I held the pineapple over the flame just enough to roast the sweet flesh. I breathed in the aroma of the warm, juicy fruit as it caramelized. Carefully, I dripped honey over the succulent morsel. There were several small bowls of spices beside me, and this time I took a pinch of chili powder, accidentally spilling the cinnamon on the floor. No matter. The servants would clean it up tomorrow.

Blowing on my tasty treat, I leaned back against the jaguar fur that padded the back of my throne. I can't remember now exactly what I was thinking at that moment, but I'm fairly certain it centered around me and how I could best please myself.

I enjoyed the Night of Sacrifices only because it meant everyone would be gone and I could come out of hiding and pretend for a little while that I actually mattered to the world. The room was different without the Speakers—magnificent, welcoming, warm, pleasant. The recliners were soft and plush, upholstered in the most luxurious pelts. The floor was clean (except for my recent spill), and the tiled mosaic of the sun glittered in the flickering torchlight. Best of all, Raven's chain lay empty on the steps. (She being yet another reason I don't attend court with the Speakers.) I liked to visit the throne room when they were all gone. I liked to sit in my throne, gazing at invisible Speakers and priests and ordering them to do whatever I asked of them. I liked that they always agreed with me.

I finished the mouthwatering morsel and wiped the juice that dribbled down my chin. I was just beginning to roast a new one when I heard the creaking of the great door downstairs. Footfalls sounded in the stairway, soft and stealthy, the kind of hesitating steps that indicated that someone was either lost or attempting an assassination. I braced myself.

The tapestry opened, and to my surprise, in walked a young woman. She saw me and froze, unsure if she should approach or retreat. I recognized her immediately as the Messenger that had performed the innovative dance at the Flower Festival the week before. I saw her eyes—those strange eyes—take in my face, my robes, my jewels, until they finally fixated on the piece of pineapple at the end of my stick.

"What are you doing here?" I said.

She said nothing. Naturally, I assumed she was in awe of my magnificence and therefore too stunned to speak.

"You are the Messenger, are you not?" I said.

She nodded, slightly, still gazing at my pineapple in the same way the Speakers ogle a gold coin.

The Messengers are famous for their beauty, since that is one of the qualities that the Speakers take into account in the selection process. We'd had some ravishingly attractive Messengers in the past, but this one was somewhat disappointing. She was sickly and looked almost skeletal. The Speakers must not have had a good pool to select from this year.

"Do you know who I am?" I asked.

"You are the Anointed One?" she ventured, her voice sounding small and meek in the grand room. "The one that they call the half-god."

"That is true," I said, raising my noble chin. "You are fortunate to still be living after seeing me without my mask. You must have a strong spirit. By this time most people would be a pile of ashes." I thought it sounded believable, but she only raised her eyebrows weakly. I changed the subject. "You have a strange accent, girl. Where are you from?"

"An island you have never heard of," she said with a sigh.

"And what are you doing out of your tower?"

She said nothing, but only looked at my pineapple and sighed again.

"Why are you here?" I said impatiently. "Do you need something? We give the Messengers every luxury possible. Are you in need of something more?" As future king, I do my best to exercise civility with those who are destined to die.

Her lips pursed slightly, "Yes . . . I am in need of something."

"Well? What is it? I'm sure the servants can accommodate you and then you can go back to your tower to enjoy your last remaining months." Or was it weeks? I do lose track of time so easily.

Her eyes never left the fruit on my stick and her stomach rumbled so loudly even I could hear it. Embarrassed, she clutched her abdomen and looked at the ground. "I am hungry."

"Hungry?" I asked in disbelief, leaning forward and raising one eyebrow. "Do we not feed you three times a day with the best food in Zitól? Are you *really* hungry? Or just ungrateful? I don't think they even feed *me* as well as they feed the Messengers," I said bitterly.

As I said this, I noticed her protruding collarbones and the shadows that darkened her eyes and cheekbones. There was no doubt that she was altered since I had seen her dance at the Flower Festival, only a week before. Little did I know they were barely feeding her enough food to keep up the beating heart of a cockroach.

"Aren't they feeding you?" I asked, softer this time.

"No," she said.

"Here, then." I took some chunks of pineapple and tossed them. They splatted on the floor at her feet. She raised her head in surprise.

"For me?" she asked.

I nodded. She immediately scooped up the fruit in her hand, brushed off the dirt, and began to eat. The scene was so pitiful that I took the bowl and held it out to her. "Here," I said reluctantly, "have more." I'm not *completely* heartless.

She walked cautiously up the steps and took another wedge, but her eyes went back to the piece on my stick, warm and dripping with golden honey.

"Very well, have this too," I handed her the skewer. She took it and the bowl, walked back to the center of the floor, and ate. I watched with a frown as my snack disappeared before my eyes.

"Thank you," she sighed, after licking her fingers. "I feel a little better now." The floor beneath us vibrated. Through the walls, the sound of the drum began the death rhythm, when the sacrifice walks up the stairs to the pyramid. I knew every beat of the ceremony by heart; I had been to so many. Even through the walls we could hear the cheers of the people. The young woman closed her eyes and shook her head.

"Do those sounds trouble you, Messenger?"

"How could the sounds of death *not* trouble me?"

"Those are the sounds of *worship*. Don't you believe in the gods?"

"What gods?" she asked.

"The gods of the universe, of course. Do you mean to tell me that you do not believe in a higher power?" I could see her mind thinking about this.

"I believe in gods . . . but I do not think they would ever want people to be murdered for them."

I laughed. "They are not being murdered. They are being *sacrificed*. There is a healthy difference. Besides, *you* just feel that way because *you* were chosen as the sacrifice. Just keep reminding yourself that it is a great honor to be chosen. Think of the blessings you will have in the world to come. You should be grateful."

"This is something I was never taught," she said quietly, shaking her head. "It is something I am not accustomed to."

"You'll get accustomed to it, just like I have." I took a leisurely sip from my cup.

There was an uncomfortable silence. I wished she would go away, but she didn't, so I decided to hasten her departure. "Is there anything else you are in need of? Before you go?" I picked up my mirror again, examined my handsomely prominent nose and plucked a renegade nose hair.

"Yes, there is," she said, her face hopeful. "I would like to know what has happened to my friends. I want to know if they are all—"

I held up my hand before she finished. "I understand how you must feel, but I am afraid that I cannot help you. The city is massive and my connections with people of *that* class are limited. But perhaps I could make it up to you in another way. Is there anything else that you need? While I am feeling generous?" To avoid seeing the disappointment on her face I picked up my mirror and checked my teeth.

The girl was silent. When she spoke, the hope in her voice was gone. "I would like someone to talk to," she mumbled. "Or something . . . to do."

Although I didn't admit it, I understood her request. Being in a tower by yourself is the apex of tedium . . . though I had recently taught myself to juggle.

"Do you have any books?" she asked after a while, her face brightening. "I would like something to read."

The mirror slipped from my hands. It bumped onto the edge of the throne and crashed on the tile floor, making her jump.

"You . . . you can read?" I asked, astonished.

She bent down, picking up the shining, broken pieces.

"Leave it," I commanded. "I don't care about that. Tell me, where did you learn to read?" The question came out sharper than I meant it.

"On my island. My grandfather taught me. He lived in Zitól as a young man. He had this book—"

"I don't believe you," I said, glaring at her. "No one in Zitól has been able to read for centuries."

She looked at me, her face confused.

"I *can* read," she said calmly.

"Then prove it to me," I demanded. I stood and walked behind the throne where a rope with a large tassel at the bottom hung from the ceiling. I pulled the rope, and the curtains all along the walls began to part. They opened to reveal the bare stone walls that encircled the throne room. All along these walls, from ceiling to floor, were hieroglyphs, chiseled in the rock.

"Read these," I said.

The girl seemed startled at first, and then curiosity sparked in her eyes. Eagerly, she climbed the steps up to the rostrum, made her way around the priests' recliners, and ran her fingers along the walls. Envy trickled under my skin as she gazed at the pictures and her face seemed to illuminate with excitement. "I can't *believe* this," she murmured.

Her excitement was irritating, as if now she, too, was in on a secret. There were seven panels in all, but I was impatient and stopped her after three.

"That is enough," I said, snapping my fingers. "Come back down." She reluctantly walked back down the steps and stood before me. Her eyes were bright and shining.

"Well, what do they say?"

"They are the Seven Songs." She was so filled with emotion her voice squeaked.

"Well, *of course* they are," I retorted. "There is no reason to get emotional." I had no idea what the Seven Songs were.

"Why are they carved here?" she asked excitedly. "And why do you keep them covered up? They should be out where everyone can see them and read them."

"Because they are only for the Speakers to read and interpret," I said easily. After all, I had heard it said dozens of times.

"Well, that doesn't make any sense," said Rishi.

"It doesn't *have* to make sense," I snapped.

She didn't say anything to my terse remark, but only gazed at me steadily with her lips tightened.

"Go," I said. "Get back up to your tower. Our conversation is over." She didn't move.

"Go! And if I find you sneaking around again I will have you beheaded."

She turned and disappeared into the shadows.

CHAPTER 35

I Ask the Messenger a Favor

Other than the ball captain of the losing team, we don't normally behead people in Zitól. It was not the custom. Hearts are what the gods desired, and hearts are what we gave them. I remember the first time I stood at the top of the temple, the machete in my hand.

I watched the feathers on his headdress bob up and down as the sacrifice was led up the steps. Beads of sweat glistened on his blue skin. He would not look at me, but kept his eyes lowered. And when his headdress was removed and he was laid on the stone he continued to look past me, up at the black sky, tears seeping out of his wide, frightened eyes. His chin was trembling too. I remember that well, for I knew he was trying not to cry out. The drum beat in my ears like a hammer and rattled my ribcage. I felt as if I belonged to another world. It felt as if the hand that held the machete was not my own, and the arm that raised the knife in the sky was powered by some other force. Only when I heard his screams did I really feel connected to what I was doing.

I sacrificed many men after that until it became disgusting to me, and left the task to the Speakers, who never seemed to tire of it. I can't remember the faces of any of the others the way I remember that first man. I saw him when I closed my eyes at night; I saw him when I woke in the morning. And when I was truly being honest with myself, I saw him every time I looked in the mirror.

The next day I went to talk to Leema.

Leema was the meanest person I had ever known. As a young child her bent-up shape and troll face terrified me and I took great pains to avoid her. But by the time I was eighteen I had learned how (and how not) to approach the old crone and even looked forward to finding ways to irritate her, which I think she secretly enjoyed. No one liked her, but she was one of the few servants who wasn't afraid to look me in the eyes. That pleased me.

I also liked that Leema seemed to have the same distrust of the gods that I did. Except her distrust went even further than mine. I don't think she even believed gods existed at all.

From what I could gather, Leema worked at the palace for two reasons. The first was, like I said, she was as mean and ugly as a monkey and she kept the Messengers captive with her crankiness. The second was that she possessed a great talent.

No one could weave like Leema. She sat at her loom day after day outside the Messenger's tower, weaving the threads that were no thicker than spider silk. Because she was so meticulous about her weaving she only wove one special garment a year. And that one garment was the dress the Messenger wore to the water sacrifice.

I never understood why someone would want to take so much time and energy to make something that would just end up rotting underwater. But her skill was legendary. Those who missed the sacrifice would first ask not about the Messenger herself, but about what she wore.

But when I approached the tower, Leema was not outside weaving as usual. I stood outside the tapestry and called her.

There was no answer.

I took the tapestry in my hand and rattled the bells hard against the stone doorway.

"Good morning, Leema!" I said. "Where are you, oh gorgeous one?"

A moan came from within. I took that as an invitation. I opened the tapestry wide, letting the sunlight fill her cell, and stepped in.

The moment the light hit the old hag's bed she shrieked and then started into a fit of coughing.

"Who is here," she hacked, "disturbing da sleep ob a sick old woban?"

"It is I, dear princess. I've come to marry you and make you my queen."

Leaning up and squinting, she saw that it was me. She sank down into her bed and put her arms over her face. "Go away, you biserable boy," she said.

"I want to ask you a question."

"Get on wid it, den. Get on wid it. Den go away and leab me alone to die."

I sat down on a chair next to her bed.

"Die?" I said. "Well, I'm sorry to hear that. We'll all miss you."

"Ask your question, and den leab me alone."

"What have you been feeding the Messenger?"

Leema moved her arm off her sour, brown face and scowled at me. The sun was so bright she could hardly open her eyes. I could have moved my chair over a bit to block the sun's light but I didn't, just to be mean.

"She is nod allowed food," the woman sniffed.

"Why is that?" I asked.

"Because she offended Speaker Dungan."

"How? Was it because of what happened at the Flower Festival?"

"I do nod know, holy one. I just do as I'm dold."

"If someone told you to slit your wrists would you do as you were told?"

Leema glared. "If id was Speaker Dungan," she retorted.

"What if I did?" I asked.

"When you are king, Adoinded One, you can have me do whade-ver you like, bud undil then I only dake orders from da Speakers." Her coughing started again and I could see that I would not be getting any more information from her.

I left her room. I walked out to the cistern, filled a gourd with cool water, and returned, placing the water next to her bed. She would never say "thank you" to me, but her glance of gratitude was enough. Then I walked thoughtfully back to my tower. Leema was loyal, but not impenetrable. I knew her weakness, and I would deal with her later.

Everyone in the palace knew about Tungan's visits to the Messenger's tower, even Speaker Riplakish and Speaker Gula. His methods of persuasion eventually found success with most of the Messengers. I knew the objective of obtaining a virgin to speak to the gods seemed pointless if, by the time the sacrifice came around, she was no longer a virgin. Just another paradox of palace life, I supposed. Every now and then there would be one who was determined and resilient, but there never was one such as Rishi. I had watched as Leema brought her the usual gifts and offerings Speaker Tungan used to achieve his desires. I was there at the Flower Festival—the only festival I can tolerate because there are no sacrifices—when Tungan decided to take advantage of Rishi's close proximity. I watched the entire scene . . . It wasn't the first time that had happened. I'm always curious about how the Messengers react, and I had to admit that Rishi was the first to spill a Speaker's blood. I was so impressed that I had one of my servants retrieve the comb and I kept it as a souvenir.

Now, as I sat in my tower, I turned the gold comb over and over in my hands, thinking about this unusual woman. It was clear she needed food. She wanted someone to talk to. She wanted something to read. She wanted to know where her friends were.

A plan started to formulate in my mind. I could grant her all of those things, in exchange for something I desperately desired. Perhaps the Messenger and I could make a deal.

I spent the next day trying to figure out how to find audience with the Messenger without attracting suspicion. It was crucial that no one know my intentions, especially the Speakers.

The sun was slowly swallowed up by the horizon and the light from the sunset faded from the walls of my room. I paced back and forth, waiting for the sounds down below in the kitchen to die down, and for the Speakers to come home from their nightly romps in the city. Sleep did not tempt me, not with the opportunity that was holding out its open hand.

Finally, everything was quiet. Tonight the moon was full and brilliant, like a bowl of light. Lifting the tapestry, I could easily see across the blue courtyard to Rishi's tower, and I could hear Leema in her little room at the base of the Messenger's tower, snoring like a dog.

My only option was to climb the stairs to the second story of the palace, where the Speakers' chambers were, and then get onto the roof. The Messenger's tower was covered with thick vines, and perhaps from there I could climb up the tower to her balcony.

I slipped through the courtyard, clinging to the shadows and walls. I reached the stairway to the Speakers' chambers and climbed up to the top. Now was the hard part.

Using the face of a large stone jaguar that jutted out of the wall, I climbed up and onto the roof. The roof was made of thickly thatched palms, and each time I stepped I sunk into the roof and the twigs snapped noisily. After six tremendously loud, crunching steps I made it across to the vine-covered tower. I looked up. The Messenger's balcony was above me.

The vines were as thick as my forearm. I put my foot on one and tested it. It gave a little bit beneath my weight, but it held. Slowly, I climbed up through the leaves and branches, finding foot holds on the thickest vines. If I fell, I would go right through Speaker Gula's room, and *that* I did not want to do. Finally I could reach the windowsill with my hands. I pulled myself up enough that I could hook one leg over the railing and within moments I was standing in the Messenger's tower.

I cast my eyes around the chamber. I had never been in the Messenger's tower. In the dark it looked almost identical to mine.

I searched the room with my eyes, examining the shapes and shadows, looking for the sleeping Messenger among the many cushions and pillows. Her voice gave her away. With a jolt I thought she had seen me, but her words didn't make sense. I exhaled in relief when I realized she was only talking in her sleep.

I stepped softly, following the sound of her voice, and there, in the blue-gray shadows I saw her thin body draped over silken pillows with the moon shining on her face. Carefully, I sat so that I would not disturb her. She was having a vivid dream, and since I knew that waking someone from a dream resulted in bad luck, I sat there, patient, and while she dreamed, I studied her face.

I could tell it was a troubling dream. From time to time she would murmur incoherently and toss her head, her brows knit together in frustration. I had never witnessed anyone dreaming like this, and it was . . . amusing. This, of course, was before I understood the nature of Rishi's dreams. Had I understood then what I know now, I would not have been so amused.

After a few moments her features relaxed. Whatever the dream was, it seemed to be over. I moved my hands to wake her but stopped quickly, for her expression softened and a smile appeared on her face, making her almost look pretty. She softly laughed. Her eyelashes fluttered. She rubbed them with her hands and yawned, the smile still teasing the corner of her mouth. Then she opened her eyes, saw me, and screamed.

My hand silenced her mouth.

"Shhh," I whispered. "I'm not here to hurt you. I just want to talk with you."

Her eyes were wide and fearful and even in the dark, her one blue eye gave me the chills.

"Listen to me," I continued. "I am going to take my hand away from your mouth, but please, do not scream. I promise that it will be better for both of us if you just listen to what I have to say. Besides, I brought these." I showed her two sugar apples. "I have corn cakes too."

Upon seeing the apples her face relaxed and she nodded. I took my hand away from her mouth, slowly, just in case she decided to scream again. Then I gave her one apple.

"What are you doing here?" she said, rubbing the sleep from her eyes.

I smiled. "Just now I was watching you dream. Did you know you were laughing?"

"I—I was?" she said, startled. She looked down, as if reviewing the dream again in her mind. Then she lifted her head, her eyes narrowed. "How dare you sit there and watch me sleep."

"Listen," I said in my most pleasant voice, "Let's be friends. What is your name?"

"Yesterday you said you wanted to behead me and now you want to be *friends*?" she said, folding her arms.

"I'm sorry about that. I got frustrated. Would you like to know my name?" I asked.

"Not really," she said. "I would like you to leave me alone."

"That is not what you said in the throne room, if I recall it correctly. You said you wanted companionship, and here I am."

"I meant another *girl*. Not *you*, in the middle of the *night*, in my *room*," she said, wrapping her arms around her knees and pulling them to her chest.

"Messenger, I believe I have a solution to all your problems."

"You do? But why would *you* want to help *me*?"

I ignored her. "I have carefully considered your wishes. As I remember it, you wanted something to eat, you wanted books, and you wanted someone to talk to."

"And I want to know where my friends are," she added.

"Of course," I said. "Now, I have graciously given you food—*twice*—and I can give you the other things you desire if you would only hear what I have to say."

"You climbed into my tower in the middle of the night to tell me that?" she replied with suspicion. "Why couldn't you have just summoned me to the throne room like a normal royal person?"

I ignored her question. "In exchange for food and companionship, books, and information on your friends, I will require something in return," I paused as Rishi pressed her lips together. I could tell she was expecting the worse possible request. But she was going to die soon anyway. What could be worse than that?

"On the first night of each month, the Night of Sacrifices, I want you to come to my tower."

"No," she said firmly. She handed back the uneaten apple. She stood and walked away from me.

"Wait—I'm not finished."

"You don't have to finish. I know exactly what you want, and I will not let you touch me. You keep your slimy hands to yourself. I am not so desperate for activity or companionship or even *food* that I would make a bargain with you and give up my bead. Do you know what I have gone through to protect it? Do you know that it is the last thing I have that is really *mine*? Is that all you men can think about?"

"But I—"

"No, no, *no!*"

"Stop for a minute and listen to me," I said, grabbing her arm.

She glared up at me fiercely. "Release me," she commanded.

I didn't.

"I'll scream if you don't."

I released her. She turned her back to me and folded her arms.

"Listen," I said. "I don't want your stupid bead."

Slowly she turned and gaped at me, astonished. "You don't?" Lowering herself onto a cushion, she grabbed a pillow, hugged it under her chin and frowned. "Why not?"

"I don't care about your virtue," I said. "I don't care if you keep it, and I don't care if you lose it. It means nothing to me."

She looked at me as if I had just crushed a hummingbird.

"Listen," I said, trying to be patient. "You *must* come to my tower . . . because . . . I need . . ." I took a deep breath. "I need you to teach me how to read."

"You want me to teach you to *read*?"

"Yes. Because . . ." I paced for a moment, wondering if I should let her know everything. She watched me intently.

"Because . . . once I know how to read then I can kill the Speakers."

CHAPTER 36

My Secret Plan to Rule the World

Y ou want to *what?*"
I repeated myself again very slowly so she could understand.
"I—want—to—kill—the—Speakers."

Now she looked at me as if I had just crushed a hummingbird and eaten it.

I sat down on a large pillow and rubbed my face with my hands. She had no idea how complicated this was.

"All right. I will explain," I began. "First you must understand that the only reason I am going to tell you what I am going tell you is because you are unable to speak to anyone else and before long you will be dead anyway."

"Um . . . thank you," she said.

I scratched my head and thought of where to begin.

"I . . . I am not half-god."

She didn't seem shocked. "Why do they say that about you then?"

"To intimidate people. To them I am all-powerful and divine. Everyone fears me. And what people fear, they respect."

"I see," she said, weighing this last statement.

"Even though I am the Anointed One, the one who is to become king one day, the most powerful ruler in the *known world*, even though I am so *important*, so *revered*, why don't I ever *speak* to anyone?"

Rishi shrugged. "I don't know."

"Tell me, Messenger, have you ever seen me make any decisions? Have you ever seen me enter the throne room when court is in session? Have you ever seen me do anything besides hide behind masks and attend a festival twice a year?"

Rishi knit her eyebrows. "I haven't been here very long."

"No, you haven't. Maybe," I cracked my knuckles, "maybe I should start at the *very* beginning. Here. Eat this so you don't interrupt me." I gave her back the apple and then stood up and walked toward the balcony.

The whole city was quiet and the moon lit the tops of the temples so they had a dull sheen, like opaque glass. Somewhere a dog barked. I heard her bite into the apple. I turned. She was sitting on a cushion, chewing and looking up at me with those huge, strange eyes.

"My name is Nadal. The king before me had no sons, and left no heir. But before he died, he told the people his heir would be found in the first infant that was born after his death. When he died they searched the city and found me."

"What about your family?" she asked, taking another bite of the apple.

"I only had a mother, and she came with me, to take care of me, and she lived at the palace. But she died when I was very young. I became the Speakers' responsibility then. They called me the Anointed One and wouldn't let anyone outside the palace see me. In the meantime, they have been acting as my regents, making all decisions for me. The Speakers used to tell me when I was a child, 'When you are sixteen you will give your first speech to the people.' Or, 'We are only guardians of your throne until you are able to rule. Be patient, and your turn will come.' Well, you know what? I'm sick of being patient!" I shouted.

"Shhh," Rishi said.

"I'm sick of being patient," I whispered. "I should have seen them for what they were, but I was too young. And they indulged me. They were very permissive. I had no worries, no problems. I could do anything I wanted, have anything I wanted. I thought this was what it meant to be ruler. When I did turn sixteen they told me I was not yet ready. I was frustrated and spent my time in idleness, sometimes getting into mischief. The Speakers always talked about teaching me this or teaching me that, but all they wanted to do was eat and lounge in their bedrooms with women from the city. I had no one to teach me anything. As I grew older I realized that if I were to be ready like the Speakers said, I would need to *know* something. I needed an education, training, something that would make me credible in the eyes of the people. I would ask them, 'What do I need to learn so that when I am eighteen I will be ready to rule?' But they never had the desire or energy to educate me. They did let me officiate in some of the sacrifices, but always at night, wearing a mask, and I was not allowed to speak. At first this was thrilling. For the first time in my life I felt power over something. I was sure I was about to take the reins of the kingdom, and I confronted the Speakers about it. I told them, 'It is time for me to assume my throne.' But they wouldn't listen. They laughed at me. They asked me, 'Do you know the ancient writings? Do you know the history of the gods? Do you know how to read the symbols in the night sky? How can you assume power when you know nothing?'"

I was pacing back and forth in front of Rishi, my hands waving around as I spoke.

"Are you going to eat those yourself?" she asked, pointing to the corn cakes I had brought. I handed them to her.

"Of course they were right," I continued. "I felt like an idiot. I finally realized that all the freedom the Speakers gave me as a child had been my undoing. They had purposely neglected teaching me anything that would give me any advantage over them. Without being able to read I was powerless."

"Couldn't you learn from someone else?" she said with her mouth full.

I shook my head. "Messenger, I don't know what it is like where you come from, but in Zitól, no one is allowed to read except for the Speakers."

"Yes, I was told that at the banquet," Rishi murmured.

"They say it is because only those that are holy are allowed to read the sacred writings written in the stone."

"You mean the stone walls in the throne room?"

"Not just those, all the stones, all over the city. There is writing everywhere. A long time ago everyone could read, but teaching people to read was done away with years ago at the time of the Great Coward."

"The Great Coward," she said, licking her fingers. "Who is he?"

"Where are you from, the moon?"

"Don't be silly. Are you going to eat that other—?"

"Sugar apple? Here." I tossed her the apple. "Centuries ago there was a man who was called to be sacrificed at the temple. I know you don't understand what a great honor this is. They took him to the temple to be sacrificed, but instead he escaped and fled."

"Of course he did. He was about to be killed!"

I stopped pacing and stared at her. "Refusing to be sacrificed is an unforgivable sin against the gods."

"To *your* gods, remember?" she said with her mouth full. She swallowed. "My gods don't sacrifice people."

"You say you don't believe in sacrifice, yet you seem willing enough."

Rishi looked down. "It is complicated."

I said nothing and waited for more of an explanation.

"I . . . I . . . have had a lot of time to think about this," she began. "I am to blame for a great tragedy on my island. I have tried to think of a way to redeem myself. I decided that by sacrificing myself I can at least show the gods the depth of my remorse, and perhaps my people will forgive me."

"See? You have a debt to pay! You want to redeem yourself! You are to blame for an unforgivable tragedy! Those are all excellent reasons to be sacrificed. I wish all of our sacrifices had your positive attitude. Now, what was I saying?"

"The man who fled because he was only trying to save his life."

"Oh, yes. The Speakers called him the Great Coward and his rebelliousness caused unrest for months. His supporters wanted to tear down the temples and stop giving sacrifices. But the gods were angry and demanded more sacrifices."

"How did the people know the gods wanted more sacrifices?" she interjected.

"Because the gods told the Speakers and the Speakers told the people."

"Ooooohhhh," she said, giving a slow nod. For some reason I got the feeling that she didn't believe a word I was saying.

"So now we have a temple sacrifice every month of the year, and every spring equinox we have a water sacrifice."

"Which this year is me."

"Precisely."

"But I still don't understand why it is that people aren't allowed to read."

"Well, it gets confusing when many people have information. The Great Coward and his followers read the same words as the Speakers, but they interpreted them in a different way. So it was decided that no one would be taught to read, so that there would only be one interpretation of the writings." I crouched down next to her and lowered my voice. "I have made plans," I said. "I am going to poison them, in small amounts in their food. It will seem as though they just got sick. When the Speakers are dead, the people will naturally turn to me for authority. But I know that there is no way I can retain the throne without being able to read. In Zitól, he who reads, rules. Knowledge is power, Messenger. Take it from one who's spent his life in the dark. I can't even *think* about being king until I know how to read," I paused and then added, with emphasis so that she could not misinterpret, "and *you* will teach me how."

Rishi frowned. "I do not want to teach you to read if it means you will use that knowledge to take lives."

"Only three lives. Three *worthless* lives. You must agree that they are detestable leaders."

"And you will be better?" she said, arching one eyebrow.

"I am not asking your opinion," I snapped. Then I chastened myself. If I was going to get her to cooperate, I had to be nice. I took a deep breath. "Listen. I will give you want you want. You will have food. You will have books. I know where there are lots of books." I saw her eyes sparkle. "And you will have someone to talk to. Me." She frowned. "And we will do it the first night of every month in my tower when everyone leaves to attend the sacrifices."

"No. Not in your tower."

"Fine. In the throne room, then. That way you will not be able to hear the sacrifices as well."

She studied me for a long time. Finally she said, "How will I get out of my tower? Leema doesn't go anywhere."

"Leave that to me."

"There is one thing you forgot."

"What is that?"

"My friends. I want to know where they are, and if they are alive."

"Of course they are alive."

"There are four of them, and I want to know that they are safe."

"I will do my best to verify that for you, but I cannot promise you anything."

"I only ask you to try."

"You have my promise. It is agreed, then? You will teach me?"

She looked at me for a long time. "Yes," she said finally. "I will teach you to read."

CHAPTER 37

Leema's Great Weakness

Leema had recovered from her illness and had started weaving again. Her favorite place to set up her loom was in the sun, just outside her tower door. Because of her sickness, she hadn't progressed far on the Messenger's dress; it was only scarf-size. I stood in the shade, leaning against a wall, and watched her weave, trying to decide on the right words to open our conversation. (She responded the best to outright insults.) I had a theory brewing inside my brain as to why she was so grumpy, especially on the Night of Sacrifices. If my hunch was correct, then the Messenger and I would be in luck. At least it was worth a try. I abandoned my spot in the shade and walked toward Leema.

"I see Tungan hasn't asked you to slit your wrists yet," I said pleasantly.

Leema didn't even look up from her weaving. "Not yet," she said. "What do you want, Monkey Dung?" Ah, Leema. How sweet she was to me.

"I just wanted you to know that the gods visited me in my bedroom last night."

"That so? And what did they say to you?"

"They told me to tell you that you better start feeding the Messenger or they will afflict you with skin boils." As I said that I glanced at her skin and grimaced. Perhaps she already was afflicted with skin boils. I should have used a different threat.

She seemed unaffected. "Well, they visited me in my bedroom too. They told me to tell you to take a big leap out of the top of your tower and see if you can fly." She still hadn't made eye contact with me. "Why do *you* care what the Messenger eats, Anointed One? You never cared before."

I shrugged. "I just want to make sure everyone in my kingdom is happy and well taken care of . . . including you, lovely Leema."

"Humph."

"Aren't you happy?"

"I would be if you'd leave me alone."

"I don't think so. I think that would make you miserable. You like talking to me, Leema. Admit it."

"Go away, pest."

"Leema, you've got a problem."

"Yes I do. He's got black hair, a really big head, and he's standing right in front of me."

"No, you have a problem and it is deep down in your soul. It is what makes you so bitter all the time. You don't know what it is, but I do."

"I'm dying to hear what you know about my soul."

"You've spent every night here at the Messenger's tower for the last—how many years?"

"Longer than you've been alive," she said bitterly, shoving the shuttle back and forth through the strings.

"Very well, we'll say twenty. You've spent the last twenty years here, weaving. And how many times have you been able to go to the Night of Sacrifices?"

Finally Leema stopped weaving and looked up.

"That is what I thought. Zero."

She frowned. "Are you trying to make me cry?"

"You have wanted for years to go watch the sacrifices, haven't you?"

"You know nothing about what I want," she said, and started moving the shuttle again, back and forth, and then taking a flat wedge to push the threads together with more force than was probably necessary.

"I can go to the sacrifices whenever I want. They are *thrilling*, Leema. Not a dull moment. Sometimes up on the temple there is so much blood spilled on the ground my sandals stick to the stone." I watched for her reaction.

She rested the shuttle on her weaving and stared up at me. "Why are you telling me this? What does this have to do with the Messenger?"

"I want to make a deal with you."

"What kind of deal?"

"You promise to feed the Messenger more food. It doesn't have to be much—just more than what she is getting now, and a greater variety."

"You mean go against Tungan's orders."

"Remember, the *gods* told me to tell you this."

"Of *course*," she said slowly, her voice heavy with sarcasm. "And what will you do for me?"

"I will guard the Messenger each month on the Night of Sacrifices so that you can go and watch."

Leema's black eyes glittered. I had broken through.

"You will not allow her to escape?" she asked, narrowing her eyes.

I put my hand on my heart. "She will not escape on my watch."

"And all I have to do is feed her more?"

"Yes. Feed her more. We don't want the Messenger dying before her time, do we? The gods would not like that."

Leema started weaving again. "No, you have a point," she said, looking up at me and smiling her endearing rodent smile, "the gods would not like that."

CHAPTER 38

Reading Lessons

The weeks crawled by.

Finally it was the first day of the month of the Serpent. I had two books in my tower that I had "borrowed" from the Speakers' library that I often flipped through, trying to teach myself the characters. I figured out some, but most of the words were a mystery to me. Now, as I looked at the characters I felt restless anticipation. Soon this jumble of pictures would make sense.

That evening, a meal of fish, fresh peppers, roasted potatoes, and a bowl of berries drizzled with agave nectar was brought to my room. I picked over the food, deciding what I would eat and what I would save for the Messenger. At first I set aside the berries and the fish for her, but then I noticed how red and ripe the berries were. I had never seen berries so bulging with juices . . . and then it struck me that they would only be in season for a little longer. The fish also looked extraordinarily fresh and succulent with its perfectly cooked, white, juicy meat. Taking into account all of these things, I reconsidered. After all, if she is so *very* hungry, she probably doesn't care what she eats as long as it is food. So I ate the berries and the fish myself and reserved the potatoes and the peppers for her in a small bowl. But an hour later I was still hungry and I ate the potatoes. Now all I had left were the red peppers, but I firmly abstained. For the sake of the Messenger I was *absolutely determined* not to eat these, for she was clearly in need of nourishment. I considered for a moment if they might be too spicy for her (which, in all honesty, is the main reason I didn't want to eat them), but I felt like the appealing color and crispness would make up for any other fault she might find in the fruit.

I put the peppers in a bowl, and luckily, after foraging around my room, I also discovered a bowl of forgotten cantaloupe slices. Two days ago this cantaloupe was juicy and supple and melted in my mouth. I couldn't finish it all so I left it for later. Now flies were buzzing around it. I sniffed it. I inspected it thoroughly. Once I was fairly certain that there was no mold or fly larva in it, I took the cantaloupe, artfully arranged it with the peppers, and waited for night to come. When I could hear the drumbeat of the first sacrifice, I tucked the books under my arm, grabbed the bowl, and made my way to the throne room.

I arrived first and lit the torches. I put the books on the throne, sat on the steps, placing the bowl on the small table next to me, and began tapping my foot. Finally I heard the door creak and footsteps climb the stairs. Rishi appeared out from behind the curtain like the moon emerging from a cloud.

"Welcome, Messenger," I said.

"I am here, Anointed One," she said, bowing her head. When she saw the bowl of colorful fruit she smiled.

"Did you have any trouble with Leema?"

She shook her head. "She practically threw me out."

"Has she been bringing you more food?"

"Do fish heads and potato peels count?" she asked. Then she looked down. "I'm sorry. I don't mean to sound ungrateful. Did you . . . did you find out about my friends?"

"I am working on that," I lied. "It isn't as easy as it seems to get out of the palace, you know."

Her face slid into the saddest expression I had ever seen. "Don't worry," I added quickly. "It might take some time. You just need to be patient. Come sit down. I have something to show you."

We sat close together on the steps, and I opened one of the large folio books and rested it on our laps. It was hard to decide if Rishi was more eager for the book or for the food, for she devoured both with equal enthusiasm. With each bite she became more animated. She pointed to characters, telling me what they meant and how they fit in with the rest of the text. It turned out I had brought a book about commerce and trading. She taught me how the numbers worked, and what the characters were for certain valuable commodities like corn, jade, gold, and cacao beans. After a while we had to move on to the next book, for this one, she said, was making her too hungry.

She picked up a red pepper and opened up the second book.

This book was a series of lists of occupations in the city, and I learned words like butcher, ring maker, weaver, cook, slave, priest, and king.

"What is the symbol for 'messenger'?" I asked as I watched her crunch into the pepper. I waited politely for her to finish chewing.

She started to answer, but instead her hand came to her mouth. Her eyes grew wide and her nostrils flared. She chewed quickly and, with great effort, swallowed.

"Are you all right?"

She nodded briskly, her eyes beginning to water. "The symbol for 'messenger' is . . . " She stopped speaking and instead started blowing air out her pursed lips.

"Yes?" I asked with a smile.

"Hahh—hahh—haaaaht," she panted, waving her hand in front of her face.

I copied her. "This is the sign for 'messenger'? Hand-waving-over-face? How is that written?"

She closed her eyes and shook her head. When she opened her eyes again they were brimming with tears. She pointed to the bowl and choked out the words, "What *are* those things?"

"They are red peppers," I said. Then after a pause I narrowed my eyes. "Don't you like them? I could take them away, if you want."

"Yes—yes—I mean *no*," she said. "Don't take them away. I like them. I *love* them. Thank you. Very . . . juicy." And to prove it, she took another hearty bite.

She turned her focus back to the book, all the while blinking away tears and wiping her face with her sleeve. After swallowing, she exhaled her air in rapid puffs that bounced off the book and into my face. Her breath was *tremendous*. Those peppers must have been hotter than I thought. I had been wise to pass them on.

Yet she continued to eat them. After a while she took one hand, grabbed her opposite shoulder, buried her face in the crook of her arm, and started to hyperventilate. "Are you sure you are all right?" I said with concern. "You seem to be having trouble."

"Yes," she squeaked. "Just give me a moment."

So I waited.

After a while she raised her head and asked, "What were we learning about?"

"The sign for the Messenger," I said.

She flipped through the pages of the book, saying "hah, hah, haaaht" every other page, while she searched for the sign. Giving up, she scooted away from me, wet her finger, and drew on the stone step between us. The sign for "messenger" was an opened mouth. Inside the mouth was a small star.

"The star means 'truth' or 'intelligence,'" she said. "When it is written inside the mouth it becomes 'messenger.'" She placed her hand on her chest and took a deep breath. Then, to my everlasting admiration, she bit into yet another pepper.

I learned all I could that first night. Then I had her review everything with me twice. Finally, when the bowl was empty and Rishi could barely hold her eyes open, I allowed her to go. The others would be coming back soon, anyway; it had started to rain.

After she left, I chuckled softly to myself as I extinguished the torches. If I could be *half* as determined as the Messenger, I would know how to read in no time at all.

I took the books back to my tower, where I lit a candle and continued to pore over them, hearing Rishi's voice in my head, explaining each symbol. By the time the rain stopped and the birds started their noisy morning chatter I was asleep, my face pressed against the precious words.

I continued to review the characters she'd taught me throughout the next month. Finally, when it was time for us to meet again, I reserved a loaf of stale bread (I tore off the moldy parts) and some tomatoes for her meal.

"Did you find out about my friends?" It was the first thing she said to me.

"I will," I said. "Don't worry."

I brought two new books and we studied until our eyes burned and our brains ached. When we were finished she gave me an assignment. The assignment was to walk the courtyard and look at the stone carvings above the palace's tapestry doors.

As soon as I woke up the following day, I threw on my clothes and headed down to the courtyard. The ground was wet and the morning air was rain-fresh. I was pleasantly thrilled to see that above the kitchen it said "Kitchen." The words above the bathhouse said "Bathhouse." The words above the throne room said "Throne Room." This may not seem astonishing to you, but for me it was very exciting. I smiled when I saw that the words above the tapestry on my tower said "King." As I made my way around the courtyard I passed the Messenger's tower. Leema was sitting outside weaving Rishi's dress. I watched her weave for a while, admiring her work and her quick fingers. I was surprised to see that the dress was nearly halfway finished. I felt a small, uncomfortable stirring in my stomach as I looked at the fabric, knowing its ultimate purpose and the destiny of its wearer. But I pushed the feeling away before it could affect my optimistic mood.

Just before turning to leave, I looked above the tapestry door, expecting to see the symbol of the star inside the mouth, the word for "messenger." But it wasn't there. Instead there was a different word. It was a picture of several stars, and below the stars, two arms outstretched. This was puzzling. I stood looking at this for a long time, trying to guess the meaning myself until Leema told me I was annoying her and to *go away.*

There is a special corridor that the Speakers used when they didn't want to attract the attention of the public. The corridor led to several key locations outside the palace including the ball court, the treasury, and the house of concubines.

I didn't want to see Rishi disappointed again, so I watched for a night when I knew that the Speakers had been hosting their consorts. When the music faded and lights died down I put on my brown cape.

I hid in the shadows near the gate of the corridor, knowing that the women would eventually have to pass that way to return to their own apartments, and waited for a very long time. Just when the sky was starting to lighten and I was about to give up and go back to my tower, I heard voices coming from the palace courtyard. Three uncloaked figures moved across the courtyard, heading straight for the gate. I flattened myself into the alcove and watched as they passed: three young women, one of them crying.

"Be strong, Sepya," one was saying to the other. "This can't last forever."

They continued to whisper softly as they passed and I saw the dark beads hanging from their waists, confirming their royal position as consorts to the priests and Speakers. I let them walk a few paces before I slipped out from my hiding place. Keeping some distance between us, I followed them down the corridor. My foot kicked a pebble and one of them stopped. I smeared myself against the wall, trying to melt into the shadows.

"Are you coming, Lantana?"

The woman who stopped looked straight in my direction and whispered, "Venay, I think I heard something."

They huddled together and whispered to each other, while I held my breath. I might have been able to hear what they were saying had my heart not filled my head with its drumming.

Then, all of the sudden, they took off in a run.

"Wait!" I said, trying not to disturb the early morning peace. "Come back!" The last thing I wanted was the Speakers finding out that I had accosted their concubines in the night.

They did not stop, however, so I had no choice but to pursue. It did not take me long to catch up with the slowest one, for she couldn't run well, and I grabbed her and held her.

"Don't be afraid," I said as she struggled against me. "I don't want to hurt—"

All of the sudden my cape was flung over my head and someone grabbed me by the neck. I let go of the woman in surprise, only to have a fist jammed into my stomach and a foot kicked in the back of my knees. I lost my balance and fell to the ground. Swiftly my arms were pinned down on each side of me, and then, without warning, a whale sat on my chest.

"I can't breathe!" I said through the fabric.

The cape was lifted off my head and cool air was once again flowing through my lungs.

"Who are you and why are you following us?" said the woman on my chest.

"Are you the girls from the islands?" I croaked. "The newest ones that came with the current Messenger?"

The woman glanced at her two companions, who were each holding down my arms. Then she looked at me again, her moon-shaped eyes like slits. "Why are you interested in those girls?"

"I just wanted to ask them something."

"Who are you?"

I had not anticipated this question. "I am . . . a cook. I work in the kitchen. I bring food to the Messenger. She sent me out to find her island sisters."

"What is the Messenger's name?"

"Rishi."

My captors relaxed. "What do you know about her?" they asked. "Is she all right?"

"I can tell you after you get off of me," I croaked.

The girls moved away and after my lungs had returned to their normal shape I struggled to my feet.

"What are your names?" I said, as I straightened my cape and dusted myself off.

"I am Venay," said the one who had been sitting on me. "And this is Lantana and Sepya."

"But there should be four of you," I said.

Venay frowned. "Isra was sold to a different house. We have not seen her since the Test of the Jaguar."

"Tell us what you know about Rishi," Lantana said. "Is she all right?"

"Rishi is fine. She has everything she needs and is very content," I lied.

"Is it true that she is going to be sacrificed into the cenote at the end of the year?"

"Yes, it is true."

They were silent.

"You are all doing well, are you not? You have plenty to eat? You have a good place to stay? You are . . . happy?" They glanced at each other, their eyes loaded with meaning that I couldn't decipher.

"They fill our stomachs," Lantana said, "but our hearts are as hollow as drums."

"We are nothing more than slaves," said Sepya, her eyes starting to brim with tears.

Venay put her arm around her friend. "We are worse than slaves," she said.

I have never been good with words of comfort, but I tried to put things in perspective for them.

"At least you won't have to die, like the Messenger. And you get to work in the palace. There are worse places to live."

The girls' expressions became dull at my words. One of them put her hand on my arm.

"Give her a message from us," she said. "Tell her that she is the fortunate one."

"Tell Rishi that we hope for the best for her. Tell her that she will always be our sister and that we are glad her fate is better than ours."

"Tell her to be strong."

"And tell her," said Lantana, "that there are worse things than dying."

CHAPTER 39
Religious Differences

I didn't tell Rishi any of those things, of course. But I did reassure her that her friends were alive and safe, which, after all, was the main part of the bargain, for she said nothing about inquiring after their level of happiness. I felt that if I told her any more than what she requested it might create needless anxiety, and being as she had enough to worry about, I felt I was rather merciful keeping some of the information to myself.

As we continued to meet, I became less stingy with my food, sometimes bringing enough so she could take some back to her tower to supplement the increased portions that Leema was giving her. Within time, the dark circles under her eyes disappeared, color came into her cheeks, and her arms became soft and round like a woman's arms should be. Gradually she seemed less wary and I became less cynical. Once she marveled at how much I had studied and retained since our last lesson. Another time she said she was impressed at how quickly I learned. Her praise was like water on a withered plant and it made me want to work even harder, just to please her. I made lists of questions in my mind to ask her at our next lesson. I wanted to learn more just to hear her say that she was impressed, again and again.

The only thing that distracted me during my lessons was Rishi herself. Like the time she looked up at the ceiling, trying to remember the word for a particular character, and I let my eyes slowly pass down her neck. Or the first time I made her laugh and saw her smile a *real* smile, not just the suspicious smiles she used around Speaker Tungan.

Her bead was also a distraction. Sometimes I caught myself looking at it while it rested between us. I wanted to touch it, to feel how smooth it was in my hands, but I didn't dare. I felt as if something might happen if I touched it, as if it had power. So I left it alone. But after my encounter with her friends in the corridor, her bead made me even more curious. What was it about the bead that made it so vital to keep?

"So why do you have to wear that bead all the time?" I asked one night.

Her finger was going down a page in a book. "It means I'm a virgin," she said, turning to the next page.

"I know that. But couldn't you be a virgin and not wear it?"

"Yes, but it is a symbol. I wear it so other people will respect my virtue." She turned another page.

"Do the women from your island wear them their entire lives? I mean, what happens when a woman is not a virgin anymore? Does she still wear the white bead? What happens when a man takes it?"

She shut the book with a *thwap!*

"Did I say something wrong?"

"On my island no one *takes* a girl's white bead. She *gives* it. She gives it to her husband, and he replaces it with a blue bead."

"Oh, I see. She gets married. Well, even if you weren't going to be sacrificed you still would never get a blue bead here. No one in Zitól gets married anymore."

"Why not?"

"Marriage is too binding."

She seemed surprised. "I would think that people who were in love would want to be bound to each other."

"Well, yes, of course. Until they became tired of one another."

She shook her head and opened the book again. "All the more reason for marriage to be binding. Marriage is a lot more than just two people being in love. Shall we continue with the lesson?"

"Wait. Did you just say that marriage is more than two people being in love?" I was surprised. It wasn't like a girl to take the romance out of it.

She went on. "Well, *of course* it is about loving someone. But it is more than that, because it affects so many others. By being virtuous I bring honor to my parents, respect to myself, and protection to the next generation."

I chewed on this for a moment while Rishi went back to examining the characters in the book. She had a point. Except that here in Zitól we had taken care of the "next generation" problem.

"Since we are asking nosy questions," she said, abruptly closing the book and turning toward me, "why do you wear masks every time you go out in public?"

I shrugged. "It's my job."

"Don't you want people to see who you really are?"

"'Anonymity gives you power,'" I quoted dutifully.

"And you don't go to the Night of the Sacrifices. Why not?"

"I've been. Plenty of times. They are all the same. Loud, bloody . . . and they don't need me. I get in the way. Besides I don't like it."

"Why?"

The memory of that first sacrifice reappeared in my head. "I just don't like the way it makes me . . . feel."

She shrugged. "Then maybe it isn't right."

She was beginning to get on my nerves. "Who made you the authority on right and wrong?" I asked.

"I'm not an authority. But I can feel it inside, just like you can. Some things feel good. Some things feel bad."

"I can think of a lot of things that feel good," I said with a wicked grin. "For instance—"

"Let me rephrase that," she said, cutting me off. "Doing something that feels *good* isn't the same thing as doing something that feels *right*." She held up corn cake and smiled mischievously. "I could smash this into your face right now and it would feel good. But it wouldn't feel *right*. Just like laying people on altars against their will and pulling their hearts out doesn't feel *right*."

"It is terrifying, I agree," I said. "But we are *commanded* to sacrifice. It is written in stone. Everyone knows that the gods require us to do that which is difficult. Could there be anything more difficult than giving up one's life? Just because something doesn't feel right to *you* doesn't mean other people don't feel right about it. We do what we believe is right. When we do, we have the blessing of the gods. If the gods tell you to do something, you must do it, no matter how you feel."

"But how do you *know* it is right?"

"I told you. Because it is written in stone."

She studied me closely, as if she were deciding whether or not to say something. Finally she said, "I was always taught that the gods love us like children, and they want us to be virtuous because they know that ultimately it will make us and the people around us happier."

"Of course you believe that," I said. "You are from a backward, primitive island, and consequently have backward, primitive beliefs."

Her eyes flashed. "And *you* come from a prideful, wicked society and your rituals exist to satisfy your own barbaric entertainment. The people I saw in the plaza weren't being obedient and religious. They were *insane*. The only person who was *really* sacrificing something was covered in blue paint, and *he* didn't seem enthusiastic."

I lifted my chin. "That man was noble and brave."

"At least *that* is something we can both agree upon," she said. "But there is no way that your gods and my gods can exist together in the same world."

"It appears that way," I said coldly.

"So that means only one of us is correct."

"Precisely."

"Which means we should not be arguing over which of us is right and which of us is wrong, instead we should *both* be searching for whatever is *true*."

I opened my mouth to speak but nothing came. Her words reached deep, for to me truth had always been like a beautiful bird, something so desirable yet always flying away. I folded my arms across my chest and sulked for a few moments, trying to appear unfazed. Then I had an epiphany. "I can *prove* my gods are the true gods," I said with fresh confidence. "How do you explain the fact that rain always falls from the sky after a sacrifice?"

She took a bite from the last corn cake and chewed thoughtfully. "That used to bother me at first, but I've had a lot of time to think about it."

"And?" I asked as she swallowed.

"The gods are not sending rain to reward your obedience. They are weeping over your mistakes."

CHAPTER 40
The Golden Comb Reappears

Rishi wasn't like the smoky-eyed women in the city with whom I was acquainted. I always had the feeling that they knew their worth to me was in the way they moved, the way their eyes were painted, and the amount of skin they could reveal. They laughed at all my jokes and agreed with everything I said. But not Rishi . . . She rarely agreed with me about anything. For some reason that made me like her more. And though she was as stubborn as the Speakers, she wasn't demeaning like them.

Despite our disagreements, I will never forget those nights when it was just Rishi and me, leaning over the books, watching her finger slide across the pages and bringing my brain to life. It was as if my mind was finally waking after years of deep sleep. Every now and then we would hear the muffled roar of the crowds down at the temples and she would stop speaking for a moment and sigh. She never learned to tune that out as I had.

I was learning so quickly that sometimes we spent the time just talking. She would tell me about her island. I had her describe the ocean to me several times, for it seemed so unbelievable that there could be so much water in the world. Rishi had a way of telling stories that could make me feel the spray of the surf on my face and the warmth of the sand, white as salt under my feet. I liked to hear stories of her brothers, for they seemed a little like me, and when she spoke of her grandfather I could tell she had a great respect for him, unlike the feelings I had for my own mentors.

When she spoke of her home and her family, her face became radiant. I had never wondered before about where the Messengers came from, or what had to take place in order for them to be "snatched" and brought against their will to Zitól. When she spoke of her island sisters I tried not to remember the things they had told me in the corridor or the look of hopelessness in their eyes. In the end I always had to remind myself that I shouldn't get too interested in her life, since she would, after all, be dead in a matter of months. But the more I saw her and the more I listened to her speak, the more I thought I might actually miss her when she was gone. She was more interesting than the Speakers, and much more pleasing to look upon.

Sometimes we didn't even open the books I had brought, but ate and laughed. Or cried . . . like the night I brought her bean soup and tamales and she told me about her abduction and how her brothers had given their lives to save her.

"Are you sure they died?" I asked, patting her back as her tears and other facial fluids soaked my shoulder.

She sniffed loudly. "For a while I thought they might have survived, but if they were alive I am sure they would have come for me. But they have not come for me, which means . . ." And then she erupted again into inconsolable sobbing.

This created a bit of a conundrum for me, being both her confidant and captor. What this situation needed was a change of subject. I looked around at the fruit I had brought that evening and grabbed three sugar apples.

Moving to my feet I said, "Do you want to see a trick?"

She wiped her tears away and sniffed.

"I'll take that as a yes." I began juggling the apples. Out of the corner of my eye I could see her watching me. She didn't seem impressed enough.

"Toss me something," I said. She looked around and tossed me another apple, and without stopping I added it to the spinning circle.

"Well done!" she said, wiping her tears.

I stopped juggling, catching each fruit without letting one fall to the ground. I bowed as Rishi applauded.

"That was wonderful! You are just like the jugglers at the Flower Festival."

"Not quite as good as them," I admitted. "They juggle fire."

She gazed at me thoughtfully. "Why is it that the Speakers do not want you to have any power?" she asked. "You are obviously talented."

I laughed. "Juggling does not qualify you to be king. If that were the case there are a half dozen men in the city who would sit on the throne before I would."

"No," Rishi said, her eyes shining. "I don't mean the juggling. I mean you are intelligent. You learn quickly. I would think they would *want* someone like you to be the ruler."

Her unexpected praise surprised me, and I did not know what to say. She leaned her head to the side, watching me and tapping her finger on her lips. "Perhaps that is why they will not let you take power."

"What do you mean?"

"Because you are smarter than they expected, and they are afraid."

I laughed and sat down next to her. No one had ever said anything like this to me before. I was shocked yet flattered, proud but uncomfortable. To mask my sudden embarrassment I took one of the sugar apples and pried it open.

"Here, have some. This one is very sweet, and I took out all the seeds." I gave her half of the apple.

She ate thoughtfully and then said, "Why do the Speakers hide the Seven Songs?"

I shrugged. "Because they are so sacred, I suppose."

"But your Speakers never even speak of them. They know them, but they do not teach them. Instead they tell the people, 'Let your instincts make your decisions. Follow the pleasures of your body, and as long as it doesn't interfere with the public peace it is acceptable,'" she said, imitating Gula's voice and accent.

I smiled. "What is wrong with that?"

"It is not your body that should control your choices; it is your mind."

"I still don't see how denying yourself something your body craves can be good. That is unhealthy."

"No, that is *self-control*. Withholding anything from your body that it desires creates self-discipline, and that is what makes one more pure. It is good from time to time to withhold something that your body yearns for; it shows you have power over yourself. It shows the strength of your spirit. Like having the discipline to wake up early in the morning when you could sleep all day. Or showing mercy to someone who has wronged you, or even something as simple as being in possession of a delicious sugar apple and giving half of it away to someone else." She looked at me gratefully and smiled. "Even the smallest acts of self-deprivation can strengthen your spirit. Even . . . even holding your breath."

"Holding your breath?"

"Of course. What could be more depriving than denying yourself of air?"

"Tell me. Do you hold your breath often?" I said as I scraped the last bit of apple from its peel.

"My family gathered oysters from the ocean. This was how we found our food and pearls. It was exciting to see how long we could hold our breath and gain mastery over our bodies."

"Exciting?" I said, raising one eyebrow.

"Yes, and I'll bet I can hold my breath longer than you."

"You cannot. My lungs are larger."

She laughed. "It doesn't matter how big your lungs are."

Now, I didn't mind being nice to the Messenger, and I didn't mind bringing her food. But I would not let a girl beat me in *anything*. "Fine," I said. "Let's have a contest."

"Do you want some tips before we begin?" she said, looking much too confident.

"No." I snapped. *Anybody* can hold their breath.

"Very well. Are you ready? On the count of three. One . . . two . . . three!"

I sucked in as much air as I could and held it.

The room was eerily silent. Rishi gazed at me steadily. One corner of her mouth lifted in a sly smile.

There was no way I was going to let her win this contest. Her constant self-righteousness was getting annoying. I didn't like how she was always acting like she knew more than me or like she was wiser than me. She acted like she already knew the truth. But I could find truth for myself. My lungs started to burn and I could feel my face redden. Across from me, Rishi sat, still and serene. I closed my eyes, partly to concentrate on keeping the air in but mostly so that I didn't have to look at her smug face.

It was getting difficult now. How my body yearned for air! I opened one eye and she was still there, gazing at me the same way Riplakish's jaguar gazes at me during the Speakers' meetings. It is a steady, ominous expression that says, "*When I break free of these chains, you will be the first person I eat.*"

Yes, it was the exactly same look.

I pinched my eyes together and clenched my fists. My head ached. My lungs cried out in pain. But I was *not* going to let her beat me. I would show her that I could indeed deprive myself of something. I *do* have a strong spirit. My body does not control me *all* the time. I opened my eyes a third time but this time the world around me was blurred and filled with tiny flashing stars.

Then everything went black.

"AAAAAAHHH!" I screamed. The most terrible sensation rushed over my body. I sat up and found that the upper half of my body was soaking wet and Rishi was standing over me with an overturned jug.

"What happened?! Why am I all wet?"

"You passed out," said Rishi, calmly sitting down across from me. "I had to wake you."

I held my throbbing head in my hands and moaned. "You could have patted my cheek or shouted my name or something."

"I did," she said with an innocent smile. "But you wouldn't wake."

I moaned again and lay down on the stone floor, putting my hand over my eyes.

"I really am sorry," said Rishi, not sounding sorry at all.

I was not going to let her get away with this. I rocked up to my feet and stepped up to the thrones, feigning anger while she knelt behind me, feigning remorse.

There was another large pot of water that was always kept behind my throne in case of a fire. I picked it up in my arms, walked back down to where Rishi was kneeling contritely with her head bowed. She raised her head just in time to see the entire pot empty over her face.

Her shriek was glorious and satisfying.

"Sorry," I said. "My mind just wasn't powerful enough to keep my body from seeking revenge."

She looked up at me through her wet hair and we both laughed. Kneeling down in the puddle of water I moved her black hair out of her eyes, securing it behind her ears.

"You look pretty with your hair wet," I said, without even thinking.

She looked down and the color on her cheeks bloomed. An awkward silence followed. "Well, then," I said, biting my lip and looking around for something to do or say. We had created quite a large lake on the floor. "Maybe we should clean up a bit."

Rishi nodded. I helped her to her feet and we gathered the empty bowls and sugar apple peels. Using a couple of the robes left by the priests, we soaked up as much water as we could. While leaning over, something fell out of my shirt pocket. It clamored against the wet floor and bounced toward Rishi. Before I could take a step to retrieve my treasure, Rishi had it in her hands. She turned it over, gazing in wonder at the golden comb like it was a long-lost relative.

"Where did you get this?" she said with questioning eyes.

"I . . . I was planning on giving it back to you," I stammered. "I kept it for a while because . . . it gave me so much joy to hear Tungan scream like a girl." Then I quickly added, "Not that screaming like a girl is a bad thing."

Her smile was like sunshine.

"Keep it," I said. "I mean, it is yours, after all."

She took the comb and was about to put it in her pocket.

"Wait . . . ," I said. "You should wear it. It is a like a trophy . . . a trophy for defending yourself . . . and your virtue." Again, her face beamed.

"And for holding my breath longer than you," she added.

I nodded my head graciously, acknowledging her victory. I took her hand and gently pulled the comb out of her fingers. I didn't really know how women's combs worked, but I did my best to fit it into her dark hair. When I finished, her hair was slightly ratty above the place where I stuck it in, and it bulged up a bit. I tried to pat it down but my hand just made things worse, so I let it be.

We looked into each other's eyes for a moment and I was about to say something when the rain pattered on the roof above us and we both sighed. Time to go.

"Well . . . good night," said Rishi.

"Good night," I said. "I guess you won't have to worry about getting wet."

She walked to the tapestry, but then paused as if she had forgotten something. She whirled around, came back to me, and leaned her cheek against mine.

"Thank you," she whispered in my ear.

Then she left, leaving me alone. My arms were filled with the dripping robes; my body was cold, wet, and shivering.

But inside, I was on fire.

CHAPTER 41

Passing by the Cenote

I spent the next several weeks obsessing over the motive for Rishi's "thank you." Did she say it because I had given her back her comb? Or did she say it because I had tried to make her happy by juggling? Or because I had let her win the breathing contest? I doubted it was for pouring water over her head, but you never know.

The next time we met, Rishi acted like nothing had happened. She sat, prim and proper, straight as a tree, and made sure she stayed an arm's length away from me, at least at first. But today I had brought a new book, and before long we were together, side by side, and she didn't seem to be bothered by the fact that our knees were touching. She pointed to different characters, asking me how many I recognized.

She turned the pages slowly and then stopped. "Oh! This is one of my favorite ones. What do you think this means? Can you tell by just looking at it?" She was pointing to a picture of an arrow broken in half.

"Let's see . . . how about 'broken arrow,'" I said.

"Think a little deeper."

"Let's see . . . if I had a broken arrow, it would mean I was in trouble. That is what it must mean. Trouble. Danger."

She laughed. "Actually, no. It is the opposite. A broken arrow means 'peace.'"

I shook my head. "The only way to have peace is to be the one with the most arrows," I said.

"You think that by using force you will ultimately get your way, don't you?"

"That is how the Speakers gained their power. Force, manipulation, seduction, intimidation, fear . . . that is why they call it *power*."

"Perhaps it can be achieved that way . . . but I don't think that is how it can be maintained. You yourself said that he who reads, rules. I think power comes from enlightenment, intelligence, persuasion, and truth. And then after it is obtained, power is only maintained by virtue and integrity."

"Let's move on," I said. She was getting preachy again and I wanted to change the subject. "What does this character mean?"

It was a figure of a small person; the oval that made its head was very large in proportion to its body.

"That character means 'child.'" This same character was repeated several times on the page.

"What is this story about?" I asked.

I watched Rishi's eyes read the characters. I liked the way her eyelashes touched each other when she blinked her eyes, like black butterfly wings.

"This is a story . . . ," Rishi said, her butterfly wings opening and closing for me once more. "It is called 'The Three Obedient Children.' It goes like this: 'There was once a man who had three children. He loved them. He gave them water when they were thirsty and food when they were hungry. He taught them to work and they were obedient to him. But they were obedient for different reasons. The first child was afraid that if he didn't do as his father asked, he would be beaten or mocked or forced out of the home. He obeyed his father out of fear.'"

"'The next child recognized that his father had given him everything he had and he felt a great obligation to him, and obeyed his father out of duty.'"

"'The third child admired his father, loved to work with him, to learn from him, and to listen to him. This child obeyed out of love.'" Rishi paused and then took a small breath as if she were about to say something else, but then stopped.

"What is it?" I asked.

She shook her head. "Nothing."

I couldn't stand not knowing what she was thinking. "Tell me," I implored.

"I was just wondering why there are no children in the city. Where are they?"

"Ah . . . ," I said, "there are *some* around . . ." Why did I feel so uncomfortable answering this question? Everyone in Zitól knew the answer, and it wasn't as if it were a secret or anything. But for some reason telling Rishi about the infants tied my stomach in knots. Somehow I knew she would not approve. And by this time I actually cared about her opinion.

"Where? I would think that in a city that places such little value on virtue, there would be babies everywhere. You know," she said, giving me a big wink and smile, "even virgins like me know where babies come from. So where are they? Who takes care of them?"

"Ah . . . they are in a place that is more suited to their needs," I stammered. "City life is designed for individuals, not families."

"What do you mean? Every individual is part of a family. You can't be born unless you have a mother and a father and a family."

"Perhaps, in the old days. Things are different now. Families are burdensome. It is harder for people to achieve their potential and enjoy the good things in life when one has such obligations."

Rishi watched me as I said this and then slowly shook her head.

"What?" I asked. "Why do you shake your head?"

"I just think it is sad, what you just said."

"I will show you the children if you want," I said. "Then you'll see that they are happy where they are."

A sudden smile spread across her face. "When? How?"

I hesitated. "I don't know . . . sometime."

"How about now?"

"Ah . . . now? How do I know you won't just run away? This could be an opportunity for you to escape," I said.

"I won't escape," she said.

"How can I believe you?"

"Because I promise I won't. And I always keep my promises."

I forced a yawn, "It is late . . ."

"It isn't that late." She stood and pulled my arm. "Come. Show me where the children are."

The crescent moon hung in the sky like a shining silver hammock. We were crossing the courtyard when I noticed that Rishi was dressed in a light blue tunic that made her form glow in the moonlight.

I stopped. "You can't wear that," I said.

"Why not?"

"Because someone will recognize you as the Messenger. The only person allowed to wear blue is the Messenger, just as the only people allowed to wear white are the priests and Speakers. You and I are important people, so we've got to stay disguised in public. See?" I was wearing a dark brown tunic and a brown cape that I wore only for outings such as this.

She shrugged. "I don't have anything that isn't *some* shade of blue," she said.

"Come with me," I said.

I pulled her into my tower and we climbed the stairs, passing my masks that hung in the stairwell. When we got to the top she hesitated. "I'll wait here," she said.

I dug through my clothes until I found a dark cape. I draped it around her shoulders. The cape was huge on her and covered her like a tent, but it would have to do. Rishi stood so still while I fastened the cape around her neck and I could feel her warm breath on my collarbone. My heart was beating so hard I thought perhaps she could hear it, she was standing so close to me. I took my time tying the cape, and although I didn't have to, I reached my hands around her neck and gently pulled her hair out of the cape and raised the hood over her head. How I loved touching her hair.

"There," I said. "Now the only way anyone could recognize you is if they looked in your eyes." At that moment our eyes locked. I gave myself two luxurious seconds to study them before my knees started to dissolve. Then I ducked down the stairs.

We exited the tower and I led her around the wall to the back of the palace. There was a passageway there that opened to a steep trail that led down the palace mound. At the base of the mound it joined up with the wide cobblestone path that led to the cenote.

I had often been to the cenote at night. I would go on hot nights when I couldn't sleep. It was cooler there, standing above the pit. I never got too close, of course, but sometimes a cool breeze swirled out of the hole, bringing with it a moist, wet smell. Tonight, with the bright moon, shining stars, and glowing clouds, it was easy to see the black outline of the hole. Rishi followed me around the cenote, a good three paces from the edge. I looked back at the palace. It was high on the hill, with my tower and the tower of the Messenger poking up like arrows against the dark purple sky. Though there was an orange glow coming from where the sacrifices were being conducted, there were no lights on in the palace, which made me a little more at ease.

Once we passed the cenote, the trail led into the trees. I had walked about five paces when I turned and Rishi wasn't there. I felt a prick of panic. I retraced my steps back to the cenote.

There she was, standing near the edge, peering down into the hole.

I walked up beside her, making sure my steps were noisy enough that I did not startle her. Deep down in the hole the water was still and black.

"Isn't that strange?" she murmured.

"What?"

"Look down into the cenote. Look at how you can see the moon and the stars reflected in the water. It is as if we were on the other side of the heavens, where the gods dwell, looking down on the night sky instead of up. It is like a piece of sky has been trapped here in the ground."

"We could go back, you know." I wasn't thrilled at the thought of going to the village. I had been there once before, and it wasn't my first choice of where I wanted to spend my time. On my bed, surrounded by food and beautiful women was my first.

"I could do it right now," she said to herself.

"Do what?"

"Jump."

"Ah . . . um . . . let's not be too hasty. We are *weeks* away from the spring equinox. Believe me, you can put a lot of living in that amount of time. Besides, I can't swim, so don't expect me to go and fetch you out."

She looked at me incredulously and then turned her head back to gaze into the negative space.

"Come on. Let's step away from the big dark scary black hole of death," I said with a nervous laugh.

She gave a great long sigh that seemed to last forever, and I thought I saw her lean forward a bit.

"Um . . . Rishi . . ." It was the first time I had called her by her name. She wasn't listening to me. She was whispering something to herself.

"Rishi?" I said again. She turned her head with the distracted eyes of someone who has just been woken from a dream. She blinked a few times and then looked back into the hole.

"I'm sorry . . . ," she said. "I was just thinking that if I jumped right now I could get it over with and I could do it without being decorated and tied with all of those people staring at me like that other poor girl."

My heart started beating fast. The thought of her jumping made my palms sweat. A reckless idea came into my mind. I looked up at the palace, and then to Rishi. "Why don't you just . . . ," I lowered my voice, "run away."

"What did you say?" She blinked and turned to me.

"Run away. Just go." It was a wild suggestion, and one worthy of death, but I was serious. I would much rather let her escape than be tossed into the well like the other Messengers. "I won't stop you."

"But I can't," she said gravely, her eyes big and solemn.

"Why not?"

"I gave you my word."

What did she just say? Was she serious? I didn't know whether I should pull her away from the edge or push her in. Instead I rubbed my face in anxiety, and let my fingers pull down my cheeks in baffled frustration. The depth of this woman's integrity was inconceivable.

"I told you I wouldn't," she said simply.

"Very well, I changed my mind. You have my permission. Go. Get out of here."

"It isn't just that. I *need* to be sacrificed. It is my duty to my people."

"The people aren't going to care, they'll just get a new Messenger . . ."

"Not your people, *my* people. I owe it to them to make up for what I did. Besides I have a message to give the gods."

"You do?" I asked.

She turned and looked at me with earnest eyes. "Ever since I became the Messenger I have thought about what I might say to the gods if *I* could decide on the message, instead of the message that the Speakers want me to bring . . . I didn't have to think for very long."

"You said your gods didn't believe in sacrificing. What makes you think your gods are even down there?"

She sighed. "I don't. Or I didn't . . . I don't know. This place with all of its strange customs confuses me sometimes. Everything seems backward. But I have imagined many times what it would be like to have an audience with the gods, and to be able to ask them whatever I wanted. I don't know if sacrificing myself in the cenote will make that happen or not," she looked at me, "but I can't let an opportunity like that pass."

I nodded my head sympathetically, but I wasn't comprehending one word that was coming out of this crazy girl's mouth.

"What would you ask the gods if *you* had a chance, Anointed One?"

I rubbed the back of my neck. "I . . . ah . . . well . . . I . . ." It was a question I wasn't in the mood to contemplate. "I don't know," I said finally.

"I'm sure if you were faced with the possibility, you would come up with something. So whether it is true or not, I at least have a message, and that makes me feel better about my future. Besides, I don't have any other options. I have prayed to them that they would hear me, and listen to me, but I don't *know* if they are listening. But if I could go and meet them face to face and tell them that my brothers didn't mean to—" her voice filled with emotion and she took another step closer. Without thinking I reached out and grabbed her hand.

"Rishi. Stop," I said softly, my voice breaking. "Don't go any closer. Please." I gently pulled her away from the cenote. "Come on . . . we made a deal, remember? There is no need to rush into things. Once I know how to read, you can go jump off any cliff you want, understand?" She nodded and to my great relief she stepped away from the cenote. I led her into the forest and as soon as my heartbeat returned to normal I let go of her hand. "You don't have to call me that, you know," I said.

"Call you what?"

"Anointed One. You could just call me Nadal."

We had been traveling through the forest for a while, tripping over roots and tree trunks, when we both stopped at once. There was a sound coming through the trees. It was singing.

> *Giving it increases me.*
> *When I keep it I shrivel,*
> *What is it? What is it?*
> *It cannot be held*
> *Yet it binds us together*
> *What is it? What is it?*

We continued walking as the voice drifted around us, soft and mystical, and I was surprised when Rishi started humming along.

> *It keeps us safe from harm*
> *Yet it harms no one*
> *It keeps us warm*
> *But it does not burn.*
> *What is it? What is it?*

We walked a few steps more when suddenly I sensed someone behind us. I felt for the knife I had concealed in my belt. But before I could draw it out I felt the tip of a spear jab my rear end.

CHAPTER 42

The Invisible Village

W ho are you? State your business," said a small, fierce voice. I tried to turn but the spear pushed deeper against my buttock.

"We mean no harm," I said.

"We'll see about that. You better do just what I tell you to or you'll never be able to sit down again. What about you?" This time the voice was directed at Rishi.

I glanced at her and I could tell from the look on her face that she too was being held by spearpoint in an uncomfortable place.

"We are not here to harm anyone," she said. "We just came to look."

"I will take you to Gabber Gerta. *She* will know if you just came to look or not."

We moved through the trees very slowly, the spear prodding me along with annoying, punctuating jabs. I noticed an amber light blinking around the tree trunks and soon the cool smells of the forest were overwhelmed with the smell of burning wood. The singing was getting louder.

The forest opened into a clearing. In the middle of the clearing a small fire glowed, illuminating an old woman in a chair. I could tell she had seen us, for her singing lowered to a hum. In her arms were two sleeping babies. Three older children lay on a mat curled up at her feet. Behind her and beyond the firelight were a dozen miniature huts.

"Chi-chi," said our escort, "I found strangers in the forest."

"Bring them to me," called the woman's raspy voice. "No need to be too rough with them. These two will do us no harm."

I felt the pressure stabbing in my behind ease and heard the spears clatter to the ground.

I turned to see my guard—a boy no more than seven or eight years old.

"Now, Zymee, pick up your spears and go put them away somewhere safe so the younger children don't play with them," the old woman said.

"You don't want me to stay? They look dangerous." The boy eyed me especially.

"I will be fine. I have been expecting them. Off to sleep, now."

"If they aren't nice to you, just let me know and we will tie them to the poisonwood trees."

"*Thank you*, Zymee. Good night."

The boy glared at me and stalked away toward the huts, dragging the spears behind him.

"You may sit down," said the old woman, nodding to the dozen or more tiny stools scattered around the fire.

Rishi seated herself without hesitation, and I carefully lowered myself onto a stool, wincing as it creaked under my weight.

"Forgive me for not standing and greeting you properly," the woman said, smiling gently and looking down at the babies in her arms.

"May I hold one?" asked Rishi.

"Certainly," said the woman. Rishi gathered one baby into her arms. She swayed as she walked carefully around the fire and lowered herself back onto the stool. The disturbed infant stretched, smacked its lips together, and then gave a deep sigh before melting against her body.

I had never been in such close proximity to a real baby before. They were so small and hairless. "When do their eyes start to open?" I asked.

Rishi laughed. "Babies aren't like dogs. They are *born* with their eyes open."

"Oh," I said, feeling stupid. I glanced over at the woman, who was also trying, unsuccessfully, to hide her grinning face. When she lifted her head she looked straight at me, amusement twinkling in her eyes.

Her brown and *blue* eyes.

Rishi must have noticed at that moment too, for she let out a small gasp. The old woman chuckled, making the baby bob serenely in her arms.

"You are the woman I saw at the Flower Festival," said Rishi in a low voice, ". . . and also the woman that is in my . . ." She didn't finish her sentence.

"In your dreams?" The woman smiled, making her cheeks rise up on her wrinkled face like little hills. "I have been dreaming too, my dear," she said. "That is how I knew you would come. But dreams don't tell me everything, you know. They often leave out important details . . . like names, for instance."

Rishi spoke first. "My name is Rishi. I come from the islands. And this is—"

"I am Nadal," I finished. I didn't want Rishi to introduce me and give away too much information. "I am . . . of Zitól."

"Very good. You can call me Gabber Gerta, though my children call me Chi-chi. Now, what brings you to the invisible village?" she said, directing her question to Rishi.

"The invisible village?" Rishi asked. "Why do you call it that?"

"Because the Zitól authorities like to pretend we do not exist."

"Why?"

"Because we remind them of their mistakes."

"She wanted to see where the children were," I interjected, trying to get back to the original reason we came.

"Yes!" Rishi said, pressing her cheek against the baby's forehead. "I knew they had to be somewhere. How many do you have here?"

"Fifty-four," said the woman with pride. "It was fifty, but we picked up four more —including these two—just last week."

"And why do they not stay with their parents? Why do they give them to you?"

The woman glanced meaningfully at me and I shifted uncomfortably, making my tiny stool creak. The knot in my stomach tightened. Once again the conversation was going in exactly the wrong direction.

"I can see you have not yet learned all the Zitóli ways, young one. These babies are unwanted."

"Unwanted?" Rishi said, perplexed. She kissed the baby in her arms. "How could a child be unwanted?"

The woman did not answer her question.

"And there are so many. How do you take care of them all?"

"The older children help out a lot," she said. "They do much of the work, including catching the babies."

It seemed very hot. I should have known the topic of the children's origin would come up and I regretted not explaining it to her first. It was too late now; Rishi was hanging on every word the woman said.

"*Catching* the babies?" asked Rishi. "What do you mean?"

I shifted pebbles around with my foot.

"We gather the babies from the cenote," the woman said, as if it were as common as gathering mushrooms or flowers.

"I don't understand," said Rishi. "Why would there be babies in the cenote? A baby can't survive in water."

"Precisely, child."

Rishi was silent. We listened to the crackling of the fire while we waited for the dark clouds of understanding to break open over her head. It didn't take long.

Rishi slowly shook her head back and forth. "No . . . please tell me the people of Zitól don't do *that*."

"Rishi," the old woman sighed, "the people of Zitól have chosen a path of passions. But one cannot walk down this path without consequences. In this case the consequences come in the form of a woman's round belly. In another day and age women would see this as a blessing, but not for the women in Zitól. Here a baby is as unwanted as a disease. When they can't make it disappear in the womb, they do what they can to make it disappear soon afterward. The women of Zitól have paid a heavy price for the social expectations of the city. But there is a bright side. I do not think it is possible for a mother to completely forsake her child. It is known in the city that we try to save the babies, so sometimes we can purchase them as the crowds gather to watch the Messengers. Those babies usually make it back here and have a good chance. Other mothers put the babies in leather bags before throwing them into the water, hoping the leather will keep the water out long enough for us to grab the child after the crowds leave. Those babies sometimes have a chance. But then there are women who choose to come to the cenote at other times of year. They come by themselves and throw their baby into the pool when we are not aware. Those babies never have a chance."

"What is *wrong* with these women?" Rishi said in astonishment.

"The problem is not with the women. No woman *wants* to give up her baby, and in a balanced world no mother would even dream of it. No, the problem lies not with the women, but with Zitól."

I heard a cough from one of the huts. Out of the corner of my eye I saw a movement. A little bare foot appeared out of one of the doorways. It wiggled for a moment and then flopped to the side and relaxed.

"I suppose the Zitóli gods have something to do with this?" Rishi asked.

The woman nodded soberly. "Sacrifices must be made."

"I understand now," Rishi said in a quiet voice.

"Not *every* child is sacrificed," I said defensively, with an uncharacteristic surge of patriotism. "Many wealthy families decide to keep their children and raise them as their own. If we kept every child, children would overrun the city. They'd be everywhere, like rats. People wouldn't have time for anything else."

Rishi and the old woman turned and looked at me with strange expressions on their faces. Having two blue eyes staring at me was unnerving.

"What?" I said. "Did I say something wrong?"

"And just when I was beginning to like you," said Rishi. "How would you feel if *you* had been one of the infants tossed out?"

The old woman shook her head. "There, there . . . You mustn't blame him for living. He does not know better. He was raised Zitóli. But I remember a time when there were many children in Zitól. We would run through the streets playing games—" she smiled, "—much like rats, I suppose. And we were all such good friends. Back then all the children went to school and—"

"School?" I interjected. "You mean you learned to read and write? Like the priests and Speakers?"

The woman's eyes sparkled. "*Yes*," she said.

"But that is impossible. It has been centuries since the common people could read," I said.

The old woman chuckled softly. "Is that what they are teaching now? Evidently I'm older than I thought I was. No, child. In addition to obscuring the old Zitóli ways, they've also warped your sense of time. When you stop educating a people you can fill their heads full of whatever you want and they'll believe it. There are not many who can remember as far back as I can, and I remember the way Zitól was before they took away knowledge, and before they started the sacrifices. It was a place of learning and laughter and love. That was long ago, though, even before Yelgab left . . ."

I heard Rishi inhale sharply. "What did you say?"

"Zitóli used to be a wonderful place of learning."

"No," said Rishi, "that name you just mentioned. What was that name you just said?"

"Who?" said the old woman. "You mean Yelgab? Oh, everyone knows who Yelgab is . . . The Speakers may have stopped teaching people to read, but they've always made sure everyone remembered who *Yelgab* was."

"Who was he?" Rishi said, breathlessly.

The woman's eyes sparkled. "Why, ask your friend from Zitól. He will tell you."

Rishi turned to me, her eyes like two enormous moons.

I cleared my throat. "Yelgab," I said, "is the name of the Great Coward."

CHAPTER 43

I Make a Mistake

R ishi looked at me as if I had announced the end of the world.
"Yelgab was the—?" she murmured.

The old woman let this idea sink in for a moment and then she said, "Is there something you'd like to tell us?"

"Ah . . . ," said Rishi, who was still in some strange trance. "Yelgab . . . is that a *common* name in Zitól?" she asked.

That made me laugh. "No one would name a child after a *traitor*."

Rishi glared at me and then turned to the old woman. "It is just that . . . Yelgab was the name of my grandfather."

"I was hoping you'd say that." The woman smiled. "Yelgab was my brother. I am fairly certain that your grandfather and my brother are the same person."

It was all coming together for me. They had the same eyes; they sang the same songs; they shared the same opinions; they both gave me the same icy stares whenever I opened my mouth.

"You are my *aunt*," Rishi repeated, breathless.

"So it seems," the woman said as she winked her blue eye.

"Are you . . . are you a dream child too?"

"Dream child? What is a dream child?" I asked, feeling left out.

"Someone who can dream the future," Rishi said.

"A seer," added the woman.

"You are a seer?" I said, turning to Rishi. "You can dream the *future*? Why didn't you tell me this before?"

Rishi ignored me. "Can you also dream the future?" she asked the old woman.

The woman nodded. "I have known for months that someone would come to Zitól with a special message that would bring a restoration of all things."

"What kind of message?" I asked.

"The dream never said," she sighed. "You know how dreams can be sometimes."

Rishi nodded with understanding.

"But I do know that the message will put everything back into balance."

Just then, the baby in Rishi's arms began to stir. Its face wrinkled and twisted, and it started to whimper and then cry. Rishi tried soothing it by standing and gently rocking it back and forth in her arms, but the cries only intensified. Another cry was heard from one of the huts, and fearing that the baby's cries would wake all fifty-two children, Rishi brought the baby back to Gabber Gerta. It continued to sob, its loud wail rattling my ears.

"You two get back home, I must calm him before he wakes the others," Gabber Gerta said.

"I will be back," Rishi promised.

"Yes. Come back as soon as you can. We have much to talk about. Now, go."

"I have an aunt!" Rishi said jubilantly as she skipped into the cool forest. "And she knew my grandfather! It all makes sense to me now—why he talked about Zitól so much but never wanted to go back, and why he knew about the temples and how to read . . . "

"Rishi, your grandfather was the Great Coward."

"I know! Isn't that wonderful?"

I shook my head. I should never have taken her to see the village.

"When can we go back?" she said, hopping after me.

"We aren't going back," I said. I was angry.

"Why not? Aren't you glad that I found a relative?"

"Not especially. You are related to one of the most disgraceful men in history. He defied the gods." It bothered me that Rishi was so exuberant about being related to someone who was so obviously treacherous. But it wasn't just that. I had actually started to like having Rishi all to myself. It was as if she was my own secret friend that no one knew about. I looked forward to our lessons more than she knew . . . more than I really knew, until that moment. I liked that I was the only person she could talk to, and that she depended on me for companionship and food. I had never had to share anything in my life, and I wanted Rishi all to myself.

I walked ahead of her. I wanted to get back to my bed as soon as possible, back to a place where I could think and sort this all out.

"Wait, Nadal. I want to tell you something," she said.

I kept walking.

"Nadal," she said, trying to catch her breath. She grasped my arm and put herself in front of me, placing one hand on my chest and looking up into my face. "I just wanted to tell you . . . no, to *thank* you. This has been the happiest night of my life. I am so, so grateful to you and all you have done for me. I'm grateful for the food you've brought, and for being my friend, and for making me laugh . . . I . . ." Her eyes glistened and filled with feeling. "I have never had a friend like you before."

When she stared at me like that and said those words, it was like someone had just poured cool water over a throbbing burn and I felt the heat inside me melt away. The moonlight shone on her face. She seemed to be waiting for me to say something, waiting for some kind of answer. I did not know what to say, so I did the only thing I could think of. I put my hand on her cheek, pulled her toward me, and kissed her.

The kiss lasted only a second, but her eyes stayed closed long after our lips parted. Her freshly kissed lips shone like polished stones.

Slowly she opened her eyes and gazed up at me with a look I will always remember. Then she spoke words I will never forget. In a voice as soft as a summer breeze she said, "Do that again."

I did. I kissed her again, cradling her face with both hands this time, and as I did I felt my blood beat through my veins. I had kissed many women, but I had never felt like this before. The skin on her cheeks was as smooth as the inside of a seashell, and her lips were soft and salty. I put one arm around her and pulled her closer. As I felt her body lean against mine, the blood in my veins turned into fire, and I felt the control of my passion shift from my mind to my body. I kissed her harder. Then, I felt for her bead belt around her waist and I shoved my hand in between the belt and the small of her back. When I did, Rishi suddenly pulled away.

I was left standing there, my arms empty. My heart was still beating like a hammer, but all the soft, beautiful feelings I had just a moment ago were gone.

"Take me back to the palace," she said quietly, looking at the ground.

"I—"

"Just take me back."

I was so confused that I just stood there for a moment until she started walking away from me. I followed her, and my anger returned. Why was it that I could never do anything right? And what had I done wrong this time?

We walked through the forest in strangulated silence. The clouds had thickened and thunder rolled through them like a distant wave. We passed the cenote, exhaling its cool breath into the hot, pressurized air. Neither one of us said a word.

What had just happened? How did I lose that moment? There wasn't enough time left for Rishi and me. Thinking these thoughts as we walked up the hill made me boil inside and just before we came to the passageway I caught her hand.

"Rishi," I said. "I'm not sure what happened back there, but whatever I did wrong, I'm sorry." The words were hollow and forced and I didn't mean them, for I found it strange apologizing for putting my hand on a girl's waist when I had done so much more than that in the past.

She looked at me and nodded, but turned into the passage.

I wouldn't let go of her hand. "Come back. All I want to do is show you that I care for you too. There has got to be a way around this whole virgin thing."

Rishi pulled away. "*What* did you say?" she asked as the crease in between her eyebrows became deep and dark. "This . . . *virgin* thing? What do you mean by that?" Her voice cut like a knife through the thick air.

"Rishi, we don't have much time left. I have never felt feelings like this for anyone before. I . . . I . . . actually think I am falling in love with you."

"What are you talking about?" Rishi asked.

"You and me . . . you *know*," I said. "I want to share myself with you, completely. I want to show you how much you mean to me."

"Nadal, you have forgotten who I am. *I* don't *do* that."

"But no one would know but us. Please, Rishi. We . . .we don't have much time left to be together. Besides, we wouldn't even have to worry about any consequences."

"What do you mean we wouldn't have to worry about any consequences?"

"Because," I stammered, ". . . you . . . are going to . . ." My mouth went dry.

Her eyes were hard as stones. "Say it, Nadal."

I couldn't finish.

"Because I am going to *die*. Is that what you were going to say?"

Thunder rolled above. I opened my mouth but I couldn't speak.

"You are saying that my virtue doesn't matter *because I am going to die anyway*," she repeated in disgust.

"That isn't exactly—"

"You are just like *them*." The wind picked up and tossed her hair so that she had to hold it back with her hand.

"What are you talking about? Just like who?"

"The Speakers. The priests. All the people here in this horrible city. I was beginning to think that you might be different. Don't you understand?" She wrenched her hand from mine and held out her bead for me to see. "*This* is my offering. I don't have anything else I can give the gods but *this*. If I don't have it, I will be dying for *nothing*." The luster of tears gleamed in her eyes.

"I'm . . . sorry," I said awkwardly. Lamely. Stupidly. Drops of rain fell onto my arms.

"*You* will stay away from me," she said, and I knew she meant it. "It isn't about whether other people would *know* or not. It is not about whether or not there would be *consequences*." She lowered her voice, "And it is *not* about you and me. It is a lot bigger than that. It is about trust and promises. It is about keeping the balance of the world. It is about honoring all the people who have come before me and all the people who will come after me."

"But, Rishi," I said softly. "No one *will* come after you."

At this her nostrils flared and she looked at me with such an expression of pain that I was ashamed.

A great clap of thunder boomed above our heads and the lightning flashed through the sky with so much brilliance that I shielded my face. When I opened my eyes, she was gone.

CHAPTER 44

Two Cups of Chocolate

I sat on the edge of my bed all night, my head in my hands, staring at ants going in and out of a crack in the floor. What went wrong? What catastrophic error had I committed? Was it something I had said or something I had done? Perhaps I had moved too quickly. Or perhaps it was simpler than that . . . perhaps it was only a matter of hygiene. I smelled under my arms. I quickly calculated how many hours had passed since my last bath.

But perhaps I wasn't to blame. Perhaps she was. After all, I had never known such a snobby, self-righteous, self-glorified, egocentric person in my entire life. What could you expect from someone who has been locked up in a tower for so long with nothing to do but obsess about her virginity?

Whatever the reason for the disastrous moment, misery cannot describe the way I felt the following day. It was as though I had locusts swarming inside my body, chewing me from the inside out.

Later in the afternoon I left the tower to get some fresh air. I paced around the courtyard. Each time I passed the Messenger's tower Leema eyed me suspiciously.

Finally, on the fourth time around she asked, "So what is your problem?"

"Nothing," I snapped.

She shrugged and leaned over her loom. Taking a knife she began cutting the strings that held the delicate fabric in place.

"How is it coming?" I asked. I reached down to touch it and she slapped my hand.

"It is finished, so keep your filthy hands away from it."

"Finished?" I said. "So soon?"

"What do you mean 'so soon'? The Messenger's sacrifice is less than a month away. I am lucky I finished today. I will barely have enough time to sew it together and add the beads and bells."

I swallowed. I had not realized the sacrifice was so soon. The thought of that day made me sick. I left Leema and her loom and headed back to my tower where I could pace up and down the stairs in privacy.

On the next Night of Sacrifices, in the month of the Rabbit, I brought my entire dinner of meat-filled tamales, corn, guacamole, squash, and several slices of jicama. I had raided the kitchen and found some pineapple, the fruit I knew Rishi liked best. I took these things in a big basket to the throne room and laid them out on a colored cloth in the center of the room. I waited for her, but she never came.

Eventually I gathered up the food and took it back to my tower. I tried to study for the rest of the night, but found it impossible.

For the first time in my life I tried to look at the situation from someone else's perspective. Perhaps I had hurt her more than I thought. I remembered back to the stories she had told me of her island. How important it was to them to stay virtuous. My recent experience told me that she meant what she said, and that when it came to her virtue, she was as immovable as a mountain. I still didn't really understand why it was so critical, but I decided I would try to show her respect, regardless of my feelings about it. I wouldn't do this for just anyone. But I would do it for Rishi.

Rishi was different. When I was with her I thought about great things. She respected me and treated me with kindness I felt that I didn't deserve. Because she was so adamant about doing what was right she was easy to trust. I remembered how selfish I had been with the food I had brought her, but she had not been selfish with her knowledge. Not only that, the knowledge awakened a feeling inside of me—a feeling that I hadn't had since I prepared the speech that ended so pitifully, so many years ago. This feeling was a desire for truth, and now that Rishi had opened up that thirst again it could not be quenched.

The more I thought about all of these things, the more remorse flooded into my heart. I hated myself for being so self-centered. I made up my mind that I would never again offend her, if only I could be given another chance. What I had told her was true: I was falling in love with her. To me she was more than just a woman; she was a queen. And if she only would let me love her, I would build her a palace, stone by stone, with my own two hands.

But practicality had to come first: she needed more food than what Leema was giving her. She *needed* to see me, whether she wanted to or not.

There were some blank books in Riplakish's library. With a piece of obsidian I carefully cut a square of paper from one of the large pages and took it to my tower. Then, taking a wooden skewer from my food tray, I blackened it with the flame from my lamp. With the skewer I scrawled out some characters on the paper the best I could.

I rolled the paper into a scroll and went down to the kitchen. The servants were there, busily preparing food for the entire palace. I asked one woman which food was going to the Messenger. She pointed to a plate of scraps, and it was just as I suspected. Rishi had been eating not much more than what we give the dogs. When the cooks weren't watching, I took the note I had written and hid it inside the food.

Late that night, I saw a candle glowing on her balcony. I grabbed my cape and a large bag that I had spent the last two days filling with food, and tied it across my back.

I knew that Rishi didn't want me in her tower, but I didn't care. How else was I supposed to talk to her? After crossing the courtyard I went up the staircase that led to the second floor of the palace, then onto the roof. The bag was cumbersome and very heavy and I readjusted it so that one strap went across my chest and under one arm. Then I started to climb up the vines that clung to the Messenger's tower.

As I climbed, the pounding of my heart grew stronger. What did she think of my note? Would she be glad to see me? Would she tell me to leave? I came to the railing and hoisted myself over the side.

I expected to see her right away. But when I got to the top I found I was in a room by myself, for Rishi had pulled the gossamer curtain across the chamber, dividing it in half. I could see her form through the translucent fabric. She sat close to the curtain, beside the pool. She had lit candles all around the pool, and they reflected off the top of the water like golden stars.

"I received your note," she said coolly.

"Good. I'm glad," I said. "You've . . . quarantined yourself."

"I do what I have to do to protect myself, so don't even *think* of coming to my side of the room. You can tell me what you have to tell me on *that* side," she said. I could barely make out her face in the glowing candlelight, but I could tell by the tone of her voice that she wasn't joking.

"I brought you some things," I said, lowering my sack. I crept up to the curtain and sat cross-legged on the ground. I opened my bag and pulled out some tomatoes. As cautiously as if I were reaching into a jaguar den, I lifted the bottom of the curtain and rolled the tomatoes to her feet.

She sat as still and silent as a pyramid.

I reached in my bag again and pulled out some papaya and passion fruit and slid them underneath the curtain. Then came the corn, the nuts, two prickly pears, and the dried fruit. I rolled under two red hot peppers, but they were quickly tossed back, so I replaced them with some dried meat and a small bag of baked seeds. I pushed each item underneath the curtain, one at a time, until there was quite an impressive pile on the other side.

"How did you get all of this without anyone noticing?" she finally said.

I smiled and reached deep down into the bottom of my bag with both arms and pulled out a pumpkin. This time, as I pushed it under the curtain she laughed.

"I can't eat this!" she said.

"I know. I thought you could use it as a decoration."

"Nadal . . . if you think this food is going to—"

"Wait—I have more," I said, trying to contain my excitement. "I want to make something for you. Something special." I pulled out of my sack two goblets and a small pouch. "We call it chocolate."

Rishi folded her arms. "I've had chocolate before, at the Flower Festival, and I didn't like it."

"That is because you had it the Zitóli way."

"Is there another way?" Rishi asked dully.

"Yes. The Nadal way."

I carefully shook some of the powder in each goblet and the smells of cinnamon, chili powder, and cocoa filled my nostrils.

"Do you smell that?" I told her.

"It doesn't smell good to me," she huffed.

"I'm not finished yet," I said. I poured a small amount of water in each cup and then I reached into the bag one more time and pulled out the ceramic vase. Carefully, I loosened the stopper.

"Rishi, let me tell you something. Everyone else mixes this drink with only water. But it is much better this way. You see . . . I have a secret ingredient." I held up the vase for her to see. Then I tipped the vase over the cups, adding a generous amount of thick, golden honey. Then, holding both cups in front of me, I poured one into the other, repeating this over and over until both cups were mixed and frothing. I took a sip from my cup, and let the foamy liquid fill my mouth. I swallowed. The honey made it mild and sweet and the chili powder and cinnamon added just enough heat to make my mouth tingle.

"There," I said, licking my lips. "I have tasted it myself. Now you know it isn't poisoned."

I picked up the other cup and lifted the curtain. I wanted her to come down closer, so instead of setting the cup down, I held it out to her, the curtain draped over my arm. I would hold it there for as long as it took.

At first she hesitated, but then she lowered herself down from the edge of the pool and sat opposite me on the tiled floor. Carefully, she took the cup from my hands. She held it to her nose and sniffed. She put it to her lips and was about to drink when she stopped and lowered the cup, eyeing me suspiciously.

"Are you sure this isn't going to do anything bad to me?" she asked.

"Only if you pour it into your ear instead of your mouth," I said. I could see her better now that she was closer to me. I marveled at how beautiful she had become since I had first met her.

She slowly put the cup back to her lips and sipped. Then she lowered the cup just a little, staring at me over the rim. Lifting it, she sipped again.

"See?" I ventured. "You like it, don't you?"

She drank the rest of the cup in five gulps. When she finished, she said, "I . . . I don't suppose you have more?"

I smiled and passed her mine. She set the cup down once she was finished. "I must admit," she said, "I enjoyed that."

"Rishi," I said, lowering my voice and leaning as close to the curtain as I dared. "Last time we were together you said I was just like them. Just like the Speakers and the priests. Well, it is true. I am Zitóli, just like them. But before I am Zitóli, I am myself. I don't do everything they do, and I don't believe everything they believe. I may not be perfect, but my whole life I have searched for truth and goodness, even if I have had to come up with it on my own, even with dumb little things like this drink. But it has been so hard to find, Rishi, and so far the only *real* truth and goodness I have found has come through you."

We were facing each other. Though I could see her features through the curtain, her expression was obscured. It was maddening to not see her face clearly, that I might perceive her reactions to my words.

"Now, Rishi. No matter what happens, I want you to know that I will never disappoint you again. I will always honor and respect you. I will never take advantage of you." She leaned closer to the curtain, so close that it moved slightly when she exhaled and I could smell the spicy chocolate on her breath.

"But, I want you to listen very carefully. In a few moments I am going to lift this curtain, and I am going to kiss you. Not because I can't control myself, but because I want to show you that I *can*. For I am going to give you the most glorious kiss you have ever or will ever receive from me or any other man. You will able to feel it from the crown of your beautiful head all the way down to your toes. You will feel as if your blood has turned into light. And after I kiss you in this most sublime and exquisite way, then I will *stop*. All I ask is that you hold as still as you can, and please, please don't run away."

Before she could react, I lifted the curtain, letting it fall behind my neck. There was Rishi's face, lovely, surprised, and—thankfully—still.

I put my arm around her and pulled her closer. Placing my other hand on her jaw, I gently brushed my thumb against her slightly open, perfectly shaped lips. Her sweet breath caressed my face. I leaned forward, hovering over her mouth until she finally closed her butterfly eyes. Then I gently pressed my lips against hers and pushed my hand up into her hair.

When we finished she was breathless, and I licked the taste of chocolate from my lips. Slowly she opened her eyes and when she did, her gaze lingered on my mouth. "Do it again," she whispered.

"Not this time." I smiled and ducked back under the curtain, letting it fall between us.

"Just once more."

"Sorry."

Now *she* lifted the curtain. She crawled onto *my* side of the room and leaned into my face, getting so close to my lips that I had to scoot backward to safety.

"Please, Nadal," she purred.

"Get back on your own side, woman," I said. "I know you are testing me."

She laughed and sat back on her knees and folded her arms. Her face was beautiful, pure and glowing.

"Well, it is time for me to go." I stood.

"What? Where are you going? You just arrived," she said in surprise. She started rising to her feet. I held out my hand and helped her up.

"I'm going to let you get some sleep."

"I don't need to sleep."

"Then I'm going to let *me* get some sleep."

"You are?" She seemed incredibly disappointed, which filled me with secret delight. "Wait! I almost forgot," she said. She took something out of the pocket of her dress and unrolled it. I recognized the note I had stashed in her food.

"Sorry it is so greasy," I said, leaning over her. "I didn't know any other way to get it to you."

She started to read out loud.

"Oh please don't." I cringed. "It is too embarrassing to be read out loud."

"This is important, Nadal. Just listen." Then she read the note:

> *"I am as stupid as a three-footed tree.*
> *You are crazy mad at me. I understand.*
> *You teach me so much.*
> *It makes my heart cry to hurt you.*
> *Put a candle in your tower*
> *If I can come and see you again.*
> *I will be there fast like a flying monkey."*

A pretty pathetic note, I know, but you have to understand I could only use the words in my limited vocabulary.

"Nadal, do you mean this?" she asked, tilting her head to the side.

"Every word, Rishi. I'm sorry. You are the best thing that ever happened to me, Rishi. I—"

She put her finger on my lips. "No," she said. "I don't mean that. I know your note is sincere," she said. "What I mean is *this*." She handed me the paper and pointed to the character "heart" that I had written. "This word means 'heart,'" she said.

"Yes, it does," I said, politely echoing her statement of the obvious.

"Now, do you really mean that your heart was actually crying? With tears?" she said, her eyes sparkling.

I was confused. Was this a test?

"Were tears coming *out of your heart?*" she asked gently.

"No . . . but you knew what I meant."

"Not really." She leaned over me and pointed to the paper in my hands. "The character you wrote here means your *literal* heart. Tears can't come out of hearts." She was using her teacher voice.

"Is this a lesson?" I asked unenthusiastically.

"This is the most *important* lesson, Nadal. There are *two* characters for 'heart.' One is literal. One is figurative, meaning not your actual heart, but your soul, your spirit, your desire."

"Well, that is what I meant. My soul, my spirit, and all that."

"Very well. I have one last assignment for you. I want you to find the characters for 'heart'—literal or figurative, somewhere in the city."

"I think I got the point. I know the difference. I don't need to go hunt for it."

"Yes, you do." The playful light in her eyes was replaced by something more serious. "It is my dying wish, Nadal. As soon as you find it, the *moment* you find it, come back to me."

"All right then. I'll look for it."

"Promise?"

I touched her cheek with my hand. "I promise. Good night, Rishi."

I left her and climbed back down the tower, my chest glowing like a sunrise. I succeeded. I was forgiven. All was right between us again.

As I walked across the courtyard I heard a loud whisper calling from above me.

"Promise!"

I turned and waved up at her. "I promise!" I said.

Little did she know, I made another promise that night. I made a promise to myself that somehow I would not let her die.

CHAPTER 45

The Last Assignment

The next morning I put on my common clothes and left the palace. I could tell by the spicy, peppery smell in the air that it was market day. Everywhere I walked there were good things sizzling or beautiful trinkets to browse. I ambled down a street filled with carts and booths laden with colorful rugs and fruits, baskets and clothing, and as I perused the wares I eavesdropped on the conversations of the people. This was how I often gathered my news, for in some ways I felt I could gain more information from the gossip of the crowd than I ever could from the Speakers. The people always had something interesting to gab about, whether it be a new law the Speakers decided to decree, a new village our armies had burned to the ground, or even what the next fashion would be. Today everyone was talking about three men who had escaped from the prison.

Beyond the booths were shops in stone buildings. Many of the buildings had characters written above the doorways. On one wall I saw it said "House of Instruction." Perhaps this was an old school. I looked in the doorway. Now it was a busy butcher's market, reeking of blood, with animal carcasses hanging from the rafters.

I left and kept walking through the crowd. Over another doorway I saw the words "House of Memories." I wondered what had been in this building, for now it was divided into many small shops for jewelers, clothiers, and sandal makers.

There were some buildings that still housed what the walls indicated. The Great Aviary was still thriving, with many birds, and also the Great Menagerie, where the animals were kept until they were needed for pelts or meat.

It was hot, and the sun sizzled in the clear, blue sky like a giant fried egg. I walked all over town until my feet ached, but couldn't find either form of the characters for "heart." I paid a man for a bowl of young coconut slices sprinkled with chili powder and I sat down to rest. I was tired and desired to sleep. It would be cooler in the evening, I decided. I should go back to my tower, take a nap, and come back later.

On my way back to the palace I cut through the temple plaza. Most people avoided the plaza during the day because it was so hot and bright, choosing instead to skirt around the temple via the shadier streets. Today it was nearly deserted.

I had to squint as I walked, since the brightness was almost blinding and the heat unbearable. But as I passed between the temple and the Speakers' Circle, something caught my eye. There were carvings on the stone steps.

I guess I had always known this; I had climbed this temple plenty of times, but always in the darkness by the flickering light of torches. Not only that, but this was the first time I had been at the temple since the writing actually meant something to me. I read the first step. It began, *There was once a man.* I read the next step up. *He was alone.*

I was intrigued. I desired to keep reading, but it wasn't appropriate to climb the temple stairway unless you were a priest, a Speaker, or a sacrifice. My disguise didn't make me look like any of those qualified to step foot on the white stones. If I started climbing, someone was sure to be suspicious. I glanced around. There were a few people on the outskirts of the square. I stepped up on the first step, trying to read as far up as I could see. I stepped up another step, and the white heat radiated off the stone as if it were trying to evaporate me. If I was going to find out what all the steps said, I would have to climb to the top of the temple. I paused for a moment, deciding whether this was wise, while an iguana that had been sunning itself on the steps flicked its tongue at me. I looked back at the plaza. Then I looked up the steep stairway that rose heavenward. And I began to climb.

The steps told a story. It was about a man whose profound loneliness caused him to cry to the gods. The gods made him perform tasks for them. He dug wells for them, he built altars to them, he built cities for them, but each time he performed a task, the gods would reply that it wasn't enough.

By now I had climbed halfway up the temple. The hot wind ruffled my hair but offered no respite from the blazing sun's heat. Sweat began to seep into my eyes and I wiped my forehead with my arm. I turned around to see if anyone below seemed interested in what I was doing, for surely I stood out on the temple like a black spot on a white cloak.

But I had to finish reading. What else could this man do to gain respect of the gods? What would satisfy them? I kept climbing, my eyes hungrily eating the words written across each new step. The man built a temple, painted himself blue, and climbed to the top. He raised his hands high above his head, calling out to the gods and offering up the only thing he had left. My pulse started to quicken for I knew the answer was at the top of the pyramid, and I only had a few more steps to go.

In agony he cried, hoping the gods would hear him and answer his prayer.

I came to the last step. I was gasping for breath. My thighs throbbed and my blood thundered through my veins. Without reading the characters I knew what the last step would say. And I knew that once I saw that last word and read it for what it really was, my life would never be the same. I would be accountable to the gods for the word's interpretation. That word in the stone would change everything about my world: the lives of the Speakers and the children in the invisible village, and every person in the city. I could step over it, closing my eyes, pretending to have read it, and carry on with the way things had been, or I could read it and face the truth. I had wanted knowledge and truth and here was my chance to really understand, but I hadn't realized until now that knowing the truth also meant I might have to change. I was petrified with fear. Finally, my whole body trembling, I looked down and read the word, and as I read, I felt my chest swell and burn.

The man in the story gave *his heart*. But it was not the heart shown cupped in a hand; it was not the heart of his body. He gave to the gods the heart of his soul.

CHAPTER 46

My Least Favorite Person

Who's there?" said a voice. It startled me so much I almost lost my balance and fell backward down the steps. I leaned forward in time, though, and I stepped over the last step and onto the top of the temple platform, just as Speaker Tungan strode out of the cloister.

"It is just me, Speaker," I stammered, my mind still reeling from what I had just read.

"You?" he squinted. "Nadal? What are you doing here? Where is your mask?" he regarded my tunic, "and why are you wearing such ridiculous clothes? You look like a street vendor."

As it always seemed to happen with me around the Speakers, I was at a loss for words, so I said nothing.

"I came to tend the fire and then I thought I'd clean things up a bit. Those ceremonies do get messy, wouldn't you say?"

"Yes," I said, looking down at the altar and the dark red stains that streaked the sides.

"Once it took my servants an entire day to clean the blood out of my fingernails. Sometimes I think we should wear gloves. Cleaning it out of toenails is the most unpleasant, though."

I watched him as he organized the bowls inside on the dark shelves, my mind too consumed in thought to pay attention to what he was saying.

"The month of the Jaguar is approaching," said Tungan pleasantly. "Soon it will be the spring equinox and we shall sacrifice the Messenger."

"Yes," I murmured.

He turned and looked at me. "You know . . . it is immoral to fraternize with a sacrifice."

"What?"

"I know what you've been doing, Nadal. All of us know. Things can get dangerous when you develop relationships with those who are meant for the gods. Gods are very jealous. But that will all come to an end soon enough once she has performed her ritual." He sighed loudly and then added, "Unfortunately the gods will not listen to our pleas this season, since she won't be a virgin." He took a wet cloth and began washing the knives on the altar.

"What are you talking about? The Messenger is—"

"Don't lie to me, boy," Tungan said. "We know you've been visiting her tower for your own carnal satisfaction. I would have thought more of you, a future king."

"You—you think I have defiled *the Messenger*?" I pointed up toward the palace. "*That* Messenger?"

"Don't look at me like I'm an idiot," he said. "It's obvious. But for your sake we will go ahead and sacrifice her just as any other virgin. No need to stir up a scandal. No one will ever know she is unworthy."

I clenched my fists. "I have *not* dishonored her," I said through my teeth.

"No? Then what was it you two did in her tower last night? Stargaze?"

Anger swelled inside of my chest like a volcano. "There has never been a truer, more virtuous maiden taken to the cenote, and *you* know it."

The Speaker acted shocked. "My dear boy, what are you saying?"

"You always try to pollute the Messengers before they are sacrificed. You are bitter because Rishi refused *you*."

"Oh, it is Rishi, is it? That just further proves how familiar you have become with each other. Let me tell you something that is important for you to understand, Nadal. As a Speaker I have been consecrated. I am holy. My touch will not contaminate her like any common man. In fact, my touch probably sanctifies her even more."

I spat in his face. "You are as holy as a ringworm, Tungan."

He stood there, stunned, as my spittle slithered down his nose and chin. He took out his mirror and a cloth and slowly wiped his face.

I had a great desire to push him from the top of the pyramid. It would be easy to do and there would be no way he would survive as his body was smashed on the steep steps. But I stopped myself. This was not the right time. Not yet.

Instead I leaned close to his face and hissed, "Tungan, your days are numbered. Soon it will be *my* turn to rule this people. And when that happens, everything will change. *Everything*. I am not as stupid as you think I am."

"Oh my—!" Tungan said, pointing down the temple staircase. "Who is that coming up the steps?"

Twisting around, I looked and saw no one. Just then, a sudden searing pain flashed across my side. I turned just in time to see the edge of Tungan's knife leaving my body, red with my blood. I reached for my side, too surprised to speak. I felt as though I had been cut in half.

With the same cloth he used before to wipe my spit from his face, he now cleaned his knife. "What were you saying about being stupid? Think twice before you threaten me, Nadal."

He turned and went back into the cloister and as he did, he said over his shoulder, "Better get back to your tower, son. Stick around here any longer and I'll turn you into a eunuch." He left me standing there, clutching my ripped side, my blood dripping on the stone.

It took a long time to get my trembling body down the pyramid steps and make it back to my tower. I passed several people on the way, each of them looking at me in pity or disgust, but none offering an arm or shoulder to help. Such was the state of our city. We, after all, were a city of individuals.

In my tower, servants brought salves to rub into my wound. They never asked how I had received it. For days after that, I lay on my bed, even when I saw the candle lit in Rishi's tower. I knew she was waiting for me to come back, to tell her I had fulfilled the assignment she'd given me. But the thought of seeing Rishi again made me feel ashamed. And it wasn't because of the gash in my side.

I had been wrong about everything. Zitól was not a city of gold; it was a city of glass, and I could feel it shattering all around me. Up to this point, all of my goals, my dreams, and my aspirations had been patterned after the examples of liars and built upon foundations of smoke. We were all fools, the entire city. The permissiveness the Speakers granted me was the same they indulged on the people and we had all wallowed in it with carefree ignorance. It was as if I had been in a dark pit and now light was suddenly shining down on me, but the light was focused and searing. I had no idea how painful truth could be.

For days I lay in my sweaty bed, feeling like a tomato thrown against a wall. The words I had seen on the temple steps flashed continually before my mind. What did it mean to surrender to the gods my will and my desires? What *were* my will and desires? I desired for power, for wealth, for praise. I desired the death of the Speakers, now more than ever. I desired to only worry about myself and not to have to concern myself with the problems of others. I desired Rishi, in more ways than one. If I had never seen that top step, if I had never known what it truly meant, I could have gone on living my life with its luxuries, free of guilt, free of responsibility. I could have killed the Speakers with my bare hands and not felt any remorse. But now I knew what the gods knew and there was nothing I could do to make that knowledge go away.

Slowly the pain in my body began to heal, but the bitterness in my heart did not. I stayed in my room, lying on my back with my hands on my face. How much easier it is to sacrifice someone else to the gods than to surrender the desires of my own heart! The fibers and sinews that held my sins to my bosom were so much more complex than those that held my heart to my body. To tear out all of my lusts and desires would be like death.

When I was awake my body throbbed with pain. When I was asleep my mind was filled with nightmares. I dreamt of snakes in my bed. I dreamt of Riplakish's jaguar eating through my wound. Mostly I dreamed over and over of standing on the temple steps, the knife in my hand, thrusting it into the victim's chest, though now the victim wasn't some nameless person, it was Rishi.

My understanding was growing, even if my willingness to comply was not. For so long I had let my body do what it pleased, guided by whatever whims and urges seemed most appealing at the moment. I had never thought of trying to restrain myself and turn the power over to my mind and my heart. If the writing on the temple meant the gods wanted us to master our will and desires, then as a people, we were doomed. I marveled why the gods had not already struck us off the face of the earth.

One night during my delirium, thunder shook my tower. My eyes flew open as lighting electrified everything around me. My curtains were open and the rain poured down so hard I could feel mist on my face. I slowly sat up in bed and watched the jagged tracks of light cut through the black night outside, as if the gods were trying to crack open the sky. I wondered if there had been a sacrifice that night and the gods were sending rain. We wanted the rain. After all, that is what the sacrifices were for, was it not? But perhaps we had been wrong this entire time. Perhaps the gods weren't sending rain to water our crops. Maybe the lightning was the glimmer of the sky they wanted us to see, to crack away the darkness from our eyes and see the light beyond. And maybe Rishi really was right; the rain wasn't an answer to our offering, but tears for our error.

Scritch, scratch. I awoke the next morning to the fresh smell of wet earth and a strange noise outside. *Scritch, scratch.* Crawling from my bed to the balcony, I leaned over the railing and saw half a dozen men surrounding the Messenger's tower. Some were in the courtyard; others were on the roofs of the Speakers' apartments. With machetes they were hacking at the vines. The scratching sound came from the long rakes the men were using to pull down the loosened tendrils. I crawled back to my bed, vaguely aware that I would have to find another way to speak to Rishi.

The Speakers were behind this, of course. The Speakers were behind everything. I could see why they had twisted the language of the temple pyramid and took knowledge from the people. The Speakers and the people were not beholden to the gods for anything as long as there was a sacrifice. They could lie, steal, and cheat as long as there was a sacrifice. As long as there was a sacrifice, morality wasn't an issue, for the gods cared not for the purity of the people, but for sacrifice. The sacrifices provided the Speakers with a way to live a life without restraint or integrity and still be given the blessing of the gods.

Only they *didn't* have the blessing of the gods. That much the writing on the stone made clear. I realized I had to know more about what the Speakers had changed when they took power so long ago.

I knew only one person who was old enough to have the answer.

CHAPTER 47

A Kingdom Upside Down

By the time I had healed enough to walk in a straight line, it was only a week before the spring equinox. Going down steps was still painful and I winced with each movement, but I managed to leave my tower, a hood over my head. I walked through the passage and around the back of the palace, taking breaks in dark shadows to rest. Finally I had climbed down the steps and was on the road to the cenote. I passed around its large, vacant mouth, willing myself not to look at the platform where Rishi would be standing in one week's time.

I entered the forest and walked until I could see the red glow of the fire.

When I came to the clearing Gabber Gerta was there, sitting by the fire as if she had never moved since the last time I saw her. In her arms were the two babies and around her feet were more children, curled up under old blankets like little snails.

I cradled my aching side and leaned against a tree to rest. The hike to the village had taken more energy out of me than I expected. I listened to Gabber Gerta sing.

> *Giving it increases me.*
> *When I keep it I shrivel,*
> *What is it? What is it?*
> *It cannot be held*
> *Yet it binds us together*
> *What is it? What is it?*
>
> *It keeps us safe from harm*
> *Yet it harms no one*
> *It keeps us warm*
> *But it does not burn.*
> *What is it? What is it?*

Then she stopped. "There is no use hiding in the trees, dear," the woman murmured. "Gabber Gerta knows you are there."

I reluctantly dragged myself out of the forest, keeping my hood over my face. As I approached the fire I could see other forms, sleeping on the ground in the semi-darkness, and they were definitely not children.

"So what is it?" I asked quietly, not wishing to disturb any of the sleepers.

"What is what?"

"The answer to your song. You keep asking 'what is it?'"

"Oh, yes." She chuckled. "It is love, of course."

"Hmm," I said, holding out my hands to feel the warmth of the fire. "I suppose it is one of the Seven Songs Rishi is always talking about."

"It is indeed," nodded the old woman. "Where is your lovely friend?"

"She . . . couldn't come tonight."

The woman clicked her tongue. "Such a pity."

"Who are they?" I motioned toward the sleeping figures.

"They are . . . visitors, trying to locate something they've lost." She smiled warmly. "Now, tell me, child, why have you come?"

"I was wondering if you could tell me the history of Zitól. From before the Great Coward."

"It is a long story."

I removed my hood and lowered myself on to one of the stools, feeling as heavy as a fallen pillar. "I like long stories," I said softly.

The woman studied me with her wise eyes. "You look different this time, Nadal. You look . . . weary. Weary in spirit and body."

I nodded. Weary was a good word. Broken would be better. But talking about myself was the last thing I wanted to do. "Please tell me. Tell me about the Great Coward . . . about Yelgab," I said.

The old woman nodded and leaned back in her chair.

"Long ago, Zitól was very different. Children were required to get an education. We were expected to one day learn to read and to write the characters you see all about you on the walls of the city. Food was in abundance. Gold was as common as corn. Everyone shared. It was a time like no other.

"But there were some who wanted more. Through wealth and power they were able to get more and when they had more, they would not give what they had to those who had less. Our society started to break up into classes. The rich became richer and the poor became poorer. Then there came the drought."

"Month after month no rain fell. People began to starve and then die. Our parents and the other adults were desperate for the gods to hear them, to bring rain, but they refused to change their behavior. They enjoyed living as lavishly as they could, and doing away with any and all virtues that had once held together our society. They didn't want to do anything that restricted them from enjoying their luxuries or that put them at the same level as the poor.

"But they would not be able to continue in this way if it did not eventually rain. There was one priest, a good and just man who deeply loved his family and his people, who suggested that a sacrifice should be made. 'And is not our own blood the most precious thing we could give up?' he asked.

"This brave man volunteered to be the first sacrifice. It was regarded by all as an act of great unselfishness. Soon after, it rained. The people of Zitól saw this as a sign, and the Speakers saw it as an opportunity.

"Now that the rains were back, people no longer thought sacrifice was needed. But the Speakers convinced the people that sacrifices were imperative as a preventive measure against future calamities. They instituted a sacrifice every year. Then every six months, then every month. The Speakers gradually made sacrifice an art form. Candidates would be chosen from the healthiest, the most beautiful. They would live what was left of their life in luxury beyond imagination. In addition, the Speakers promised they would be generously rewarded in the next life. This proved tempting to many who wanted to live a life like the wealthy but were too poor to afford it. I think some were sincere in the offering of their bodies to the gods. Sincere, but misled.

"We grew older and we found to our delight that they had stopped teaching schools. Of course to our young minds this was wonderful. We had heard our older siblings complain of the work they had to do. We were more than happy to live carefree with no studies, no obligations . . . all except my brother.

"My brother Yelgab was troubled by the sacrifices. He was older than me and had studied hard to become an astronomer. Believe it or not, the original purpose of the Messenger's tower wasn't to sequester maidens for sacrifice. It was the astronomer's tower, and my brother spent many hours there, studying the stars. While living in the palace he became acquainted with the Speakers and he learned their true motivations for dismissing education.

"With each year his contempt for the Speakers grew. The words he always used for the sacrifices were 'upside down.' He said that the priests and Speakers were twisting the words of scripture to fit their own desires, and that they were telling us the way they wanted us to *perceive* the gods, and not how the gods really were. He never told anyone but me about his opinions. He knew that it would hurt his chances of being elected."

"Elected?" I asked.

"Yes, at that time the Speakers were elected by the people. Yelgab hoped to bring Zitól back to balance by becoming a Speaker himself. He had a gift with words and was liked by many. No one was surprised that he won. He was an excellent Speaker, and he was respected for his knowledge and his fairness. The people recognized in him something special. Ironically, the qualities that made him special—his integrity, his knowledge, his virtue—were the very things the people were eagerly giving up.

"But soon another drought lay waste to the land. This was discouraging, for just when my brother was in a position to reason with the people that the sacrifices were wicked, the people demanded more."

"Yelgab was determined. He spoke many days from the steps of the temple that the priests were in error. Of course, to speak out against the government was not only illegal, but blasphemous, and the penalty was high. I begged him to stop. But he would not. Finally, a priest publicly suggested that *Yelgab* was the reason we were now in a drought, and that if they really wanted the gods to listen, they should sacrifice *him*.

"When Yelgab heard of this plan he was distraught. For many days he fasted and kept to himself, trying to find the best answer to this problem. But a group of elitists and priests broke into his home and dragged him up the steps of the temple. If I had not warned him in advance, he would have certainly died. There was a terrible fight on the steps of the temple." I touched my waist where my own bandages were.

"Yelgab escaped and disappeared into the forest," Gabber Gerta continued. "I found him in the jungle and healed his wounds. He knew he could not enter the city again and remain alive. I asked him where he would go and he said he would walk until he found a people that were humble enough to listen to the truth. From what we discovered the other night about your friend, it sounds like he had to not only walk but also *swim* before he found anyone who would listen.

"From that time onward the Speakers made an example of Yelgab. They made sure he was known by all as Yelgab the Coward and that anyone else who refused to be a gift to the gods would be disgraced.

"After that the sacrifices accelerated. People wanted to show their devotion. By then they were so under the spell of the Speakers that they didn't know better. They added the cenote sacrifices later. When the sacrifices were first begun they were quite grand affairs, with feasts and dancing and speaking. But increasing them took some of the pageantry out of the event. My theory is that they added the spring equinox sacrifice just to have a big event again. Only this time they would make it more sensational. To throw a beautiful, untouched virgin into a well . . . What a dramatic way to begin the planting season."

"So you are saying that there is nothing sacred about the cenote at all? That the Messenger's sacrifice is just a spectacle? A pageant?"

"I don't doubt that there are many people who sincerely believe she will be able to talk to the gods in the well. They used to say that the gods would send the Messenger back to the surface if they wanted to reply, but not one of those girls has ever risen to the surface with a message," she said bitterly, "and now the people don't even bother waiting to see if she might."

"You know she is the Messenger, don't you?" I blurted out before I could stop myself.

"I know. She is famous. You don't have to be a dream child to know that. Everyone knows who Rishi is."

"I can't let her drown," I said, trying to push away the emotion that was swelling inside of me.

"Do you have the power to stop them?" the woman asked eagerly.

"I don't know. I don't know how," I moaned, rubbing my face. "I don't even have a way to speak to her anymore."

The woman sat back in her chair, lost in thought. Neither of us spoke for a long time. I sat there with my head in my hands, listening to her creaking chair and the soft breathing of the sleeping children. One of the large figures snored loudly. Finally she spoke. "Some day things will be restored, young man. Someday Zitól will be balanced again."

"Balanced," I said. "What does that mean?"

"Have you ever wondered why it is that men rule over the animals on earth?"

"Not really," I said. "People are smarter than animals. That is all."

"People are not *smarter* than animals," the woman said. "Have you ever seen a wolf track its prey? Or watched a jaguar locate water? In many ways animals surpass humans with the things they know. What makes people different from animals is not our knowledge, but our restraint. Take this ability away and people become animals. I know of tribes who have already succumbed completely to their carnal selves." I thought of the Snatchers that Rishi had told me about.

"Our patience, our ability to take command of our instincts, making our bodies do what our minds tell them to is what makes us superior. *That* is self-mastery. *That* is intelligence." She looked up at the stars. "And that is why man is the only living thing with the potential to become a god."

CHAPTER 48

The Sacrifice of the Messenger

I trudged back up to the palace, thinking about all of the things Gabber Gerta had said. Who would have ever thought that this diminutive forest woman, wrapped in shawls and babies, could unstitch everything I had understood about the world, seam by seam? Was everything she said true? And if it was, now what? Listening to truth is one thing. Acting on it . . . that was a different game altogether. And it was a game I was not ready to play.

But Gabber Gerta's enlightening narrative still did not help me solve the immediate problem at hand: the Sacrifice of the Messenger. It had to be stopped.

I woke the next morning to the sound of conch shells announcing it was the week of the spring equinox, the month of the Jaguar, and the most festive time of the year. This week there would be parties and dancing. Madame Xoca would bring her "Daughters of Paradise" to be tested by Riplakish's jaguar, and finally the Messenger, *my* Messenger, would be cast in the cenote.

I heard a clap in the stairwell.

"Come in," I said.

It was one of the Speakers' attendants. "The Speakers sent me to summon you to the throne room," he said.

This was a surprise. I quickly put on my white clothes and went down.

They were all there, reclining on their sofas, deep in serious conversation. As I walked into the room the voices abruptly changed tone.

"Anointed One!" said Speaker Riplakish, smiling. "Welcome! We have exciting things to discuss with you."

Since when were they so eager to discuss things with me? I stood in the center of the room, standing on the mosaic of the sun. All the Speakers looked at me, their eyes bright, glistening like volcanic glass. I deliberately avoided Tungan's face. His skin was not worth looking upon.

"Nineteen years ago you were brought to us as a tiny babe," began Speaker Riplakish, nostalgically. "From the moment you were born you were destined to one day rule the great city of Zitól."

I narrowed my eyes, sensing something rotten in Riplakish's statement.

"You were placed in our care, and we have done our best to be attentive guardians to you while serving as your regents."

"We knew that one day it would be time for us to step aside and let you have your rightful place," added Gula.

They sounded so perfect. So flawless. So . . . rehearsed. I waited for the "but."

"We have waited for you to show signs that you are truly ready for this magnificent and weighty responsibility."

"Speaker Tungan told us of a recent encounter with you on the temple," said Speaker Gula, nodding at Tungan. I still did not look at him, nor did I need to. I could *feel* his darkness.

"He said that there was a disagreement . . ."

I stiffened.

". . . And that you handled it most manfully. That you showed courage and resilience."

Finally I turned to Tungan. His expression was the pretense of a man welcoming home a long-lost brother. But there was no brotherhood here. Beneath our calm façades our eyes locked in mutual hatred.

"We have discussed this and we unanimously agree that it is time for you to ascend to your rightful place as king."

I blinked. "You . . . what?" I said in disbelief.

"Yes, yes . . . it must be quite a shock, and I'm sure you are full of questions." Speaker Riplakish smiled so wide I thought his face would crack apart. "You are probably wondering when this will all take place. And we thought there would be no better time than now, during the week of the spring equinox," he said, monitoring my expression.

I swallowed. My eyes traveled from face to face. I had never seen the Speakers watch me with such rapt attention. I couldn't tell if they meant what they said or if they were trying to stifle their laughter. Perhaps this was some joke.

"What are the conditions?" I asked.

"Conditions?"

"Yes. What do you want for it? What do I have to give you in return? You don't really think I believe that you are willing to relinquish control completely."

"Of course not, Nadal. We will continue to advise you and serve as your faithful counselors. That is the only condition."

So in other words, nothing would change except that their puppet would finally have a face. *Snakes*, I thought.

"The announcement will be made public at the sacrifice. Of course, this will just be the beginning of the preparations. You won't actually be *crowned* king for another month."

I again examined their faces, knowing that I was being fed half-truths. But I didn't have the desire or patience to second-guess the Speakers and their mysterious agendas. The only thing that mattered right now was Rishi. I had to find a way to free her and take her far away from these men.

But I didn't have a chance. From the moment I was escorted from the throne room, I was never alone. Every minute there was someone attending me, briefing me, dressing me, feeding me, measuring me for new clothes. I was required to be present for every session of court and to listen to the Speakers' speeches. I sat there in my throne, sweating with anxiety, wanting more than anything else to escape and be with Rishi, but the Speakers made it impossible.

I had never cared before about the sacrifices. I had never known any of the people that died; I hadn't even spoken to them. To be honest, killing them wasn't even much of a sacrifice for me. But now, for the first time in my life I felt as if part of me would drown with Rishi at the week's end.

Like a child, I was escorted wherever I went. Guards stood at the base of my tower, night and day. Only when I was up in my tower would they let Rishi out to be washed and fitted for her dress and regalia. In dismay I looked out at the smooth walls of the Messenger's tower, regretting that I hadn't rescued Rishi sooner.

I had some paper left. I wrote to her that the Speakers planned to make me king. I wanted to write more . . . that my life would be worth nothing without her. That I never knew how to love someone until I found her . . . I couldn't think of anything to write that could convey my anguish, so I folded the paper, intending to deliver it to the kitchen, but I was not allowed in. In frustration I walked toward the Messenger's tower, looking for Leema, but my escorts blocked the way.

"I just want to speak to the Messenger's keeper," I growled.

I was tersely informed that Leema had been "removed" and that armed guards had taken her place.

When I learned this I immediately went to the Speakers.

"What happened to Leema, the Messenger's keeper?" I demanded.

"She has been found unfit to guard the Messenger."

"What did you do with her?" I said.

"She has been . . . dispatched," was the answer.

This made me angry. I liked grouchy Leema and her peculiar ways. It made me hate the Speakers more than ever.

With each dawn my resentment for the sun grew. If only time could stop long enough for me to figure out a plan.

The night before the sacrifice I tried praying to Rishi's gods for the first time. In my mind I tried to picture them, not as I had been taught to know them, gnarled, terrifying beings, but as Rishi knew them, benevolent and merciful. I asked that if they were really gods of love rather than lust, they must help me find a way to save Rishi.

I was up before dawn on the day of the spring equinox. As the sky turned from grey to blue I paced around my room, going from my bed to my balcony, checking Rishi's tower every time to see if she would come out where I could see her, but she never did. I scrambled my brain, trying to think of something I could do to take her away, to rescue her, but I had no solution.

Down below in the courtyard they were lining up the litters. As was the custom, my litter was first, then the litter for the Messenger.

I leaned out on the balcony, searching the people below. Finally I caught a glimpse of her when the female servants led her out across the courtyard to the bathhouse to be bathed and clothed. Her figure passed through, and I watched, pounding my fist against the stone railing with frustration. There was a clap at the stairs, making me jump. It was the women coming to dress me for the ceremony. Reluctantly, I let them come in.

They undressed me down to my loincloth and massaged fragrant oils into my skin. I knew they were doing the same for Rishi, except after the oils they would paint her body with the thick blue pigment. The women held out a pure white garment for me, fresh and pristine. Their quick hands wrapped it around my body, fastening it into place. Rishi would now be fitted with the light blue gown that had taken Leema a year to make. They would also be combing her black hair, plaiting ribbons through it, and fitting her ears with earrings that sparkled like fireflies. They tied a blue sash around my waist, the only blue I ever wore, and only on this day. The women had brought three different necklaces for me to choose from. I knew that Rishi would be draped with necklaces too, and rings and anklets and bracelets. The women clasped the necklace around my neck and I felt it cold and heavy on my chest. I wondered if Rishi realized that the heavy jewelry given to the Messenger was not just for ornament, but to make her body sink.

Another sharp clap came from the stairs.

"The procession is ready, Anointed One," said the servant.

When I emerged from the bottom of my tower more women were there, holding a giant, fanned headpiece made with bright red spoonbill feathers. They had to stand on stools in order to place it on my head. The weight pressed down on me, forcing me to adjust my balance. Then came the mask. Today I was to wear the mask of power, the mask of the jaguar. Once it was fastened on my head it was as if I became a different person, and everyone in the courtyards sank on their knees as I passed them and mounted my litter. To my surprise, Tungan and Riplakish were waiting for me and when I sat down they surreptitiously tied my arms to the arms of the chair with tight cords.

"Just to make sure you don't do anything you would later regret," Tungan said. He draped a jaguar cape over my arms and shoulders, concealing the ropes.

Conch shells blew. My chair floated off the ground and the procession began. We were on our way to the cenote.

My heart beat in my throat. I stared straight ahead, knowing she was watching me from behind. There were no pumpkin seeds to throw this time. *This* was not a celebration.

My chair rocked and tipped like a ship in a storm as we headed down the hill. When we reached the cenote there were more people there than I had ever seen before. They rimmed the circumference of the pit, holding their baskets of golden riches, each trying to outdo his neighbor with his offering. And now that I knew to listen for it, I could hear the muffled cries of babies coming from the closed bags.

The procession halted and my litter was positioned in a deliberate manner so that I might have the perfect view of the platform from which Rishi was to be sacrificed. This is where my litter was always placed, and this is where I always sat. I was now on my way to becoming king, but little had changed. I was more powerless than I had ever been.

The other litter was set down beside me, and, as always, the Speakers helped the Messenger out. The people all around the cenote let out a collective gasp at her beauty. This was all part of the tradition, of course. She was magnificent. Her beautiful blue body was slender and perfect, and her pale blue dress shimmered like sunlit water. On her head was a magnificent, plumed headpiece that transformed her from a girl to a goddess.

For one moment she glanced up at me, and I thought I saw her smile. I would have run out to her at that moment, seizing her in my arms, if it were not for the cords holding me down.

They led her up to the platform.

I felt as if I were about to suffocate. My palms were wet as I gripped the arms of my chair. My stomach churned inside me like a great snake, and I felt as if at any moment I would vomit. Worse than the thought of Rishi dying was the thought that there was still time to do something to stop this, but I did not know how. It was like trying to stop a wave from washing over me, or to stop the rain falling from the sky. I could do nothing but watch, silently screaming.

She reached the platform, with Speaker Riplakish and Speaker Tungan beside her. Riplakish held up his arms and the people's admiring murmurs hushed.

"Great citizens of Zitól!" he announced. "We are about to perform the most sacred sacrifice of the year. This holy and chaste Messenger will plead with the gods to sanctify our city and our crops, that we might once again enjoy their great generosity."

I was barely listening to what he said. I did not care about the sanctity of our crops. I doubted the gods did, either.

"But before the sacrifice I have another, historic announcement to make," continued Riplakish. This was a break in tradition, and I listened.

"I am here to announce that preparations are being made to crown the Anointed One. And by the end of this month, Zitól will once again have a king!"

A gasp of surprise reverberated through the group that quickly grew to an enthusiastic roar, but the Speaker held out his hands to quiet them. Before he spoke again he looked down in my direction and smiled.

"And to show his devotion to the gods, *our new king* shall have the honor of performing this year's sacrifice of the Messenger."

Hundreds of faces turned to me. I felt a shock wave flash through my body, and the life drained from my arms and legs. How could I have been so stupid? Did I suppose that the Speakers really wanted me to take the throne without first making me prove my loyalty to them?

Gula was standing beside my litter. Slipping his hand under the jaguar cape, he cut the cords that held me to the seat. Then, with a mighty flourish he gestured for me to move forward.

This unprecedented change of protocol created absolute pandemonium in the crowd. Never before had the Anointed One varied from the established tradition of being present, stoic, and impotent. And now here I was, finally coming of age and blossoming into my long-awaited, well-deserved role as their next bloodthirsty leader. They were wild with excitement.

I remained in my seat, as if the cords still bound me to the throne. I could not move. "Your sacrifice awaits," said Speaker Gula pleasantly in my ear. Then, taking my wrist, he pulled me from the litter.

I didn't know what to do except move forward. I stumbled out of the litter and made my way to the steps of the platform in a trance. I ascended the steps with the nobility of a prince, but under my royal robes I trembled like a rabbit. I looked up at Rishi. She was staring into the cenote, while Tungan and Riplakish bound her hands and feet.

By the time I reached the platform and faced Rishi I felt as if not one of my bones was properly connected with its neighbor and that at any moment my legs would fold under me. I glanced off the edge to the water below and felt myself sway. Riplakish and Tungan finished tying Rishi and brushed past me as they descended off the platform. I heard Tungan chuckle softly. Finally, when the Speakers had reached the bottom of the stairs and Rishi and I were alone on the platform, she looked up at me.

She was dazzling. Up close, the details of her regalia were exquisite. Her blue skin was the same shade as the blue in her eye. Gold dust had been blown on her eyelids and lips, making her seem otherworldly. A beaded headband wrapped around her forehead with tiny golden bells and above her head, the headpiece blossomed with blue and white feathers, like a great fountain. Her dress was the most amazing Leema had ever made, and hanging down at her side, her bead swung, smooth and white. I could smell the cool water far below us in the void. I looked down for a moment, into the deep space, and thought I saw something move close to the edge of the water, near the steep, white walls. Chills crept up my back. I fixed my gaze back on Rishi's eyes.

I expected Rishi's demeanor to be terrified, fearful, or at least anxious. But when I looked into her eyes I saw none of these emotions. She was as tranquil as the eye of a hurricane. Her face was serene and determined. She did not look like someone who was about to lose her life. If anything, *she* looked like the royal one and I looked like the one who was jumping into the cenote.

The mass of people that surrounded us was hushed now, watching to see me perform my first act of power.

"Nadal. Are you in there?" she asked, peering into my mask.

"Rishi," I swallowed. "This wasn't my idea, I hope you know." My mouth felt as dry as sand. Inside the mask my voice seemed so loud I felt that everyone could hear me.

I had never seen her face shine with courage like it did that day over the cenote. She was brave. Braver than I had ever been in my life. "Nadal," she said solemnly, "I will be all right. You need to believe me." The bells on her headdress tinkled and glimmered in the sun.

For once I was glad I wore a mask, for I could not stop my chin from quivering. My hands shook and my heart was breaking in my chest. Suddenly it was so important to tell her what I had learned. "I read the writing on the temple," I said, my voice trembling. "I understand now. I was wrong about everything. You knew what I would find, didn't you?"

She smiled and her eyes looked up at me with a yearning I had never seen before, "I want you to be a *good* king, Nadal. I want you to have the truth on your side. Zitól wasn't always like this. You can restore it to the way it was."

I felt like the First Man in the story on the temple steps, except instead of looking for a companion, I was losing mine. I would give anything to keep her with me. Anything. Nothing mattered if I didn't have her alive and safe. But I was out of choices.

I could lift her up and throw her into the well, walk down the stairs, and be the king I had always wanted to be. Or I could do what my heart and soul screamed out for me to do: to take Rishi in my arms and carry her back down the stairs, where, if we weren't killed immediately by the Speakers, we would be ripped to pieces by the people. If the gods truly wanted a sacrifice of the soul, I was willing to give it, but how? Tears stung my eyes and wet my cheeks. How could I show them that above anything else, all I wanted was love?

Then it happened, like a clap of thunder over my head. I knew what to do.

I put my trembling hands on Rishi's headdress and lifted it high in the air. The people cheered, since to them this meant the ritual was about to begin. I glanced down at the Speakers. They smiled and nodded approvingly, and I could almost hear their words in my head: *The first step in sacrificial protocol: save the headdress.* I placed the headdress on the ground.

The second step to sacrificing a victim was to present her to the people and acknowledge the crowd. I skipped this step. Instead, with my heart beating in my chest, I raised my hands over my head and removed *my own* headdress. I set it on the ground, next to the Messenger's. Confusion in the audience was palpable, and their whispers sounded like wasps.

"What are you doing?" Rishi's eyes were wide and liquid.

Without answering her, I reached behind my head and unfastened the jaguar mask. Sunlight fell upon my face, reflecting the silver rivers running down my cheeks. The people muttering crowd became mute. I let the mask fall at my feet, and with a loud crack it broke in two.

When Rishi saw my face, her brave composure faltered and tears spilled from her eyes, making tracks through the blue paint on her cheeks. I placed my hands on her wet face and slid my fingers across her cheeks, wiping away some of the blue. Then, with my fingers covered in paint, I rubbed blue across my own forehead and down my cheekbones. I wiped more blue paint off her arms. Then I smeared it onto my own chest and shoulders.

The people watched me, spellbound. It was only when I wrapped my arms around Rishi's body, slipping my hands under her bound arms that they started again to buzz. And then murmur. And then rumble.

"You will not go alone," I said, emotion filling my lungs so that the words barely squeaked out. The air around us filled with the screaming crowd. "I go where you go."

"Nadal . . . ," she said.

I held her close and kissed her forehead. A roar erupted from the surrounding onlookers, not understanding what was going on, but loving it.

"Nadal," she said more firmly, looking up into my face.

"Yes, Rishi." I couldn't see a thing; my eyes were so blurry.

"Are you sure you want to do this?"

"Yes, Rishi," I said. I had never been more sure of anything before.

"Then you've got to pull yourself together. I want you to know that we are going to be all right. We are not going to die."

"I highly doubt that," I said, closing my eyes and holding her close to me. I tried to recall if I had ever told her I couldn't swim. It didn't matter now, though, for I had my whole world right there in my arms.

"But you must listen to me. If you want to come with me, you need to stop shaking and breathe slower." Her eyes became deadly serious.

"What—?"

"Do you remember that silly breathing contest we had so long ago? We are going to do it again. But this time you need to do as I say. You are breathing too fast. Match my breathing. And pull your breath in as deeply as you can. Every time you breathe, make your breath go deeper down inside your body. Your last breath needs to be the biggest because you are going to have to hold it for a long time."

"A long time? What do you—?" I asked.

"Just do it," she said. I felt Rishi's body slowly expand and contract against my chest. I tried to breath more slowly, to match her breathing.

"Yes, that's it," she said after a few moments. How could she stand there so calmly? "Are you ready?" she asked, her eyes set and resolute.

"Yes," I said. *No*, I thought.

"Now take the deepest, lowest breath you've ever taken in your life," she directed, "on the count of three. One . . . two . . ."

Together we breathed deeply, together we held onto that breath, and as one we leaned our bodies over the edge.

CHAPTER 49 ·

Into the Underworld

I will never forget the unpleasant feeling that rushed through my body as I fell through the air. My stomach lurched up to my throat and I felt like I was being pulled inside out. The terror was so intense my only desire was to scream, and if I did, the sound was swallowed up in the thundering of the crowd that screamed all around us as we fell. Within moments we plunged deep into the dark water, separating from each other in the rush of bubbles, and the world became muffled. I opened my eyes, seeing the round light circling above me. Then I reached for Rishi, removing the heavy necklaces and bracelets from her body. I tried loosening the ropes that held her arms and legs trapped. If I could just loosen it a little, perhaps she could wriggle free. I turned her body over, looking for the knots, but I couldn't find them. My lungs were starting to burn and I yearned to scramble upward toward the crown of light above us. At last I found a knot and started tearing at it with my finger-tips, when something happened that I never expected.

Something yanked me backward.

Strong arms grasped my shoulders, pulling me down and away from Rishi. I panicked. To my horror, other dark forms gathered around Rishi, handling her, pulling her. I tried to pry off the hands that gripped me but it was impossible. They were dragging me deeper into the water. My chest burned and I knew I needed air or I would explode.

I did everything I could to suppress the urge to open my mouth and take in a breath of water. I twisted away and fought to ascend up to the glimmering light above me but a hand gripped my ankle, jerking me downward again. Then all around me the water became much cooler and seemed to move with a life of its own. The water was pulling me now and I was moving quickly away from the surface and into the belly of the cenote. Those familiar stars started to sparkle and drift around in the dark water. The last thing I remember was watching Rishi disappearing ahead of me, leaving behind her ropes that floated through the water like ribbons. Then everything went black.

"Is she alive?"

"I think so. Her heart is beating. She's breathing."

"Let's see if we can wake her up."

"No, let her rest. She's had a rough year."

"We've *all* had a rough year."

"What about the other one over there. Is he breathing?"

"Who cares?"

Someone laid his head on my chest. His wet hair stuck to my face.

"He's breathing."

"That's a pity."

"Whose idea was it to save him anyway?"

"He's Rishi's friend. Didn't you see what he did?"

"Yeah. He just doesn't seem like Rishi's type."

"Well, he'd better not cause any trouble. It almost killed me to get him out of there."

The voices sounded vague and far away, and when I opened my eyes all I could see were dim, waving lights. It was very cold. Somewhere water was dripping. I tried leaning up and got as far as my elbows when water came gushing out of my mouth. The entire contents of my stomach plus enough water to sail a canoe flowed out around me. Wave after wave, the choking and gasping continued, echoing off the walls like the retching of some terrible monster, until my quivering abdomen relaxed and I finally lowered my face against the cold rock.

When I awoke again someone was nudging me with their foot.

"Wake up, royal fish face," said a voice. *Was it just one voice?* I thought. The echoes made it sound like hundreds.

I opened my eyes. Three men were peering down at me. Strong men. They wore no clothing except for cloths about their waists, which were wet and clung to their legs. Waving lines of light rippled over their bodies.

"Are you . . . are you the gods?" I asked.

The three men laughed.

"I like this guy," one of them said.

I sat up and tried to rub the pain out of my temples. "Where is she?" I asked.

"Rishi? She's over there. She's all right. She looks a lot better than you do, anyway."

"What place is this?"

"You, fish face, are in a cave."

"Yes, but how—"

"It is a cave that connects to the cenote," the other explained. I leaned up and looked around me. It was dark and cold and cavernous, and the ceiling was covered with long, cone-shaped rocks that seemed to grow out of the roof of the cave like giant crocodile teeth. Light fluctuated on these great teeth in undulating lines, reflecting off the surface of a small, jade-colored pool. I had been lying on a small bank nestled next to the wall of the cave. Further down the bank, lying on her side with her back toward me was Rishi. Beyond her I could see a crack of white daylight in the distance.

Just then, something in the pool glittered. Rubbing my eyes, I looked deeper into the water. I couldn't believe what I was seeing. The entire bottom of the pool was covered in gold. Not only that, but jewels, pearls, necklaces, and . . . skeletons.

"As delightful as it is in here, we really don't have time to make ourselves comfortable," said one of the men. "Zitóli priests will be here soon to gather their spoils."

On my hands and knees I crawled over to where Rishi was lying and gently lifted her head. She shivered and uttered a soft moan, but she did not open her eyes.

One of the men worked his arms under her body and gently lifted her up. I stood too, hitting my head on the ceiling of the cave.

"Oh," said the skinny one. "Watch your head."

We made our way out of the cave, toward the crack of daylight that looked like a great keyhole. Rishi's hair and dress were wet and her arm hung limply, swinging back and forth with every step her bearer took. I followed, clutching the mossy cavern walls for balance.

I hadn't realized how cold it was in the cave until we emerged into the bright afternoon and the sun bathed us in warm light.

The young men turned into the forest, seeming to know exactly where they were going. I staggered behind them like a drunk man, blinking at the brightness and still finding it hard to believe I was alive. That Rishi was alive. I had no idea what was about to happen to us and I didn't care. We were both alive and the looming terror of the cenote that had plagued me for months was now gone.

Several children spied us first. They were watching for us from the trees, and initially they just stared at us, their eyes wide and their mouths hanging open. Then one of them shouted, "They did it, they did it!" and they dropped out of the branches and ran off like deer through the forest.

Before, when I had visited the invisible village, it had always been as peaceful as a sanctuary. Now the village was bursting with color and life. Everywhere I looked there were children. Every size and age was represented. They ran, jumped, laughed, fought, and when they saw us, they came flocking to our sides like brightly colored birds. They sounded like birds, too, all speaking at once, chanting, yelling, every one trying to make his or her voice heard. Little hands were all over me, pulling me forward, rubbing the blue paint that still clung to my arms and between my fingers, patting my clothes . . . They were friendly and had no reservations. One even swatted me on the behind.

Gabber Gerta was cooking great pots of food over the fire, with several babies strapped to her back, and when she saw us, relief washed over her face. The children who had first seen us were now swarming her and pointing to us excitedly. She bent low and spoke to the children and they all started running to different huts on little errands. When they returned, some came with blankets and others brought gourds of water. In no time they had a bed made under a shaded canopy for Rishi, stumps were rolled out for the men to sit on, and food was served. The man who was carrying Rishi set her down gently on the blankets. A child handed him a gourd from which he took a long, gulping drink.

There were adult women there too, but they did not look like women from Zitól. They were modestly dressed and wore simple headbands around their heads. Their faces were bright and anxious and they couldn't take their eyes off Rishi.

The children buzzed and chattered until Gabber Gerta clapped her hands and silenced them. They obeyed her immediately but still wiggled and hovered around us like dozens of little owls, their eyes full of curiosity.

We must have looked like we had just washed up on the beach; our clothes were still soaking wet and our hair was sticking in all directions. I felt wasted and exhausted. But when I looked at the men beside me, they were all grinning.

"Well done, nephews," Gabber Gerta beamed.

"Nephews?" I asked as something clicked in my head. "Does that mean—?"

"Oh, we're sorry. We completely forgot to introduce ourselves. My name is Eno."

"My name is Cotyl."

"My name is Quash. And we are Rishi's brothers."

CHAPTER 50

The Brothers Tell Their Tale

Rishi started to moan.

The young women moved to her side, brushing the tangled hair from her cheeks, touching her shoulders, and cradling her hands. Rishi still had blue paint on parts of her face and arms, and as they wiped it off she fluttered her eyelids and gazed up at her friends. "Sepya . . . Venay . . . Lantana," she said, blinking in disbelief. She rubbed her eyes and looked again at their beaming faces. "You are here! I was so worried about you! But . . . ," she said, her expression of relief darkening to concern. "What about Isra? I don't see her. Where is she?" The women smiled and looked over their shoulders toward another young lady, still dressed as a Zitóli consort. She stood with her head down, her hands behind her back, and her eyes brimming with tears.

Rishi pushed herself up into a sitting position. "Isra," she beckoned warmly. "Oh Isra!"

Isra knelt beside Rishi and grasped her hands, pressing them to her wet face. "I'm so sorry, Rishi," Isra cried. "I will never forgive myself for what I did not do. I wish I could have been strong, like you!"

"What are you talking about?" said Rishi, wiping the woman's tears. "How can I thank you enough? You *were* strong—and brave! If it weren't for you, I never would have known that my—my—" Realization dawned on Rishi's face. She bit her trembling lower lip. "Where are they?" she whispered. She put one hand over her heart as if to guard it from the words she might hear. Her hopeful eyes searched Isra's face. "Did they really— Are they *really*—"

"As handsome as you remembered?" said a deep voice. Rishi's eyes flooded with tears as the three men rushed around their sister, smothering her in their strong arms.

"Is it really you?" she gasped, laughing and choking as tears poured down her face. Pulling back to see their faces, she fingered each of their grinning cheeks, her eyes drinking in their gentle, earnest expressions.

"We are so sorry, Rishi," Eno said. "Can you forgive us?"

Rishi couldn't speak. Instead she put her arms around them and pulled all three men to her so that their heads were touching. With a voice as fragile as glass I heard her say, "I knew you would come for me."

I thought I should look away and not intrude on Rishi's moment with her brothers, but I couldn't. As I watched those four black heads huddled together with their arms holding each other close, an ache grew in my chest and spread out through my whole body. What would it be like to have someone to come home to? I noticed that Gabber Gerta was watching them too. Her eyes glistened, and I wondered if she was thinking of her own brother and the reunion that never was.

Finally the heads came apart and the brothers sat on the ground next to Rishi, each young man's brawny face wet with tears.

Rishi wiped her cheeks. "I knew you were out there somewhere. But how did you get off the beach? How did you find me? How did you get into the city?"

"Well," said Eno. "It is quite a story."

With that, the children all started to speak at once. They surrounded Quash, gathering around his feet and tugging at his tunic.

"Please, Uncle Squash, tell us the story," begged a little girl with big, black eyes.

Wiping his face with his great big hands and sniffing loudly, he looked down at the children and smiled. "You all want me to tell you a story?" he asked. "Are you sure? It might be a little scary."

The older children pleaded. The littlest of the children scrunched up their shoulders, their eyes big and bright and their hands covering their smiles.

"Well, all right," Quash said. "Gabber Gerta, stoke the fire. I've got a tale to tell." The children cheered.

The children packed themselves as close to Quash and to the fire as they could get without getting burned. There was no place on the ground left, and a little girl climbed into my empty lap.

Quash cleared his throat. "Once upon a time, there were some hideous creatures called Snatchers," he began. "They looked like men but acted like animals and their purpose was to kidnap beautiful maidens from the islands and bring them to a golden city where the maidens would become sacrifices."

"Oooooooo," said the children.

"One day the Snatchers arrived on the shores of a certain island and found it full of maidens, including a strange girl with one blue eye. This girl is very important in this story, because she had three extremely attractive and intelligent brothers. These brothers tried to stop the evil Snatchers, but due to some unfortunate errors in judgment, they failed."

"The brothers woke to find they were the only survivors of the terrible raid. Immediately they planned to find these men and seek revenge. No one steals *their* sister and gets away with it. But first they had to figure out how to walk again." He smiled at Rishi.

"It was not easy. After traveling to the mainland, the brothers paddled up and down the beach at night looking for lights. Finally they found where the Snatchers had taken the maidens and they hid in the forest, waiting for their chance.

"But, even though the brothers were very strong, with muscles of iron, their bodies were still weak from the Snatchers' poisoned darts. There were opportunities to rescue the maidens, but the brothers had learned from their previous experience that to stage a rescue without a plan was like jumping into water without knowing how to swim. They decided that stratagem was their best weapon. They waited and watched, and when the girls needed protection they helped in what ways they could. But then they had some setbacks."

"We got lost," said Cotyl.

"And Quash ate poisonous mushrooms," added Eno.

"It became even more difficult after the girls disappeared into the city of Zitól," Quash continued. "The brothers were not allowed in the city. Over the next few days rumors came out of the city that a virgin had been sacrificed by being thrown into a well, and that a new one had been chosen and she had a blue eye. The brothers tried disguising themselves as vendors, priests, and traders, but every time they were turned away. Finally the only way they could get into the city was to set fire to a corn field and be thrown into prison."

"For *months*," added Cotyl.

"It was only because of a smooth-talking female—" Quash nodded to Isra.

"Who happened to know the captain of the guard—" said Eno.

"That they were able to escape," Quash continued. "Now they were free, but they were back on the outside of the city. Eventually they found a charming old woman hiding in the forest, raising hundreds of children all by herself." The children cheered and Gabber Gerta nodded graciously.

"It was the children who taught them how to enter the city unnoticed. Once they were in the city, Isra helped them find all the women from their island and they snatched them back."

Cotyl elbowed Rishi. "I told you I wanted to be a Snatcher."

"Then there was only one maiden left—the one with the blue eye. But how could we—I mean they—get to her? The palace seemed impenetrable. They pondered this problem for days."

"Meanwhile the nice little old lady in the forest turned out to be a slave driver. She made our handsome young heroes chop firewood, haul water, and tell hours of stories to her noisy, dirty-faced children."

The children laughed.

"As they fetched the water from the cave, they couldn't help but notice the gold at the bottom of the pool. The children informed them it was 'blood gold,' washed out of the well inside the city, and they were forbidden to touch it. But the brothers were not interested in the gold as much as the well. For if the pool and the cenote really were connected, they had found a secret exit, one that only *they* had the skills to navigate." All the children grinned and nodded to each other.

"They decided they needed a trial run first. So when no one was around, they dove into the cenote and practiced swimming through the underwater passage."

"It is harder than it looks," said Cotyl.

"And it gives you a massive headache," added Eno.

"It took several attempts for these intrepid swimmers to finally get through the cenote and surface in the cave. But once they had succeeded, they knew they had discovered how they would save the last maiden."

"But how did Rishi know that you were going to rescue her through the bottom of the cenote?" I asked. "How could you get the message to her without someone suspecting?"

"Isra warned me," said Rishi, beaming at her friend. "She was one of the women who dressed and prepared me for the sacrifice. She told me that it was time to become a 'true brother.' As soon as she said those words I knew who sent the message, and what I needed to do."

"But Isra, how did you get into the palace?" I asked.

"The woman who usually dresses the Messenger had been removed. They were scrambling to find replacements and I volunteered. They must have forgotten that I knew the Messenger."

Quash continued, "When the day of sacrifice arrived, hundreds of people gathered around the cenote. No one noticed the brothers, clinging to the cenote walls, half submerged in the water and hidden behind the dangling vines, because everyone's eyes were on their magnificent sister. And in the midst of all the Zitóli mayhem, Rishi searched out her heroes below, making eye contact with each one.

"Everything was going as planned until the man who was supposed to sacrifice the blue-eyed maiden surprised everyone and decided to *jump in with her.*" Quash cast an annoyed glance my way. "But no matter. The brothers by this time were undaunted. Neither deep water, nor underwater cave, nor masked man would stop them now. Beneath the dark water of the cenote, they caught their little sister and her tagalong and pulled them through the underwater passage to safety. And here we all sit."

The children applauded.

"Now we want to hear *your* side of the story," said Eno, adding a few more logs to the fire.

Rishi started at the beginning, telling them about the Snatchers, Mama Xoca, the selection process, and her year of isolation.

"I never gave up hope that you would come. There was a night on the beach when the dog men were teasing us. Someone came and tied the gate shut. I knew it must have been you, Cotyl. I would know that knot anywhere. It was the same one you used to tie my hands together when I was little."

Cotyl smiled and shrugged, "I'm good at what I do."

"But then when they put me in the tower and you never came, I started to think that something had happened to you. I hoped I would have a dream or something that would tell me if you lived and if you were coming for me, but I never did."

"We told you we'd come back for you," said Cotyl, tugging her hair.

"We just didn't know it would take such a long time," said Eno quietly.

By now the fire had burned down to the coals, and the children started to yawn. I hadn't even noticed how dark it had become. The little girl in my lap was asleep.

"All right, everyone," said the old woman. "Time for dreaming."

The children moaned and grudgingly got up and headed off to their huts, some singing and holding hands, some shoving each other. Rishi's friends went to help the younger ones get to sleep, and her brothers carried off the ones who had already succumbed, like the girl on my lap. Even Rishi left the fire. Only I stayed, by myself, watching the smoldering coals and feeling like I didn't belong among these wonderfully good people. I couldn't stop thinking about how happy Rishi looked when she awoke and saw her brothers. The whole last hour she seemed so calm and content, and it made me think that now that Rishi had her brothers, her aunt, and her friends, she wouldn't need me. What was I to her, anyway? A pupil? A food bringer? Just another corrupt ruler?

While these worries were eating at me, I felt a hand on my shoulder. It was Rishi. She had changed into a fresh tunic, the color of the earth, and she had brushed through her hair and cleaned the blue off her face and neck. She sat down next to me and took my hand.

Once the children were in their huts it still took some time for the noises to calm down. Then, one by one, Rishi's brothers and friends made their way back to the fire. Finally, Gabber Gerta came, still rocking a tenacious baby who wouldn't close his eyes. The huts were quiet and everyone around the fire was lost in their own thoughts, relishing just being close.

Finally Quash murmured softly, "So that is the end of the story. Now what happens?" He stirred the burned logs around and they blazed back to life.

Cotyl smiled. "We are all together again. I think we should go find ourselves an island to populate." He winked at Lantana, whose face flushed scarlet.

"Actually," said Rishi, "the story is not over."

"Do tell, sister," said Cotyl, who had stood up and walked over to Lantana. He sat next to her, put his arm around her waist and pulled her close to him. Lantana leaned her head on his shoulder and closed her eyes.

I saw the corner of Rishi's mouth raise in a sly smile. "I have to tell you about my meeting with the gods." Everyone looked at her. For a few moments the only thing that could be heard was the crackle of the fire.

"Rishi," whispered Eno loudly. "I hate to break it to you, but the gods don't live in deep, dark, watery holes in the ground."

"Perhaps. But I had a message for the gods, and I delivered it." She smiled at her bewildered audience. I was happy that she still didn't let go of my hand. "I don't know if it was a dream or not, because it seemed so real. All I know is that from the time I fell into the cenote to the moment I woke up surrounded by all of you, I was with the gods."

"What did they look like?" breathed Sepya.

"They shone like they had sunlight pulsing in their veins," said Rishi.

"And what did the gods tell you when you asked them to water the Speaker's corn fields?" asked Eno.

"I didn't give them *that* message," she smiled. "I had my own message for them." Rishi paused.

". . . and the message was . . . ?" prompted Cotyl.

"That is my secret."

Everyone groaned.

"But they gave me a message in return. They told me that I—we—all of us—were to deliver a message to the people of Zitól. The message is the Seven Songs."

"What?" said Cotyl. "The gods want you to teach the Seven Songs to the Zitóli crazies?"

"Not so fast, nephew," said Gabber Gerta. "I think this is something the Zitóli people have been waiting for, even if they do not realize it."

"What are you saying?" asked Eno. "That she needs to go *back* to Zitól?"

"If the gods asked her to deliver a message, then that is what she must do. What do you think, your highness? After all, they are your people," asked Gabber Gerta, addressing me.

I sighed and shook my head. "I don't think Rishi's message is going to make any difference to these people. I know them. They are not like all of you. They are heartless. They have no sense of self-control or restraint. They are governed by their lusts. They are past feeling remorse for anything they do."

"There's nothing like a king who believes in his people," said Quash to Eno.

Rishi looked at me and I could tell from her expression that she was thinking about what I said.

"What do you think could make them believe Rishi's message?" asked Isra.

I shrugged. "A miracle."

"A miracle will not change their hearts, either," said Lantana. "The change must come from the inside out."

"Then it's impossible," I said. "The people of Zitól will never listen to her. Don't you understand? She will be rejected. She might even be killed. They are full of madness. They can't even control the speed at which they eat or the amount that they drink. Nothing will change them from what they are."

Rishi turned to me and in a soft voice said, "But if that is what the gods want me to do, don't you think they will help me? They wouldn't ask me to do something unless I had their protection." Rishi's faith astounded and confounded me. I knew she believed she had the power to change the people of Zitól, but I did not.

I shrugged. "This is not a job for one person. We would need an army."

There was a long silence while everyone watched the fire. I was beginning to regret the pessimistic impression I was making on all my new friends.

"I have an army," Gabber Gerta said softly.

Everyone looked at her.

"You forget how long I have been pulling babies out of the cenote. I have *hundreds* of children. Some of my oldest children are almost as old as you all are."

"Where are they?" I asked.

"They work in the surrounding villages, and some of them live in the city."

"Then their hearts have turned to stone, just like the rest of the people," I said hopelessly.

I saw something flash in the old woman's eyes. "No, not *my* children," she said. "I have taught them the Seven Songs since the moment they entered my arms. My children go to the city to work, but they were not raised on the city's diet of beliefs. They have their own minds and their hearts are not controlled by the Speakers' smooth tongues."

"How many children would you say you have altogether?" asked Eno.

"Over two hundred."

"This is getting more promising," said Quash.

"Would they be willing to help us?"

"They would do anything I asked them to."

"Aren't you afraid that they might get hurt?" Rishi asked.

"I don't worry about my children's bodies as much as I do about their souls."

"Well?" said Eno, looking at me and Rishi. "What do you think?"

"I think . . . I think we need to come up with a plan," I said.

Quash then gave a great, loud yawn. "Excellent idea. You all come up with a plan and wake me up when you've decided what to do. There is something about being a hero that just wipes me out."

Gabber Gerta nodded. "Yes. I think it is time for everyone to get some sleep."

Gabber Gerta found as many extra blankets as she could for her guests. She came to me with a mat and a blanket. Rishi's brothers had curled up on the ground, giving their mats and blankets to the women, and so I also refused.

"You are our king," she said and she set them down next to me anyway. Reluctantly I laid out the mat, but I still didn't feel like sleeping.

Rishi spread out her mat next to mine and sat down, our shoulders touching. Gabber Gerta made slow, meandering circles around the group of sleeping people, still trying to lull the baby in her arms to sleep. Finally the baby succumbed and Gabber Gerta sank down on her chair by the fire.

"Would you like to know the message I brought to the gods?" Rishi said. Gabber Gerta smiled sleepily and nodded.

Rishi's voice was low and soft. "When I was taken from my island, all of my people were massacred. If it hadn't been for my brothers and me, my people would still be alive. I promised the gods I would make up for our mistake. I thought that by offering up myself as a sacrifice that would help. At the very least I could beg the gods to forgive my brothers, because they were only trying to save me. When I saw the gods, I knelt before them, and I told them I had given my life so that they would forgive my brothers."

Gabber Gerta smiled. "Why is it young people are always thinking that one must gain the attention of the gods by dying? The gods do not want us to die for them. They want us to live for them."

Rishi looked at Gabber Gerta in amazement. "That is exactly what they said to me. And then they told me that no sacrifice would bring my people back or make up for what was lost. But, they said, there are other people that need to be saved now. And it is not their bodies that are in danger, but their souls. They said the people in Zitól have goodness in their hearts, but the Speakers have smothered it with ignorance. They need knowledge and light. They said my duty to them is not atonement, but *action*."

Gabber Gerta closed her eyes and nodded her head. "This is a new generation of Zitóli people. They are not their parents or their grandparents. They are not bloodthirsty because they were born that way, only because they were taught that way. They need to be retaught. And once they know the truth, the truth will change their hearts, just as the truth has changed the heart of your king." Her tired eyes met mine.

"It is true, Nadal," said Rishi. "Your heart was changed. Why couldn't theirs be?"

"My heart was changed by watching you and your determination to live a pure life. At first I just thought you were good, but when I understood the writing on the temple steps I knew you were more than good, you were right. Although the change felt immediate, it took months of your careful brainwashing to reach that point."

"Then somehow we need to show them the truth, and show them in a way that will make them feel it deep in their hearts."

"But how? It would take us months to teach them to read, and once the Speakers found out, they would stop us," I said.

By this time Gabber Gerta's eyes were closed, and she was breathing heavily. The baby was nestled in the sling like a seed in a pod. Finally Rishi yawned and lay down next to me and closed her eyes. I stayed up, listening to all the sleeping sounds around me, lost in my own thoughts.

"Nadal?" Rishi asked sleepily.

"Hm?"

"Do you remember when you first came in to my tower and you watched me while I was sleeping?"

I smiled. "Yes." I took a stick and stirred the coals.

"You said that I was laughing."

"You *were* laughing."

"Well, I was, but not at first."

"It is true." I remembered the look of pain and terror on her face.

"At first it was a terrible dream. A nightmare. And I have had the dream several times since then." She paused.

"Will you tell me what it was about?" I asked.

"In my dream I was standing on a small mountain and all around me were children. They were everywhere, and extended as far as I could see."

"What were the children doing?"

"Just watching me. As if they wanted to see what I was about to do," she said. "The Speakers were there too. And when they spoke, fire came out of their mouths and burned some of the children. They did this while I watched, and they thought it was fun."

I squirmed. I hoped that I was not in her dream.

"Then," she said, "one of the Speakers turned toward me. I was terrified. I knew he would start speaking and when he did fire would come out of his mouth. I didn't know what to do so I did the only thing I could think of."

"What was that?" I asked.

"I sang," she paused for a moment and leaned up on her elbow. "And do you know what came out of my mouth?"

"Fire?"

She laughed. "No. Feathers."

"Feathers?" I asked.

"Yes, feathers," she said. "And the feathers covered everything. They were white and beautiful and they piled up in great heaps everywhere. The feathers smothered the flames and protected the children." Rishi rolled to her back, her profile pointed up at the sky.

I smiled. "Let's just keep our expectations low," I said. "I think this will take more than songs, feathers, and an army of children."

Rishi yawned. "You know what, Nadal?"

"What, Rishi?"

"I don't dream very often, but when I do, my dreams always come true."

"I'm beginning to understand that now," I said. I lay down next to her and brushed her hair away from her face. She smiled sleepily but didn't open her eyes. For the first time since I had met Rishi she seemed completely at peace. I knew it was because she was with her family again. I wondered what it would be like to finally be reunited with someone that you thought you had lost forever. I thought of my mother who died so long ago. It always made me sad that I could barely remember her face. What would it have been like to have had her in my life? Perhaps I would have been a better person if I knew she was there to love me and teach me. What would it have been like to have a father? Were they up in the stars somewhere, looking down on me?

I didn't know what it was like to have a family, but I knew what it was like to be lost. And I wasn't the only one. It seems that I had spent my entire life among people who were lost. Every person in Zitól was lost. Even the Speakers were lost. And the only thing worse than being lost is when no one *cares* that you are lost. But not Rishi and her brothers. Her brothers had done everything they could to find Rishi and become a family again. She was needed. They were needed. And only when they were together were they complete. It was there in that relationship where Rishi belonged and where she felt the most love.

My thoughts came together and started to form an idea. The idea rolled back and forth in my mind as I watched Rishi breathe. I thought of all the options; I weighed the risks. It could work, I thought, but the idea still was not complete.

What would people be willing to do to be reunited with people they loved and lost? Would they travel through jungles? Would they swim an ocean? Would they sell all they had? Would they sacrifice themselves? Perhaps. But perhaps it was simpler than that.

I wanted the people of Zitól to feel joy. The same joy that I witnessed between Rishi and her brothers. I wanted them to know what it was like to be needed and to belong. Then, finally, the last part of my idea finally clicked into place. I knew how to bring families back to Zitól.

And I would need a lot of blue paint.

CHAPTER 51

The Day of Miracles

I t took us two days to make all the preparations to carry out my idea. Before the sunrise of the third day, Rishi walked up to Zitól, alone in the cool cerulean darkness. She wore a white dress that trailed behind her on the ground. At the end of her dress Gabber Gerta had sewn half a dozen large, brass bells. Rishi entered the quiet, sleeping city, holding up her dress to muffle the bells. Then, when she stepped on to the flagged stone streets she lowered her dress and began to walk slowly through the city. With each step the bells clattered and bounced against the street, filling the still, cold air with their raucous noise. She walked, passing the bathhouse, passing the empty marketplace. She walked up and down the roads lined with apartments, around the fountain, and up through the merchants' quarters.

Soon windows began to open. Sleepy Zitólis peeked out from behind tapestry doors, rubbing their eyes. Who was making all this racket so early in the morning? When they saw her, a lone woman, walking through the mist-filled streets, her long hair hanging down her back, with no jewelry or ornaments besides her bead belt, and wearing the Speakers' holy white, they were at once intrigued. They threw on their cloaks and stepped out of their homes into the cold morning air. *Could it be?* they wondered. They began to follow her.

Rishi kept walking, looking straight ahead, making sure she covered every street in the city. More and more people gathered to follow her, trying to get close enough to see her and still maintain a safe distance. At one point she paused, letting the jangling bells rest. The crowd shuffled to an awkward stop and slowly she turned to gaze at them, her blue eye sparkling. *It is the Messenger. It is the Messenger,* they whispered. *She has returned from the well. She is alive! It is a miracle.* Little did they know that this was just the beginning of the miracles they would see this day.

Rishi raised the corner of her mouth in a half smile. She nodded and beckoned them to follow her.

From where I was standing, alone in the temple plaza, I could hear Rishi's bells echo eerily in the distance as she made her rounds through the streets. Finally the noise became louder, and I knew that any moment she would arrive in the plaza. I held my head up high and stood as straight and tall as I could. I prayed to the gods—Rishi's gods—that my plan would work and that this would all end well. When I finished, Rishi entered the plaza, followed by the entire city of Zitól.

I stood in the center of the plaza, on the great round stage where the Speakers stand to give their orations. I glanced up to the pyramids, where the others were waiting, but the morning mist had shrouded the temple tops and I could only see partway up their great stone steps. In spite of the crisp morning air I started to sweat.

Rishi walked toward the Speakers' Circle. On her face was a look of perfect serenity. She climbed the steps that wrapped around the stage until she finally stood by my side. Our eyes met and she winked. "This is so exciting," she whispered.

The people streamed around the stage until they surrounded it on all sides like a great sea. Hundreds of curious faces turned toward me. They could feel that something special was about to happen, something different than what had happened in the past.

All went well when I had rehearsed my speech in Gabber Gerta's village, practicing for her children and Rishi's brothers, but this audience was different. Their expectations were so much greater and their wrath was much more lethal.

The Speakers made speaking seem so effortless, and I always hoped that when my turn came I'd somehow inherit their confidence. I remembered my carefully crafted speech so long ago, and how they had ripped it apart. I could only imagine that this group of people would be ten times worse. If I couldn't convince them at this moment, I would never have another chance. But this time I was without my mask. Would they believe a mere man? I had to get as much truth into their ears before the palace awakened and the Speakers came down to the plaza with their guards.

"You can do it," said Rishi, placing her hand on my back. "Just open your mouth. When you are telling the truth there is nothing to fear." She gently pushed me forward. I cleared my throat.

"People of Zitól," I began. "I have watched you for many years. Do you recognize me? I am your king. Today I come before you with my face naked, wearing no mask and bearing no pretense. It is time for you to see me as I am, rather than how I seemed."

"Long before I was your king, I was a witness. Behind the many masks I wore I witnessed the Speakers teach you things. They taught you the nature of the gods, that they are demonic and bloodthirsty and that we are constantly at their mercy. They have told you to sacrifice yourselves, your gold, even your children. You were taught to believe that this was the right thing to do, and the only way to appease them. But things are about to change. For I am the witness to something else too."

"In the past few months I have witnessed goodness, integrity, and courage. These qualities came from a source that had not been defiled by our Speakers' flickering tongues. This source taught me that we have forgotten the true nature of our gods. Like lost children, we have estranged ourselves from our divine heritage. We must come back to them. And the only way to come back to the gods that we deserted is with a great and precious offering. It is more precious than gold and jewels. It is more precious than even the beating hearts of well-prepared sacrifices."

No one moved. No one blinked. They were still as stars.

"We must offer the gods our will. Our heart. Not the heart of flesh from our bodies, but the heart that drives our passions. It is time to end the killing and horror that has been done to the people and children of this city, for the true gods are gods of light and happiness. They desire us to be true to each other, as spouses, brothers, sisters, and parents. They want us to live in love, not fear."

I paused for some sort of reaction. I could not tell what they were thinking, if they were dumbfounded, amazed, or ready to bind my hands and carry me up to the temple altar. Just then a murmur rippled through the audience and one by one their gaze shifted, looking past me and beyond the stage. I turned. There at the end of the plaza I saw the Speakers striding across the plaza, flanked by dozens of armed guards.

The guards split up and surrounded the multitude, and the Speakers walked straight through the crowd, pushing men and women aside until the people scrambled to open a corridor for them to pass through.

Up the stairs they came, each man hot-faced and angry. "What is the meaning of this? Who are these people? Get off this platform!" shouted Gula as he reached the stage.

When Rishi and I turned our faces toward them they gasped, and the blood drained from their cheeks, leaving them ashen.

"You're . . . alive," gasped Riplakish.

For a moment they just stood there, with their mouths dropped open and their eyes as big as coconuts. I had wondered what they would do at the moment they first saw me again. Would they bow? Kneel on the ground and worship me for coming back from the dead? Tell me they were sorry for treating me like I was invisible all those years? Turned out I was being optimistic.

Gula walked straight up to me and slapped me across the face. The multitude gasped.

"What sort of treachery is this?" he demanded in a booming voice. "You have deceived these people. How dare you snatch a sacrifice out of the hands of the gods! They will send down their wrath upon all of us. Our city is doomed, because of you!"

Gula and Riplakish took a hold of my arms and Tungan held Rishi.

"Guards!" Gula cried. "Seize these traitors!"

"Wait!" I shouted. "The Messenger has returned. She did not shrink from her duty. She gave her message to the gods. In return the gods have sent her back with a message for you, and they will protect her until she gives that message."

Riplakish hissed in my ear. "I don't know how you did it, Nadal, but we will have your heart for this, if I have to rip it out with my teeth." Then, much louder, he said, "There is no way he could have spared himself and also retrieved the Messenger. I tied her up myself. She can't be the real Messenger. You have brought an imposter. You are a liar!"

"No, I am a king," I said. "But whether or not you believe me does not matter. You only need to believe *her*." I nodded to Rishi. "No one can change the color of their eye. She is the real Messenger. She did what she said she would do. Let her speak. She must give her message."

The people looked at us up on the stage, not knowing whom to believe.

Then someone yelled out, "Let the Messenger speak!" and more voices joined in, shouting and calling out until the whole plaza was a sea of hammering fists and shrill voices. The guards tried to make their way through the people to the stage, but they were pushed aside and their spears were sucked into the powerful mass.

Sweat broke out in beads on Gula's forehead. He glanced at Riplakish as the people's demands became louder. Finally I felt Gula's grip loosen and then he released me. He held up his arms.

The crowd hushed at the familiar signal. "We will do as you wish," said Gula. "We will let this girl—whether she is the Messenger or not—speak. Tungan, release her," he muttered. "She won't be going anywhere."

Reluctantly Tungan loosened his grip on Rishi, and she shook herself free. There were white marks on her arms where Tungan had held her.

Rishi stepped forward. She swept her eyes over the enormous mass of people as if trying to make contact with every person there. When she could feel that all eyes rested on her face, she opened her mouth and started to sing.

She began with the first song, the Song of Birth, and then the second, the Song of the Bead. Her voice sailed through the plaza, fearless and clear. The crowd listened, motionless, their faces filled with wonder, their focus entirely absorbed on her, the way one would stare at the light of a candle burning in a dark room.

Then, as Rishi continued through her songs, the next miracle came walking slowly down the steps of the temple, looking as if they were walking straight out of the clouds.

They came down the steps, slowly and carefully, the older ones helping the younger ones. At first the Zitólis were astonished and afraid, and none of them moved.

The children kept climbing down the stone steps. There were only a few at first. Then ten. Then twenty. More and more and more came down from the mist, until the stairway of the temple was filled with children. But more were coming. They spread out along the platforms of the temple. Finally the temple was covered with children, teenagers, and young adults, all painted cerulean blue, all peering into the multitude below that concealed their lost parents.

At that moment the words of Rishi's songs stimulated something in the souls of the people that will never be forgotten. They did not know why, but something stirred inside of them, feelings they had suppressed for many years. And when this happened, the children and parents regarded each other with deep gazes on which travel words only known by the heart.

Rishi came to the sixth song:

> *Give me a new heart, oh gods.*
> *A new spirit put in me.*
> *Take out this stony heart*
> *Replace it with a heart of flesh*
> *For I see my evil ways, oh gods,*
> *I see my evil doings.*
> *And I want to turn to them*
> *No more.*

It was painful, this stirring, but also hopeful. And finally, when Rishi finished and the last notes echoed off the blood-soaked pyramids, the people pulled their wet eyes away from the children and turned toward me, looking for an explanation to the stirrings they felt in their hearts.

For my entire life I had seen the masses of Zitóli people as one large organism. But now for the first time I saw individuals. I saw a man wiping tears from his eyes. I saw a woman hiding her head in her hands. I saw others earnestly looking at the rows of children's faces, as if searching for something lost and precious.

"The Messenger has sung to you these sacred songs," I told them. "They are your heritage, but you do not know them. You do not know them because you were never taught. But the words of these songs are written on the walls around this stage. They are written in the walls of the palace. You have seen these songs every time you go to the market and pass by the market gate. They are written on the temple steps and around the cenote and in many of the buildings and houses you now live in, but you did not know this because no one here, except for the five people standing on this stage, can read."

"The Speakers knew that if they filled you with lies they could also fill you with fear, and governing by fear is the quickest road to power. But the gods do not want us to be afraid."

"The gods have given you a gift. These children standing on the steps of the temple, as if they have just come down from heaven—" but at this moment I was rudely interrupted.

"You are being deceived!" bellowed Gula. "This is trickery. Those children are not children from heaven. This isn't a miracle. These are tricks!"

I glared at Gula. And turned back to the audience. "I was going to say that these children that you see standing on the temple steps are *your* children. But as I look in your shining eyes I know I don't have to tell you that. They were given to the cenote, and you forfeited your right to be their mentors, teachers, and parents. But I know you have not forgotten them. I know that there is not a day in your life that you do not think about them and what they could have become. Now here they are. A wise woman taught me that children are a gift from the gods, and to prove to you the gods love you, you are fortunate enough to receive that gift a second time. You will find them healthy and loved and well taught. Listen to them. Turn your hearts to them, as their hearts are turned toward you. You will learn much from what they have to tell you."

"As your king I will give you the choice. You may choose the Speakers to rule over you as they have for the past decades. If this is your choice,

I will leave this city forever and you can continue this life of constant sacrifice and butchery. Or, you can accept me as your king. I will teach you to read so that you will understand what is written in the stone, as long as you understand that you will be held accountable for the truths you find. To the gods you will be required to offer your own heart, an open heart, filled with meekness and sincerity, instead of offering up your neighbor's heart of flesh. For in my kingdom there will no longer be sacrifices of blood."

"You can't do that!" Gula shouted. "The gods were pleased when we offered sacrifices. How else do you explain the rains that always followed the ceremonies?"

I wanted to say something brilliant here, but Gula had me. He was right. This was something I had never been able to completely understand. I looked at Rishi, and I could tell she did not have the answer either.

"*Ha!*" laughed Speaker Gula. "You see?" He pointed at Rishi and me. "They are wrong. They are making this whole thing up to confuse you all. *They* can't make it rain." He turned back to me. "If you want people to believe you there *must* be a sign."

"The change that occurs in their hearts is enough," said Rishi. "That is where all the real miracles happen."

"No. There must be *physical evidence* that the gods accept your offering." Gula shouted, spit flinging out of his mouth. He was pacing back and forth across the stage, pointing his fingers at Rishi and me, the people, and the clouds. "There must be a sign! There must be something from the heavens to prove that they are even listening to you. There must be evidence! There must be—" Gula stopped mid-sentence, for something strange started to happen.

Smoke was coming from his mouth. And when he realized it, he abruptly stopped speaking. But even then, smoke billowed out of his mouth every time he exhaled. And it wasn't just him. Wisps of smoke were curling out of everyone's mouths. A coldness like I have never felt settled over the plaza. And then, the final miracle happened.

Tiny bits of white started to fall from the sky.

They were like pieces of ash that floated down by the thousands, only much whiter. It was as if someone was whittling at the clouds and the shavings were drifting down to the earth. They whirled and fell, getting larger and more numerous by the second. I held out my hand to catch one, but it melted on my skin and disappeared, leaving behind a cool drop of water. Rishi looked at me and smiled, and held her arms up to the sky. The white things floated all around us. Like bits of paper. Like tiny white butterflies. Like feathers.

We are used to having the thunderous roar of rain in our ears, but this was not like rain. It was strangely silent, and its gentleness calmed everything around us. Even the constant chatter of the birds and monkeys in the trees was hushed. Amazingly, even the Speakers had lost the ability to talk, and they gazed around the plaza in awe, with what seemed like a growing pile of popcorn on their heads. I had never felt such a stillness in my life as I did at that moment. It was as if we were being embraced by the heavens.

Before long the bloodstained pyramids were covered in a white mantle. The children scooped up the white powder from the ground in wonder, pressing it in their fingers, smelling it, tasting it. It covered the ground for as far as we could see. I could do nothing but gaze at the miracle all around me and feel the gratitude swell in my heart. The gods had given their sign. They had listened to our message. And to show their satisfaction they had made the entire world white. As white and as pure as Rishi's bead.

CHAPTER 52

Raven's Revenge

Carefully the children descended down from the temple and at the same moment the people ran forward to greet them. I savored the moment, watching the children and adults look for common eyes, common noses, and other features that might help them find their long-lost loved ones. I smiled and turned to Rishi, but she was gone.

To my surprise, I was alone on the stage. I whipped around, darting my eyes into the mingling people, but Rishi was nowhere to be seen. The white flakes were still coming down thick, and beyond the group I couldn't see anything but cloud. Panic filled my chest. I flew down the stairs, through the dispersing crowd, and into the white oblivion.

It only took a few steps before I was completely lost. The forms of the Zitólis had faded away in the whiteness and it muffled their low voices. For a few moments I could hear nothing but the crunch of the white flakes beneath my sandal. I turned around and around, hating myself for letting Rishi out of my sight. I prayed to the gods that I would find Rishi before the Speakers did something to her.

Then I heard the bells.

Rishi's bells—the ones that were tied onto her dress. The sound of the bells was faint and ghostly in the white expanse, like it was coming from the other side of a mountain. I sprinted in the direction of the sound and soon I found footprints that led me out of the plaza and up the ramp to the palace.

The tracks led through the wide gates, into the courtyard, and through the doors of the throne room. I flew up the steps two at a time and ripped the tapestry from its holdings. There I saw them—Gula, Riplakish, and Tungan. Rishi was tied and gagged, sitting in Tungan's throne. The Speakers were opening the chests kept under their chairs, filled with jewels and gold, and stuffing as much as they could into large bags. Pacing up and down the steps as far as her chain would allow, Riplakish's jaguar watched the commotion with eager eyes.

When they saw me they stopped. Immediately Gula dropped his bag and strode down the steps, shaking his fat finger at me. His eyebrows pointed up into triangles and he exclaimed, "Who do you think you are? Embarrassing me in front of my people?"

"They are *my* people," I said. "And you embarrassed yourself."

"Watch what you say, boy," said Riplakish. "Remember all that we've done for you."

"And what have you done for me?" I replied. "You taught me how to look down my nose at others. You taught me to be lazy and incompetent."

"We gave you freedom."

"No, you gave me ignorance."

Reaching into a scabbard at the side of his robe, Gula drew out a knife, and I stepped back.

"You have *always* been a problem, Nadal. Ever since you were born." He stepped toward me, flashing the blade.

I was completely unarmed. I glanced at Rishi and for the first time I saw fear in her eyes.

"Let's make a little arrangement," Gula said, casting a sideways glance at Rishi. "You give yourself up to us as a sacrifice, and we'll let the girl go."

"I already took my turn," I said. "I'm sure it is bad luck to be sacrificed twice."

"Tungan," Gula called sharply over his shoulder, "take your knife and put it to her throat."

Tungan obeyed.

"If you don't want your Messenger to be harmed, I suggest you go take a seat." He pointed his knife to my throne, next to where Rishi was tied. I hesitated. I knew they were lying. They would not release Rishi, even after they killed me. I knew that if I allowed them to bind me, neither of us would make it out of the room alive. But how could I save her without a weapon? Just then Rishi let out a muffled cry. Tungan had one hand grasping the back of her neck, the other pushing the tip of his knife into her skin. A bead of bright red shimmered at the tip.

"The longer you stand there, the closer she is to being dead. Get up to your seat or I'll tell Tungan to redecorate this room with her blood," Gula hissed. I had no choice but to trust him. I clenched my jaw and walked up to the throne. Raven hissed and snarled as I passed.

"Yes, Nadal, great king of Zitól. This gilded chair is your rightful throne . . . or should I say *altar*? Riplakish, tie him." Speaker Gula gleefully rolled up his sleeves. "We are going to have a sacrifice."

"You will gain nothing by killing me," I said as Riplakish cinched ropes tightly around my arms.

"You are wrong. I will gain huge amounts of satisfaction." Gula laughed. Then he paused. "There is only one thing that would give me more pleasure . . ." He licked his lips and looked at Rishi and then back at me. "Hmmm . . . I've changed my mind. We shall sacrifice *her* first. I want to see the look on your face when I rip her beautiful beating heart out of her body. Tungan, bring the girl down here to the floor and hold her down."

"You told me you would let her go!" I said.

Gula shrugged. "I lied."

Tungan untied Rishi from the throne, dragged her down the steps to the center of the room, and forced her to the ground. By this time Riplakish had finished tying me and hurried down to hold out Rishi's arms while Tungan pinned her legs. Rishi struggled the best she could but all the men had to do was hold her tight and wait until she became too exhausted to resist. Overpowering a victim was not something new for the Speakers.

Once they had her restrained I watched in horror as Gula knelt beside Rishi and raised his knife high above his head. He was about to thrust it down into Rishi's chest when a low, slow voice sounded in the chamber.

"*Get—away—from—my—sister.*"

Eno stood in the doorway, flanked by Quash and Cotyl.

Astonished, Gula stared at them for a moment, his mouth as wide and as gaping as the cenote. Then his face became so red, I thought his brain would erupt out his ears. He glared at me hatefully, and then back at Rishi. I knew he only had time to kill one of us. It didn't take long for him to decide which. With a loud yell and an astonishing leap for a man his size, he hurdled over Rishi's body, no doubt intent on climbing the steps to sink his knife into my heart. But just before he could clear her body and touch the ground with his feet, Rishi raised her knee, catching Gula's fleshy ankle. His great frame came crashing against the ground and his obsidian knife skidded, spinning across the stone floor.

The brothers fell upon the Speakers. Powerlessly I sat tied to my throne, watching the tangle of men and arms and flashing knives. Rishi's brothers fought like dragons against the Speakers. Desperate to join in the melee, Raven pulled on her chain, baring her white teeth, flattening her black ears, and swiping her steely claws at anyone who came within reach.

It did not take long before the three Speakers were restrained and the brothers heaved them up to their respective thrones, where Cotyl secured each man to his chair. Quash cut me free and I ran down the steps to Rishi, ungagging her and lifting her up into my arms.

We left the Speakers there, tied to their thrones, screaming that the gods would avenge them, while Raven sat slinging her tail crossly back and forth, her ears still flat against her head.

Before I left the room I paused. I couldn't leave without taking a moment to relish this long-awaited victory. But when I turned around, it was not the captive, cursing Speakers that caught my attention. Instead my eyes locked on the piercing yellow eyes of the jaguar. Her teeth were no longer bared and she sat there staring at me with an intensity so humanlike that it stifled my feeling of triumph. My eyes then went to her jeweled collar glittering in the torchlight and the heavy chain that held her fast. A low whine came from her throat and with one foot she lightly pawed the ground.

As I turned and followed Rishi and her brothers down the stairs, I considered the reasons I had always been so frightened of Raven. In reality she was just like me—a neglected and manipulated hostage whom the Speakers used in order to exalt themselves. Now I was free—free not only to be king, but to be king on my own terms. Perhaps Raven was not so different. Her gilded collar could not hide the fact that she was an abused, pitiful creature who had the potential for a different destiny.

Rishi and her brothers stepped outside into the bright courtyard, but I didn't follow them.

"Go on," I said. "There is something that I need to do."

Turning, I climbed the stairs back up the dark passage to the throne room. The three Speakers could not suppress the hope that came to their faces upon my reentry. Instantly they began begging, imploring, pleading with me to free them. But I hadn't returned for *them*.

When Raven saw me she rose up on all fours and pricked her ears. For a few moments we carefully regarded each other.

"Release me and I promise I will never let any harm come to you," Gula was saying.

"No—release me and I will give you anything you want," said Tungan.

"They are liars," said Riplakish. "Untie me and I will forever be your faithful servant until the day you die."

I did not acknowledge them. My eyes were still on the jaguar who, save for the gentle swelling of her ribcage as she breathed, was as still as black marble. Her golden eyes followed me as I made my way toward the place where her chain locked into the floor. Bending down, I put my hands on the large clasp.

"Nadal—*son*—what are you doing?" said Gula, his voice rising to a panicked pitch. "You are not going to do something you might regret, are you?"

But his voice was as far away as a forgotten dream. I looked up at Raven from where I crouched and she was still staring at me, her eyes eager and unblinking. I saw no savagery in her gaze—only desperation. I was not afraid of her now. I knew now that she had never wanted to hurt *me*.

I lifted the chain.

"Nadal—please—please don't do it. Don't do it! We will give you anything! Do not release—"

Gingerly I unhooked the clasp and let the chain clatter to the ground. For the first time since I entered the room, the Speakers were finally silent. Slowly I stood, barely breathing, bracing myself for Raven's reaction.

But the jaguar still did not move. She only watched me. It was as if . . . as if she were asking permission.

"Nadal," Riplakish said in a hoarse whisper, "revenge is never a good idea."

But this was not about me. It was about Raven. And it was about the past Messengers and the children and all the sacrifices who had died from either the Speakers' hands or their order. I looked into Raven's eyes and granted the permission she desired. In a low whisper I said, "Help yourself."

A gleam of gratitude flashed behind her golden eyes.

Then I turned and walked out of the room, shutting—and barring—the great wooden doors.

Just because I'd changed didn't mean I was perfect.

EPILOGUE
The Color of Your Heart

It took me many days to get the bead exactly the way I wanted it.

I had selected the finest turquoise stone in the treasury. Then I shaped and polished it until it was as flawless and smooth as a songbird's egg. I strung it onto a fine leather cord and slipped it into my pocket. In only a few days I would see the fulfillment of my greatest desire: to make Rishi my queen. Permission from her brothers had been granted, and preparations were being made for a ceremony. There was only one problem.

The problem had been discovered the day before the wedding. I was sitting with Rishi's brothers, eating a meal, when the island women approached us with solemn faces.

"Rishi cannot be married," Isra said.

"Why not?" asked Eno.

"Remember the washings?" Sepya asked.

"The washings?" asked Quash. "What washings?"

"*All* brides are washed before they are wed," said Isra, annoyed that she must explain what the brothers should have already known.

Venay looked at me earnestly and added, "It is a very sacred and necessary part of the ceremony."

"And why is it that she can't be washed?" asked Cotyl.

"She must—" Isra paused, "she must be washed by another woman who wears a white bead."

Without meaning to, all of our eyes slipped down to the deep purple beads that hung from the girls' waists. Purple: the bead of a concubine.

Eno slowly nodded with grim understanding. Cotyl sat back and frowned. Quash gave a deep, troubled sigh. They looked at each other, perplexed.

"She must be washed by someone who is worthy to wash her," Lantana said quietly.

"They are right," Eno murmured. He turned to his brothers. "What is to be done?"

All were silent.

Panic pulsed through my veins. I reached into my pocket and cradled the precious blue bead in my fingers. How could this be possible? To have sacrificed so much, and to have come so far, only to be stopped by a mere washing ritual? My old self would have seen this impasse as something to ridicule. "Just change the rules. Do away with the washing," the old Nadal would have suggested. But through Rishi I had come to know these men and women, and I knew their desire to be pure and worthy was part of who they were as a people. If they abandoned the customs that gave meaning and order to their lives, they would become as the Zitólis had been: confused and backward. If Rishi had taught me anything, it was that the significance and symbolism of their customs were not to be mocked or taken lightly.

But, I thought as I smoothed my thumb over the bead in my pocket, it was important to see things clearly. It was not the color of the bead itself that was the real problem here. No, the real problem was that virtue had been taken from these innocent women without their desire or consent. The thought of such an act now repulsed me like nothing else.

The brothers were still brooding and troubled, not knowing what to say. But I knew the story was not to end like this. For all the wisdom and truth that this small group of believers had, there was one thing that even they had put backward. I released the bead in my pocket. I turned to the brothers and spoke.

"I am in the process of learning about the nature of the heart," I said. "Now, I know I am new at this, but I have an idea."

"Please—speak," Eno said encouragingly.

I gazed at the young women who looked at me with expressions of sadness and shame. "Rishi has told me many stories about you, so that I feel as if I know each of you very well. I am going to ask you a question and I want you to answer it within yourself as honestly as you can." They all listened intently to my words. "Ask yourself, what color is your heart?"

"What do you mean?" Isra asked.

I stood. Walking around the table, I faced them and gestured to their beads. "Is this the color of your heart? The color of a concubine? Is that your desire? Was that *your* choice?"

With eyes wide and liquid and expressions of intense sorrow they all shook their heads.

"Was it your choice that your white bead was taken by the man with the shark mouth, Lantana?" I asked her softly. "Did he not only replace your bead but your heart also?"

Tears swelled in her eyes. She glanced at Cotyl. "He did *not* replace my heart," she said, her voice filled with emotion.

"What do your beads symbolize anyway? To have a white bead is significant, for it is a representation of what is in your heart, is it not? And what *is* in your heart, Sepya? What is in *your* heart, Isra and Venay?"

I stepped toward Lantana, who was staring at the ground. Softly I repeated my question, "What is in your heart, Lantana? You think it is the color of your bead that tells the color of your heart. But I think it is the color of your heart that should determine the color of your bead. If this is true, what color would your bead be?"

Now the women had tears running down their faces, and the words I had spoken astonished even myself. Perhaps I was finally growing up. Perhaps I was finally understanding how all truths fit together.

I turned to the brothers. "It is my opinion that the woman who washes my bride should not be measured on the purity of her bead but on the purity of her heart. Tomorrow Rishi will be my queen, and she will be washed by one of these pure women you see before you."

I sat back in my seat. The women looked at the brothers, their faces shining with hope. Eno smiled. "Well, you heard the man. Go decide who it will be."

When they were gone Eno put his hand on my shoulder. "I can see now that you were meant to be king."

The next morning when the Zitóli sun stretched its bright arms across the sky, the moment I had been waiting for arrived. A rope was placed on the ground in the center of Gabber Gerta's village, forming a circle that was only big enough for two people. I sat cross-legged inside this circle, surrounded by Rishi's brothers, Gabber Gerta, and the many, many excited children. The word was that Lantana had completed Rishi's washing ritual and the women were finishing her hair.

I held the bead nervously in my hand, stroking its polished surface. Then a whisper passed among the children like wind in the trees. "She's coming!" they said, and I rose to my feet, slipping the bead into my pocket. My heart was a pounding drum.

The crowd parted and Rishi appeared, wearing a dress the color of coconut milk. Her hair was pulled back from her face in a long, ebony braid. The only pieces of jewelry she wore were a band of tiny shells that graced her forehead and her bead belt that adorned her waist.

Following Rishi, their heads bent down, hands behind their backs and smiles on their cheeks were her island friends, all with swinging white beads at the hip. Venay whispered something to the others and for the first time since they had left their island, Lantana laughed.

Rishi and her small entourage approached the place where I was waiting and stopped just outside the circle of rope.

After Eno had welcomed everyone, he recited the seventh song.

> *Keepers of the past*
> *Guardians of the future*
> *Here in this circle of rope*
> *Two halves unite*
> *To form one unbreakable whole.*
> *Holding hands,*
> *Their arms become a circle and*
> *A sanctuary*
> *For voices not yet heard*
> *For faces not yet seen.*
> *Let this circle of love be unbroken*
> *Oh, ye keepers of the past,*
> *Ye guardians of the future.*

Then he invited Rishi to step inside the circle. Everyone was so still you could have heard the wings of a hummingbird. I looked into Rishi's dazzling eyes, framed by her butterfly lashes and beaming face. Reaching to her side, Rishi took her white bead and with a small knife gently cut it off her belt. She slid the bead from the old, worn rope. Cotyl handed her a strip of newly braided leather and with trembling fingers she strung the bead onto the new cord. Then she stood on tiptoe and fastened it around my neck.

"With this white bead Rishi gives you her heart and promises to seek for your happiness and the happiness of your posterity," Eno said, bowing his head to me.

It was my turn. I pulled the perfect blue bead from my pocket, and after holding it up for everyone to admire, I knelt to the ground and tied it onto Rishi's belt. As I tied, a drop of water fell onto my hand. I stood and Rishi looked up at me, smiling, another crystal tear forming in her eye like dew on a flower.

Eno bowed his head toward Rishi, my bride and my queen. "With this blue bead, Nadal gives you his heart and promises to seek for your happiness and the happiness of your posterity." Then he added, "And if he doesn't, just let us know and we will break his legs."

There is a saying on the island of Talom that when you love someone they carry your heart. I loved Rishi ever since she walked into my city. I loved her when I saw her dance, when I saw her stab Tungan with her comb. I loved her every time she was pleased with the food I brought, and every time she taught me a new word or told me a new story of her people.

But it wasn't until the moment she off cut her bead that I understood that Rishi had loved me for a much longer time. Rishi's bead was more than a pledge of honor, more than just the desire of her pure heart. She knew that all the time she spent carrying that bead, she was actually carrying *my heart*. And whether it was the heart of my body or the heart of my soul, I couldn't say, for when it comes to my love for Rishi, they are both the same.

We have come to the end, and as you can see, dear reader, I misled you from the very beginning. I let you believe that my beloved Rishi would die somewhere between the covers of this book.

Often I still reflect on Speaker Gula's advice on speaking. He was wrong in so many ways, and in one way in particular. It is not the beginning of speech that is the most important; it is the end. Just as it is not how we start out that matters as much as what we become. There is hope for me yet.

Acknowledgments

There is an ancient Aztec saying that describes children as a "necklace of precious stones." I want to first thank three of the precious stones in my necklace. Sophia, Syrena, and Naomi Dyreng probably read this manuscript more times than I did, and their influence illuminates these pages.

I want to thank my other beta readers: Casey Atherton, Kay Brown, Scott Dyreng, Shelly Dyreng, Nicole Empey, Lillian Fitzgerald, Aubrey Hampton, Jessica Heath, Angie Kelly, Abigail Kunz, Connor Kunz, Eli Morse, Olivia Morse, Eliza Nelson, Korinne Nelson, Erin Newton, Holly Penrod, Emmaline Rhodes, Amy Robinson, Sarah Smith, Eliza Stewart, Sophia Stewart, and Liza Wilson. Your insights and suggestions were invaluable. I especially want to thank the teen reader who gave me the greatest compliment of all by leaving her tearstains on my manuscript.

Thank you to my aunt Liza Wilson for letting my sister and me tag along with her in Mexico while I researched this book. It was a magical trip I will never forget.

Thank you to the people at Cedar Fort, especially Emma Parker for championing Rishi's story, and Michelle May Ledezma who designed the beautiful cover. I would also like to thank Emily Chambers, Justin Greer and Kelly Martinez.

I am grateful for excellent parents, wise sisters, and three heroic older brothers.

Most of all I want to thank my greatest hero, Scott Dyreng, for asking me to marry him so many years ago. It continues to be the best choice I've ever made.

About the Author

CHELSEA BAGLEY DYRENG is the daughter of a fireworks salesman and Miss Malibu. She was raised in Wyoming and Idaho and earned her BA at Brigham Young University. She worked for several years as a librarian before moving to North Carolina where she and her husband are raising five God-fearing, book-loving, adventure-seeking kids. She is also the author of the allegorical novel *The Cenote*.

0 26575 18960 5